# THE WONDROUS LIFE AND LOVES OF NELLA CARTER

# ABOUT THE AUTHOR

Brionni Nwosu is a joyful creative based in the musical city of Nashville, where she enjoys making memories with her husband and three children and crafting compelling stories to share with the world. An educator by training, she's spent over a decade supporting students and teaching teachers how to teach, all while shaping her stories on the side. She was recognised as a 2021 We Need Diverse Books Mentee, working with the esteemed Rajani LaRocca. *The Wondrous Life and Loves of Nella Carter* is her debut novel.

# THE WONDROUS LIFE AND LOVES OF NELLA CARTER

BRIONNI NWOSU

HODDERSCAPE

First published in Great Britain in 2025 by Hodderscape
An imprint of Hodder & Stoughton Limited
An Hachette UK company

The authorised representative in the EEA is Hachette Ireland, 8 Castlecourt Centre, Dublin 15, D15 XTP3, Ireland (email: info@hbgi.ie)

1

Copyright © Electric Postcard Entertainment, Inc. 2025

The right of Electric Postcard Entertainment, Inc. to be identified as the Author of the Work has been asserted by them in accordance with the Copyright, Designs and Patents Act 1988.

Author photograph © Brionni Nwosu

All rights reserved. No part of this publication may be reproduced, stored in a retrieval system, or transmitted, in any form or by any means without the prior written permission of the publisher, nor be otherwise circulated in any form of binding or cover other than that in which it is published and without a similar condition being imposed on the subsequent purchaser.

All characters in this publication are fictitious and any resemblance to real persons, living or dead, is purely coincidental.

A CIP catalogue record for this title is available from the British Library

Hardback ISBN 978 1 399 74631 1
Trade Paperback ISBN 978 1 399 74632 8
ebook ISBN 978 1 399 74633 5

Typeset in Adobe Garamond Pro

Printed and bound in Great Britain by Clays Ltd, Elcograf S.p.A.

Hodder & Stoughton policy is to use papers that are natural, renewable and recyclable products and made from wood grown in sustainable forests. The logging and manufacturing processes are expected to conform to the environmental regulations of the country of origin.

Hodder & Stoughton Limited
Carmelite House
50 Victoria Embankment
London EC4Y 0DZ

www.hodderscape.co.uk

*For Sam, who believed. For Mom, who believed first.*

# Contents

**THE BARGAIN** — 1

Savannah—June 1784
    Prologue — 3

**PART I: SAVANNAH** — 15

June, Present Day
    One — 19
    Two — 25
    Three — 39
    Four — 49
    Five — 53

**PART II: NOUVELLE-ORLÉANS** — 61

The Figures—1795
    Six — 63
    Seven — 85
    Eight — 95
    Nine — 103
    Ten — 111
    A Visit from Death — 115
    Eleven — 121
    Present Day: Savannah, June — 127
    Twelve — 129

**PART III: PARIS** — 131

The Sketch—1871
    Thirteen — 133
    A Visit from Death — 139
    Fourteen — 145
    Fifteen — 157
    A Visit from Death — 163

| | |
|---|---|
| Present Day: Savannah, June | 167 |
| Sixteen | 169 |

## PART IV: LONDON — 171

The Dupatta—1901

| | |
|---|---|
| Seventeen | 173 |
| Eighteen | 187 |
| Nineteen | 191 |
| Twenty | 199 |
| A Visit from Death | 205 |
| Present Day: Savannah, June | 209 |
| Twenty-One | 211 |

## PART V: NEW YORK — 213

The Gloves—1920

| | |
|---|---|
| Twenty-Two | 215 |
| Twenty-Three | 227 |
| Twenty-Four | 233 |
| A Visit from Death | 237 |
| Twenty-Five | 243 |
| Present Day: Savannah, June | 251 |
| Twenty-Six | 253 |

## PART VI: MONTGOMERY — 261

The Postcards—1955

| | |
|---|---|
| Twenty-Seven | 263 |
| Twenty-Eight | 275 |
| Twenty-Nine | 285 |
| A Visit from Death | 297 |
| Present Day: Savannah, June | 301 |
| Thirty | 303 |

## PART VII: BUENOS AIRES — 305

The Golden Sun—2005

| | |
|---|---|
| Thirty-One | 307 |

| | |
|---|---|
| Thirty-Two | 317 |
| Thirty-Three | 329 |
| A Visit from Death | 335 |
| Present Day: Savannah, June | 341 |
| Thirty-Four | 343 |
| Thirty-Five | 351 |
| A Visit from Death | 353 |
| Thirty-Six | 359 |

**PART VIII: SAVANNAH** — 361

A Final Visit from Death—2084
    Thirty-Seven — 363

# THE BARGAIN

### Savannah—June 1784

# PROLOGUE

Death kept his pace on the lane to Hampstead House—gait steady, limbs just the right amount of loose.

The time was marked by the bright June sun hanging high overhead, beaming down on the tender green cotton shoots, the first true leaves bursting through. Three vultures circled lazily on the horizon, black slashes on the blue sky, as they spiraled lower toward their prey, doing their job—as was he.

He'd materialized a moment before, appearing alongside the gutted road etched with wagon wheel tracks and the hooves of many beasts, on his way to collect his next soul.

His deeply bronzed skin glistened in the light, sleek muscles stretching, as they had on the body of his last collection, taken from a fazenda outside Rio de Janeiro. That man had been beautiful before an unwieldy load of sugarcane crushed him.

Death had admired his form and taken it as his own as he arrived in the teeming, swampy marshland outside Savannah, Georgia, falling into step and his duty. Trying on bodies had become a habit, all stemming from his desire to understand.

Though he was far from human, his work consisted entirely of contact with the species. From the start, they'd perplexed him. Most were messy, chaotic, and cruel, so, he thought, if he could assume their shape, perhaps he might better grasp their perspective—find some reason for their barbarity toward themselves and most life on Earth.

Irrational in the end, for the practice yielded no answers, at least none that satisfied.

But the custom turned to habit, and so he'd continued ever since.

He paused along the edge of the road, no stranger to these parts. Typhoid and yellow fever had done their rounds this summer, spreading stealthily from the swamp into fresh water, creeping into the white wooden main house, claiming first the master and his new wife before slipping into the cabins that dotted the surrounding fields, each ringed with a small garden. Death had collected souls from each structure, by ones and in twos, leaving neat rows of red-humped dirt to mark each earthly resting place.

Now someone else's allotted hour was at hand.

It was *always* at hand for someone, somewhere.

That was the problem he'd been considering for some time, and he'd finally landed on a solution.

It was perfect.

He needed only to think of a suitable method of execution.

A clatter of hooves interrupted his thoughts as a wagon rattled toward him, the wheels churning through the thick mud, a pitiful brown mare staggering, straining against her load, her jutting ribs heaving as if each breath might be her last.

The driver, Murray, ignored the beast's struggle and flicked his crop; a new lash leaked red on the mare's hindquarters. He hunched over the reins, a brown rifle perched by his feet, glazed eyes shifting, scanning the empty road ahead. Death watched him passively, knowing of the deep and unabating infection that lurked within him.

Soon, the spasms would start, pain that would tear at his insides, making him wish for a swift end to his misery. Murray would find it at the end of the week, jerking and gasping for air in a pool of his own blood and vomit.

Murray did not know his fate as he snapped the crop again, urging the poor beast forward—his jaw clenched, his left hand twitching.

His cargo would fare no better.

A man called Scipio lay in the wagon bed, huddled in the sawdust, his broad brown hands and feet rigged in ropes, eyes closed. A gash on his head bled freely as angry welts marched up his arms, his white canvas shirt cut to ribbons, red blooming across it like a field of summer roses, guaranteeing that Death would collect him, too, before the day was through.

Death watched as the wagon rattled along its miserable way.

A feeling ticked through him—hot and rough—knowing what their imminent demise meant for him.

More work.

Always another soul to fetch and ferry.

Time and again.

For eternity.

Small plagues seemed to keep them in check, ushering the masses to the afterlife without much intervention from him, but then the humans always came back, more than ever, loud, pushy, conniving, and horrible—forever killing each other off with their unending wars, filth, and pestilence, their crimes replete with cruelty and violence.

Even now, they were inventing new ways to die.

Cannons.

Muskets.

Amputations.

How many men had he collected from surgeons' tents that stank of rotting meat as the surgeon hacked off limbs? How many from the battlefield? What used to be dozens of souls had become hundreds, all at once. One would think gathering them in batches would make it easier, but the work never ceased.

Life squandered for no good reason.

*Wouldn't it be better to scrub it all clean?* Death wondered. One final plague to rid the world of them once and for all.

A lot of effort up front, but surely the world would be better for it. Humans could be formed again over time and improved. Not by him, of course. But it could make his job a bit better. As far as Death could see, no redeemable one existed in the bunch.

He considered his plan as he turned down the familiar lane, his steps silent and sure, with only the buzz of blackflies and the whine of mosquitoes for company.

All other life had fled at his arrival. The birds stopped their chatter, and the white-tailed deer turned, leaping into the thick brush. The gray rabbits burrowed deeper in their dens, and the fox squirrels darted for the tallest treetops. They needn't have feared him, for his dominion was over human souls affected by age, accident, or disease, while other beings were tasked with collecting animal souls. Only the lone mountain lion, shaded in the tree's low branches, didn't flee, for he, too, was a purveyor of death.

He'd almost reached the cabin to enact his latest reaping of the day when a tingle pricked at the edge of his awareness, sharp and keen. He slowed, scanning the land, seeing only the wave of low green branches bending in the wind.

Nevertheless, he was being watched, and not because he'd decided, as he did on rare occasions, to show himself to a human.

He winked out, slipping into the endless in-between, searching for the source.

A woman, on the young end of the human spectrum, stood not fifteen feet away, her body hidden by a wide gray oak, her eyes trained on where he used to be. He eased closer, studying her.

Sickness clung to her, scented through her sweat, marked by the red rash scattered on her neck and face. Her golden-brown skin was pale, several shades lighter than his own. She squinted at him with keen eyes, grown glassy with fever, as she held herself still. He watched her realize he had disappeared from the road, her gaze darting to see where he'd gone.

He cocked his head.

Most humans were blind to him, only catching a glimpse while on the edge of their death. He preferred it that way. She behaved differently altogether. His ennui melted away as his curiosity grew, his questions abounding.

*How can she see me? Why can she? More importantly, what does she see?*

The woman was his next soul to collect. Although the time of her reaping was near, he found himself . . . reluctant to take her. Surely he could spare the time to learn a bit more.

He shifted behind her, back into view. "Hiding from me, Nella?"

She jumped, twisting and falling back against the tree's rough bark, her honey-colored chest heaving. Her homespun dress gaped at her shoulders, exposing a heart-shaped birthmark and the telltale reddened spots that crept across her collarbone and neck. A kerchief covered her thick black curls, which, slick with sweat, had escaped their binding. He noted that her pulse quickened at the use of her name, but she didn't run or look away. He sensed no *true* fear, which conjured even more curiosity.

"Mama always said there's no use hiding from Death—but best keep out his way when he's about his business." Her voice was quiet but rough, made worse by coughing.

"Your mama was a smart woman," he murmured.

"If you're here, I expect I'll see her soon," Nella said, her meaning plain.

"Smart woman," he repeated, this time a compliment.

She trembled, even as she tried to stand tall. "You're different than I thought you would be."

He considered the statement. "Different, how?"

She paused, breathing with effort. "I saw you take the master's littlest baby, Maybelle. You were a redheaded woman dressed in green muslin standing on the big porch. Then, another time, when you took Missus Carter's sister in the front tearoom, you had skin the color of day-old corn bread. But I knew they were both you because your edges are hard. Almost black."

Death nodded, struck. Never had someone seen him so plainly. "Is that what you see now?"

She nodded, pointing to his form. "I see it plain as day."

"Have you always?"

Her eyes pierced him, the brown vibrant in the slant of light through the tree branches. "I've always seen you. Mama saw you too. Never knew why, but I reckon those sorts of things weren't up to us. Must be God given."

An unfamiliar sensation twitched in his chest. This was not the regular begging of the sickroom, the damned pleading for him not to take them to their final resting places as he claimed their souls. This was simply conversation. "You believe in God?"

"Sometimes." She gazed off in the distance.

"Come, let's get you ready." He held out his arm, firm and dark brown, as real to her as it was invisible to others.

They didn't speak as they reached her low cabin, situated at the far back of the plantation, edged by dense forest and brambles. The cabin's condition was poor—even by human standards—with rough-cut windows providing little light and poor ventilation. A shoddily hewn door that gaped, somehow managing to both trap the heat of the day and allow in the creeping chill of night. Wooden wattle peeked through the rough white tabby walls as jagged bits of oyster shell glinted in the dim light. A crude fireplace sat at one end, a pair of lumpy pallets at the other, next to a small stand holding a washbasin, a pitcher, and two chamber pots, the fetid smell of sick rising in the cabin's thick heat. A square wooden table, two chairs, and an assortment of pans and dry goods comprised the rest of the cabin's contents.

He helped her to the closest pallet, where a small book rested on the stained cloth, its cover bright yellow. He moved it and settled her down. Once she lay back, it was as if all the strength had fled her body. He sat in one of the spindly chairs, surveying her.

"Where is everyone?" he asked, more for conversation than anything else.

"Once the overseer took sick, they moved everyone healthy to Master's brother's home and boarded up the Big House."

"Why didn't you go?"

She gestured to her skin, mottled with rash. Her eyes gleamed with fever; she had sweat through her dress. He'd seen humans abandon their young for less.

"So, what now?" she wheezed. Blood covered her hand where she'd coughed.

He considered her question. "I take your soul, and we transcend this place."

She nodded, accepting the fact. "Will it hurt?"

"You'll leave this pain behind."

"That would be good. It's all I've known."

She reached for her book, and Death handed it to her, first reading the title.

*Robinson Crusoe.*

"Is that important to you?"

She nodded. "My father—I mean, Master Carter—read from it when I was small. I can read it myself now, having listened to his stepdaughter Mary's lessons." She dragged it up to her chest. "It brings a bit of comfort."

"You can't take it with you." Although people were always trying. Gold, jewels, papers, and once even a prized pig. Worldly goods held no value in the next place. He nodded toward the book. "What's it about?"

He didn't particularly care, but he wasn't ready to collect her—not yet.

She wiped her hand on her skirt, the blood smearing. "A man who goes on an adventure and sees all the sights to see. He is made a slave and then finds himself free."

Death examined her. "Is that what you would do?"

She nodded adamantly, wincing at the effort. "I'd give anything to see the world. My brother and I dreamed about it when we were young. How we'd leave our old place and travel. Silas was so sure there must be more to life than this." She gestured weakly to the rough, craggy wood floor where she made her home. A coughing fit filled her lungs, wet and thick.

It wouldn't be long now.

By rights, he should take her and ferry her soul, but . . . he found he didn't want to. All he wanted to do was carry on speaking with her.

"Tell me, where would you go if you could?" he asked, delaying the inevitable.

"Away from here."

"Anywhere more specific?"

She was quiet as she considered the question, probably having never been asked anything like it before. "I'd want to go everywhere. Places I've only heard about, like Paris or London or where my mother said her father was from. I'd like to see the world and its wondrous things. I'd like to be free," she said, her breathing ragged.

Death shrugged, slightly miffed at her answer. "You're not missing much. Places are places and humans are humans, everywhere they live."

"I don't think so. I want to believe there is a better sort—at least better than I've experienced," she challenged.

Death snorted. "I can assure you they're not." His mind wandered to the men he'd seen south of here who had set whole towns on fire to dominate those they thought inferior, leaving only destruction in their wake. Nothing about those men was worth saving, but it hadn't been their time. When it was, Death would have something special for them, indeed. They would learn that no one was crueler than he.

"What about me? What have I ever done to anybody?"

Death's gaze swept over her, studying her like he was seeing the core of who she was, deep in her marrow. It was true. She'd been born in bondage during this godforsaken time. Her soul, for all its ill treatment, was still pure.

This fact didn't fit Death's plans, so he conveniently ignored it.

"You are only one person. Millions more are wretches, waiting for their chance to inflict themselves on other humans. Living is more trouble than it's worth."

Her mouth fell open with shock. "How can you say that? Of anyone, *you* should know how precious life is."

"It's because I know that I am an authority."

Nella shook her head forcefully. "Then you don't understand it at all. Life, I mean. I've seen my fair share of trouble and terribleness. But Mama always reminded me there's still love to be had, even in humans, even in this terrible place." No doubt she meant the plantation she and others had been forced to labor on. "There's family . . . even if they're gone. There's the people we love and who love us . . . even if it's all just memories. There's the things we leave behind. It's the only way my people survived this hell. Holding on to dawn. All you have to do is pay attention."

He quirked his eyebrows at her spirit. Even while dying, even in the face of all the horror she'd endured, she was willing to disagree with Death himself. "So, I can't see people's goodness?" he asked. "And you . . . could show it to me? Is that what you're saying?"

Her eyes sharpened with clarity. "Let me live—and do this life over again. I'll show you. It's all around us."

Death scoffed, but her proposition surprised him. She hadn't lived long enough to see the fallacy of her words. If she'd existed as long as he had, she'd see this was the only conclusion. She, born enslaved, should know better than anyone.

But he paused as he considered her bargain. Many prayed to him for this sort of rescue, though he'd never answered. "So, you would like to live?"

She glanced at him. "Yes."

Death was strangely animated; he'd never had to share his thoughts, let alone his plans, with anyone else. He played it out in his mind. It was an exquisite solution. "I've grown quite weary of humans. I could collect your soul and bring you to the new world, and that could be your new life."

"What new world?"

"The one that will be created after I destroy this one," Death said as a matter of fact.

She lurched up, eyes wide, using the last of her energy. "But you can't do that. What about all the people? My brother, Silas? He's out there somewhere. You're going to kill them all?"

He frowned. She didn't seem to appreciate the simplicity of the plan. "Precisely the point. I am quite sure there is no one and nothing redeemable among them. It will be good to start again," he explained. "You would see if—"

"I bet I wouldn't!" Nella's chest heaved at her effort. "There's me, Silas, my late mama, and surely others. We all can't be as bad as you say."

"I assure you this is the case."

"I'll find proof. I'll show you what you cannot see. Give me a second chance . . . a new life."

Keep her living . . . on the earth as it existed. Death thought it over. Could she do it? Make him care about them? Show him something he didn't already know? Her arrogance amused him. "So, if I save you, grant you life, you'll bring me this evidence you speak of? And I will decide if humanity should continue its existence?"

Her eyes widened, but she nodded. "What kind of proof do you want?"

*What kind, indeed?* His eyes dropped to the slim yellow volume.

Death grinned, more excited about this than anything he could ever remember. "Like your book—you'll be Crusoe. Record your adventures, show me that man is redeemable—worth saving." He hadn't paid much attention to the inane scribblings of humans and their vain attempts at remembrance. But this would be different. This would be written for him, and only he would know.

"What's the catch?" Her eyes narrowed. "There's always a price."

Nella continued to amuse Death. He thought she might not have seen much of the world beyond the Carter plantation in Georgia, but she knew that fundamental rule of life: There must always be an exchange for a deal to be honored. "I will give you the second chance you seek. A true chance outside of the shackles of this current existence. Several lifetimes of freedom and a gift to help you be understood, no matter where you might land. And you will write for me. Prove your lofty ideas about redemption and love—"

"What do I lose?" she interrupted.

Death leaned back, the shock of her irreverence increasing his curiosity tenfold. A slow smile crept into the corner of his mouth. "You shall have no descendants. No family. No tangible legacy on this earth. Only the words you write for me. And you can tell no one of our bargain." He extended a strong brown hand, tickled at the idea. "What do you say?"

"How will you see these words?"

"You will publish them along the way, and I will meet with you to discuss them and anything else you want to show me."

She took a deep, ragged breath. "How will you know the writing is mine?"

"I will know." He liked how she underestimated him. "Any more questions?"

"For how long?"

"As long as you are able." His smile deepened. "Given the task, I doubt it'll be very long."

"And if we don't agree?"

He shrugged. "Then you die. I'll take your soul and collect the rest of the world as planned."

He watched memories rush through her mind: her brother and first friend Silas, sold away to the outskirts of New Orleans five years before. Her mama died not soon after that. Her lonely life left behind as Master Carter's enslaved daughter. "You can't do that."

"I can, and I will." He smiled at her, pleased with his solution despite her turmoil. "Whether I do so or not depends entirely upon you and the bargain you put forth. If I am not compelled by what you write, what you show me, then you'll come with me, and the rest of this world will end too."

The small cabin filled with her heavy breathing as she weighed his offer—the gift of life or a certain death.

Slowly, Nella put out her hand. "I'll do it."

He took her slender hand in his. He wondered how long it would be before she broke—before she saw the world as he did and surrendered to his will.

"I'll check in from time to time—I'll let you know when. Until then, I look forward to your efforts." He reached out one long brown finger, brushing it across her forehead.

Nella shuddered. He watched the cooling sensation ripple across her skin as the pain receded. She rose, taking her first easy breath in days, lungs clear. She stared at her hands, spots gone, her rich brown skin smooth, every movement effortless. He relished in his power to change her.

Death stood, pulling Nella to her feet. She staggered a bit before she steadied, clutching her book to her chest.

She faced Death, eyes wide, uncertain. "What now?"

He smiled, his teeth white against his tanned brown skin. "What, indeed?"

# Part I: SAVANNAH

## June, Present Day

## The Savannah Tribune

### Dust Tracks Column

### A CROSSROADS CITY
### THE REAPER IGNORES THE HOSTESS CITY

#### Vivian Edwards

The haunted rumors about Savannah have always been true, despite reports to the contrary. Tourists' claims of spirits standing above their beds in the Marshall House Hotel or lurking beneath the oaks of Madison Square, their business unfinished or their confusion about their demise ever present, have been debunked by the city council for years. The mayor and aldermen wish to keep ghost hunters searching for paranormal activity out of the city, in favor of a higher caliber of visitor. But perhaps the Hostess City of the South is a crossroads between this life and the next . . . or, worse, has been ignored by Death—the reaper having grown lazy in his collection pursuits, leaving behind untidiness and restless souls.

If seeing the otherworldly is on your vacation wish list, Savannah has all you'll ever need. See the guide starting on page . . .

# One

I sit in my favorite café, as I do every day, and wait for Death to arrive. It's a nice enough place to pass the time while I anticipate our usual meeting and his assessment of my latest writings.

Sunlight streams through the wide front windows, bathing the Parisian-themed café in a warm, pleasant glow. The bell jangles as new customers crowd in, decked out in crop tops, shorts, and flip-flops, drawn by the scent of fresh pastries and strong coffee.

They flock to the counter, their cameras out, diligently recording their authentic Savannah experience as they linger over tempting displays of rainbow-hued macarons, pain au chocolat, and fresh croissants. The place hums from their conversation and the soft music that floats from hidden speakers, mingling with the whir of the bean grinder and the gurgle of the espresso machine as it spurts smooth streams of richness into white cups.

I lift *The Savannah Tribune* and reread my latest weekly column, Dust Tracks, revisiting the hidden Black history in the city and surrounding area. It's odd, this need to see the words in print, but I can never resist.

I look up every few minutes to eavesdrop on the tourists babbling about the antebellum mansions and cobblestone streets and the rumors about ghosts roaming the national historic landmark district. The noise of it all is a welcome distraction from the spirits chasing me.

This café is a good place to wait until I can face Death again.

And wait, I have.

I didn't think it would be this long.

I'd thought Death would come see me the instant Winston died.

I imagined looking up from his bedside to find Death leaning against the hospital door, his head tilted, arms crossed, mouth smug, eyes glinting with the knowledge that he thought he'd won—that he might've been right all along.

He should've come.

Winston was my last person to lose. The last straw to break me, to make me write less and less.

But he didn't.

Not then.

Not now.

Not for the three years, two months, six days, and sixteen hours since I left that hospital room. I've gone years without seeing Death, sometimes with more than a decade between visits. In the beginning, I used to fear him showing up, never knowing when he'd appear, uncertain if the words I'd published would be enough to please him and continue our eternal wager . . . leaving my soul and the souls of all at stake.

Even with the momentousness of the task, I can't deny that there have been perks, in the wondrous things I've experienced. I've watched Marian Anderson sing on Easter Sunday at the Lincoln Memorial, sat with Langston Hughes as he wrote "The Weary Blues," detailing one of our nights out, and ridden with Ollie Stewart on the convoy behind Charles de Gaulle during the liberation of Paris in 1944. I've covered the signing of the 1965 Voting Rights Act by Lyndon B. Johnson.

I've watched on a grainy black-and-white TV as men took the first steps on the moon and then written about it. I've gathered and recorded mountains of evidence attesting to humanity's goodness—our miraculous wisdom and inventions and our redeemable nature—for more than two centuries. The task has always been difficult—cobbling together stories from all the people I've met and the places I've been, scrambling, hoping I've found enough proof to save everyone.

We're two weeks from the 240th anniversary of our first meeting in the cabin. I wonder what he thinks of my latest little column. A tiny blip of a piece, in contrast to the travelogues and articles I used to write and the grandiose publications they appeared in. But writing for a Black newspaper has always felt bigger, as if my words might linger forever. I should be working on the next one, my deadline imminent, but I ignore my notebook.

My phone pings. A reminder. The lecture tonight. I flip back to the front of the paper and trace my finger along the black-and-white write-up of Dr. Sebastian Moore, historian of international journalism specializing in Black journalists. The headline haunts me: THE MISSING VOICES—EXCAVATING THE BLACK WOMEN OF HISTORIC JOURNALISM THROUGH THE WORK OF JIMI IRELAND AND BEYOND.

That name is a firework. One of the many iterations of myself. Even after all this time, it still startles me to see my past self in print.

I trace the four letters of my old name, so small, that lifetime so far away now, and I can't resist the tide to return to a sliver of it. I've kept internet alerts for all my names in case they pop up in scholarly databases or online. Apparently, some overinflated academic decided my work was worth critiquing—in the *New Yorker*, no less—with all the smugness of someone who's never left their ivory tower. I intend to find out who, exactly, he thinks he is.

I check my phone for the hour and eye the thinning line at the register. I'll have barely enough time for another cup if I'm going to make the lecture on time. I have to know what he plans to say about me and my work.

"Vivian!"

I glance up. I've been isolated for so long I've nearly forgotten this name, my current one. I push back my pen and notebook and scoot off the high stool, grateful for the distraction.

Ruby waves from the pickup counter, holding a to-go cup in my direction. She's the closest thing I've had to a friend in the time since I moved back here, checking in as she fills my cup and asks about my work—always curious about what I'm writing next.

Perhaps it will be her. She deserves to be written about. The hardships she's had to endure hidden beneath her beauty. Her sunny disposition radiates out, enveloping the customers in its glow, as she efficiently manages the café. There's no hint that she's picked up the pieces since the fire that took her mother's life and nearly took hers, or the struggle of raising her brother. Ruby is one of those people, the redeeming ones who do things despite the challenges, still believing that life can be good. She reminds me a bit of myself.

"You must be a mind reader," I say as I approach.

"Tough writing?" she asks, nodding to the open notebook back at my seat.

I shrug, taking the offered cup. "You know, one of those days."

I've struggled with writing anything serious as of late, Dust Tracks being my latest attempt. Mostly it's been reviews of bed-and-breakfasts and restaurants or informational visits to obscure historical sites. After Winston, I stopped traveling and stopped collecting other people's stories. But I couldn't *not* write, a habit centuries in the making. Now my notebooks hold only false starts of things I'd love to write, the messy drafts of my column, and mostly a smattering of memories—vignettes of the lives I've lived and people I've lost. My mother, my brother Silas, all the loves I've had along the way—little parts of the centuries leaking across the pages and sometimes feeling more like fantasy than reality. If someone ever got to read my scribblings, they'd never believe them.

Ruby nods sympathetically. "It'll come. You have to have the best to write for *The Atlantic*! Inspiration will strike soon, and you'll have plenty more stories to tell," she says, beaming.

"Some days, I'm not so sure," I reply. Especially as I wait for Death and his latest assessment.

"You have all the time in the world to leave your mark. As my mama used to say, 'You're a spring chicken.'"

"Not hardly. More long in the tooth."

Ruby laughs. "Sometimes you sound a hundred years old."

I smile. *If you only knew.* I sip the coffee, a heady mix of espresso and lavender bloom, the honeyed deliciousness sliding over my tongue. "How much do I owe you?" I juggle the cup and riffle through my purse, realizing I've forgotten my wallet. "I don't—"

"Allow me." A hand appears with a fistful of dollars.

I glance up at a tall man. He's wearing a white button-down that contrasts against his rich, dark-brown skin, and his square glasses give him the look of a Black Clark Kent. His hair, cut in a fade on the sides, the top a touch longer, forms tiny curls, the shadow of a beard along his jaw. In his early thirties, I'd guess, he's in shape, the lines of his biceps visible through his shirt. He clutches a yellow legal pad and a red book. I wonder what he's reading. A tendril of curiosity unfurls in me.

His arm grazes mine as he places the money on the counter.

I startle. Surprised at his gesture and how the feel of his skin sends a rush of heat through me. It's been so long since I've been touched. It's been so long since another person has had that effect on me.

"Th-thank you," I say as Ruby's eyes cut back and forth between us. "But I can't—"

"You don't have any money," he teases as his intense gaze holds mine, and a small, hopeful smile grows on his lips.

My face flushes, leaving me mixed up inside as we stand there frozen, his eyes examining me and mine examining him. The glances . . . the elevated pulse . . . the heightened emotions . . . I can almost hear the faint whir of destiny and wonder *What if?* A tiny question I haven't pondered for years, one I thought I might never ask again.

I've forgotten what it feels like to be seen and admired.

"Do we know each other?" His eyebrows lift. "I have the strangest feeling we've met."

"No." I finally find my words. "And I couldn't possibly accept. Ruby, could—"

"You'll just owe me." He smiles. "Perhaps you can buy me one another time?"

I start to answer him when a thin edge of darkness snatches my attention away. A tall man with milklike skin and thinning auburn hair stands on the other side of the window, milling with the other tourists—his shadowed edges distinct, but only to me. Heat rushes through me as he passes, just out of sight of the windows, my breath coming in quick bursts.

It's *him*.

Death.

"Are you okay?" The handsome man trying to buy my coffee looks concerned, his eyes kind. He reaches out but stops just short of touching me.

Ruby's eyes narrow.

I swallow, struggling to breathe, blinking my eyes clear. "I'm sorry," I blurt out. "I'm sure you're great, but I have to go . . . I'm late."

I jam my notebook in my bag before the man can respond.

The bell on the door jangles behind me as I run into the afternoon sunshine. I stop outside the shop entrance and scan the street, the air thick with dust and exhaust from the neighboring construction.

Tourists mill about, sitting at the wrought iron tables or admiring downtown Savannah's architectural gems as traffic streams past the café. I search the crowds, anticipation humming inside me. I'm chilled despite the hot, humid sunshine, and hug my bag closer, my papers rustling, knowing what this means.

It's time to find out if the world is about to end.

# Two

I search for Death until it's time to attend the lecture. I think about skipping it, the mix of expectancy and apprehension and curiosity about seeing him after all these years almost too much to bear. But I enter the jam-packed lecture hall, the hairs on my neck still prickling.

The lights are already dimmed as the university dean climbs the metal stairs to the podium. I scoot into the last seat in the back row, hands twisting in my lap, gooseflesh running up my arms. My eyes drift over the audience, but no one is paying attention to me. Everyone is facing the stage, watching the dean.

I look for Death. *Is he here too?*

I don't feel him.

The space is missing that inexorable gravity he holds—that pull that makes the breath hitch and the heart pound, that primitive knowledge of being in the presence of a tangible threat to your existence.

*Why did Death disappear?*

I glance around the hall, my gut twinging again. Why did he appear only in my periphery earlier? This time feels different. Or maybe after Winston, everything is different.

*Was it a statement of some kind?* Letting me know I couldn't summon him, no matter how hard I tried? That I wouldn't find him unless he wanted to be found . . . wanted to be seen?

I shake my head and sit back. Despite knowing him for centuries, I still can't guess what Death is up to. There's been no invitation to a formal meeting. Those are special.

Every decade or more, an item will appear, usually on my night table or desk, with an address on white card stock, a reminder that he can go wherever he pleases and that I will come when called.

I replay the morning in my mind. There was no object waiting, but I felt in my marrow that a meeting was imminent.

What finally drew him here?

*Could it be the warning shot in my column? Or the man flirting with me?*

We barely spoke at the café, but maybe that didn't matter.

The memory of what Death did to Diego tightens around me.

I know what Death is capable of. I know how to anger him.

A photo of a familiar face flashes across the projection screen, distracting me from my thoughts.

Dean Sutton, the head of the journalism department at Savannah State University, continues her introductions. She's stunning in a deep-blue suit, white silk blouse, low heels, and a double rope of pearls, her sister-locs looped elegantly into a chignon as she gazes at the crowd.

"And we have to thank the Reynolds Foundation for hosting this wonderful series, created in honor of Winston Reynolds, a noted economist, financier, and alum of our proud university."

Winston's gently lined face graces the screen with his characteristic bow tie, his skin deeply bronzed, his white mustache thick, his eyebrows wild, his midnight eyes still holding the mischievous sparkle of the boy I met all those years ago, amplifying his absence and all I've lost in the three years since his death.

I close my eyes for a moment, hearing one of his silly jokes and remembering how he'd make me a cup of tea before listening to me ramble about my latest piece. I squeeze my hands to my stomach as if to hold in that anchor of grief. After living so many lifetimes, I should've been used to losing someone, the knife wound to the heart dull, more paper cut than puncture. But his death was one of the hardest to take, the closing of a final chapter.

I gaze up at the screen as Dean Sutton continues detailing his work and achievements and his mother's legacy before she pauses, waiting for the big reveal, coordinated over dozens of emails.

"To support his legacy, I'm delighted to announce that in addition to this generous summer series, the Reynolds Foundation has gifted twenty-five million dollars, enabling us to renovate the east wing of this building and fund an endowment to provide *full scholarships* for all students in the journalism field in perpetuity."

Thunderous cheers crash over the auditorium as the crowd stands, their shouts and whistles echoing off the rafters. I stay seated as the wave of energy washes over me, soaking in the moment, a warmth building in my chest.

No soul in the room could know that I was responsible for this money, earned and compounded over several lifetimes. I've spent millions to help others, always in the background, always anonymous, so I rarely get the chance to experience the appreciation of it all. This feels good, the joy spreading, a sensation I've craved for so long.

Dean Sutton beams as the applause dies down. "We are truly grateful for the gift and what it will allow us to do for the many, many, many years to come."

With her sincere thanks, a pall of reality descends, and the chilly touch of guilt returns.

It *is* a wonderful gift—for a future that won't exist if I don't continue to hold up my end of the bargain. I glance at my bag again, the newspaper crinkled from my obsessive reading and rereading of my column. Will it be enough? It has to be.

Dean Sutton continues, "Today, I'm excited to introduce you to our newest addition to the journalism department. He comes to us from Mullins University, where he lectured on African and African American history, his work focusing on historical narratives, the Black press, and digital journalism. His first book, *Black Travel Narratives*, is a

*New York Times* nonfiction bestseller and has been put into production as a series with the Discovery Channel. He's working on a new project about the Black women journalists of the past. So, without further ado, I introduce the esteemed Dr. Sebastian Moore."

The crowd claps wildly as the professor climbs the steps to shake hands with the dean. As he turns away from the glare of lights, my stomach flutters.

The man from the coffee shop.

~

I freeze as he places his papers on the stand, the red book peeking out from under his legal pad, and he straightens to address the audience. I swallow the worry that he might've recognized me in the café . . . a dead woman. My brain toggles through the memory of pictures of Jimi, of me, printed at times in the periodicals and newspapers I once wrote for. *If he did recognize me, he would've said so, right?* He would've been shocked. I try to cling to that thought as he begins his lecture. He's changed his clothes, now wearing a black suit jacket that fits him perfectly, accenting the breadth of his shoulders. Under the white fluorescent light on center stage, it's as if he's been made smoother, shinier, and more confident in his clear brown skin, flashing his matching dimples and easy smile. He's transformed into Professor Sebastian Moore, a seasoned PhD of history and an accomplished academic.

One who's about to lecture about me.

Dr. Moore lays his hands on the podium's edge, entirely composed, at ease in the limelight, his presence intriguing. He clears his throat. "First, I want to thank the dean, my colleagues, and the SSU community for this warm welcome." He smiles down at us, and we can't help but smile back, his enthusiasm infectious. "During our time, I want to go deep into our subject; today, I will feature some of the divergent voices in Black journalism. Not just the bylines of your typical journalist or the editor's words, but the voices and lives of everyday African Americans as they shared their travels." His voice rich and deep, the cover of his book on the screen. He eases around the podium, and the room seems to shrink, drawing us all closer like we're in a living room, having a casual chat.

He continues, "I wrote *Black Travel Narratives* because I'm fascinated by how we traverse life and the stories we tell, based on the rich experiences we have as we explore this world and embrace all that it has to offer, despite the limitations that others place on us."

His words ripple through me, the baritone of his voice ringing with sincerity. He's a good orator and storyteller, artfully weaving together the disparate threads of history and tying them into a cohesive narrative of strength, resilience, and possibility. He has that quality where you can feel as if he is speaking only to you—just you—and having a normal conversation, even though he's addressing an entire audience. "And so many voices, especially those of women—Black women—have been erased and silenced."

The crowd claps at his words. An easy rhetorical flourish to endear a mostly female crowd. The words from his *New Yorker* piece flutter through my head: *"From all Jimi Ireland's notable travels and firsthand accounts of the gargantuan historical events that shaped the modern world, she transforms solely into a naive eyewitness, neglecting to showcase the cracks of humanity . . . the dark places where the light cannot roost or take hold and destructive decisions rain down. She ignores the human appetite for the bittersweet, the pain, and our everlasting tug toward selfishness."* I snort at the thought. *What is he even talking about?* His assessment of me is wrong. If he only knew why . . .

I grind my teeth, hoping I can make it through the entire presentation if he continues to hammer his thesis home. As he clicks through the slides—images of Black and Brown writers in exotic locations—I'm hooked on every word despite myself, and the rest of the audience is, too, having fallen under his spell.

I fall back in my seat, clutching the armrest as my own words and a grainy picture of me grace the projection screen.

"Here we have the work of Jimi Ireland, a writer for prominent Black newspapers, notably *The Chicago Defender* and *The Montgomery Advocate*. Her work in travel writing and the Civil Rights Movement was featured in *Ebony* magazine, bridging World War II, civil rights, and pop culture until her death in the early 1990s."

I can't hear as he continues, a buzz building in my brain.

Her death.

My "death."

I fight away the memory of all the small methods I've used to erase myself before moving on to a new city, a new country, time after time. Having to leave everything and everyone behind. Having to be unable to take credit for many lifetimes' worth of bylines.

A shiver of misgiving worms its way up my spine as he continues. All the coincidences could've been explained away before, but what might explain him selecting my words, written under another name in another life, for his article and for the talk I'm attending today? Why me?

As if he can hear my thoughts, he continues: "I've centered Jimi in my talk and my current research because her writing was some of the first travel writing I encountered during summers at my granny's house in Alabama. I was flipping through old newspapers because I was bored and, as you probably guessed, hot. When I read Ms. Ireland's works, I wasn't roasting in the living room under the box fan, but I was transported to a place beyond, somewhere my mind could take me that my body had not yet been. All the things she'd seen were awe inspiring."

He pauses, the weight of his statements pressing upon us all, and perhaps me the most. I begin to feel the hard grudge inside me soften. "This experience was the spark that lit my passion for travel and the search for something bigger than myself, proof that I could explore the world beyond what others had set out for me. I saw that my experiences could be shared and potentially resonate with someone else—and that revelation brought me to where I stand today."

He reads aloud, his voice carrying my words through the auditorium. The crowd around me dissipates, and it feels like he's only talking to me. "'Travel is the bridge between who you were and who you've yet to become. If you live your life in just one place, it keeps you there, holding you small, limiting you to the scope of its reality. But once you glimpse the bigger life—the possibility to, perhaps, dream a little more and go a little farther—then maybe you will meet yourself on the other side of the globe, the true you, the one who was there all along.'"

He pauses, facing my direction, though he can't possibly see me this far back and through the lights.

"This is the power of travel narratives. You can experience a place, a time, or a people through another person's eyes and feel the truth of their lives as they traversed through time. But as much as I've hunted for all things Jimi Ireland . . . and other Black female journalists of her ilk like Tessa Thorpe, Maria W. Stewart, Vivian Edwards, Ida B. Wells-Barnett, Arden Bell, Josephine St. Pierre Ruffin, Hazel Garland, Carmella White, and so many more whose names have been lost to history . . ."

My skin warms as I hear several of my former names folded in with those other great women.

"I have a bone to pick with her. With how Black diasporan writers have a narrative urge to clean up the terrible parts of what it means to live and travel and exist as a person of African descent on this planet and all that comes with it. Our greats often clean up the untidy bits, sweep them away by folding the suffering into the language of God and the devil and pious struggle for the sake of our legacies . . ."

I ball up my fists, trying to keep myself from interrupting him, his words tinged with Death's point of view on humanity. He clicks through his final slides, where he's dissected a travel series I did in which I followed Victor Hugo Green's *The Negro Motorist Green Book* through the American South. He misinterprets the beauty I noted in the impoverished Black communities listed there for neglecting reality.

"You're wrong!" The words leave my mouth before I can catch them.

"What was that?" He cups a hand across his forehead, squinting to see me.

The auditorium spotlight finds me.

He smiles so wide I can see all his perfect teeth.

A roving microphone appears before me. "I said you're wrong."

"Is that so?" he challenges.

"Jimi Ireland, like so many other Black women, shouldn't have to solely focus on the hardships of being a woman, or of being Black, in order for their words to be of value or understood." My upset is a shaken bottle of champagne. "They should be able to witness beauty. Why should they only report suffering?"

"I never said her words held no value. But rather that they neglected to capture the entire portrait. That she, like so many in our community, glamorize to appease—"

"I . . ." I clear my throat, trying to cover the silliness of my mistake. The entire day is rattling me. *Jimi Ireland is a dead woman,* I remind myself. *I cannot explain myself.* I swallow. "Jimi Ireland, like the others, should be able to write as they please, write their truth. Is that not the role of the artist . . . the writer? To be free?"

My question lingers between us, between everyone in the auditorium. He nibbles his bottom lip, and I crave his answer. I'm about to press him again when Dean Sutton appears onstage, signaling the end of our public spat. The heat of curious glances from fellow audience members sends a deep blush through me.

"Well, we've run out of time for more Q and A. But wasn't that a wonderful lecture? Let's give a round of applause for Dr. Sebastian Moore," Dean Sutton says. The crowd climbs to its feet, filling the room with thunderous applause.

The rest of the auditorium lights come up, and the audience breaks apart, gathering their things and making their way to the buffet piled high with crackers, fruit, hot appetizers, and desserts. A secondary line forms for the professor as he greets each person.

I stay in my seat, unsettled.

First, the article in *The New Yorker*, and second, the coffee shop, then finally, my words on the screen . . . I don't know what to make of it. It's as if the universe is aligning, planning for us to meet; honestly, I don't trust it. The universe's plans rarely break my way. I think of Death, unable to shake the feeling that he might have something to do with this. A new iteration of our game.

The heat of my debate with Sebastian leaves behind a warmth: a surprising kindling, of sorts. I haven't had anyone to discuss my writing with since Winston . . . and since Death didn't show up. As I stand to slip out of the room, Dr. Moore glances over from his adoring crowd, spotting me. He holds up a hand, signaling to me to wait as he wraps up his conversation. I could still leave, blending in with the last of the lingering admirers, but curiosity keeps me in place. I'm already here. I might as well figure out why he keeps popping up and continue to tell him he's wrong about the writings of Jimi Ireland.

He strides over, his scent enveloping me like a fall day—spiced cinnamon, crunchy maple leaves, and rich, oaky leather—bringing to mind Sunday afternoons wrapped in a cozy blanket with a good book and a tall glass of wine. His eyes are distinct, velvety, teddy bear brown with smile lines that crinkle in the corners.

The surprise of him unexpected.

He smiles, his teeth white and even. "Glad to see you made it where you needed to be, Cinderella," he says.

"Cinderella?"

He nods. "That's who I thought of when you rushed off, saying you were late. That, and the fact that you left something behind." He reaches into his pocket and withdraws a black-and-gold fountain pen. *My* pen.

"Thank you *so* much, Dr. Moore!" This particular pen was a gift from Gabby. As I take the pen, our fingers brush, a tendril of electricity sparking between us again. I hurriedly tuck it in my bag.

He coughs and tugs at his collar. "Call me Sebastian, please . . . I saw it was a Montblanc and know those can cost a pretty penny. I thought, as a writer, you'd like it back."

"How did you know?"

"Only another writer would argue with me like you just did in front of everyone." He winks.

"I could be a scholar like you," I quip back.

"So, are you?" He reaches out a hand for me to shake.

"Vivian," I say, reminding him of my name in this time. "I write a small column for *The Savannah Times*."

"Look at you. Great paper."

"Not quite *The New Yorker*, though."

He smiles in confirmation. "You hated my article?"

"I did, in fact."

He laughs. "Care to join me in the hors d'oeuvres line so we can continue our discussion?"

I should go, but something about him holds me in place—that, and my reporter's instinct. There's more to the story of Dr. Moore and how my past as Jimi has shown up in his studies. I can't leave until I've gotten to the bottom of it and set the record straight so he'll write about her—me—correctly.

I get in line on one side, him on the other. We're quiet as we head toward the tables.

"I do have one confession," he says, selecting a canapé. "When I saw you in the café, it's just that . . . I could swear I've seen you before."

I nod. "I just have one of those faces." My standard response whenever anyone looks too closely. I stick to the edges of history, recording it while fading into the background. The secret to a long life like mine—that, good hair-graying powder, and being handy with makeup too. People tend to get suspicious when one stays perpetually twenty-four.

He shakes his head. "I never forget a face and would never lose track of one as unique as yours."

I bite my bottom lip, fighting to keep my expression neutral, enjoying the tiny thrill of his words. A challenge crackles just beneath them. I haven't been flirted with in ages, and I can't fight the pull. "Does that line work for you often?"

He laughs. "Why? Is it working now?" His eyes search my face, still trying to place me.

"I couldn't say. It might only encourage you further, and you have bad opinions."

His mouth opens with shock, but I can tell he enjoys this sparring. And perhaps I do too.

I focus on filling my plate with deviled eggs and crudités. We reach the charcuterie board of salami roses, cubed cheese, and artfully displayed grapes. I pluck a few with tongs as his questions continue. "So, Vivian, what do you write?"

"A bit of this and that."

"I'm sure it's more than that, given your spirited defense of Jimi Ireland."

"I may have done a bit of travel writing."

He grins, his dimples revealing themselves, and drops a few slices of rolled salami on his plate. "Where?"

I pause, as always, my brain doing its usual dance as I decide how much truth to share. "My last piece, outside of my column for *The Savannah Tribune*, was on the Dahomey in Benin and was published in *The Atlantic*."

"Wait. Are you *the* Vivian . . . Edwards?" His eyebrows practically reach his forehead, and he almost drops the tongs into the cheese dip.

"Are you going to call my writing naive too? I'll save you the trouble," I say.

Sebastian sets his plate down. His eyes are hopeful, his grin earnest. "All right, let's have it out. I suppose you take umbrage with my findings?"

"I think you don't *see* as much as you think you do."

He straightens, and I know I've struck a nerve. "I have read, studied, and collected the travel writings of Black people spanning from the present to post-antebellum. I've seen a lot."

"Hardly." The word slips out, unleashing a flood. "You seem to believe people like Jimi Ireland should've woven suffering and pain into their experiences of the world, their travels. Why can't they enjoy walking along the beach without drawing attention to ragged stones that may have left behind a cut on their feet?" The thrill of arguing with him sends a surge through me.

"Then what is the truth? Is life simply wonderful? Are we supposed to lie? Wrap our legacies in pretty bows and ignore the rot?" he says. "Our community owes the next generation more than that."

"Owe?" My voice raises, and for the first time I realize everyone around us is watching and listening.

He notices, too, then leans forward to whisper, "Maybe we should continue this conversation in my office. I want to show you something."

Unable to resist the urge to prove him wrong, I agree. This is providing a wonderful distraction from anticipating Death's arrival.

He beams. "Just give me a second with the dean, and we can talk in my office." He juggles his plate and lecture notes while walking over to her.

I stand by the door, my pulse fluttering at my wrists. Running into Sebastian twice in one day is a bit too lucky, but I'm curious about the coincidences.

All too soon, he is back at my side. "Ready?"

His office is three floors up from the auditorium. The buzz of the hall fades as he escorts me into the elevator. His cologne wraps itself around me. The energy of our argument was electric, but something about being in close quarters with him feels like the quiet before a storm, only I am not yet sure which one of us is the storm.

His office is at the end of the hall. He fumbles with the keys, then welcomes me inside as he clicks on the lights. He sets his plate and papers on the desk next to a thick leather journal. "Forgive the mess. I'm still getting settled in."

I sink into the chair opposite his and admire every detail. "Nothing to forgive. It gives me time to admire the art." I gesture at the large painting that dominates the wall between the windows. It's a sketch of a man's face in black ink, the eyes piercing as he gazes at you, direct and knowing.

Sebastian smiles.

His large brown desk anchors the office, with a plush navy couch on the left side and a textured orange carpet running underneath. The open shelves above reveal his diplomas, awards, and a jaunty plant with the name "Lennox" Sharpied on its pot, its leaves trailing down. A large bookshelf covers the right side of the office, half filled with books, four cardboard boxes stacked underneath, half unpacked. Several books are familiar from my own shelves at home, and some are on my to-be-read list. Everything in the space says he's intelligent, curious, and well read.

He sits across from me, fidgeting with a pen. "So where were we?"

"You were about to lose our argument?" I sit back in the chair.

"Oh, was I?"

My stomach flutters unexpectedly, and he rummages around in his desk before removing a large album. "Maybe this will prove that I do love nothing more than our history and only the things *we* see."

I flip it open, finding expertly preserved clippings from Black writers spanning hundreds of years. We tumble into deep conversation about history, journalism, and writing. His words set off a light inside me that triples when he touches me again, directing my hands to find certain pages and passages. I continue to soak in the words as we spar. Here, among these greats, I find myself reminiscing. The memories wash over me as I find one of the pieces I wrote before learning that Winston was sick.

I run my fingers along the protective plastic preserving the article as if I can feel the words and remember the typewriter I used: *"Beauty exists in all forms, all around us. Though the world's darkness may dim our sight, we should always know beauty is there."*

The sentences may as well be a stranger's. I fight the surge of emotion as Sebastian watches. I don't know if it's the day, if it's the waiting on Death, if it's seeing my words, or if it's Sebastian.

He stands, moving to sit in the vacant chair beside me. "Did I say something to upset you?"

"No," I say, though his closeness rattles me. It draws up a want I thought had long since faded, buried by time and quiet years. The intensity of it surprises me—it's been so long, I'd almost forgotten how good it could feel.

His eyes burn into mine as if he's searching them, but for what?

"There's something so familiar about you. The way you talk. Your turns of phrase. I can't place it. Part of me feels like I've met you before . . . or read—"

I press his accusation back into his mouth with a kiss.

# Three

I button my shirt as quickly as possible while watching the office door, anticipating Sebastian's return from the bathroom. My mind cycles with a million thoughts: how much I liked the way his mouth tasted, how his hands found every curve of me as if he'd been touching me for years, how his smell slowed the beat of my heart, how resting in the crook of his neck felt weirdly like home. I shake my head as if I can empty those thoughts right onto the floor. I can't believe I had sex with him. *What was I thinking?* I know I have to get out of here. I hustle into my shoes, grab my purse, and scribble a note on his desk pad with my phone number.

*I'm sorry. I had to go.*

I don't stop running until I'm back in my car, then race out of the parking lot and back home before my body tries to turn around and explain myself.

The clock ticks in the hall as I sit on my couch, wrapped up in a blanket and my anxiety, Sebastian and Death and seeing my articles again all spinning on a loop.

My phone trills with a notification. My heart flutters. It's an unknown number, but I know it's him.

Hey Vivian,

It's Sebastian. Sorry to see you go earlier. Everything alright? Was it because you lost our argument and needed to save face? ☺

I can't fight away a grin.

No problem. It was good to meet you too. I thought you might be embarrassed after I poked holes in your carefully constructed thesis.

I toss my phone away before I type anything else. The phone has landed face up, and three dots are wiggling under his message. I can't help watching them start, stop, disappear, and start again.
I don't move, waiting to see what he will say next.
In another minute, my phone trills again.

Well, we should continue this debate of ours. A proper date. I found an invitation to First Fridays at the McMullen Art Gallery downtown tomorrow at ten a.m.

They're featuring some works from the artist who painted the piece in my office, and I thought it would interest you.

I'm sure he sees my many stops and starts before I finally hit send.

If you want to have your entire scholarly career up for debate, then I guess we should go and continue our discussion. You might have to write a letter to the editor of The New Yorker with clarifications and edits.

I pad along the hallway into the kitchen as a guilty thrill ripples through me. There's a wrongness to this feeling, an echo of something I used to chase. Sleeping with a man who knows my words—my soft spots, my ghosts—should scare me. Instead, I crave it. He's like a gorgeous blue fire, dangerous and beautiful, and I'm already reaching out, knowing full well I'll burn but craving the heat all the same.

Maybe I need it, just to feel something sharp again.

The phone vibrates in my hand. I'll see you there, Vivian. Looking forward to proving you wrong.

⁓

I arrive at the exhibition late, debating with myself the entire time. I am wearing a white dress and low heels, my curls piled high on my head, with a few pieces at my temples pulled out to frame my face. I walk in and spot him dressed in a white polo, dark-blue jeans, and navy-and-white sneakers. He's holding a bouquet of white hydrangeas, pink roses, and tangerine daylilies.

I almost laugh. It's been decades since anyone's brought me flowers. It's such a simple gesture. Yet, the flutters have returned to my chest.

"You look beautiful," he says, kissing my cheek. "I thought these might help soften the blow when you lose our argument."

I laugh and inhale the flowers' delicate perfume. "Is that what happened?"

We loop around the exhibit, indulging in some mimosas and exquisite mini pastries. This is one of those moments that begs to be written down. I remember how captivating he was speaking to last night's audience. I feel that pull again as he explains the work of Shawn Bines, the vulnerable but strong charcoal lines of his male models.

We talk for hours and don't find our way back to our argument. I learn he's decent at chess but will crush an opponent in checkers, has an aversion to every kind of artificially processed cheese, and has a scar on his left knee from falling from an apple tree when he was ten. He's warm, charming, and considerate at every instance. But when he turns the tables on me, I do what I've always done and stick to vague details about my past.

We are among the last to leave, lingering in the magnolia-scented breeze.

"Lunch?" he suggests. "I know a great local West African restaurant owned by the family of one of my students."

I have an article that needs to be written, and as much as I've missed this feeling, this possibility, I hesitate for a moment. *Only* for a moment.

We walk to the car, he opens the passenger door, and we drive.

"So, what's the catch, Sebastian?" I ask.

"What catch?" he says while changing the music.

I enumerate the facts on my fingertips. "A PhD, seemingly unattached, loves history, appreciates my writing, has a taste for adventure, and, not to stroke your ego, is sort of handsome."

He purses his lips. "Based on eyewitness accounts, I'd say definitely handsome."

"You rely on biased sources to make your case," I say with a wink. "I have to dock you points. But I have to be missing something."

He leans forward. "So, you do think I'm handsome?"

"*Sort of* handsome. I thought scholars paid attention to detail. Facts."

He tilts his head, glasses glinting, the sun kissing his skin. "I know what you're doing," he whispers. "You're searching for the big flaw, my secret shame. Is that right?"

"There must be one . . . like, how many women currently believe you're in a relationship with them right at this very moment? How many children do you have? How many baby mamas?"

He laughs, the sound deep and rich, how chocolate would sound if it made noise. "No baby mamas. No children. Not that I'm opposed," he says, holding up his hands. "No wife, and no girlfriend." He pauses, the twinkle in his eye slipping, replaced with sadness. "I wouldn't do that to anyone." He glances away, and I barely hear his next sentence. "No one alive has a claim on me."

I follow his gaze to the window.

I know that tone. I've lived that tone.

Only losing love to death hurts like that.

We sit in traffic, the shrieks of laughter from a nearby school bus full of children at odds with the heaviness of the moment. I put my hand on his before he shifts the gear. He looks over gratefully, brushing his thumb across the back of my knuckle, the awkward moment sliding away. I'm not one to press him. I have my own secrets and pain to bear, but in that instance, we share the weight. It feels like a bit of relief.

"How about you?" he asks in return, the moment gone but not forgotten. "I'm not keeping you from anybody, am I?"

I shake my head no because what else can I say? *I am waiting for Death?* I give him the semblance of the truth. "I moved back last summer. A friend passed away, and I wanted to make a change."

"Sorry for your loss." He waits a moment before continuing. "You said 'back.' Are you from Savannah?"

"Yes," I admit. "But, with all the changes, it seems like another lifetime. It felt like coming home was the right thing to do." I don't speak my secret thought—of how fitting it would be for it to end where it all began.

"I can understand that. It's part of why I came back to Georgia too. My mom's from here and has needed more help than she'd like to admit ever since my dad passed away two years ago. The move was unexpected, but when the position became available, the dean contacted me to interview. Just another example of the good luck I've been experiencing lately." He winks at me.

"Good luck?"

He lists things off on his fingers, miming me. "The sun is shining. I met this infatuating woman who loves to argue with me. The food is about to be great. The day's glorious." He draws attention to the sky like the day is perfect just for him—for us. "All good luck."

When he grins, I can't help but smile back. Part of me feels like I'm awakening from a deep sleep, seeing the world with fresh eyes again. After Winston, I've been barely living, barely writing, hovering on the edges of existence, and Sebastian makes me want to take part again. To spend less time thinking of Death and far more relishing the present moment—planting a seed deep down in my heart once more, a fallow ground where I swore nothing could grow again.

We arrive at the restaurant and feast on jollof rice, egusi, and spinach stew. I forget myself while conversing with the owner, slipping into Igbo and then French when his wife from Côte d'Ivoire joins us, astounding Sebastian.

He gapes at me as we leave. "You're a puzzle, Vivian. All the things you know, languages you can speak, and to be so young. How?"

I just smile and grip his hand tighter. "Testament to a life well lived."

"Up for one more adventure today? Since we both are fans of history?"

I can't back down from his challenge. This time I don't hesitate. "Lead the way."

Before heading to his surprise location, we grab lattes and pastries from Ruby at the café, then traipse along Broughton Street, perusing the stores, stopping to peer into Leopold's Ice Cream and to finish our coffees under the shade of the SCAD cinema marquee. "Is this what you do every day?" I ask as we continue down the street. "Surely you have classes to prep for."

He tosses his cup in the trash. "Summer sessions don't resume until the seventeenth, and I can't think of a better way to spend the time." He holds my free hand as we walk across the street. "Why? Are you trying to get rid of me?"

I fight a blush. "No, of course not. Well, not yet," I tease.

I'm so distracted by how he looks at me that I don't realize we've stopped at the Telfair Museum.

I freeze and drop his hand. Even though the Owens–Thomas House & Slave Quarters are open to visit, repurposed as an educational center sometime after I left for Paris over a century ago, I don't need reminders of my early life here, especially while I'm with Sebastian. For once, I want to leave the past in the past and live fully in the present.

"Everything okay?" He looks puzzled.

"Fine." I take a deep breath and enter. I should relax. Maybe, for once, the past can stay in the past.

We tour the other exhibits hand in hand, studying sculptures, displays, and artifacts from the eighteenth and nineteenth centuries to the present. It's like viewing history in reverse. I bite my tongue, trying not to share too much, as he watches my every reaction. What is he searching for? And what do I see when I watch him right back?

Sebastian laughs after I get too detailed about World War II photographer Jack Delano recording life in the 1940s, the evidence I shared with Death in our meeting in 1952. Death pointed to the evil of war and all his work collecting souls, while I pointed to the good that had won in the end. "How can you know all this, Vivian?"

I shrug. "I'm a student of history like you."

He accepts my answer, but a strange part of me wishes I could tell him the truth. It's been so long since I've said the words out loud.

As an academic, his knowledge of and interest in the past nearly rival my own. His fascination and curiosity excite me. He's riveted by every part of the exhibit, reading all the descriptions and then using his phone to research more—like it hurts him not to know something. The wonder inside him is infectious.

It's late afternoon as we finish the main tour. "Why don't we duck in here," he says, pointing to a burgundy sign that reads SAVANNAH COLLECTS. "One last exhibit. That is, if you're up for it."

I know the museum's collection is like my own, with bits of history captured for posterity. Paintings, knickknacks spanning from early colonial history to the present, museum-quality items from local homes putting their treasures on display. Any other time, I'd be looking forward to searching, seeing what objects might be interesting for Death, but this time, I'm content to exist with Sebastian at my side. I can't think about what could happen next. Instead, I'm just glad the moment exists. Besides, I'm not tired in the least. A buzzing runs through me, near electric at his touch.

We're standing near the entrance, bodies close. No matter what I do, a force keeps drawing me back to Sebastian, back toward the light. He only has to lean down, to adjust his head just so, for his lips to find mine.

"You make me feel up for anything," I admit softly, gazing up at him, giving him the permission he's asking for.

He smiles, leaning in those few and final inches. His kiss is as good as I remember—better, even. His lips are warm and taste of chocolate from the croissant we shared earlier, and he cups my left cheek, holding me close. I wish I could hold on to this sensation, the delicious frenzy of wanting someone, a bond deeper than a one-night stand on his office desk.

I forget that I'm in a museum.

I forget we're not alone.

Nothing exists except for us at this moment.

As he leans away, I realize how much I've missed this—all of it.

A coughing fit from an elderly woman brings us back to reality. We break apart, but our fingers remain intertwined. I'm not used to such public shows of affection, but won't apologize for this surprising, beautiful day.

"Vivian." I like the way he says my name. The admiration is nearly too much to bear.

"Sebastian."

"After this collection, how does dinner sound?" He checks his watch. "I seem to have kept you out all day, and something tells me you forget to eat when you're on deadline."

I stop beside a table of displays, my heart hammering. How can he read me this easily? Everything about him and this day has felt so right. Could I have another love after all this time? "On one condition."

He waits eagerly.

"We can eat at my house." The words feel foreign, inviting him into my space too dangerous, but something inside me can't stop making these sorts of mistakes.

He beams, nodding. "You know, I—"

I freeze and don't hear his response.

The light falls, streaming through the slatted windows, on a smaller display. I step away from Sebastian, leaning closer to the case, my lungs shuddering, all the warmth disappearing.

"What are those?" I can barely get the words out.

An older gentleman, one of the tour guides, slides over, his face rosy and round.

"Good eye! Hand-painted tin figurines from the late eighteenth century from a private collection, artist unknown. It's rare to find objects like these in such good condition. You might have seen them on the promotional materials."

A piercing cold spreads from the center of me.

The glass display holds a set of painted tin figures. Not soldiers, but instead men and women of the day—businessmen, servants, as well as the elite—painted as if they're going about their day-to-day lives. In the middle is a woman, skin bronzed, hair brushed up into black curls, dressed in a blue-and-white-striped gown with a red rose at her waist.

I bring my hand to my lips. My fingers tremble.

I'd thought these were all lost. How are they here?

I don't need an exhibition label or didactic text to know whose these were.

I knew the creator.

I loved him.

I never thought I'd see work by his hands again.

"How much for them?" My voice is rough and doesn't feel like my own.

The tour guide stands back, pale blue eyes wide. "Th-they aren't for sale, ma'am," he stutters. "They're on loan from a private collection."

"Then contact the owner," I say sharply. "I'll pay for them, whatever the price."

Sebastian appears at my side. "Vivian, are you okay?"

"No." I grip the glass, staring at the figurines. I'm not okay. Sebastian reaches for my hand, but I keep it firmly on the case.

If I touch him, I'll fall to pieces. I've never wished so strongly and so urgently that the ground would open and swallow me whole, plunging me into darkness, where at least I couldn't feel pain like this.

How stupid could I be?

To his credit, Sebastian remains by my side, respecting my space, as the guide goes to get his manager. A petite blond woman breezes in, at first smiling; her frown becomes more pronounced the longer they talk. Soon, she picks up a phone to make a call. I watch it all like an out-of-body experience. All I want is to get the figures and get out of here. I can barely breathe past the lump in my throat.

After ten tense minutes, the guide and his manager return. "This is highly unusual, but we've spoken to the owner, who wishes to remain anonymous. These pieces are quite rare," the manager says, gesturing to the display. "And, unfortunately, the seller won't sell for less than half a million dollars." She holds her hands up in a display of helplessness, as if that will resolve the matter.

"Done." I open my purse and pull out my checkbook. "Who do I make it out to?"

Sebastian's eyes widen, his expression more than curious.

The tour guide and his manager both drop their jaws, and they scramble to do the necessary things to secure my purchase.

The manager wraps them up carefully, places them inside a gift box, puts that in a bag, and hands over my acquisition as gently as if handling a bomb.

It's apt.

Any inkling of an idea I had for a future, any future, for myself or the world went up in smoke as soon as I saw the figurines.

"Vivian, what's going on?" Sebastian asks, his gentle voice easing into the silence between us.

"Sebastian, I need to leave. I can't explain this." I gesture to the bag. "But I can't do this either," I say, gesturing between us. "I thought I would have more time to figure it all out—what it is, what could be—but I don't."

"Vivian, wait! You can talk to me. Let me help you." Sebastian is bewildered. He reaches for me, but I jump back, tears stinging.

How could I have been so stupid? I was *this* close to giving in and starting it all again—the story that's played out over and over as the decades and centuries have passed.

Sebastian doesn't know the favor I'm doing him by leaving. If he knew the truth, he would already be far away.

Death will find anyone I love and take them. These figurines are more than enough of a reminder of that.

"You need to leave me alone. For your own good," I say as I grasp the bag and flee.

# Four

Everything is frighteningly clear and straightforward on the walk home—the alarm sounding in my brain is high, and piercing. "Shock" is the only word I can use to describe the feeling of finding the figurines. I don't even recall leaving the museum, when suddenly I'm home, under the shady trees of Jones Street. I storm up the front steps of my town house and slam the door shut, barricading myself inside.

My phone pings with notifications, likely Sebastian wondering where I am and confused by what happened. I turn it off and sink into the quiet, with only the white noise of the air conditioner. My papers are scattered all over the table—all the notes I've taken for my latest article on the Cluskey Vaults, part of it now inspired by Sebastian and his challenge put forth to Jimi to show more.

It's laughable in hindsight. I thought I could offer this as evidence. Why would Death be moved by words inspired by another potential love when he's so committed to seeing me alone? When he keeps taking the loves I've had?

I sag onto the couch, reliving the image of Sebastian standing there, the confusion and hurt on his face as I ran away. I imagine what he thinks of me: crazed, clutching a thin plastic bag like it was my life preserver. I hate that I can't tell him what's wrong.

The bag lies on the floor, listing open. A strangled laugh burbles up inside me at the sight of it. I suppose I should take more care. I just paid half a million dollars for seven tiny pieces of tin.

I slip onto the floor to pull the gift box from the bag. I open it and touch each of the metal pieces. Up close, the paint's faded in spots, but I picture them as they were when they were new, vibrant colors mirroring real life. William bent over the workbench of his shop, sweating from the forge's heat, the coals glowing red hot as he steadily poured the tin between the slate plates, setting up the molds to harden. I remember him painting all the fine details with a tiny brush, in awe of how the same huge hands that fixed massive wagon wheels, shod horses, and forged iron could do such delicate, intricate work.

I pull all the figures into my lap. We're all there, represented in the set: Eulalie in her green gown and golden hair, holding hands with Eugène, Jacques with his black hair and blue eyes in his dark coat.

I pause, holding William himself, skin brown, shirt white, with a hammer in his hand. I trace my finger over the tiny face, the one I once caused so much pain. I push away what it has always cost me, what it cost William, what it cost all the others.

It was unthinkable. The happiness of the last twenty-four hours feels fleeting and idiotic.

How did I imagine I could pursue something with Sebastian?

How did I think Death would let me?

How did I think I could endure another love . . . when they always die?

When I lost William, I thought these figurines were lost as well, stolen along with his life. How did they get all the way from New Orleans and into that case? Their beauty admired by museum patrons and a cruel reminder for me. My life has never been my own, from my birth into forced labor to my bargain with Death.

The irony is that I finally have what I wanted. My collection is complete. Something from each of my loves—my own evidence of beauty and cruelty. I take a deep breath, pack the figurines in the gift box again, and head to the trunk—the one I keep covered with a weighted blanket, as if it were thick and heavy enough to hide the past.

I drag it off and gaze down at the leather steamer, patched and scarred from decades and decades of travel, a fitting final resting place for all my memories.

I unsnap the locks and push open the lid, plumes of dust whirling in the light, angered at being disturbed. The scent of old leather, cedar, and cardamom rises toward me with a faint whiff of mothballs. Inside lies a smattering of objects that, at first glance, look like junk destined for the trash heap.

A weathered sketch ripped in half.

A red silk dupatta edged in broken golden thread depicting birds, flowers, and vines.

A pair of embroidered silk gloves, the fingertips yellowing with age.

A bundle of faded postcards from destinations all across the globe.

A small wooden sun painted gold, the snapped rays carefully glued back together.

A scrapbook collecting clippings of every piece of writing I've ever published.

An album of secret photographs of me through the decades.

My life in objects.

My life fractured in pieces.

The room is quiet, just the whirring of the air-conditioning, the faint whoosh of cars passing in the street, and, if I listen closely enough, the sound of my broken heart. No one would know how much any of this means to me. But my entire heart is locked away in here, splintered between each item and the person it represents.

I ease the gift box in front of the sketch, and I'm sure now of what comes next. I stand and retrieve the book from the bookshelf, my worn, weathered copy of *Robinson Crusoe*, and nestle it inside at the front, everything in order. Now the collection is complete, a timeline of my long life.

Seeing it all makes me think: What's next?

Is it time to end this? Is that why Death is teasing me, prolonging his arrival?

A knock comes at the door, breaking the silence with perfect timing. He has always appeared at his whims, and not a moment too soon.

I stand, brushing my hands on my skirt, and let the trunk slam shut.

It's time to face whatever is supposed to come next.

# Five

I fling the door open, the knob slamming into the wall. Instead of Death smirking at me in a new form, Sebastian stands there, wide eyed, chest heaving. "Vivian?"

I flinch and swallow the name, grating against another reminder of how little he knows, how little I can share. "What are you doing here? How did you know where I live?"

My tone's sharper than I want it to be, but I can't seem to keep anything under control right now.

"You were so upset . . . I just wanted to make sure you got home safe."

Even as I'm pushing him away, he's here, steady. I'm falling to pieces and being mean to him, and he's still standing here, concerned. I wish I could tell him my secret. Not just because I trust him, but because I know he'd *get it*—he'd see the story in it, the history, the wonder. I think he'd see the beauty in it—the meaning others would miss. But even the thought is an impossibility.

"I appreciate you coming, but I really need to be alone."

"Are you sure? Of course, you don't owe me an explanation . . ." He approaches cautiously; his face is crestfallen and confused. "But I can't shake the feeling that something happened. One minute you were inviting me here for dinner. The next—well, I'm not sure. For what it's worth, I'm here."

Guilt bubbles up inside me, and I can't push him away.

"It's just my past," I say, trying to hold back the emotions. "And there's nothing you can do about that."

He studies me, unflinching. "Can I help? The past is sort of my specialty."

"I just met you yesterday." A hot tear streaks down my face, landing on my collarbone. He reaches, wiping it away with the pad of his thumb, still managing to make me smile despite the overwhelming pull of my past and my present.

"Your birthmark—so unusual and beautiful. Just like you." His fingers gently trace the heart-shaped mark.

I want to lean in, but our touch sends sparks, and I snap out of the reverie. "This isn't your problem. You can't help me with it. No one can. You should go."

"Are you sure? I'll go if that's what you truly want, but every part of me is saying that I shouldn't. That I can't just let you disappear."

"That's what I'm best at." I clutch the door, trusting it to keep me upright—the emotion of everything running through me. I don't want to disappear. I want to let him in. I want to understand how it's still possible to feel this way after all these years, all these lifetimes.

I turn to go, stepping into my foyer, but he reaches for me again, like he did at the gallery, brushing my curls from my eyes, his touch soft and sweet. The ease of it disarms me. Tears erupt from deep inside. In a swift motion, he cradles me in his arms. Any sane man would run, but he stays, stroking my back as the tears come endlessly. The seconds turn to minutes until I'm empty and wrung out.

"I don't know where to begin," I say finally.

"Perhaps we can start from the beginning."

I shake my head, unable to even fathom how I'd explain it all.

"Vivian, I said you could trust me." I gaze up at him, his arms still wrapped around me. Deep in my core, I know I can. I'm not sure that he should trust me, though. I think of Diego. Sebastian will only end up hurt in the end. Or worse. I study his face, wishing it could all be different. "I'll understand."

His promise lingers as I leave his warm grasp. A new resolve fills my heart. I start to walk toward the kitchen, then turn back. "You coming?"

A half smile tucks into the corner of his mouth. I fill the kettle and make us both a cup of tea. He carries the tray into the living room. It is a strange feeling that he seems so at home. He examines each wall painting, remarking on my pieces; then he turns to the shelves to run his fingers across the spines of my books. "You've amassed a collection of quite rare books. I thought my library was impressive, but this is . . ." He fills the charged silence with praise as he soaks in the details of my world.

He pauses by the open trunk, glancing at me for permission. I wait as he peruses the objects, gently handling the albums of photos. Photos of every version of me. He flips through. "Are these your ancestors?" He flashes one at me.

"No, they're me." The words feel distant, but now that they're out, I can't take them back. They're me. They're *me*. It's one of the first true things I've said to him since the moment we met.

I watch him marvel, his passion for history bubbling up inside his chest, before a wrinkle of confusion mars his brow. "Period-costume parties? Is that your thing, Vivian? Is that what you were too afraid to tell me?" He chuckles nervously.

My mouth is dry, so I take a gulp of tea. "That's the thing, Sebastian . . . you should know my name's not Vivian."

He rubs the ridge of his brow, confused. "So, you're not Vivian Edwards? Esteemed journalist and writer?"

"I *do* go by Vivian, and I wrote all those articles. So, it's not about that." I swallow hard, the truth on the tip of my tongue. "It's just that . . . Vivian's not my original name."

"So, what is it? A pen name? What do you mean?"

My heart hammers like a bird is trapped in my chest. Once I do this, there isn't any going back. Despite the cost, I only want to go forward.

"I mean that the answer to your question . . . none of it is going to make sense."

"I'm a historian. I can puzzle together a lot." His eyes widen with deep trust.

"My name is Nella May Carter, and I was born in February of 1760."

∼

Sebastian paces around my coffee table. He's on his fifteenth lap. Hands pressed against his head, soft mumbles under his breath. "This is a prank, right? Is it because I'm new to the history department? Is this some kind of . . . initiation?" He glances at me again, searching for the gotcha.

"It's not." I fuss with my dress, the nervous energy in my hands looking for an out. "It's one of the first true things I've ever told you. Ever told *anyone* this decade."

I wait for him to run. A normal person would run or, at the very least, search for the number for the nearest psychiatric unit, but he stays put, staring down at me, his brain, no doubt, trying to reason it all out. "Let me explain." I shift on the couch to make space for him.

He eases beside me like getting in a too-hot bath, wary, a little fearful. "But . . . how?"

I've forgotten where to begin. It's been so long since I've uttered it out loud. "Have you ever read *Faust*?"

His eyes bug out. "You made a deal with the devil?"

"Not the *devil*." I shake my head. "Death. There's a difference." It's subtle, but I understand his thinking. I haven't met the devil in all my life, but I've seen enough evil to believe there is one.

"Okay . . . so you made a deal with Death for . . . immortality?" He rubs his temples and doesn't touch his tea.

"I was dying of typhoid, and I asked Death to save me," I say matter-of-factly, knowing how implausible it sounds.

"Typhoid?" He makes a face. "What is this, *The Oregon Trail*?"

"Hey!" I say, wagging a finger at him. "It was pretty common back then. You should all be more grateful for clean drinking water and antibiotics."

"Okay, okay." He holds up his hands. "I apologize. Typhoid is a perfectly reasonable and respectable way to die."

We laugh and the tension breaks. Not quite belief, but a tendril of faith stretches between us.

"So, Death saves you from . . . death—I'm still wrapping my head around that—and wants what?"

"I told him I could show him the beauty of humanity. I'd find evidence that humans are worth saving."

"So, all of your writing was to please Death—and allow you to live?" I sense him wrestling with the reality of my story, lingering on the cusp of belief.

"Me, yes, but also you. Everyone."

"I'm going to need a little more than that."

"He wants to end the world. He will if I don't continue to win our argument."

"And how long will this go on?"

"Until I can't do it anymore."

He cocks his head, examining me. "And this is not a joke? I'm not on some show getting punked? *Do* people still do that?" He sounds more inquisitive than repelled.

I shake my head as the emotion of the truth floods me. He can finally see it.

"You've been alive . . . all this time?"

I grab the photo album from the trunk with shaky fingers. He helps me open it between us. "See for yourself."

He flips through it again, his jaw dropping with each turn as his brain makes sense of what he's seeing. I edge closer, experiencing the album through his eyes.

The past smiles up at us. Kerchiefs and hats give way to a 1920s flapper bob, 1940s Hollywood waves, and a picked-out Afro from the height of the 1970s. Though my hairstyle and clothes change, my face and the heart-shaped birthmark on my collarbone remain the same. The woman in the photos is, unquestionably, me.

"These images are from their period. Ambrotype, tintype, celluloid, Polaroid. And it is you," he breathes, flipping faster. "It's all you." He points to one from 1973. "Your birthmark." The album remains open in his hands. He's frozen that way, absorbing the impossibility of all this. The seconds feel like an eternity. Then, all at once, he jumps to his feet, animated, pacing again. "God, the things you must have witnessed! When were you born again? What were the conditions like? How have you managed to escape notice all this time?" He sits again, turns a page, and freezes, his eyes on one picture. "I knew it. I knew I'd seen your face before." He shakes his head in disbelief. "You *were* Jimi Ireland? All the stuff I said in the lecture . . . that was *you*?" He scrutinizes me, his mouth a beautiful wry smile. "You arguing with me. It was all . . ."

I delight at his expression, like a kid's at Christmas, or, more accurately, as if all his Christmases have come at once.

"I'm sorry, I'm just so . . . excited. You are living history." He gazes at me, eyes clear, no hint of repulsion, just intense curiosity. "I must be going crazy, but it all makes sense. The languages, the travel, the history?" He laughs to himself and leans back on the couch. "My God. All you've truly seen . . ."

I close my eyes for a moment. Time has trickled by, adding up like grains in a sandglass, and I've withstood it all, faithfully recording my travels. The album in Sebastian's lap tells the tale—a picture of me at the 1893 Chicago World's Fair listening to a speech by Frederick Douglass, and me in the front row at the Savoy, watching Ella Fitzgerald perform . . . dozens of images of me drifting through history. All those people gone now, with only me left to truly remember.

"Will you tell your story one day?"

"I want to tell you."

"And I want to hear it."

I gaze at the window as if Death stands there watching me invite someone else into our game. The repercussions and consequences of telling Sebastian every single detail crash inside me, a storm I'm unable to escape on the horizon. It will anger him. He will come.

"I need to say the whole thing out loud one time. I need to remember it all." I close my eyes for a brief moment. Death has given me a gift many have dreamed of—a long life free of disease and physical pain, unchanged appearance, the gift of tongues—as long as I can please him. But the true cost sits between Sebastian and me, thickening in the silence. The devastating reality is that if I fall in love with him, I will lose him. There will be nothing either of us can do about it. Do I want to do this again? Living as long as I have, I now know it's a curse to want to live forever. A long life isn't, as Sebastian thinks, about all you've seen. "I believe you could understand the most."

"I'm honored." His face is somber and sincere. He puts his hand in mine. "So, how should we start?"

"Record it." I steady my voice, calm but certain. "I want to hear it when all is said and done."

"Give me one second. Don't go anywhere."

I'd ask *where* I would go, except I've already run out on him once.

Sebastian dashes out the door to his car. It's only a minute before he's back, out of breath. He sets the recorder on the table as quietly as possible, the steady red light staring at me. The glare a warning beacon. A rule broken. Unlike the words in my notebook that could be cast off as the ramblings of a lonely, unwell person.

But this old-fashioned device makes it feel real, capturing my story like Zora Neale Hurston did in *Barracoon* or as Ernest Gaines did for the fictional Miss Jane Pittman. Something tangible left of me when I've spent my life as a ghost. Something Death said I would never have.

I smooth my skirt and lick my lips, throat suddenly dry. Where will I even begin?

He senses my tension and eases it away with only the sound of his voice. "We can start wherever you like. I'm here to listen."

The knot in my chest loosens. I think through all of it for a place to start. New Orleans. Paris. Sierra Leone. Decades of history stretching into centuries flash before my eyes.

*Where to begin?*

The gift box sits there waiting, calling me to start at the beginning. I open it, brushing away the tissue wrapping.

Sebastian waits, his beautiful eyes filling with a deluge of questions as he bites back the urge to ask. I will unspool the truth. I glance at him again, hesitation suddenly cropping up in my chest. If I do this, he'll see me. *The real me.*

"Where do you want to start?" Sebastian teases to fill the silence between us.

I remove three figures, running my fingers over the painted tin. Might as well start with what tore the day apart. "Let's use love."

Sebastian's nose crinkles. "Love?"

"Yes. The truth of this story starts in New Orleans."

# PART II: NOUVELLE-ORLÉANS

The Figures—1795

# Six

I rechristened myself Noelle Carbonnier. I thought it fitting, since I was beginning a new life in La Nouvelle-Orléans, and it had been eleven years since my first meeting with Death. The journey from Savannah had been long and slow, mirroring my search for Silas. My first task was to find a job—no small task—and learn the lay of the land. Miss Hortense was instrumental in teaching me the customs of the place. I had found a room at her boardinghouse at the outskirts of the city—clean, neat, and far more comfortable than the shack where Death had found me.

As gruff as Miss Hortense was, she taught me how to get by in a place so foreign it might as well have been a different world. The law then commanded that all free women of color in the city wear their hair in tignons to show their status. They made their wrapped scarves things of beauty, with elegant twists and curves that looked as if tropical birds had landed upon them and graced them with their plumage. Miss Hortense instructed me on how to tie mine, how to wear my dress, and how to live in a city that was a mixture of the French, the Spanish, and the newly made American.

I had sold whatever valuables I could take from the main house to pay my way, but the money I had in my pocket wouldn't last long, and if I didn't want to be on the street, or worse, I would have to find a way to earn.

And of course, I'd need money if I was to find my brother. A young slave couple fleeing through the same forest pathways I'd discovered had told me they knew Silas, and that he'd been traded to a branch of Master Carter's family in Louisiana. My aim was set.

After a week, I donned my best white cotton dress, the least mangled from the trip, and paired it with a white tignon, tied simply. Peering at the bit of reflection in my room's small looking glass, I decided my appearance was at least ordinary enough. I would blend in.

I approached Miss Hortense, asking what kind of opportunities the city offered to a woman like me. She barked a laugh. "You know what you can do. Laundry or manual labor. Anything that'll leave your body bent and broken." She gazed at her own hands sadly. The skin was rough and darker than the rest of her, and her right hand twisted in a painful-looking gnarl.

I knew the truth of her words, but I had no choice. I thanked her for the advice and asked her to be alert if she heard of anything. Then I set out, determined to find a position.

Though I had been in the city for a while, the noise and busyness still startled me. The entire town bustled with movement. A lorry driver was urging his team of horses down the avenue. Marchandes' calls rang out above the chaos, their arms full of food baskets, tempting each passerby. The more well-to-do strolled, fanning themselves in the growing heat as they picked their way across the streets. The smell of hot dung and human excrement mingled with the fresh wood of constant construction. A fire had ravaged part of town the year before, and the recovery was still underway. In other areas of the city, new grand projects were planned. New Orleans was a town on the rise, and if I planned on staying, I would have to rise with it.

By the third shop I visited—and the third resounding no I'd received—my spirits and the rest of me were dampened. The midday sun shone, spiking the humidity. Sweat leaked from my tignon, and my dress clung to me as I soldiered on, ignoring the thoughts of failure that were becoming increasingly present. What if I couldn't find a position? I had only enough money for three more weeks with Miss Hortense.

As I pondered the magnitude of my situation, a woman pressed to my side, dressed in the white cotton skirts common at the time, head framed with a yellowed tignon, a broad wicker basket in her hands, full of browned sugar cakes. "One shilling or piece of eight," she urged in Creole French, crowding me in the street. The cakes smelled heavenly to my empty stomach, the rough ground coffee from breakfast long gone. I eyed the cakes but thought of the shillings in my pocket.

I stepped back. "Not today," I said, matching her accent. My eyes landed on her basket, still pressing into me. "I'm looking for work, actually," I said quickly. "Would you know of anything?"

The woman's welcoming smile vanished as her black eyes narrowed, looking me up and down. "Work's tough enough. You won't find anything here." She brushed past me, bumping me hard in my shoulder, knocking me off-balance and nearly to the ground. I was stunned, hot pricks burning behind my eyeballs as I almost fell into the dirt.

Later, I would come to understand her reaction. With a limited market, another woman of color on the street wasn't good for her business at all.

Luckily, she wasn't the only marchande working that day.

A hand extended from nowhere, gripping mine to steady me. My rescuer rested her woven basket on her hip and grinned. Her skin had a honeyed tone, and her brown eyes sparkled warmly. Her skirts were wide, white, and full, covered by a dark-blue many-pocketed apron. The square neckline suited her stout structure. Her hair was in a red tignon, tied expertly, as Miss Hortense had shown me.

"Don't mind Adelice," she said, jerking her head at the offending woman's retreating back. "I'm Sylvie. I heard what you said." She gave me an appraising look. "You need to find Miss Eulalie de Mandéville. She has a big warehouse on Esplanade Avenue and always needs people. Go on down there."

She winked and resumed her calls, beckoning customers from across the street with gentle ease in her movements.

It wasn't much, but it was hope. I hurried from that spot, excited at just the chance of an opportunity. Her words spurred me on through the humidity, thick as soup. I followed her directions, closing the gap between me and the warehouse. I hadn't been to that area of town before, and made my way carefully, aware of my surroundings. The warehouse was near the water, the funk of the river growing stronger the closer I went. It mixed with the pungent smell of fish left to dry in the sun. Construction clamored around me as teams of brown and black bodies labored under the careful eyes of their supervisors. One of them caught my eye: a tall man near my age, a long scar running down the right side of his face. He reminded me of Silas, with his hooded eyes and prominent brow. He could have simply been looking, interested in a woman walking down the rutted street, but guilt rose inside me, spurring me forward; the expression in his eyes haunted me.

Luckily, the warehouse wasn't far, only three turns away, set in the middle of two larger buildings, crates piled just outside. My mouth got drier with every step as blood pulsed in my ears. I tucked my chemise in and straightened my tignon, ensuring my hair was pinned away, pulling this and that until I was respectable. I straightened and made my way inside.

Piles of crates and boxes filled the large main room, about the size of Miss Hortense's house. Beams of light slanted down from the upper windows, illuminating the space. Men and women, all shades of brown, bustled around like ants carting boxes or wares and stacking them for distribution. The space was orderly, filled with positive energy and the hum of activity. I tried to pinpoint exactly where the energy was coming from and realized it was the workers. They held themselves proudly, as if they had a mission, a purpose.

I scanned the space, searching for Miss Eulalie. Sylvie had said she'd be impossible to miss. I only hoped I would know her when I saw her.

I asked a passing man, a box hoisted on his shoulder, and he jerked his head toward the back of the cavernous room.

Sylvie had been right.

Eulalie stood in the middle of that great warehouse—tall, with dark-blond wisps escaping her tignon. She directed the workers around the warehouse, not unlike the supervisors from that construction site, but with a calm demeanor that spoke of assurance that her orders would be followed. She didn't have to yell or threaten. She simply consulted the papers she had in her hand and told them what to do.

I had seen the mistress of the house giving direction, but never a woman of business—and a woman of color, at that. I didn't know it, but at that time, she was younger than me, just twenty-one, the seeds of her empire newly forming. Still, a tingle ran through me, a sign I was in the right place at the right time.

Eulalie's tignon might as well have been a crown, made of a canary-yellow cotton broadcloth, meticulously knotted and twisted to the right. It marked her as the queen of her kingdom, which I quickly learned was absolutely the case. Loose curls framed her face, her light-brown skin clear and even.

What struck me most, though, was how at ease she was.

I wiped my sweaty palms on my skirt and waited for her to notice me, biting the inside of my cheek the entire time.

She turned toward me. "What do you want?" she asked in a clipped fashion, her eyes coolly taking stock of me. I resisted the urge to recheck my appearance and stood at my full height. I didn't know what she thought of me, but I knew instinctively to meet her eye and hold my place.

"A woman named Sylvie told me you needed workers. I'm here for work."

She didn't say anything but continued to assess me, the moment stretching out. I was conscious of every one of my flaws and imperfections, from my worn dress with its inelegantly hidden patches to my ragged shoes, gone thin in the sole. What would this formidable woman think of me? The tingling feeling that had flooded me quickly turned to dread. "I'm a hard worker. And I can read," I said quickly, filling the silence.

She shook her head and motioned away, shooing me without ceremony. "I have nothing. Good day." She returned to squinting at the papers in her hand.

I was baffled. What would I do now? I almost turned and left, but I hadn't had that feeling before. That tingle of the meant-to-be.

I stood my ground. "I'm sorry, miss, but I can't take no for an answer."

Eulalie stopped and frowned. "Unfortunately, it's the only one I have."

I inhaled. "I know what you said, but also . . . I—I'm not leaving."

"Is that so?"

I swallowed and nodded. In truth, I was *this* close to fleeing. "I'm supposed to be here. I know it."

Her eyes twinkled in a shaft of light, a rich hazel that sparkled with mischief, and she smiled, suddenly blooming like a flower in the sunshine. "Now that's the kind of attitude you need to succeed. Name?"

"Noelle."

She cocked her head. "Well, Noelle, let's see if I can't find something for you to do."

That was how it began. Even in our brief meeting, I could see that Eulalie was a beauty, a brain, and the boss all at once. And in that instant, I formed a new goal. I knew who I wanted to be.

I would continue to search for Silas, and I would also become the woman who could buy him outright.

∼

Months passed, and I became Eulalie's most successful marchande. I had an advantage, as I was able to speak the native language of any person on the street, and with Miss Hortense's help, I wore the fashionable goods I was selling, showing them to their best advantage.

Soon, Eulalie took me into her office, where I was able to see firsthand how she had grown her French grandparents' dairy business, left to her in their will, into the thriving trade she did today. She was whip smart, bold, and self-assured—everything I hoped to be. Time spent in proximity made us fast friends. She took me along to social gatherings at the most beautiful homes on Marigny Street—newly built, with wraparound porches and wrought iron railings ornamented with flowering vines—screaming of both abundance and influence. The gatherings were mixed, attended by some of the top Spanish officials and other members of the Creole ruling class.

My feeling in these gatherings was always the same: a swirling cauldron of contradictions. While we weren't the only free people there, most of the other people of color were serving the event, offering drinks, and bringing platters of food. People acknowledged us as we walked by, but the gaze was cool, almost dismissive. In response, Eulalie always beamed her brightest smile.

"Do you ever get used to it?" I asked as we made a turn around the room.

"I find that the more money I have, the less the gazes of small people matter." She squeezed my arm.

One Sunday, I was invited to Eulalie's church. She and her family attended St. Louis Cathedral, the great big Catholic church in the heart of the French Quarter. The white stone building reached two stories and was flanked by three-story towers on each side. A great clock in the middle marked the time. The building was new, having only recently been completed after the earlier great fire of 1788, the cornerstone marking the date. The tower was so grand, almost a stairway to heaven, that it made earthly problems seem small.

I didn't know what to expect when I sat next to Eulalie, sinking onto the wooden pew near the middle of the aisle dedicated to the personnes de couleur, free people of color. We lit candles and said our prayers. As the preacher droned on, I prayed that somehow news of Silas would find its way to me. It was easy to believe in that place, and I was glad I had come. My heart ached, but I could breathe a little.

After the service, we walked together toward the area surrounding the church, enjoying the fresh breeze and warm sunlight. We weren't the only ones.

Eulalie's beau Eugène was there, and so was his friend Jacques. In the last month, Eulalie had become absent minded, misplacing orders and repeating herself when giving directions to the staff. More than once, I'd come to her office to find her staring off into space, a secret smile on her face.

It was Eugène, her father's pick, her love, and her future.

With fewer women in the colonial city, arrangements called plaçage were commonplace—a wealthy white Creole man beginning a relationship with a free woman of color, promising to provide for her and any children the union created. I had never considered Eulalie desiring something like that. I had assumed she would have married another free man.

"Does he have a wife?" I asked, my curiosity getting the best of me.

"He does, in France," she admitted. "But you've been here long enough to know this is the way of things."

I swallowed. "Then I only inquire as to whether you love him?"

She seemed to expand in that moment, her eyes alight. I half expected her to float in the air. "'Love'? I don't know if that word is big enough to describe what I'm feeling. One day, you'll see. You'll find you won't care one whit what they call it."

When I met him that first day after church, I understood. Tall and slim, Eugène had dark-brown hair with clear skin the color of cream. He wore a dark-blue jacket tailored to fit his broad shoulders, and it suited him well, along with his open smile and cornflower-blue eyes that crinkled in the corners. He was fun, dashing, and obviously in love with Eulalie, so her distraction made sense.

"Is this the famous Noelle?" he asked in French, gasping theatrically.

I laughed, nodding in greeting. "Famous? Hardly."

"According to Eulalie, the warehouse would fall to ruin without you. Anyone who is a boon to her shall be a friend to me." His words charmed another smile from me—the man was besotted.

Eugène reached for Eulalie's hand, and she gave it gladly, intertwining her fingers with his. Anyone could see the love bursting from them like sparks from the blacksmith's forge. I had to glance away, the sight as blinding as the grief I still felt being so alone in the world. But the introductions were not finished.

"Jacques, it would be my pleasure to introduce you to Noelle Carbonnier, my most trusted personal assistant," Eulalie said, nodding to me. "Noelle, this is Jacques Boudreaux. He works with Eugène in the brokerage, managing investments." Jacques stood four inches above me, dressed like Eugène in a snug-fitting dark-blue jacket. His deep-brown eyes held merriment as he bowed in my direction.

"Pleased to make your acquaintance," I told him.

"I doubt you could be more pleased than me," he said, taking my hand, as was proper, and kissing it, his French smooth and melodic. He gazed at me through thick black lashes.

"How could that be, sir?" I asked as he released my hand, my fingers still warm and tingly.

"I have heard of your prowess with figures and reading. I find it estimable."

I blushed. "They're acquired skills. Easy with study and practice."

He tilted his head, considering his words. "Perhaps, but it puts you in a class of your own. I do enjoy the company of others who improve their mind." The compliment blossomed within me, like a seed finding sunlight.

"Now, Jacques," Eulalie said playfully, "she won't be needing your company. You are a distraction. I implore you to be on your best behavior." Her eyes connected with me. "He is incorrigible."

"Eulalie, you wound me," he said with mock distress. "I consider myself a gentleman." His stare never left me. "All I meant to say was that I have quite an extensive library and will happily lend every book in it to you, should you ever ask."

"That's generous, sir. I appreciate your kindness," I said.

I bade them goodbye and retreated to my rooming house, resuming my place in a mood that was perceptibly lighter. I didn't know it then, but the slender roots of infatuation were taking hold, wrapping around the shards of my heart. I had no clue how much Jacques would change it.

~

After that, I began to regularly attend the services at Eulalie's church.

I came to enjoy the time afterward, with Eugène and Jacques arriving faithfully each week and escorting us through New Orleans.

My favorite neighborhood was the Place Publique, where we gathered to watch dancing to the cadence of African drums and sample the beignets, a hot fritter-like pastry covered in fine sugar. Groups of the free and enslaved would gather for an impromptu market and celebration day on Sundays—dancers from Saint-Domingue, white fabric wrapped around their heads and stretched across their hips, bodies moving in unison, faces lit with joy, celebrating the only piece of the week they had for themselves.

Like a flower under a patient gardener, I blossomed, flourishing under the warmth of Jacques's affection and weekly book selections. I began to look forward to the title he would bring and discuss the one he had offered the week before. My favorites by far were Ann Radcliffe's dark and moody *The Mysteries of Udolpho* and *The Travels of Dean Mahomet*, which detailed Mahomet's travels to Europe from India, opening my mind to places I didn't know existed. I stayed up late into the night reading his accounts of the delicacies, people, and cultures he encountered.

Jacques didn't read the books, seemingly satisfied to have me recount the contents to him. I felt important as I shared the ideas and the conversation the books sparked. I didn't question why he spent sums on books, only to give them away. I was interested only in growing my own collection as I read deep into the night, learning of lands far beyond this one, grateful for Death's gift of being able to read and speak any language I heard.

Some Sundays, we broke off and walked alone, his hand lingering over mine. It felt good to be the center of his attention. It wasn't the red-hot love Eugène had for Eulalie. I didn't know if I was even capable of those kinds of feelings, but it was a warm, pleasant glow.

In September, Eulalie and Eugène moved into a large two-story home on Rampart Street. They hosted a masked ball at their house to celebrate their commitment, a celebration open to all who understood the nature of their relationship.

For the occasion, I had chosen a blue cotton dress with marigold petticoats, a white shawl tucked around my shoulders and into the neckline, and a marigold tignon to match.

Eulalie bustled by me. "Is that a new dress? Quite fetching."

I nodded, fluffing the cream cotton skirts with the dark-blue trim.

She gave me a long look. "Anyone you're hoping you'll see tonight?"

"Possibly." I blushed and straightened the row of extra masks meant for guests.

The steady stream of guests soon consumed my attention as a quartet began to play. The sound of stringed instruments mingled with lively conversation as a pair of dancers swept about the room, waltzing to the sprightly fiddle. Other couples joined them on the dance floor, and the room became an atmospheric swirl, colored with the flicker of candlelight, the spin of vibrant cotton and patterned silk, the spice of tobacco, and the titters of laughter from tongues loosened by wine and champagne. The scene was a wonder, and my place in it would have been unthinkable before Death had given me this chance.

I stood watching, until suddenly Jacques came up behind me, pulled me into his arms, and took me out through the open door into the darkened summer evening.

"Mr. Boudreaux, you forget yourself!" I yelped. But I went willingly with him into the night, my grasp on propriety loosened by the effervescence of the champagne and the atmosphere.

"Miss Noelle, I'm sorry to say that your mask does nothing to hide you from me."

"That's a shame. I paid far too much for it then."

He grasped my hand and pulled me into a twirl—my back pressed to him, his cheek next to mine, our bodies swaying to the music.

"No matter what you picked, I would always know it was you. You have utterly bewitched me."

My heart hitched as he gazed down at me, the slightest dimple visible on his left cheek, rough with a day's growth.

"Now that you know it's me, what will you do about it?" We were not the only couple strolling along in the darkness, farther away from the lamplight of the interior, slipping into the shadows that only the garden could provide.

"Everything."

No one had ever spoken to me this way. A flush bloomed in my heart and sank low into my belly.

I wasn't innocent. There had been . . . incidents at home right after Master Carter, my father, died. Sometimes memories I had buried deep returned to me in flashes, and I'd startle and struggle to remember that I wasn't back home.

But this was the furthest thing from that place, that time.

And Jacques was a good man.

Right hand on my cheek, he drew me in, brushing his lips over mine, his free hand on my back. I lost myself in the kiss, the music tinkling through the air, and the hum of the cicadas in the background, his warmth stirring me from the tips of my toes.

Then he looked down at me. His eyes lost their teasing light, becoming serious.

"Noelle," he said, his breath heavy, "would you consider something more between us? Something more . . . secure." His eyes swept over my face as he searched for the words.

He wasn't being coy. I knew true marriage was not an option, but Eugène and Eulalie had settled for the closest they could get.

"I—" I couldn't finish the thought. It all felt so sudden. He crushed his lips to mine, his kiss more urgent, his hands more insistent. Heat flooded between us. It frightened and thrilled me.

I pushed against his chest, allowing more summer breeze between us. "You can't ask me something like that and then make me lose my senses."

He grinned good-naturedly, still not letting go of my side. "Think about it, and tell me in the true light of day. We can go on a ride tomorrow." He grasped my hands, his strong, pale fingers dwarfing mine. "I will take care of you."

His earnest declaration felt heavy. To be taken care of—I hadn't even considered what that would mean.

Having someone to do all the worrying for me.

Someone to give me space for my writing and the time to complete my task.

Someone whose resources could be put to use in finding my brother.

I was still processing his words when he kissed me again, his lips soft this time, moving gently over mine, the caress making me feel whole and complete. He ended the kiss, then bowed and said, "Please consider my offer, Miss Noelle." And then he took his leave.

∽

The carriage slowed and shuddered to a smooth stop.

"Do you find it pleasing?" Jacques asked, sitting so close I could barely turn, my hand gripped in his. A fine sheen of sweat sat on his pale brow as he glanced out the window, then back at me, blue eyes darting over my face.

"It's everything you've promised and more," I said, placing my free hand on his arm.

He'd kept his side of the plaçage arrangement. I pushed away thoughts about what it would actually mean to be his, while his white French wife lived miles away on the family plantation. Though she was here in Louisiana, unlike Eugène's wife, Jacques had assured me there was no love between them. Their marriage had been more or less arranged—the union of two wealthy families—and I, he insisted, was his focus.

I believed him. Eulalie had discreetly inquired and had been told that Jacques's wife had her own arrangement, with a woman in her social circle.

Jacques beamed, wrapping me up in his arms, the scent of fine tobacco flooding my nose. I waited for the appropriate time before I leaned toward the window and gazed at the house.

"It's beautiful," he said.

And it was.

The house on Rampart Street spoke of affluence—whispering of sugarcane wealth from the thickly paned glass door to the brass lion-head knocker centered at eye level, its mane curling, a brass ring clutched in its sharp metal teeth. Long and narrow, two stories of white stucco rose skyward, supported by four white Grecian columns standing like sentinels, centered on a large corner lot, one of the grandest on the street, attesting to its own importance. A stately wrought iron balcony wrapped around the second floor, and the forest-green shutters were thrown open to catch any breeze that cut through the swampy heat. Trimmed hedges peeked from the back garden, nestled next to the carriage house and stables.

It was a far cry from that tiny cabin on the outskirts of Savannah. It almost didn't seem fair that I'd be living there—that I'd have the opportunity to call it home. What would Mama think of all this? Guilt rattled through me that while I'd been blessed, I still hadn't discovered Silas's whereabouts, but I was determined.

"And yet, it is nowhere near as beautiful as you, Noelle," Jacques murmured, distracting me. He stroked my arm, his fingers lingering, tracing a path up to my shoulder, along my jaw, his eyes on my mouth, their color like the sea after a storm, his dark hair curling forward.

I flushed at his words and his touch, jumpy as a jackrabbit, ready to bolt, but kept myself still.

From the moment our arrangement had become official, Jacques never missed a chance to touch me. The intensity of his affection was overwhelming.

Jacques had always acted honorably. But I continued to carry what had happened to me in Savannah. My body had been my own for the past eleven years: to work, write, and survive. In entering into this agreement with him, I would discover what it meant to live and lie with a man.

*We just have to get used to each other,* I thought. *He knows how to be affectionate.*

Jacques sat beside me, his hands clasped around mine. "Are you ready?"

I swallowed the butterflies twirling in my stomach and remained still, focusing on his handsome face, square jaw, curling hair, and hungry gaze. I reminded myself this was not all for me. This was also a way to find my brother, Silas. *I can do this.*

Still, I couldn't shake the tightness in my chest when he came near, as if my new corset had been laced too tight.

"Should we go inside?" I asked, one hand on the handle as I smoothed my white-and-blue-striped shirt and adjusted the fabric rose at my waist, the garment symbolic of my new station as a placée.

"I'd love to see our home." I sweetened my voice, playing the part.

Jacques blinked, the lust clearing from his eyes as a red blush traveled up his milky-white cheeks. His usual calm demeanor slid into place. The tightness in my chest eased.

"Of course," he said. "We'll have time enough together." Jacques bent quickly, grasping my hand and kissing my knuckles as the carriage door hinged open.

The driver, William, stood waiting, dressed in a cotton shirt and dark-blue waistcoat that contrasted his rich, dark skin, allowing us room to pass. Taller than us both, William had the neat trick of appearing smaller, taking up less space, hovering in the background, as silent as a shadow when he drove us on our outings before the arrangement had been finalized. I'd always wanted to speak to him. Back home, I would've acknowledged his presence, all of us tracking each other, keeping an eye out for one another. A free Black man, he cared for the horses in Jacques's stables, working as his driver and farrier, shoeing Jacques's horses and those of others in the city. He operated a small forge and fabricated the nails, horseshoes, and tools. But I struggled to find the words just yet. William didn't say much, sticking to one- to two-word responses, always keeping his attention fixed an inch above my shoes.

Jacques trundled out and reclaimed my hand to help me out of the carriage. William said nothing, per usual, his eyes forward, trained on the distance.

Sometimes I wondered what William thought of our arrangement. A free personne de couleur moving in with a white man of French descent. Did he think it strange? Did he think about it at all?

"William, make certain her effects are delivered to my room," Jacques said.

"Of course, sir," William replied, stepping back from the door and securing the horses. "I will tend to Beau's hoof. He cast a shoe on the way back." He patted Beau, a broad brown bay, with gentle, graceful strokes.

"Good man," Jacques said, leaving William behind and leading me by the hand up the walk. He had never been to Miss Hortense's rooming house on Dauphine Street. He couldn't know how far a cry this grand house was from my small, shared room there.

"Ready?" Jacques whispered as we strode toward the front door.

I didn't know if I was, but the time for hesitation had passed. My future and my fortunes were now tied with his. I inhaled to steady myself as he unlatched the door, and we crossed the threshold to our new life.

The door opened into a small foyer, a small drawing room on the right, and a narrow set of honey-wood stairs on the left that swept up to the second floor and smelled of wood polish, linseed oil, and the dainty bowl of dried-rose potpourri on the stand. Some of the nervousness ebbed as I took in the magnificence of the decor. The mirror to the right had been polished to a high shine, reflecting the both of us.

"Welcome home," he said, beaming, pulling me forward. "Come, there's more to see." Seconds later, I learned exactly how much *more* there was and what that meant to Jacques.

Green arsenic lace papered the drawing room's walls, depicting bluebirds on red flowy branches covering the room, and good-quality furniture was arranged artfully. Sets of blue-and-white plates featuring flat-roofed houses and delicate mountain scenes spanned the entire right side. Twelve golden statues of indigenous design sat on a central table, and a large battle painting dominated another. The eye had nowhere to rest. The room was packed, nary a horizontal surface uncluttered.

*How can he have so much?* I wondered.

I tried not to react as we continued the tour, each room fuller than the last. An elaborate cage made of gold wire stood in the center of a sitting room, the light slanting through its bars. A small bird rested on a wooden perch. I'd never seen anything like it—its exotic plumage fluffy white, with a bright crest of yellow feathers on its head and two orange circles on each cheek.

"This is Milly, my pride and joy." He rubbed the bird's gray beak through a gap in the wire. "She's a cockatiel. I bought her from a trader last autumn." Milly chirped, the sound happy and high as she fluttered from post to post. She hopped down, pecking at the food bowl, talons scratching the newsprint at the bottom.

"Do you ever let her out?" I asked, drawing closer.

Jacques shuddered, face paling. "Oh no. She got out once, circled the room, smashed into the shutters, and got caught up in the curtains." He stroked her beak again, his smile growing as he gazed at her with adoration. "She's much happier here, where she's safe."

I studied the bird as it hopped from post to post. It let out a cheery warble. I stuck my finger through the bars and wiggled it. "Hello, Milly. It seems we'll be sharing an address. It's nice to meet you."

Jacques seemed pleased at my reception. "Now, come," he said, tugging my arm. "Allow me to present to you the rest of the household staff."

We crossed into the dining room, where two women waited. The shorter one, tawny with wide hips, was around forty years old. The taller one was her daughter. Her skin was a rich reddish brown, her figure trim. She was close to my age—at least, the age I appeared to be since my deal with Death.

I swallowed, smoothing my skirts, flustered. He'd told me about them, but I still wasn't ready for the reality of the situation and how similar I was to these women. But for the differences in our dress, an outsider would think us related.

Jacques extended his arm in welcome. "Noelle, this is Sarah, one of the finest cooks in all of Nouvelle-Orléans. Her rice and beans are a true delicacy. She can make both French and Spanish dishes or whatever your heart desires." Sarah bobbed a curtsy in my direction, eyes lowered, a thin smile crossing her lips. "This is her daughter, Jenny, who takes wonderful direction. I'll leave the management of the household up to you." Jacques beamed over at me and gestured for me to introduce myself.

"I'm . . . delighted to be here, and I promise . . . not to be a bother." They both nodded politely, but I caught the glance between them.

Their presence unnerved me. I could too easily imagine myself in their place, stoking the fire in the kitchen, cleaning chamber pots, my arms swollen and red from boiling laundry. And for so long, I *was* in their position, doing those very tasks. Presiding over the house as mistress felt false, for I hadn't yet learned the rule of immortality—be whoever you need to be to survive.

Sarah and Jenny lived elsewhere, as Jacques paid his house servants, for which I was thankful. After what I'd lived through, I couldn't hold someone else in servitude.

Jacques's family, however, didn't mind it at all. The large Boudreaux family's sugar plantation sat outside New Orleans in St. Bernard Parish, a scant seventeen miles from where our house now stood. Though Jacques spoke in angry tones about the practice, the enslaved at the estate, managed by his older brother, numbered over 250. The pervasiveness of slavery was as thick as the mosquitoes in the city, with hundreds of thousands of people pouring in on foot, by steamship, and the cartload to be sold at one of the city's many auctions. Entire families were sold by the auctioneer's call to those who deemed themselves civilized.

But we never discussed slavery, and I had to keep the reality of the large Boudreaux plantation toward the edges of my mind.

We bade Sarah and Jenny a good day and allowed them to return to their duties. Delicious smells wafted from the kitchen as Jacques and I continued our house tour.

Each room was clean and packed near the rafters with his collections, each drawer stuffed to the gills. Of all the rooms, I liked the study the best; the furnishings were minimal, and bookcases overflowing with books covered three walls. The oddities in the room were contained to the fourth wall: an odd assortment of taxidermy, including horned bucks, a hairy, sharp-tusked wild boar, and a jewel-blue stuffed peacock. A large secretary-style desk took up most of the floor, with a burgundy rug underneath and various papers scattered on its surface. How much could I write on the large corner desk? Pages and pages, both for Death and for me.

I had not forgotten about our arrangement. All through my time in the city, I sought as many stories as possible, hoping to capture examples of laudable humans and wondrous things. Once I entered society, I began to puzzle out how to get published in *Le Moniteur de la Louisiane* so he would see I was hard at work.

The final room on the tour was his chamber—or should I say, ours. It was tranquil—the walls painted a rich cream, the space dominated by a large four-poster bed and its intricately carved headboard, complete with a mattress thick with goose down. Two small nightstands stood on either side of the bed, each holding a pitcher, bowl, and trimmed-wick candle. The soft scent of roses floated through the air from the bouquet on the bureau. Of all the rooms, it was the sparest, perhaps because it had the most straightforward purpose.

William had already deposited my chest at the foot of the bed. Jacques gestured toward it. "Here is the wardrobe and some things I had purchased for your convenience. I have a letter to attend to. You get settled, and we'll dine shortly. I've given Sarah and Jenny the evening off."

I understood the implications.

We'd have the house to ourselves.

I wasn't sure what to think. My experiences had only been ones I wanted to erase from my memory, and I'd lost Mama before it was time for those kinds of questions.

I nodded, trying to keep my smile from wobbling. "I'll refresh myself."

"Jenny will come for you when the meal is ready." He brushed a kiss against my temple and left, and his footsteps ebbed away. I sank onto the goose-down bed, listening to the steady ring of William's hammer and the twitters and squawks of Milly downstairs. I stared into the ceiling, my mind toggling through all that had transpired up until now.

I'd come a long way from when I'd arrived in Nouvelle-Orléans from Georgia, yet I was still in pursuit of Silas's whereabouts. I had amassed a bit of money. Enough, I hoped, to buy his freedom when he was found. Jacques had been managing my accounts, and they were growing every month. His name, I reasoned, would open doors to places and information that had previously been closed to me.

And here I was, in Jacques's house—my house. We'd signed the papers that very morning, with Eulalie and Eugène as witnesses. Jacques would provide for me should something happen, improving my financial situation and caring for any offspring we might have.

I couldn't tell him there would be no children because of my bargain. Death hadn't said anything about relationships when he'd left me in that cabin. He hadn't said anything since the day he'd saved my life; he hadn't yet come to visit me again.

A knock at the door in our new home startled me from my reverie. Jenny stood in the hall, brushing her hands on her skirts. "Miss Noelle, dinner is ready."

I nodded, rising from the bed, breathing deeply, knowing what would come. Would I like it? Would it be what I'd hoped for?

I followed her, slowly descending the stairs.

Though dinner was delicious—stewed rice, sausage, and greens tastefully seasoned—I left half of it in the bowl, my stomach fluttering.

All too soon, the church bells tolled, naming the hour when Jacques rose, hand extended. We didn't speak as he led me up the stairs.

"I do hope you're happy here. Now that I have you, I feel my life is complete." He sprang forward as if released, his lips capturing mine.

I tried to focus on the moment, but his hands, now loosed, were everywhere—on my back, on my stays, running up my spine, the sensations overwhelming. I wanted to slow things down and ease into each other, but it was as if he were dying of thirst, and I was the first glass of water he'd sipped in weeks.

He moaned and murmured against my neck.

*Beautiful.*

*Exquisite.*

*Gorgeous.*

The depth of his desire left me spinning. I tried to lose myself in his affection. Being with Jacques would be new and different because he cared for me.

With a few swift movements, my dress pooled on the floor at our feet. I kissed him soundly, willing myself to surrender to the moment. His stare felt like being worshipped in the dim candlelight as he dragged me on top of him. We rolled in the bed, his hands roaming again.

He took my breast gently between his teeth, and I gasped at the new sensation. He trailed kisses along my neck, nuzzling under my ear. He was a man possessed, his fingers digging into my hips. He ground himself against me. His member, swollen through his breeches, pressed into my belly. He reached down between us, adjusting himself between my thighs, and thrust forward. I couldn't breathe, startled by the foreign sensation.

He shouted almost immediately, "Noelle, my love. I adore you."

I held on to his shoulders, my voice trapped in my chest, as he groaned, then collapsed beside me.

He pulled me close, clutching me to his chest. My heart raced, my core aching, a yearning still there in the hollowness.

Was this love?

And lovemaking?

Was this what husband and wife did?

I supposed it would be fine.

After all, it was the cost of this new life.

# Seven

Life in the house soon grew to be routine. A tap would come on my shoulder each night, and Jacques would draw me close, kissing the spot below my ear. Each time allowed me to sink deep into a life with him and away from the memories of where I'd been.

Master Carter's first wife died in childbirth. After that, he'd forced himself on Mama, who'd had Silas and then, two years later, me. In time, though, he'd needed a legitimate heir, so he'd married Miss Mariah Wilcox, a widow, when I was five. I remember seeing them for the first time when the wagon slowed as it crept toward the Big House. Missus Mariah had a daughter named Mary, aged seven, and a son, Wilbur, aged twelve. Their father had died from pleurisy two years prior.

I'd peeped through the window into the sitting room, too curious for my own good about the new mistress of the house. I watched her sip from the nice china. Beautiful like one of the women in the books that Master Carter would read. Her brassy yellow hair was swept up and pinned with a black hat as she ushered the boy and girl from the carriage. Her smile had dropped the instant she saw me, her mouth turning to a thin, flat line. I never saw that smile again in my direction. My resemblance to Master Carter and his slight favor of us earned me sharp smacks or painful pinches as we passed in the narrow hallway—always a reminder of my place. But she hated Silas the most because, with his reddish hair and hazel eyes, he looked most like Master Carter.

Missus Mariah wanted her son Wilbur at his side instead, and she finally had what she wanted in 1778, when Master Carter died.

His will was ignored, and instead of freedom, the little favor granted to us was stripped away. Missus Mariah sold Silas, leaving me alone to fend for myself. Wilbur had watched me over the years—the threat of my father the only thing keeping him back. Now gone, he'd caught me a few times, hurried, pushing my skirt up, leaving me bruised, with split lips. Thankfully, I never became pregnant. Bearing his child would have been a fate worse than death. Wilbur married a neighbor's daughter, Miss Jessica Monroe, and took over the plantation. The abuse lasted for a year before Wilbur was called to war. There'd been no tears from me when he became cannon fodder at the Siege of Savannah.

Jacques's touch didn't erase the horror, but it did dim it. He showed me sex didn't have to be violent. It could be pleasant. Functional. Warm. I'd slowly gotten used to his touch. Which was good, for it was almost my only responsibility.

Once I'd moved in, I'd given up working with Eulalie, only seeing her to attend social events and parties as we mingled with other free Creoles in the city, folding into a veritable spectrum of brown folk striving to set themselves apart and assert some control in the growing city. I looked forward to those days, a break from trying my hand at being mistress of the house.

The freedom had been glorious at first. I no longer had to wake up by the tolling of the bell. Jacques dressed, and we ate in the dining room daily. In the afternoons, he had meetings, and on the days he didn't, he shut himself up in his study to work. We kept our habit of walking on Sundays, but I spent most of the days alone, left to my own devices.

I would eat Sarah's breakfast and spend the hours as I pleased, usually reading or writing. Like all his collections, his library was extensive, with more books than I'd ever seen. I read the poems of Phillis Wheatley and Samuel Taylor Coleridge and perused Benjamin Banneker's 1794 and 1795 almanacs. Eulalie pressed into my hands a copy of the scandalous novel *Justine* and advised me to save it for when Jacques was not at home.

I spent many days using the thick creamy paper from Jacques's study to record the day and the events and even cataloging Jacques's collections, still searching for the beautiful and good; I submitted letters in French to the editor of *Le Moniteur de la Louisiane* under a male pen name. I thought Death would've come around by now, but he'd left me to my own agenda.

As did Jacques. He made occasional trips back to the plantation to tend to his duties there. Before he left he would grasp my hands, hold them to his chest, and assure me of his devotion. I had no doubt of it.

Still, week by week, my world shrank, limited to the house's four walls. Despite my inquiries, I'd heard no news on Silas, and my letters to Missus Mariah's cousin, the family I was told Silas had been sent to, had gone unanswered. Still, I continued to search for him, paying for investigators and combing the newspaper for information, but I found nothing new.

I had seemingly endless time.

So, I wrote, continuing to fill my notebooks as I called up memories and recorded them. I chronicled hog butchery in the fall, watched Milly the cockatiel as she flapped and climbed in her cage, and wrote of my experience having a new wardrobe made for me, the details of my life pouring across the page. Sometimes it wasn't even my current life, but memories of the places I'd been and the things I'd seen there—the croak of frogs on the bayou, the beat of African drums on a Sunday afternoon.

Whenever Jacques returned, we would retreat immediately to our chamber, no matter the time of day. He was always at least cursorily interested in my pleasure, but almost as soon as he'd enter me, with three to four rough strokes, he would shudder, his face contorted, before he collapsed, sweat coating his brow. He'd kiss my shoulder and roll over, his soft snores echoing to the high ceiling soon after.

This left me tossing and turning until the early hours of the morning, wrestling with insomnia, searching for a feeling I could not yet put to words. I would stare at his sleeping face, the hollowness inside me growing bigger and bigger by the day.

It was during one of his trips away, long after bedtime, that I sat in Jacques's study, fresh paper before me, ready for another letter to Missus Mariah's cousin about Silas.

The crash of breaking glass lured me from my writing. I tiptoed toward the sitting room and heard something rustling inside. Had Jacques returned? I turned the knob and peered in, and a great whoosh sounded in my ears. There was a blur of white as something raked against my face.

I screamed and slammed the door. My heart beat like thunder. It was a moment or two before I heard—

"Miss Noelle?" William's deep voice came from under the door to the kitchen.

"William," I gasped, pointing. "There's something in there!"

He entered the hall, his eyes blinking away sleep. He looked at me, then dropped his gaze to the floor. "May I see to it?" he asked.

I nodded and stepped out of his way. He put his hand on the knob. Without thinking, I touched his arm. It was like rock, strengthened by his work at the forge. "Be careful."

He nodded and went inside. The rustling sound came again, and William called out in surprise. Then, after a moment, a different sound slipped beneath the door: a soft familiar song loosening memories I'd long buried. I waited there, puzzled, listening to the baritone of his voice, the melody filling the lonely parts of me and reminding me of when Mama would wash and comb my hair.

Curiosity rose, and I peeked my head inside, finding William serenading a petulant cockatiel, luring her down from a perch on a curtain rod high above.

"Milly?" I laughed. "Naughty bird! How did you get out?"

William smiled, and it was as warm as the sun. "I think after Sarah cleaned the cage, she made a run for it."

"I don't blame her in the slightest." I whistled to see if she'd come to me, but the bird continued to stare at the both of us with glassy eyes.

Finally, William warbled in a way that mimicked Milly's calls, and she flitted down to his outstretched finger. He grasped her gently around her wings and brought her to me.

"Determined little girl," I said as I stroked Milly's beak.

Willlliam rubbed her chest with his calloused thumb. "Just following her heart, I suppose."

I held the cage door open, and William deposited her inside.

Silence stretched between us, and I realized that this was the first time we'd really interacted. He averted his gaze, staring again at the rug on the floor. "I'm sorry for the intrusion, Miss Noelle. I'll be going."

"Wait—" It only then occurred to me that I was in my bedclothes. My cheeks burned. I pulled the robe's opening tighter around my waist. "It's the dead of night. What are you doing here?"

"One of the horses is due to give birth any moment. I've been in the stable, tending her. I heard you scream. I hope I haven't—"

"No," I interrupted. "No. I'm grateful to you. Thank you."

He trod gently out through the kitchen, and I heard the back door latch behind him.

From that point on, William started to find his way onto my pages. The sound of his hammer was a constant in the background of my home-centered life—swift, heavy strikes against metal as he shaped horseshoes, forged tools, and made nails to supply the constant construction. I didn't see him much, except for when we happened across each other in the garden. I'd learned about him secondhand from Jenny and Sarah and from Jacques's acquaintances as they came for dinner.

"You should see his business! Soon, he will have his own shop and work for himself."

"William is the finest farrier and blacksmith in the town. His craftsmanship knows no equal."

They painted a picture of a talented man who cared for others and worked toward his own success. When I heard his hammer strikes, I imagined him coming one step closer to his dreams with each blow.

The next week, while Jacques was at his office, I screwed up my courage and went to the stables to see him. A mare and her newborn greeted me in their stall; William was laying the floor with fresh hay.

We spoke for hours. He told me how he'd studied his trade and honed his expertise. "Good jobs are hard to come by for colored people in this city," he said, tapping his thick fingers on the handle of his pitchfork. "I was lucky to have apprenticed to a true craftsman."

I nodded. "I worked as a marchande when I first arrived."

"You?" William startled. "Figured you were a writer, since you're always scribbling in the study or reading a book."

"I got to know the city and meet so many people. It helped me ask after Silas . . ." Accidentally saying my brother's name out loud felt like another piece of shattered glass, this time a part of my heart. A truth I hadn't uttered out loud to anyone but Eulalie in months. The only truth I could share with him about my life.

William's eyes filled with concern. "Who is Silas . . . if you don't mind me asking?"

"My brother. He was sold here. I came to the city to find him." Everything I'd been doing and had learned about Silas's whereabouts up until now poured out of me. I didn't realize how much I'd needed to comb over the details with someone, to allow someone else to hear the story of our family. Telling this part of the truth cracked open a dam. Tears poured down my cheeks, and I couldn't wipe them away fast enough.

William closed the gap between us, plucking a fresh handkerchief from his pocket. He put a hand on mine, the sensation flooding me with a warmth I'd never felt before, a warmth Jacques's hands had never conjured. As he wiped away my tears, I gazed up at him, really seeing him for the first time: his dark-brown eyes, almost black, filled with curiosity and care; his soft black hair, curled like sheep's wool; the trim beard framing his jaw; his perfect full mouth. For the first time, I felt the energy I'd seen between Eulalie and Eugène. Desire. My own.

"I can ask around about him if you want," he said. "Nouvelle-Orléans seems like a big city from the outside, but it's a small town for the colored folk. We know each other. We watch out for one another. Someone's got to have seen him or heard about him. I'll help you."

⁓

As the new year came and went, I found myself outside in the garden every day, writing and waiting to see William. He tended the plants or made his way to the stables to care for Beau, Jacques's brown bay, or Winny and her foal. I'd look forward to greeting him with a nod, then stealing glances between sentences: always aware of him, where he was, and what he was doing, and unable to forget the night we'd rescued Milly together and hoping to get a few minutes with him alone.

He trundled by with a wheelbarrow, and I couldn't help but stop him. It had been weeks since we'd talked.

"William," I called out, careful to ensure that no one in the house heard me.

He paused before me. "Yes, madame?"

I balked at his formality. "Nel—I mean, please call me Noelle." The panic of almost saying my real name flooded me.

A small smile played on his lips while sweat gleamed against his brow.

I opened and closed my mouth, trying to drum up something to say to him. "How are Mr. Boudreaux's horses?"

"Would you like to go riding?"

I wanted to reply that I could care less about the beasts. "No, not at all. I—"

"What are you working on?" He gestured to the paper.

I flushed as I shuffled the papers together, wanting to lie to him but being unable to as he stared down at me. I wondered if he could read and write. "I was writing about the sunset."

"May I hear?" he asked finally.

Nerves ran through me at the thought of him hearing my work, but I cleared my throat as I plucked a page off the top. Jacques had never taken an interest in my words. I hadn't had anyone but Milly to read to.

He closed his eyes as I read:

*"One of nature's sweetest songs comes in the evening, as the golden day fades into the depths of night, when a man lays down his labors and prepares to feast and slumber.*

*"That is when the symphony begins, the cascade of sound that gives Earth her music.*

*"Her song.*

*"The cricket's steady chirp, the bullfrog's deep burble, and the cicadas' crescendo serenade a day at its end, their earthly lullaby singing the sun to sleep."*

"That's a mighty fine piece of writing," he said.

"Thank you." William's encouragement felt like much-needed sunlight. "Do you read?"

"A fair bit. Enough to order what I need for nails and things. Nothing like this, though," he said, pointing to the pages. "I've never heard anything like it before." He collected his wheelbarrow. "I hope you wouldn't mind reading your work with me again in the future." He tipped his hat and headed toward the stables.

I floated inside, delighted to have found an audience.

So that was how it started: my readings with William.

I would spend my mornings writing and then find him as he tended the garden or the horses. I watched for William's reactions as I read, hoping my words would lead to a smile, his dimple flashing, head nodding encouragement as he worked with precision.

The more time I spent with him, the more I grew to admire his nature. His gentle care showed in how he handled his horses, brushing their coats to a high shine, reshoeing them, and keeping their stalls near-perfect.

"It's good practice until I have my own space. I'll have a full blacksmith's shop with at least three apprentices, and we would have the biggest forge for miles. I'd have a shop in the front where we sold the nails, pieces, and supplies. The cities are growing. If we had one place folks could get all their supplies for building, I think it'd be a success."

I'd watch how his eyes illuminated as he described his dream, a roaring fire like the one in his forge, fed by passion and vision. The same way the hearth inside me burned with the desire to write for eternity, to see all that the world had to offer, and to beat Death at his own game.

"With you at the helm, of course, it would be," I assured him.

William at work was beauty incarnate. The forge burned, the temperature hotter than hell, as he pumped the bellows, the coals burning yellow. Black iron bars stuck out of the coals, their centers glowing red. William gripped a rod and swung it out of the fire and onto his anvil, white hot like a piece of a broken-off star. It sparked with every strike, cascades of light floating onto the floor. Once it was finally shaped to his liking, he'd smash the rod on the sharp instrument sticking out of the anvil, knocking off a glowing two-inch chunk. He plucked it with tongs and forced it into a forge, banging this way and that until he'd landed the final blow, sending the object on the floor to cool. In just thirty seconds, he'd expended all that effort to craft a single, perfect nail.

His mastery floored me. His ability to create something meaningful and useful from primitive materials like metal and fire felt like that of the ancient god Hephaestus. I'd watch the sweat drip down his muscled arms and the way he'd bite his bottom lip in concentration. The strength of his hands shaping iron to his will. My desire to know what his hands felt like, and if they carried the heat of the fire he tended to all day, only grew.

The days with William turned to playing with fire. As I tried to deny it, my heart grew fonder, and so did my dreams about where he could fit in my life. Then one day, William surprised me, inviting me into the stables.

"Close your eyes," he said as I walked in.

"What are you up to?" I teased.

"You will see." He took my gloved hand, the warmth of him still able to find its way through the fabric.

"On the count of three, you can open them." He stood behind me, the feeling of his tall frame making me want to sink back into his arms. He counted softly in French, his deep voice sending a shiver across my skin.

I opened my eyes to find a tray full of little figurines standing at attention. William stepped back, shifting from foot to foot as I absorbed them one by one.

"All your creativity inspired me. I thought I'd make something myself."

Fashioned out of tin, the figurines captured the essence of life—several were horses, while the others were human, forged from metal scraps.

One stood out, larger than the rest, buffed smooth and polished. She was the only one with color, wearing a blue-and-white-striped gown and a red rose at her waist.

"Is this me?" I held the dress up to the light, recognizing it from my first day in the house.

William ducked his head. "It's just something I do to pass the time."

"They're wonderful."

"A few weeks ago, I set to work on it. Your words greatly inspired me." He paused and spoke slowly: *"One of nature's sweetest songs comes in the evening, as the golden day fades into the depths of night, when a man lays down his labors and prepares to feast and slumber."*

My heart leaped to my throat. He'd remembered my words. Remembered them and committed them to heart. Remembered them and channeled them into his own work.

I took his hand. He startled. "It's okay," I whispered. "It's okay."

We stood in silence, listening to each other's heartbeats.

# Eight

I'd written article after article—from thoughts on the Code Noir to the marchandes to life in the colonies—and submitted them to the newspaper. I checked the post daily for acceptance, but it never came. I waited for Death to arrive filled with complaints about being unable to read what I'd written and demanding to see the evidence of our bargain. I watched for William and stole moments with him in the gardens and stables, hoping I'd be able to figure out what to do with the guilt over wanting to be with him.

Then on Mardi Gras, in February 1796, news finally arrived.

Sarah slipped into the study while I wrote. "Madame?"

"Yes," I replied, not looking up, feverishly writing about the decorated wagons that wheeled along the streets as the city prepared to fast for Lent.

"You left something in the garden."

"I did not—" I swallowed the rest of my sentence, looking up and finding Sarah's expression, a double meaning in her eyes.

She meant some*one* . . . William . . . was in the garden. I thanked her and quickly freshened up before slipping out of the house. Jacques was busy as ever, working on a new opportunity that often kept him at his office, but I could never be too careful.

A February chill clung to the garden, but I was already shivering with anticipation. I snaked through the trellises, looking for William's tall form. I spotted him along the edge.

"Hello," I whispered, trying to quell my excitement.

His eyes twinkled in the sunlight. "I have news. Good news about Silas."

My heart hammered. I rushed forward, taking his hands. He squeezed mine. "What is it? Tell me."

"He's in town with the family that owns him. They're here for Mardi Gras."

The impossibility of his words washed over me. My knees buckled and I slumped forward. William caught me in his arms, holding me in place as the truth of his news settled into me. "Is it truly real?"

He nodded. "I was told by three different people. There is a man who fits his description and goes by that name with the Cormack family."

Missus Mariah's kin. It had to be him.

"Will you take me?"

Apprehension filled his eyes.

"Please."

"What if we are seen? What if—"

I stepped back, his arms falling away from my shoulders and waist. "I can't miss this chance to find my brother. I've come all this way. I haven't seen him in more than fifteen years. I've . . ." I bit back tears. "I will go alone if you will not accompany me."

William shook his head. "You cannot do that."

"Then I guess you're coming with me."

∼

The afternoon and early evening passed as slowly as grains shifting from one side of an hourglass to another. William and I were meeting at half past nine to ensure the celebrations were finished, when Silas would most likely be back from escorting the Cormacks, but it felt like a thousand hours away. When Jacques returned home for dinner, he burst into the study, and I startled, shoving my writing aside.

"Noelle, I have news!" he announced.

"Yes?" I replied, trying to hide my distraction and guilt.

"An opportunity has come through. We've gotten word of Napoleon's victories in Italy and peace talks. I'm to be stationed in Paris, heading our operations there." He plucked me from the chair and swung me around, the room spinning. "We will spend some time in France!"

"What about . . ." I never uttered his wife's name out loud.

"She will manage the affairs back here, of course. Never you worry about that. You need to pack this house and prepare our things for the voyage."

A ship. Paris. Europe.

But Silas . . . If I left, who knew when I would be back? Which was why I *had* to find him right away. Figure out how to help him gain his freedom, how to bring him with us.

"When would we leave?" I asked as the idea of using some of my money to purchase Silas and free him formed. I started to ask him, but he swept me into a kiss. Betrayal and guilt and anguish drowned me, his lips not the ones I wanted.

"Come now, let's go to bed. The news of Paris has enlivened my mood."

Jacques could barely undress me before he was snoring. Once out for the night, he'd never wake up, and if he did, he'd assume I was in his study, up late, reading again, if he thought of me at all. A thin beam of moonlight danced on the windowsill, and I knew it was time to meet William.

I crept out of bed and dressed quickly, donning a dark dress, warm cloak, and hood.

A delicious hope raced through me as I tiptoed downstairs. I pulled the latch on the front door, carefully keeping it from creaking, and shut it tight behind me. I slipped into the night like the moon sliding between the clouds. I found my way to the gravel path leading to the stables.

William stood in the rough gravel that led to the stable, his hat in his hand, still as a statue, clouds from his breath rising in the night air. He took my hand. "It's not safe, so stay close to me."

"I can handle myself, I assure you," I said, thinking of my early days as a marchande, when some customers thought they were entitled to your body as well as your goods, but I let him take my hand anyway.

The beat thrummed through the streets, pounding up the soles of my feet as we got closer to the music.

The night was perfect, crisp with the edge of excitement. The festivities were still in full effect as a caravan of African dancers marched down the street. They moved to their drums, seemingly impervious to the chill. The horns from another band farther down gave voice to the beat.

It was life out loud. I spotted William smiling at me as I watched everything. Along the way, he even paused to spin me as the music grew louder. I'd never danced with a man, and relished the feel of his hands on my waist and resting my head on his chest.

I soaked it all in, so glad that I'd come. I soothed any guilt I'd had about not telling Jacques and being out in the city with William. I was my own person. The sensation felt so strange, even after more than a decade of freedom from enslavement. I had an important task. Silas.

William led me through a riot of people as we navigated the streets, turning left and right to head deeper into the Vieux Carré. Revelers raced by still inebriated and intoxicated by the celebrations. I could write about this for Death. I could remind him of the beauty of unabashed celebration.

William stopped before a sprawling mansion trimmed with thick iron lace drenched in moonlight. "My letters have been ignored," I said. "I can't march up the front steps; I am not welcome. What will we do?"

"I'll go to the back, to the quarters, and see where he's at," William whispered, squeezing my shoulder. "You stay here behind this rosebush."

"Take this." I pressed a scrap of paper into his hand. "I've written him a few lines. Tell him to send some word out to me. I must know that it really is Silas. That my search is finally over."

William nodded, and I watched him slip into the darkness behind the large house. I cowered close to the roses and out of sight. Then, like a deer stalked by a predator, I felt a tingling sensation rise on my neck.

I scanned behind me but found nothing other than the quiet house, a single candle flickering in a front window. I stared between the bushes before spotting a trio of white men in dark-blue sailors' coats and canvas breeches—one fat, one skinny, one tall—watching me.

"What are you doing over there, girl?" one called out.

My heart squeezed, and I tried to tuck myself away and hope they hadn't spotted me after all. I stayed still, waiting for the three to walk by. The frisson of my excitement at finding Silas fled, and my thoughts turned suddenly sober. I'd follow behind William and hide, then race home once these men were gone.

I waited for two more minutes but didn't see them pass.

Maybe they'd gone another way?

I gathered my cloak around me and turned out of my hiding place, only to run smack into the trio. A wobble rose in my gut. I moved to step aside from them, but the short one stood in front of me, blocking my way back toward the house.

"Look here, gentlemen," said the tall one. "A fine miss for the evening. Let's top off the night proper." He leaned toward me, leering, his tooth missing, his shirt front wrinkled and stained. The big one swayed, staring blearily at me and hiccuping, while Skinny watched me threateningly.

I stepped back, head high. "Nothing I have is for sale, sirs. I bid you good evening."

"Not for sale? Don't be coy. How much?" he said, reaching. "You're lurking outside this house. Must be waiting to be invited in to do your job."

"Don't you dare touch me," I hissed, pulling myself back. No one was close enough to hear my plight.

Tall laughed. "Hear that, boys? This colored tail thinks she's not for the likes of me!"

Skinny smirked. "Might have to disabuse her of that notion."

Tall reached out lightning quick and yanked me toward him. The other two crowded me in, blocking my view of the street.

"Let me go, or I'll scream." I yanked my arm back and pushed at him.

"Scream, and I'll knock you silly. Now, be quiet. It's only a bit of fun," the tall one said, one hand ripping off my cloak and hood, then fondling me roughly before tugging at my skirts.

"Stop it!" I clawed him, my nails doing no damage through my gloves. He smacked my hands and grabbed me by the throat. One yanked the fichu from around my neck, ripping the embroidered scarf in two.

"Now, Claude, you're being a bit rough, aren't you?" Big One said.

"Push off, Clemons," Tall snarled. "I'm not done with my celebrating yet. You can have your turn."

My breath caught in my throat. Black-and-white splotches marred my eyesight. My head lightened and my muscles turned weak.

"You there! Let her go!" William's voice rang out behind them.

Tall had just turned when a board smacked him across the face. His grip loosened, and I fell to the ground. Another blow hit Tall, sending him spinning, and he landed like a lump in the dirt.

Skinny jumped out next, snicking a blade open. He stabbed at William with three quick jabs, but they weren't fast enough, for he, too, received a blow to the head and a swift kick to the chest, sending him flying.

"Clemons! Let's go!" Skinny called out, lip bleeding, eyes low and murderous.

Big One hadn't engaged in the fight at all. He scrambled at Skinny's words and tugged at his tall friend, rousing him.

"We'll be back for you!" Skinny called, spitting blood and pulling at Tall's shirtsleeve. "You're a dead man!"

The three bumbled off into the night as William dropped the board, then pulled me up to my feet. His hands wrapped around me, holding me tight to his chest, absorbing my shivers of fear. His heart hammered in his chest, matching mine. "You're all right," he whispered into my tignon, the care in his voice finding its way deep down into me. "You're all right."

He lifted my chin, his eyes searching mine as if he could find the pain inside me and erase it. "I heard a commotion. I was so worried." He kissed my forehead, the warmth of his mouth sending a tingling flush to mix with the fear rushing through my blood.

"Silas?" I said, the realization of why we were here in the first place crashing back.

He handed me the slip of paper. My brother's full name, written in his hand, was unmistakable on the other side.

"He's gone to fetch the master. I've left him your address. The others say that if his master approves, he will come to you tomorrow." The pad of his thumb gently traced my collarbone, landing on my heart-shaped birthmark.

"You found him. You really . . ." I pressed my lips to his, and we held each other among the lingering Mardi Gras crowd.

# Nine

Jacques woke up the next morning none the wiser. He stretched and used the chamber pot, humming as he dressed, the day proceeding as planned. I donned a cream dress embroidered with deep-red flowers and emerald leaves, but I wanted only to block out the memory of what had transpired and wait for Silas to come. I gathered a thick fichu around my neck, fanning and pinning it to hide the bruises.

As we had breakfast, I stared outside to where William trimmed the hedgerow. Jacques laid out the plans for Paris as my mind drifted, tugged in two directions. I longed for Jacques to be gone so I could wait with William for Silas. After I kissed Jacques goodbye, I slipped into the garden. William still battled with the hedges, a bulky canvas bandage covering his right arm.

"You *were* hurt! Why didn't you say something?"

"It's a scratch." He shrugged as he clipped, the sound sharp.

"Such a large and reddened bandage cannot be for a simple scratch. Let me get you fresh bandages and salve."

"Please, don't trouble yourself."

"It's no trouble. It . . . it was my fault. Please," I said, holding my ground.

"All right . . . it is paining me."

I leaped up, glad that I could help him in some way. I grabbed the medical kit Jacques kept in his office.

When I returned, William unknotted the bandage, and the bloodied linen fell loose. An angry slash snaked up his arm. I used the lightest touch, though William hissed in pain when I got too near the wound.

"I'm so sorry," I whispered, the shame overwhelming. I quickly applied the salve and wrapped the wound in the softer bandages.

"Better?" I asked.

He sighed. "Thank you."

"It's I who should thank you."

"Please, let's put it past us." He nodded, his eyes meeting mine. I froze, and the same feeling from last night rose. I shivered, though the day wasn't that cold. I wanted to lay my head against his chest and listen to his heart, the way he always listened to me. I wanted him to hold me with those hands of his, making me feel like I could never fall.

He took my hand and squeezed it. "He's going to come as soon as he's able. Don't worry."

I fought away tears and nodded. "I know he will. I do."

"Mistress Boudreaux?" came Sarah's voice.

William dropped my hand. "We shouldn't . . ."

"Coming!" I called to Sarah before turning back to William. "I know . . . I . . ." At a loss for words for the first time, I couldn't make sense of what to say about our kiss. "I'll leave you to your work." I retreated back into the house.

I spent the rest of the day locked up in Jacques's study, unable to concentrate on my book, watching for Silas as I thought about William, the feel of his strong hand in mine as he guided me to safety, as the strikes of his hammer rang through the house.

～

The dusk came and the moon rose and still no sighting of Silas. William had waited around to sneak him into the stables. My heart sank as I pushed my dinner around on my plate, wishing for an alternate ending to my evening and instead listening to Jacques drone on about his plans for Paris.

"Is that your dream?" I interrupted.

"My what?" he replied mid-chew.

"Your dream for your life?"

He thought for a moment. "I suppose it is. Making and managing money. Traveling abroad. With you at my side, always." He nodded self-assuredly and continued cutting his potatoes.

"Aren't you going to ask me?"

"Ask you what?" He stopped before taking another bite, brow furrowed.

"What is my dream?"

He rested his knife and fork on the edge of the plate. "To be a mother . . . yes?"

I swallowed. "What if I can't have children? It's been months, and it hasn't happened."

He shrugged good-naturedly. "Sometimes these things take time." He popped another potato in his mouth.

"I told you I want to be a writer."

"But, my dear, don't you want to focus on our home and the possibility of a family? What kind of life do writers have? There aren't any woman writers, and certainly none who . . ."

I pushed the plate away and folded my arms. "None who what?"

He shook his head. "A determined person can do anything their heart desires, but you must be rational. Besides, there is no need for you to work. It's unseemly."

"I was working when you met me," I reminded him. "And your wife works."

Jacques's mouth flattened into a straight line, and I knew I was taking out all my upset about Silas on him.

He cleared his throat. "She reviews things for me. She is not employed. And *you* get to go to Paris while *she* stays here and makes sure my affairs are in order." He took another bite. "We each have our roles, and we should play them."

We spent the rest of dinner in silence, then Jacques returned to his study, and I returned to the gardens. I paced, my thoughts bubbling over with frustration about Jacques's plans for me, my plans for myself and Silas, and my feelings for William.

And beneath all that was the ultimate worry—whether I would please Death, or fail.

Tangled in a knot, I was trapped, with no path forward.

"You're going to walk yourself into a ditch," William called out, a horse bridle in his hand.

I tucked myself beneath a trellis. The study was on the front side of the house, but voices could carry.

William followed. "I know you're still waiting on Silas. I sent word for him. I know he's trying to get away to see you before they leave again."

"Everything is . . ."

He took my hand. "You have to be patient. Your time will come, and Silas is coming." He gazed out into the garden, beyond the fence.

"But we're leaving for Paris," I whispered so maybe it would feel less true.

"I heard Miss Sarah talking about it." His eyes flickered with sadness. "I've almost saved what I need so I can leave too."

"Where will you go?" I asked.

"Anywhere I can live and be free." I knew what he meant. The flimsy freeness of Nouvelle-Orléans was restrictive and fleeting.

"Why not come to Paris with us? I'm sure Jacques will need a good man on the ground." I wished I could pull the words back into my lips. I wasn't sure if *I* should go to Paris with Jacques, let alone with William in tow.

"Mr. Jacques is a good man, but . . ." William glanced at the house.

"But what?"

William hesitated. "The more I get to know you, the more I think that . . . and forgive me for my forwardness, but maybe he's not the right man for you."

His words sank into me, burning with truth.

"William—I don't know what to say," I told him.

"Nothing to say." He shook his head. "He treats you about the same as he does his favorite mare, same as the rest of us. Like we're his." William shook his head again. "He's not a bad man, but that doesn't make him all the way good either."

"How should I be treated, then?"

He laughed. "A damned sight better than a horse."

I thought of Milly, stuck in that elaborate cage. Was I any better off?

"You should be treated like you're the 'earthly lullaby singing the sun to sleep.'"

Tears pricked as my words fell from his mouth. "So, you see me."

"I see you as clear as day." He grabbed my hand—his scarred and rough from work, so different from Jacques's soft, pale ones. Despite William's calluses, his caress was gentle.

I reached up and pulled his head down. His lips crashed onto mine, the bridle clattering down by our feet as we wrapped around each other.

William put everything into that kiss—his passion, yearning, and pain.

A fire erupted in my soul. It filled my whole body with heat. Nothing with Jacques had ever felt like this. William's arms were warm and inviting, and I fell into them as his kisses grazed my lips and cheeks like worship.

My body was aflame, and so was my heart. We fit together. I understood Eulalie's secret smile when she spoke of Eugène. There was an aching beauty in this moment, this right now. It was as if I'd lived in the dark all my life and had finally come into the light.

He broke apart from me, chest heaving. Cold gripped me without him, guilt already curling inside my belly. My heart had started to betray Jacques long ago, and I'd been ready to let my body do the same.

"We shouldn't." He put more space between us. His chest still heaved as he held his hands to his sides, restraining himself. "I'm sorry, Miss Noelle. We shouldn't have done that." He rubbed his neck. "Maybe it's best if I find another place. Avoid temptation."

The thought of him leaving cut a hole in my very soul. "But you can't. Your—your dreams! You've almost got enough to establish your shop. You shouldn't have to change your plan."

I stepped back, struggling with the impossibility of it all, when the French doors suddenly opened behind me.

"Ah! William!" Jacques called, striding out and placing his hand on my back. "Just the person I need. Beau threw a shoe."

"Of course, Mr. Jacques," William said, hefting the bridle, eyes downcast, sweat leaking from his brow.

I couldn't tell if Jacques had seen anything.

"Splendid. What were you two discussing?"

"France," I said. "William mentioned he'd like to travel."

"Would you?" Jacques stood, eyes squinting as he did when he was deep in thought. "I could use a good man like you over there."

"You could?" I asked breathlessly.

Jacques shrugged. "They have horses in France. They'll need shoeing too." He waited expectantly.

William stood there, torn. "It is a mighty fine offer."

"Then what's stopping you?" Jacques asked.

I gulped. This was bad. If William gave anything away, my life here would be over. But perhaps it already was. If he came with us to Paris, temptation would be so close.

William straightened. "Thank you. I shall take you up on your offer."

"Good man. We'll talk it all through in the morning. I believe I have an apology to make," Jacques said, looking at me. "Come, Noelle." He extended his hand.

"Night, Miss Noelle," William said, looking over at me. I nodded goodbye, unable to speak. I wanted to follow him and relive that feeling, but Jacques's hand in mine felt like a dousing of cold water.

What was I doing? I needed to be alone and think. I didn't have the chance, as Jacques's apology came in the form of sex.

He was more tender than usual, but I couldn't help comparing his kisses to William's. My face flooded with shame at the thought and the tingles between my thighs at the idea of William's body on mine, lifting me, stretching me out. It was enough to give me vapors.

After Jacques finished, he lay back, pleased with himself. "It's all right if you can't have babies for a while. I have three already, and it'll give me more time with you." He laid his hand on my leg, thumb stroking the top of my knee. "All will be well between us."

But that was far from the truth.

I agonized over my decision as the weeks passed. I kept away from William. I focused on writing and trying to get word to Silas, who still hadn't shown. A few times, I would catch William working in the garden from the upstairs window, and every time, he would stop as if he could sense me looking.

He invaded my dreams with the things we would do together, once we were free. I woke up aching for our hopes to be made reality: walking together or reading my work, him at the forge fashioning more metal figures.

"Ma would have my hide if she knew, but as you're leaving, I had to say something," Jenny announced as she helped pack a trunk of my winter dresses.

"What?" I said, startled. We had been working in silence the whole time.

She folded another dress and packed it in the chest snugly. "I know it's not my place to say, begging pardon. But we've got eyes, Miss Noelle. We don't just cook and clean."

Heat flushed up my neck as I glanced away.

"Ma is glad it's finished," she said. "Says it's not the way of things—that Mr. Jacques is a good man." Jenny finished the last skirt, carefully packed in the shoes, and stood up.

"What do you think I should do?"

Jenny paused for a long while. "It's not my place and not my heart. William is as good a man, perhaps a better one, if that's your heart's desire. It'll be up to you to choose the life you want." She left the room, leaving me full of confusion.

I sat there, staring at the wall. Did I even know which path was the one for me?

I would have to make a choice, and my actions would hurt someone.

With a monumental decision to make, it was fitting that Death chose this time to make an appearance.

# Ten

Twelve years, with not a word or a whisper.

Twelve years of looking over my shoulder, waiting for him to appear.

Twelve years, and he was back the day before we were to leave.

The announcement of his arrival came in the form of a pocket watch. It was golden and perfect, etched with intertwining spirals and a curlicued letter *N* on the back.

It sat on my dressing table, not there an instant before.

One glance, and I knew it was from him.

As I held it, an image of William popped into my head, echoing our conversation about time. My time had finally come, and all I could feel was dread.

A pristine white rectangular card sat beside the watch, the paper silky soft. It named a local tearoom frequented by the Creole women of color I knew for tomorrow morning at nine.

I was to leave for France at one.

Why did it have to be the morning of the trip?

Why did it have to happen at all?

Sickness roiled through me the rest of the day, indecision rippling as I gathered my stories, switching them from the pile I would take, to the trash, to back again. What would he want to see? Taking the watch as inspiration, I selected everything I'd written related to time: the way I had experienced its passing and, in doing so, had borne witness to miraculous developments—the growth of my friendship with Eulalie, the flourishing of her business, and her family. The rising fortunes and prospects of the Creole women who worked beside me. The progression of my courtship with Jacques. I added all the articles I'd written for the paper, returned to me by its editor, and pulled everything together, hoping it was close to what he wanted.

The enormity of my task rushed back. What if I failed? Everything—every*one*—would be forever gone in the blink of an eye.

The day passed in a haze as the picking and packing were completed. I could see no further than nine a.m. the next day.

I slept fitfully that night, images of fire sweeping across the earth, the screams of thousands in the air, and the steady ticking of a clock in the background.

I awoke as dawn broke across the sky, dread thick in my belly. I couldn't lie there, so I pulled on my clothes.

"Where are you going?" Jacques asked, stretching.

"Just a quick stop. I want to say goodbye one last time to Eulalie," I fibbed. I'd already dropped by the day before to say goodbye and see her new babe, a little girl my friend had named after her love, very pale with wisps of blondish-brown hair and hazel eyes.

Jacques nodded. "The boat leaves at one p.m. sharp. I'll have William drive you there."

"That's not necessary."

He shook his head. "He'll need to drop the carriage with my brother for storage after taking the last trunks to the dock."

"Jacques—"

"No arguing. We'll have a smooth trip together, you'll see." He jumped out of bed. We dined on the last food in the pantry, as all the other goods had gone with Sarah and Jenny—Eulalie had taken them on.

Jacques gave his last directions to William. "Get her there on time! And let me know about the horses."

"Of course, Mr. Boudreaux. I'll take care of everything." Soon, the carriage was loaded with cases to drop at the ship, and I stepped inside.

"See you there!" Jacques called, waving.

I fidgeted in the carriage the whole way over, trying to breathe, my stays digging into my ribs. I thought my feelings toward William might have faded with a bit of distance, but if anything, they were stronger. I noticed everything—how he had cut his hair, his new coat, how his hands held the reins, and how he smelled. I clenched my jaw, unsure if I was prepared for what the day would hold.

"You okay, Miss Noelle?" he called back.

"I'm fine. Nervous, that's all."

"Nervous for what? The trip?" He half turned to face me.

"I have something I need to do first. Someone I have to meet."

"This isn't about Silas, is it?" He turned in his seat, face serious. "I told you the Cormacks took ill and went back to the country."

"I know. It's not about my brother." My shoulders tensed as the carriage rolled to a stop outside the tearoom.

He jumped from the driver's seat and opened the door. I hadn't been that close to him in weeks, but the heat had built between us. Sparks flying as if fueled by his forge. He cleared his throat, as if that would get rid of the tension between us.

"Noelle, about that day—"

"William. I have to get inside."

He nodded, but I could see the disappointment in his eyes.

"After I'm done, we can talk." If there even was an after.

"Are you going to be all right in there?"

"Of course," I said, forcing a weak smile, then gathering myself and walking in. Two women sat at a table near the far window, primly sipping tea. I chose one nearest the door to see the wagon where William still waited, the horses pawing the ground.

I pulled the watch out of my pocket for the time.

Ten seconds to nine.

As the second hand crossed the nine, my hair stood on my neck.

Death had arrived.

# A VISIT FROM DEATH

Nella glanced up at Death, her amber eyes widening.
He'd taken the shape she knew from their first encounter—bronzed skin, straight back, sinewy physique. She gripped the table for support and swallowed, her throat bobbing delicately, betraying her nerves.

Death took a moment to study her. She was lovelier up close now—well fed and rosy, having gained weight since he'd seen her last. Her wardrobe had also improved, and the ice-blue silk dress complemented her skin tone, announcing her station. She'd certainly put some distance between herself and that cabin—her life dictated by the evils of enslavement.

He pushed away a strange sensation in his chest—light and fluttering—at seeing her after all this time.

He'd secreted her in the back of his mind. The thought of her had brought welcome respite as he collected souls of Sauk warriors, women, and children from the American plains, dying on the land they'd been promised was theirs, land that they could keep. On the battlefields of Wallachia, where he had just been, malaria had done more damage than any human enemy.

He knew she was busy amassing her evidence, so Death had assembled his. In his estimation, there was still little worth saving among humans. But could she possess something that would prove him wrong? The possibility was electrifying.

He settled into the seat across from her, his form solidified enough to be seen by other humans, if only vaguely. He hadn't done it before—for what was the need?—but Nella shouldn't be seen talking to herself. It could end their arrangement prematurely.

He was surprised to find it was interesting to be corporeal in the world. He wondered if he might try it again soon—engaging with the living, not just the nearly dead.

"I trust you're well," Death said, taking her in, attuned to every breath and gesture, knowing he'd replay this meeting in the gaps between his tedious collections.

She paused, her lips parting and closing, as she thought of what to say.

"It has been challenging," she said slowly. "And interesting. Certainly not the life I would have had without you." The server poured hot tea into two cups—the china clattering in the woman's hands, though she had no idea of the reason for her nerves. Death frowned at her, and she hurried away.

Death turned back to Nella with a smile. "Without me, you'd have no life at all."

Nella grasped the cup, the tea inside sloshing as she steadied herself. "Very true . . . and while I appreciate it, I did want to ask, Why have you taken so long?"

Death cocked his head. "You think *this* is long?"

"Yes," she said, the sound strangled. "Twelve years without a word. I had no idea when you would come."

Human perception of time was fascinating.

"Well, I had to give you a chance," Death explained, picking up his cup. "I doubted you would be ready after mere months. Only with experience will you truly know all the ill that man has in his heart." He sipped delicately, the bitter liquid hot and thick with the taste of herbs. "I read the papers and found none of your evidence."

"They would not take articles written by women or colored folk. I have the rejections to prove it. I tried a French male pen name. Let's see how that works."

"Fickle and feckless. These humans are caught up in the arbitrary, wouldn't you say? Does it change how you feel about them now?"

She shook her head, the movement sharp. "I still believe as I did all those years ago." Her voice wavered at first but then strengthened. This was it. Her moment to convince him.

Death leaned forward, ready for their debate to begin. "Even with all your struggles since? The men in the alley? You still feel that way?"

She sat back in shock. "The men . . . you knew? Why did you not intervene?"

Death shrugged a delicate shoulder. "That is not my role."

Her nostrils flared. "So, would you have let me die? Can I even die?"

"Would you like to?"

She snorted. "Of course not!"

He gave her a patient look. "You can feel pain, my dear Nella, but your death is . . . paused, if you will."

She silently digested this, swirling her tea with a spoon. "You left me with no guide. What else should I know?"

He remained quiet, sensing the things unsaid between them. He could see them in her eyes.

"Have you already forgotten the finer points of our agreement? You traded your legacy for immortality."

"Ahh," she said, comprehension dawning. "So, a child . . ."

"Is legacy," Death finished. "Only your words will be left. That was our deal."

Nella pursed her lips.

Death nodded. "Could you watch your children grow, wither, and die? Our experiment would end too soon because of your devastation at this death or another. It's truly for your benefit. I'd thought it wise."

Nella said nothing, instead drawing out a parcel of papers, her hands shaking as she passed it over the table. She glanced at the window, her driver just visible in his seat.

Death knew he had been right. Given her feelings, a child would have only complicated things further.

He flicked through the pages eagerly, drinking in her words. He knew some of this, of course. He'd observed her from time to time. He didn't check in often, though, only when his need to know grew too great. Just sensing she was there, at her task, had made his work less exacting. Her experience in the world, and their bet, had given him something else to think about.

Now, with her words, he had even more to experience—a completely different perspective. She'd recorded it all, the beauty she'd seen and the good people she'd come across. He read her accounts of human kindness—being saved in the wilderness by a trapper and his runaway love; her early days with Eulalie, building a business and aiding other marchandes; the work of the Free Creole women's groups to lift up their neighbors. He had seen these sorts of things all the time but had never considered the beauty in any of them. He found it curious to consider as he continued to read.

The most interesting passages were those of human creativity. A number of the stories revolved around a man named William and the care he took in his craft: forging objects from metal and bringing them into reality. Here, Death saw more of her. He quickly deduced what was written between those lines.

She fidgeted as he read, taking tentative sips of tea and placing the cup back on the saucer. Her eyes darted around the shop, trying to land on everything but him. He took his time, savoring her nearness as he absorbed her words. He knew she remained steadfast in her belief, but she would not for long.

Death knew what was coming.

He sat back, his face carefully neutral. "Have you enjoyed the process?"

Nella hedged as she reflected. "It was hard to know what you wanted, what would count as evidence, but in the end, I enjoyed capturing those moments from life, showing you their meaning."

Death nodded. "I'm glad. Your talent has only increased," he said, pulling out a familiar bundle of folded paper from his pocket.

Shock ran over her face, followed quickly by anger. "Those are from my desk."

Death chuckled, surprised at her response. "Don't look so alarmed. I had to make sure you were on track; after all, the fate of the world is at stake."

"But you went through my things! Without permission."

He shrugged indifferently. He could take so much more if he wanted. "I had a vested interest," he explained. "And I'll admit, I couldn't resist. I can honestly say this is going better than expected. Humans are so given to speaking about nonsense, blathering on about nothing—but the written word! I can see it through your eyes and hear your voice. It's an odd sensation that I have come to like. I find it . . . refreshing. After all, this is why you're alive." Something akin to sunshine bubbled up within him. He was not familiar with it, but it wasn't entirely unpleasant.

Death watched as Nella digested this.

"So, this is it? Earth continues?" she said cautiously.

He grinned, showing all his perfect teeth. "Unless you want to end it now?"

"No!" Nella said. "I just . . . I mean, I continue? My life goes on? I grow old? I . . . die?"

Death snorted. "Of course not. You have me intrigued. I need to see what you'll do next. You're off to Paris, are you not? I think the trip will do you good; there will be more to see and more life to share. You'll learn the world is bigger than these shores, and humans of all kinds are capable of great cruelty. You will continue with your task—that is, until you can't."

Her face fell, but she schooled it back into place, the reality of what she'd agreed to dawning. Only Death would decide when, if ever, her task was complete.

Death rose from the table, taking the writing with him. He had much to read before he'd collect her next installment. He was interested to see how she would deal with what was next.

"Wait! I had a question."

Death paused, head tilted.

Nella took a deep breath. "My brother . . . Silas . . ." She looked up, so hopeful.

Death had wondered if she would ask. "Don't search further, for he is with me."

Her mouth dropped open. "How? Why? When?"

"It was not long ago," Death said matter-of-factly.

She sat, still shocked, the news reverberating, tears cresting down her cheeks. "But how?"

"Yellow fever," Death said. "Just after Mardi Gras. He'd been bit by mosquitoes when clearing out the marshes on the Cormack plantation."

Nella's gasp filled the tearoom. "That's not true!" she said, eyes glistening. "He was just here. He wrote this." She pulled a scrap of paper from her purse and laid it on the table. "He was supposed to meet me."

"I'm afraid he will not," Death said simply.

She sat for a long while as the knowledge of the loss washed over her.

"My dear Nella, does this change anything? I have your evidence," he said, gesturing to her papers, "but I'll gladly accept your forfeit."

"No," she said after a long time. "I . . . had hoped to see him again."

"You can. All you have to do is give in."

It would be easy with the pain of the news so fresh. Death waited. The world bustled around them, unaware that its very existence hung in the balance.

"No," she said, lip trembling. "I won't let you take anyone else."

Death smiled. He stood closer as he made his final point. "I don't say this to be cruel, Nella, but more loss is to come. Joy, happiness, and a little peace, but pain and loneliness will always follow. If you haven't learned that by now, you will." Death tapped the table. "This is the game we play. That's how I know I'll win."

"No, you won't. I won't let you," she said, her eyes hard, mouth tight.

"Well, we shall see," he said, more invigorated than he had been in eons. He wondered how long it would take before she finally gave in to him. Before she learned that death was inevitable. That *he* was inevitable.

He glanced out the window at the man named William, who waited in the carriage, the horses pawing the ground.

Yes, she'd learn that soon enough.

# Eleven

I stumbled into the blinding sunshine, dazed by the news.

The world marched on, unfazed and unscathed. Horses clopped by, wagons rolled past, and marchandes called, enticing passersby with their wares, the melody of the city a discordant cacophony of contrasts. I had succeeded, for now, but none of it mattered.

Silas was dead.

I gripped the doorframe on my way out, needing to concentrate on putting one foot in front of the other, trying not to faint in front of all of them.

All other sounds drained away, replaced by a piercing whine emanating from the center of my brain. I jostled forward until I reached the doors that opened to the veranda. The humid air closed around me, squeezing all the breath left in my lungs. I clutched the nearest post, dragging in deep heaves of air.

It was over.

I'd spent years searching for him, the purpose anchoring me, driving me forward. I had no family left.

William hopped down, concerned. "Are you all right?"

I would never be okay again.

"The meeting . . . It was about Silas."

"What happened?"

I swallow, wishing the words weren't true. "He's gone."

"But how?"

I shook my head. "I have it on the firmest authority that it's too late."

William's face wore anguish. "I'm so sorry," he said, taking my elbow. "Let me help you in the carriage."

I sat inside, reeling from Death's revelation. I squeezed my eyes shut, the powerlessness a vise snaking around my core. William paused, holding me for a moment. I wanted to cry into his jacket but couldn't find the tears. We just sat in the back of the carriage until my heart slowed and I could breathe again.

"I'm here." William kissed my forehead.

He lifted my chin. "You could stay? We could stay?" His eyes brimmed with promise. I could almost see what our life could be in this city: a cozy house beside his blacksmith's shop, my very own study built by him and filled with endless paper and ink, a garden spilling over with our friends. "Don't go to Paris."

A single tear streamed down my face. "I only came to this city for Silas, and he's no longer here."

A knock rattled the carriage, and an angry voice barked about moving out of the way.

William planted a gentle kiss on my mouth before slipping out. He hopped up, took the reins, and turned the carriage down the street toward the docks. I pushed back into the seat, inhaling the strong breeze through the open window, the scent making everything more real.

My brother was dead.

And I was on my way to meet Jacques to start a new life in Paris.

I couldn't go back.

I couldn't change anything.

I couldn't save Silas.

William stopped the carriage and helped me down, careful with his touch in the public eye—no passion there, only comfort.

"Are we going to Paris?"

I nodded.

"Are you going to be all right?"

I couldn't answer. I didn't know if anything would ever be all right again.

"Get on the ship. I must drop off the carriage, but I'll return with my things. We can talk then . . . I'll come and ensure you're well once Mr. Jacques gets settled in." William gathered the last of my trunks and handed them to the steward, who helped me toward the ship.

He climbed back into his seat, then turned to look down at me, his eyes full of bittersweet hope. "I'll return soon."

The ship's steward guided me to my room, one of the few proper cabins on the vessel. I lay on the bed, completely numb. It was one thing to think Silas *might* be dead, but to have it confirmed was another thing altogether.

Jacques trundled into our room close to departure, smiling. "Why don't we go up on deck?" he said. "We're casting off soon."

"You go. I . . . need a moment."

He took my hand and kissed it. "All right, I suppose I'll see what William has gotten up to. Don't worry, I won't let the ship leave without him." He strode out the door, whistling a tune, oblivious to so many things . . .

But the idea that the ship could leave without William began to gnaw at my heart. After a while, I rose and made my way to the rail of an upper deck to watch for him. The sun shone bright, warming my shoulders. The sky was robin's-egg blue, a mockery of my despair. Gulls called, beckoning our ship to sea.

It wasn't long before I saw William striding toward the pier. A small bit of my heart lifted. He would understand my pain; he would hold me in my grief.

I held my hand above my head and called to him. "William!"

He looked up, shielding his eyes from the sun, searching for me.

I began to wave, and meant to call again, but the words died on my lips.

Three men in sailor's uniforms lurched from the shadows.

My heart seized. I knew them. The men from Mardi Gras, the night we'd found where Silas was kept.

"William!" I shrieked. He continued to search for me and didn't notice as the sailors made for him. They were on him in an instant, dragging him into an alley full of cargo, until he was out of sight.

The world spun. I heard a shout from the ship's gangplank: "Stop! Stop there!" It was Jacques. He and three members of our crew ran to where William had disappeared.

None of it seemed real. It couldn't be happening. The echo of Jacques's voice calling William's name was the last thing I heard before the world went black.

～

I woke in the cabin. For a moment I believed, I hoped, the entire thing had been a dream. Then I noticed Jacques settled heavily on the end of the bed, his head in his hands.

He turned to me. Dark circles ringed his eyes. "Noelle, there's something I have to tell you."

I touched his shoulder. His body shuddered, and he went on.

"A fight broke out on the docks. Three sailors. They spotted . . . they spotted someone and carried him off. The crew and I gave chase, but they had knives and a musket. We were too late."

The silence hung in the air. I prayed to God, to Death, to any force in the universe to keep the words from coming from Jacques's mouth.

"William," he rasped. "He's dead."

Bile rose, burning in my throat. "But how? Why?"

Jacques scrubbed his face, as if he could wipe away the horror and make sense of it all. "I don't know, Nella. William was an honorable man. What trouble could he possibly have had with sailors?"

None. Except . . .

Guilt riddled my heart.

It was all my fault.

If I hadn't insisted on going out at night, they wouldn't have accosted me.

If they hadn't accosted me, William wouldn't have had to embarrass them.

If William hadn't embarrassed them, they wouldn't have sought revenge.

Jacques cupped my cheek with his hand. My tears rolled down, dampening his palm.

"Oh, my dear, you are so pale. I know, this is a terrible shock. But I am here. And I am unharmed. You are safe. Tell me, what can I do to help put this horror behind us?"

"Nothing," I whispered. "There is nothing."

First, the news of Silas.

Now William . . .

I stood unsteadily and stared out the porthole of our cabin. I felt frozen, the tips of my fingers numb.

Jacques announced he would fetch some tea. It was good he left when he did.

The moment the door closed, my stomach heaved. I retched into the chamber pot until only air was left, the tears coming then—hot, fast, and ceaseless.

I poured out every bit of me.

For William.

For my brother.

For my shame.

For what could have been.

Death had been right about life and loss.

If it felt like this, I didn't know how I would survive.

# PRESENT DAY

## Savannah, June

# Twelve

The couch dips as Sebastian inches closer.

Thunder growls outside, and it's like I'm back on the ship to Paris, huddled in moldy-smelling sheets in that dank cabin, as the walls pitch up, waves slapping the hull. I pull the coverlet closer, breathing in the fabric softener.

*I'm here. I'm safe. It was a long time ago.* But it doesn't feel that way. I've locked all the memories away for a reason.

"Did you find out what happened?" Sebastian's arms are smooth and strong, an anchor in the storm. "Did you think Jacques had something to do with it? Did you ever think he suspected something between you two?"

I blink. "I don't think so. Jacques didn't mean harm. Mostly, he was blind to his own faults. William was dead due to my arrogance. He would never have been in that predicament or have made enemies of those men if it weren't for me. I knew he cared for me. All of his plans—all of his dreams simply gone . . ."

"Don't you think you're being unfair to yourself?" Sebastian tips up my chin, his fingers soft as he holds my gaze, his touch comforting. "Love is inevitable. You and William both wanted a good thing, but circumstances got in the way. The only ones to blame here are those men and those men alone." Rain pitters against the window as I listen to him absolve me of my role in William's death.

"He was the first person since I'd lost my family to really see me." I sweep away a tear, knowing there's worse to come.

Sebastian reaches for my hand. "What happened next?"

# PART III: PARIS

### The Sketch—1871

# Thirteen

The tumultuous monthlong journey from New Orleans to Paris matched my depression and forecast trouble on the horizon. As we were shuttered away in our cabin, the portholes closed to keep out the cold wind and salty water, the darkness became welcome comfort in mourning the loss of William and Silas, but it birthed a wedge between Jacques and me. I stayed with him for a few years after leaving New Orleans, a ghost of myself, going through the motions as I accepted my lot and focused on my work. I had some means, having invested all my savings, but I was a shell of my former self, left reeling from my actions. I'd dared to try for what I wanted, and William was dead as a result. Perhaps if I hadn't met him, I wouldn't have wanted something different, something more.

Jacques chalked up my sadness to homesickness and tried to cheer me by buying us books. We made a quiet life in Paris, where I passed the time by focusing on writing for plentiful magazines and newspapers under various noms de plume, the literary options seemingly endless, passing as a socialite from the Kingdom of the Two Sicilies or the Algerian colony. But after the death of Jacques's brother, he inherited the Boudreaux plantation and returned home to oversee it, tired of France's stormy government. There was no future for me in returning to Louisiana, not when his presence at the plantation would, by necessity, be constant. He honored our plaçage agreement, leaving me with my money and our trappings as he sailed back to America.

I was an independently wealthy woman. When Jacques left, a chapter of my life—a lifetime in itself—closed. I wanted a complete break, so I rechristened myself, taking the name Marguerite Conte. The time passed, one decade blending into another as the city changed around me from a monarchy to a republic and to an empire. I was referred to a banker for the moneyed elite who worked at the kind of institution that put a premium on privacy. Exactly what I required. I lived off my investments and through submitting pieces to Parisian literary journals, newspapers, and magazines—just small articles under assumed names, some male—and moved around the city to avoid suspicion about how I stayed so young as the years stretched on.

It was a nice routine. Simple, and it helped me to pass the years between my meetings with Death. The writing and moving and watching. We met again in 1821, just after Jacques left, at the Salle Le Peletier, the home of the Paris Opera. He summoned me with a jeweled brooch left on my desk. We met again in 1832, after he'd left a journal of blue leather wrapped in gold, the ivory pages soft. As before, a small white card announced our meeting place, this time the Café de Chartres, located inside the Palais-Royal, patronized in the past by the likes of Napoleon and Josephine. And again in 1870 as the city bubbled over with the invasion of the Prussians. He'd left a piece of chocolate, rare during the siege, in my valise at a farmhouse in Tours, where I'd sheltered from the fighting with three widows.

Unlike my time in New Orleans, when Death met me in Europe, I didn't feel trepidation. My work was good and plentiful, and, living in Paris, surrounded by a different form of beauty, my life had opened up. After three-quarters of a century of grief, the clouds cleared as the beautiful era, la belle époque, began.

I moved to Saint-Germain-des-Prés onto one of its tiny streets, folding into the artists, other writers, and thinkers of the time. My three-bedroom apartment overlooked the Seine, and my windows let in snippets of intellectual arguments escaping the plentiful literary salons on Rue de Beaune. I loved disappearing into the daily crowds making their way throughout the Palais-Royal and the labyrinth of shops and curiosities. From the highest of high among Parisian society to peasants and paupers, all were seeking pleasure, for that was what lay at the heart of this city. A trio of jewelry shops stood on one corner, competing for the same passersby. Milliners with exotic fabrics stacked near to the ceiling, with silks, chiffons, and satins spilling out, called to customers, enticing bits of coin from their pockets. The best of all were the tiny bakeries, their ornamented cakes beckoning, the sweet perfume of sugar-coated air wafting through the streets, leaving bellies full and wallets empty.

I'd made a tidy life for myself as my investments continued to grow, and I kept busy sharing my writing and travelogues in various reviews, newspapers, and magazines. As you know, travel narratives were growing in popularity during that time, as they allowed readers to explore the world from the comfort of their own homes. To me, this city was still a feast, even after all these years. I'd folded myself into the social circle of salonnière Élisabeth Comtesse DuBois. Her grand monde contained a who's who of Parisian society and beyond, the invitations to her never-ending stream of dinners, parties, concerts, and balls filling the presse mondaine broadsheets for the outsiders. Many of them I'd secretly reported on myself, from the inside.

Tucked into Mme. DuBois's elaborate gardens with a tarot deck spread across a small table, I'd taken to telling fortunes to pass the time and to explain my odd presence among the white Parisian elite, leading them to believe I was an exotic honey-brown bird from a far-off place. It was necessary, as their understanding of race and color was stilted, shaped by the circus and salacious human exhibitions.

An overly powdered courtier sat across from me, her mouth a frayed rosebud on account of too much rouge and anxious biting. Her pale-blue eyes watched every hand-painted card I placed before her. "The

Hierophant and the Three of Cups together speak of an engagement on the horizon," I said, watching as her eyes twinkled.

She spilled her secrets, detailing her suitors and her heart's desire. This silly grift kept me close to fascinating stories of the people of this time as I detailed life in the city—visiting museums, partaking in fine French cuisine, attending literary salons, and recording all the wit and loveliness that humanity offered. But I always wondered what Death thought of me doling out fortunes, as if I had an otherworldly power akin to his own.

After I'd fully satisfied her with tales of a blessed future and she gave me a few francs I didn't need, she scurried off to report to her friends over sips of champagne, and I watched the elite crowd. I enjoyed the early-March breeze blowing away the miasma that rose from the city's stagnating rubbish, offal bins, and human waste. There wasn't a corner of Paris, rich or poor, without the stench as its denizens tried to conquer the sewage and water contamination problems. The women tolerated my presence, but I was never quite welcomed into their spirited conversations about the latest philosophy enlightening the elite masses or critiques of the composer du jour.

An artist set up an easel and art supplies to the right of my table. A man with creamy white skin, black wavy hair that ruffled in the breeze, and cheekbones sharp enough to cut paper. I startled, often occupying this area alone at this particular salon. His head tilted in my direction, his hand flowing over a sketch and his grayish-green eyes studying me.

"Wha—"

"Don't move," he called, "I'm almost done."

"I didn't ask for that," I said.

"Then it shall be mine to enjoy," he said. "Now, *hold* still." The way he said it sent a shiver spidering up my neck. Usually, I would have cursed him and sent him away, but I stayed put, feeling more intrigue than annoyance.

"I'm not paying," I said. It was a common scam at the time, and really any time, sketching and guilting unsuspecting marks into payment.

"I didn't ask for money," he said with a small smile and a shrug.

I crinkled my nose at him but followed his instructions, stilling myself. "Were you going to ask permission?"

He shrugged again. The charcoal never stopped moving, an extension of his hand. "Better forgiveness than permission. You cannot blame me, though. I seek beauty, and you happen to have it. Now, hold your head back again, please."

I did as he asked, resuming my position as I studied him. A fellow soul in search of beauty?

He methodically crumpled up a bit of paper and brought it to the piece, precisely smudging the lines.

How would this man see me? Would I be pleased by what I saw?

"Voilá," he called, dusting his hands. "J'ai fini."

I glanced over, ready for the hard sell, but I gasped at the image. Through the scant use of curved lines and shadows, I'd been transmuted onto paper as if by magic.

In mere minutes, the sketch had captured a certain quality of light, rendering a liveliness in my face. I felt seen.

"It's exquisite," I breathed.

"Everyone deserves to see how others view them." He smiled, a wolfish look in his eyes. "But the sketch is only a pale comparison of what I see before me." His French was silken, words tripping along my earlobes, energy ricocheting through me. "If you like this, you should see what I could do to you in oil . . . paint, of course," he said, winking. "I think all will have an enjoyable time."

"I'm sure you do." I flushed at his implication.

"Correction. I *know*." He grinned at me, the smile seductive and slow. He reached up, unclipping the paper from the easel, and handed it to me, the work even better up close.

"I thought this was for your private collection," I said, eyebrow arched.

"Something tells me I'll have the chance again. One last thing." He slipped the paper from my fingertips.

He signed it with a flourish. *René.*

He handed it back. "And you are?"

"Marguerite. Marguerite Conte." I'd been using the name for a while, publishing my stories under the name M. Conte with the growing number of magazines in the city.

He nodded approvingly. "I'm at the Palais-Royal most Tuesdays and Thursdays, and whenever Comtesse DuBois calls, I'll be here among the rest of the birds in her aviary." He handed the picture back, his fingertips brushing mine. "You should find me again if you want a proper portrait."

Heat bloomed in my cheeks. "I'll keep it in mind." I nodded in thanks and stood, ready to head home.

"Wait," René called out.

I turned back. He held a tiny, gilded peacock figurine. "You forgot this." He lifted it up, its jewels twinkling in the candlelight. "It's engraved too."

My stomach twisted. No, I hadn't forgotten anything. The peacock figure hadn't been there a moment ago. I was being summoned. "Thank you." I plucked Death's gift from his hands and slipped it into my purse before dipping in and out of the crowd to say good night to my gracious host.

I tugged at my lace collar as soon as I was out of sight, warm in my gown. There would be a note, no doubt, back at my apartment. I would soon see Death again.

I glanced down at the sketch René had done, tracing my fingers along the lines he'd drawn. Here was a man who could create beauty. A man who saw me. Did Death already know that?

As I walked away, I knew that René was right.

I would meet him again.

# A VISIT FROM DEATH

In the café, Death eased into existence beside Nella, just as he'd done for the previous meetings in public, and waited for her expression of recognition. Nella merely smiled, her eyes flicking over his new form as he casually lounged against the crimson velvet. She looked beautiful. Two plumes of butter-yellow feathers arched over her head, the ends dangling by her delicate ears. They complemented the marigold-yellow bows that adorned her sleeves and marched down her ivory gown, highlighting the pickups of her skirts. A beautiful bird in a sea of crows with her head high.

Dressed in all black, an ebony mask in hand, Death blended in with the thousands waiting for Carnival to begin. He'd chosen a different form: a man, olive skinned, with a thin black mustache and beard and cinnamon-colored eyes framed by thick black lashes. He'd collected this form from an Amazigh farmer as he'd languished at his home, the victim of a simple tooth abscess. The man had been kind as Death had taken him, his only concern for the well-being of his wife and children.

Kindness was a state Death had only recently begun to understand, after Nella had written him stories on the concept. She'd composed one about a baker who'd kept the town alive during a famine, despite people having no money to pay him. And another about the groups of nurses who'd volunteered to care for the sick during the last cholera outbreak, despite the risk. He'd come to understand that some humans chose to help one another for no reason other than that they could. Some humans had kindness—not enough to convince him of their overall goodness, but some did.

He settled back, noting the lavish differences in her dress, her regal bearing, and her confident demeanor. She'd evolved since he'd seen her last, her wide-eyed wonder gone. She knew she belonged in this world, among these people who were not worthy of her. He wondered what new lessons life had taught her and if she'd be ready for him.

Nella faced Death, her gaze clear and direct. "Off to enjoy the festivities?"

"The work of collecting souls never ends." Death leaned forward. "But I had to make time for you. I do enjoy our bit of catching up. Have you been well?"

"There have certainly been ups and downs," she said quietly, playing at the gold embellishments on her dress. She realized what she was doing and flexed her fingers to stop, slipping them out of sight.

Death nodded, noting the motion. "For you, more than most. Are you going to tell me or show me?" His eyes swept the table expectantly.

"These are for you." She pulled out bundles of parchment. He settled casually back into the seat as his eyes flew over the pages of broadsheets, magazine articles, newspaper columns, and her journals, greedily snapping up each word. He couldn't hear the tables around them, only her words as they filled his head.

*"The women of the salons, widowed and married alike, turned cages of isolation or loss into vibrancy, channeling their energy into the creation of spaces built just for their pleasure and pursuit of happiness. I'd learned how to stitch my grief and loss into . . ."*

She'd improved; if anything, her pieces had become more nuanced as she examined her life and processed the deaths that had affected her so much. Despite everything, she still believed in the good of humankind. She'd learn one day, and he'd relish her defeat.

As he watched her closely, Death paused, the papers still in his hand. "Writing is truly your gift."

Nella blushed. "I'm glad it meets your approval."

"From the bit I've read, you still believe humans to be worth saving."

"I do," she said calmly. "Even after all this time." She cocked her head, studying him. "What about you? Or do you still think us meaningless?"

Death waved his hand dismissively. She'd understand his point of view eventually. "What of the doctor who doesn't heal the poor, only the wealthy? What of the man who loses his entire wage to gambling, throwing his family into poverty? What of the people who set fires for fortune . . . or fun?" Death shook his head. While she had seen some of the world, he had undoubtedly seen more. "For every argument you make, there is a human example opposing the goodness."

Nella stood firm in her position. "The world is full of opposites. Without darkness, there can be no light. Without life, there can be no death. Without us, what would you do?"

She seemed too amused by her own question. Death steepled his hands and considered it. He'd only thought of the absence of humans, not the purpose of their existence. He and the other reapers had a role to play as they returned souls to the origin point. So had it been since the dawn of things.

Nella caused an avalanche in his thoughts.

*If there were no humans, what would become of me?*

*Do I exist only in the presence of their lives?*

Surely it wasn't possible that he needed them as they did him. The very notion made him seem weak. Vulnerable.

"I'm certain I'd find ways to occupy my time," Death said finally. Stowing the thought away for later perusal, he returned his focus to her. "And as for you, my dear Nella, once you've seen centuries, as I have, you'll come around to my way of thinking."

*Centuries.* At the word, her breath caught.

He beamed at her wan expression, his smile wicked. "What's the matter, Nella? Haven't you considered what happens if you don't give in to our wager? Have you envisioned the very long life you'll lead? It's been hard enough to this point. Imagine what more is to come. You've given me evidence now, which I'll accept, but how long can it last? I can only imagine how weary you'll find yourself in the future."

"Not likely," she said, smoothing her expression, "and not yet. The possibility still exists that I will convince you. That you'll share *my* view . . . even end our deal early. Conceding defeat."

Rich laughter bubbled from Death, loud and long enough to draw stares from the other patrons. Tears streamed down his cheeks while the sides of his solid form ached as amusement filled him. It took several minutes before he could get himself under control.

"It's a possibility," he said, wiping his eyes with the backs of his hands, chuckling still, "but my dear Nella, you shouldn't plan on convincing me anytime this century."

Nella's mouth tightened, and he relished her confidence. "I wouldn't be too sure," she said, wrenching open the black satchel that rested by her feet, revealing two canvases. She eased them out and handed them over, watching Death's face as he realized who the subjects were. "You never know when I'll surprise you."

All his mirth faded as he clasped the frames, handling them delicately, surprise evident.

*It's me,* he thought.

Two oil portraits of him from the two times she'd seen him. In the first, his eyes had smoldered as if lit from within, bright against his darkly bronzed skin. In the second, though the light was different and his dress more refined, the eyes held the same quality, simultaneously knowing and mocking. It was the first time he'd seen himself from her perspective. His throat went tight with an emotion he had not felt before.

"Why did you do this?" he said, keeping his face neutral.

Nella's smile crept across her face, slow and deliberate. "I'm tasked with finding goodness. I wanted to show you how you appeared to me. I wanted to capture the goodness I found there. A friend from the salon recommended a painter from the École des Beaux-Arts, and I commissioned him. I described you, and he . . . he brought you to life."

A moment passed between them. "From just a bit of cloth and pigment, humans wring emotion and awe. They create and make the world more beautiful in doing so."

Death swallowed against the unexpected lump. "You see me very handsomely, indeed. It is to your credit," he murmured, glancing at her. "I look forward to our next meeting. It will be interesting to see what other tricks you'll have up your sleeve."

She inclined her head like a queen to her subject. "I look forward to proving once again that we're worth it. All of us."

Death shrugged but gently gathered up the paintings. He dropped gold coins on the table—far more than necessary—and stood. She had done well. He had much to consider in their time apart.

He nodded farewell as he left, slipping into the in-between, paintings carefully in hand.

# Fourteen

Art haunted me in the weeks to come, distracting me from working on a new piece for *La Revue des Deux Mondes*. My gaze fixated on the sketch I'd pinned from the artist René in the garden. Still smug from meeting the challenge with Death, I saw art everywhere I went now. But as I stared at my likeness, unchanged from 1784, I wondered . . . How had he done it? His talent clearly surpassed even that of the artist who had rendered Death for me. How had he managed to capture me? What could he create with proper paints in a studio?

I replayed how he'd held the charcoal in his strong hands, veins running over his muscled forearms, his eyes fixed on the canvas. As the spring warmed to summer, I opened my windows and wished for a breeze, waking up sweating, imagining his fingers trailing across my skin, his lips on my neck, and my legs wrapped around his. It was a surprise, my own visceral desire after pushing away thoughts of sex and love for decades since William's death.

I lasted another week before I found myself visiting the courtyard of the Palais-Royal, where René said he worked on Tuesdays and Thursdays, dressed in my best green silk with white ruffles and drenched in a new perfume. I strolled along the edge, leisurely pretending to take in the sights.

Other artists were also out, but there was no mistaking him, stationed back toward the gardens. Families sat on spread-out blankets, enjoying the day as children chased each other, the lively playing of fiddle and accordion adding a festiveness, the mood light.

He sat in front of his easel, sketching the gardens, his hand floating across the paper as the scene sprang to life—a smudge blooming into pear trees and magnolia blossoms, a line becoming a neat trellis, all appearing as if by magic.

I didn't say anything as his hand slowed, and he turned, scanning. I wanted him to see me again. I wanted him to notice me among the crowd. The second his eyes caught mine, a smile spread over his face as sweet and slow as molasses.

"Back again, I see." He smiled as I drew near, the sunlight a beam of gold on his black hair. I didn't know how it was possible, but he was more handsome than last time; his green eyes had an apex predator's energy beneath a veneer of sleek refinement, and his black lashes were thick and long.

"You had an offer I couldn't refuse," I said, a pleasant heat feathering along my skin.

"Are you interested, then?" he asked.

"I wouldn't be here if I wasn't."

"Excellent." He reached forward and added his slashing signature to the drawing.

He dropped the charcoal back in its tray and started packing his papers frantically.

I stepped back. "What are you doing?"

He gestured to the sun. "The light will not last. I'll have more control in my studio."

"I see."

That meant I'd be alone with him . . . which probably wasn't a good thing, but an intoxicating thrill tugged me forward like a will-o'-the-wisp leading me into a dark and dangerous wood. I should've been afraid, but I cleared my throat. "How long will it take?"

"Three days," he said, folding his easel down. "One for the outline and background, the second for details, and the final for finishing touches."

I blinked. Three days? "I don't usually go traipsing off with a man I've just met."

"Don't worry. I assure you that the experience will be safe. Perhaps even pleasurable." He smiled, the movement slow and sensual. He didn't move an inch, but heat slunk through me at his gaze as if he were stripping me bare.

I waited for caution to flare, but shivery anticipation trickled down my spine. It had been years since I had been with someone. If he was interested and I was willing, what was the hesitation? There was no one here whose reputation I needed to consider other than my own. There was no Code Noir governing my every move. There was nothing holding me back.

We strolled together, our pace languid, not quite touching. His retracted easel and black portfolio swung between us, occasionally brushing my skirts and nudging me gently. I swallowed and counted the steps to his studio as anticipation built.

His voice broke into my thoughts, soft as satin. "So, do you know what you'd like?"

I shivered at the subtext in his words. "What, sir, are you offering?"

He tilted his head, his errant curls turning in the warm breeze. "That depends on you. How do you see yourself, Mademoiselle Marguerite? What kind of portrait should I create?"

I was used to being addressed by my alias, yet hearing it from René's mouth made me pause. It was the first time, I thought, it sounded like a lie. "I don't suppose I've thought about it. The regular kind?"

He shook his head. "There is nothing regular about you." His eyes traveled down my dress. "You, mademoiselle, are unique."

I flushed at the bold statement. Technically, he was right. I was a woman out of time—or perhaps lost in it. "You must see hundreds of people a day. Why flatter me?"

"There's something in the way you hold yourself," he admitted. "That day at the salon, you reminded me of Athena, beholding her subjects, observing as they lived their small lives, wise beyond your years. You've seen things. It's in your eyes. A grief, a weariness that only comes with seeing parts of the world that many do not."

The unexpected truth of his words slammed into my chest. "Are you sure you're not a writer? You certainly have a way with words."

He shrugged. "I'm French."

I laughed. I'd been here so long that French assurance had softened for me into a charming cultural bravado.

At that moment, I knew he had it, the same gift I'd come to understand all artists shared. The ability to see beyond a thing, beyond what was presented. Artists know what something is and what it can become. Unlike Jacques, he could perceive more than the physical. Potentially, he could see me . . . if I let him, if I could let someone see me again after all this time and all that had happened.

René was a thing of beauty himself. His stride graceful, he easily navigated the crowded street. I studied him as we talked, orbiting each other as we navigated the crowds, the streets thick with *life*. Vendors hawked from the corners, the fowler selling rows of plucked ducks strung upside down as carriages and wagons trundled past, sending the ripe scent of horse dung through the air. His clothes were well made, without a hint of paint; everything about him was even and precise.

He made me think about how long it had been since Jacques. With him, sex had been staid and safe. And while William and I were never together that way, I'd felt love and understanding, a shared sense of our pasts with him; this was a different sensation altogether. This felt like abandon. I'd seen others carried away with it, and despite being more than a hundred years old, I'd yet to experience that for myself.

His studio wasn't far from the Palais-Royal, located in a three-story limestone walk-up. He stopped at a doorway on the third floor, by the stairs.

"Here we are." He fumbled with the key—perhaps he was not as calm and collected as he seemed. He covered it masterfully and opened the door with a flourish, swinging it wide. "Welcome to my studio."

The entire space was an artistic endeavor: an ample central room with draping next to an open window and a smaller bedroom just beyond, both spilling over with a variety of pieces at different stages of creation. Even the side table, with a loaf of bread, bright-green pears, and yellow cheese wedges, sat in a slant of sunlight, ready to be painted.

A detailed nude caught my eye: a blond with golden curls cascading down her neck, drawn languidly on a red velvet settee, arm above her head, apple-size breasts arched high, sporting pert nipples the color of strawberries, a fold of silvery fabric the only nod to modesty as she gazed at the viewer.

A lover.

Former or current was the only question. I blushed at the intimacy of it, her pleasure on display for the world to see.

"Do you like it?" he asked, his tone teasing. "We could explore this style, should you choose."

"Uh, I think more . . . conventional for the first one."

"Ah, the first," he said, smiling. "I'm glad to know there will be others." He directed me to a small couch covered in a deep-blue fabric that contrasted with my dress. I sat delicately, fiddling with my skirts, my throat dry. Maybe this *was* all about a portrait. I should sit for it and be on my way.

He plucked a larger canvas from the stack and set it on his easel. "Since you don't seem to know what kind of piece you'd like," he said, "why don't I make it a surprise?" He chose a wooden palette, smeared it with a brown tint, and worked a palette knife across the surface.

"We didn't discuss a price," I reminded him.

"Pay me what you think it's worth." He smiled easily as he selected a brush, flicking it through a small tin of solvent.

"You don't understand business, do you?"

"I understand as much as I need to get by. This I do for . . . personal reasons."

We were quiet as he began, only the steady clop of horses outside and the scrape of his brush as he roughed in the shapes on the canvas.

"What brought you to Paris?" he asked.

"What makes you think I'm not from here?"

He smiled patiently, as all Parisians do. I wondered how he could detect what must've been the faintest of accents after all these years living in the city.

"Fine, I'm originally from America. I came here in . . . I came for business and stayed for pleasure."

His eyes twinkled, but he seemed to resist another quip. "Hold your head a bit higher," he instructed.

I adjusted, half reclining on the couch. "Do you bring all your clients here?"

"No . . . only the best ones," he said, eyes lingering.

That sent a thrill through me.

"What do you do?" he asked, changing the subject. "How do you pass the time?"

"I write articles."

"What kind?"

I'd never thought to categorize my writing, other than knowing its strange audience of one. "Human interest stories and, um, travel guides?"

He furrowed his brow, considering the idea. "Interesting. Does it pay well?"

"If you need the money."

"It sounds as though you do not. And you were going to quibble price with me," he teased. He added another slash to the painting. "I have a young cousin who dreams of being a writer one day—he's not bad. Perhaps you could help him."

"Perhaps, should the opportunity arise."

He stood back, considering his work, before turning the canvas to the wall.

"You're not going to let me see?"

"Only when it's finished. There must be some incentive for you to return."

He came over and helped me to my feet. "That's all I can do today while it dries. Come back tomorrow. At the same time." His words had a bite, a commanding tone I liked.

"And bring some of your writing," he called as the door shut behind me. "I'd like to see what goes on in that lovely head of yours."

⁓

I was back the next day at noon, papers in hand. My head swirled, filled with images of what might come to pass inside René's lair as I drew closer to his street. My hand shook when I knocked on the wooden door.

He threw open the entry and smiled in his particular way, with a hint of *I told you so.*

"Don't look at me that way. I had to come. You're keeping my painting hostage. It was this or call for the police." I brushed past, the smell of him luring me like a bee to nectar; I wanted to cover myself in all of him.

I sat for the portrait, in the same dress and position, but this time wearing my best perfume, hoping I could intoxicate him with my own presence. The conversation sparked between us as he painted, thickening with curiosity and passion. When I moved too much, he'd lift my chin or adjust my hand, his touch sending ribbons of heat through my body. The more we talked, the more enchanted I became. René was in charge of his fate, painting when he liked and what he liked, commanding top prices.

"I have an upcoming show—an exhibition. Perhaps you'd like to come?"

"Looking for a patron?" It was not an outlandish offer; I had agreed to similar arrangements with more than one artist.

He raised an eyebrow but didn't answer, instead standing and sweeping one of my long curls behind my ear. "Are you hungry?" The words caressed my ear.

I gawked at him, confused. It took all my strength to not chase his touch with my own.

"You keep nibbling your bottom lip."

I blushed but licked the swollen, tender skin I'd just been biting. He was entirely too delighted with the way I reacted to him, even as he walked to a small table, unwrapping the basket upon it. He pulled out a dark-red apple and deftly sliced it with thin, even strokes. He arranged it artfully, spreading the ripe fruit on the tray next to thick wedges of cheese and golden, crusty bread.

"Try." He held a piece of apple a few inches from my lips. "Bite this instead."

I tried not to smile at him.

"You shouldn't move from your pose," he explained, a grin dancing on his face.

My blood thrummed in my veins. I leaned forward and took the apple in my teeth, never breaking eye contact.

His gemstone eyes burned into mine, and I wanted him to kiss me, but he brushed his hands against his smock, breaking the spell. "And what of your art? Did you bring some that I might see?"

I pointed to my papers. From the top, he plucked my favorite piece and read aloud. "'My footsteps echo on the cold white marble, filling the royal chamber with sounds of life. The gold display, dull from lack of care, struggles to glimmer while the moth-bitten velvet from an age gone by molders silently. The kings don't question my presence. They can't. They've gone to dust, and the memory of their greatness slides further into nothingness with each passing moment. I breathe in. I am alive for however brief a time.

"'The Musée des Monuments Français is the perfect place to consider your fate. Where better to contemplate your life than at the feet of dead kings? People who, despite having enormous wealth, influence, and impact, could not escape Death?

"'I spent an afternoon this way, dwarfed by the high curving walls that guard the treasures within, relics of the past before the time of the Revolution. The display of the mortal remains of those who had once ruled the world held my attention the longest of all the beautiful things. Charles V, Louis XII, and Catherine de' Medici, instrumental in the direction and fate of so many lives, were reduced to bone and ash in death. What did it all signify? The pain? The plots? The pursuit of earthly goods and immortality?

"'It ends in dust, in a quiet room, on a forgotten shelf. I choose not to focus on the end, for that is long and stretches toward forever, but instead, think of the life that flared and thrived in the in-between. For who has a more cautionary tale on the importance and brevity of life than those who have already lost theirs?'"

The silence sang out as René smiled, his teeth pearl-like, as he replaced the sheet on the pile. "I am in the presence of a master. I believe as you do: Life is fleeting. We have but a moment."

Then he winked, teasing, and added, "Though it is a bit passé to refer so strongly to Death in your work, no?" I blushed, and he nodded to the paper. "What are you going to do with it?"

I squirmed in my seat. After all, this was for Death's eyes only.

"You should share your work." He leaned closer to the canvas, daubing in small strokes.

"I do . . . at least, I have pieces published in a few magazines."

His gaze was assessing. "Not as much as you should, I think."

I blushed even deeper. "It's the way of the world. It won't be accepted."

René frowned. "Why would I paint if no one could see it?" He gestured to the canvas. "It's how I make myself known. It's how I show the world the value of my existence. And in doing so, I give the world meaning. Your writings, they are the same. Keeping them to yourself is a selfish thing." He turned his attention back to the painting as I considered what he said.

I hadn't been keeping my work to myself—it was the editors rejecting them. But I had to admit that the constant rejection made me slow to submit. Maybe I was letting potential noes stop all the future yeses.

His words sent chills over me as I pondered them.

"Come now." He grasped my hands, cool against my warm skin. "Let us finish our work—so we can immortalize you in another way."

We spent the rest of the afternoon talking as he painted, and when I returned the next day, we picked up right where we'd left off.

In the late afternoon, he laid his paintbrush down. "It is finished."

I stood eagerly. He'd kept his work covered when I wasn't confined to the couch.

He nodded. I walked to the easel and gasped. He'd painted with wild abandon. Shafts of light highlighted my hair as my eyes, regal and powerful, gazed at the viewer. I sat confident in my presence—serene but strong. He'd depicted me as royalty.

"It's amazing," I breathed. "Everything you promised and more." I'd thought him talented, but this was a wonder—the work of a master.

His green eyes held me there, a question open between us. Our business was nearly finished. I had no more reason to stay, and desperately wanted a reason to.

My curiosity got the best of me. "What will you do now that our time is ending?"

He stepped closer, giving me enough time to reject him. I made no move to leave, and welcomed his touch. He traced a finger along my collarbone, pressing the pad of his thumb into my birthmark. He ran it along my plunging neckline. A pulse drummed between my legs and I gasped, my nipples pushing against the fabric of my dress. His firm hands skated along the outline of my figure, and he lowered his mouth to my neck.

"I believe our time is just beginning," he whispered, the heat of his breath caressing my skin, making me wild for his touch. "I didn't tell you the other part of what I knew when I saw you that first day."

I curled my fingers in his hair, hurrying his kiss along. But he waited, teasing.

"What did you know?" I panted.

"That you would be mine." He kissed me.

I groaned with pleasure as we crushed together, almost devouring one another in our urgency. I plucked at his buttons, him pulling at my corset. We landed on the couch in a pile, limbs tangled as we shed our clothes. He pulled me on top of him, his clever painter's fingers sliding down my body, skimming my hips, and slipping into the warmth between my thighs. I couldn't look away from the intensity of his eyes, such a unique shade of green. I sank around his fingers slowly before he filled me. I gasped with pleasure, every sense, every nerve heightened. He grabbed my hips, rocking me forward, the spark of pleasure within reach. It had never felt this *together*, this *perfect*. The sensation raced to my fingertips, through the ends of my hair. I felt ready to break apart.

René's expression only said *more*. He knew just where to touch me, familiar with my body as he was with a canvas, rocking me forward again and again, until—with a cry a century in the making—my world blurred. René shuddered beneath me, and his groan drove the ache within me, making it stronger and stronger. A wave crashed over us, our voices mingling, our sweat glowing in the golden light of the sunset.

In the aftermath, with René's arm wrapped around me, I blinked in disbelief. Sex had never been *this*. There was no pretense, no fear, no dishonesty—only truth and transcendence.

It wasn't long before I wanted more. We stayed that way, making love again and again before the day slid into the night.

"Marguerite, there is one thing."

There, the name. I yearned to tell him the truth, but instead I sat up, pulling the sheet around me. I was already thinking of the blond with the rosy breasts. Maybe he, like Jacques, had a secret wife somewhere. "What is it?"

"I hope you don't think I take this as a form of payment."

I laughed and pulled him on top of me, not finished with him yet.

# Fifteen

Days fell into weeks that melded into months as René, now a steady fixture in my life, continued working on his pieces. I hadn't expected or wanted anything serious.

When I'd started with René, I'd thought it would be a simple, if intense, affair, destined to burn itself out, but I'd come to rely on my time with him, as his passion sparked my creativity, allowing my writing to flow. Being with someone after so many decades, no longer feeling alone, eased the burden of my work for Death. All I had to do was not fall too deeply in love—not care too much.

But it endured, our time together spanning into years.

Being with René offered entrée to another world and the invitations to literary salons and art showings became endless. We were the toast of Paris, and now I was gaining access to all sides of the city, from society circles—where I was now a celebrated guest rather than an attraction—to the hidden places few knew about, exposing me to a prism of love that extended through an array of people and expressions. I'd never before considered this a possibility. René's sensuality was a force that attracted followers. After an exhibition or a show, someone would usually be willing to join us in bed. We experimented with other lovers but always found our way back to each other, so much so that I stopped waiting for the end, for him to fall for another muse and move on.

Eight years passed. We'd settled into a routine, him with his painting and his shows and me with my writing. I thought I would eventually have to confess my secret. But René always claimed that he had known I was a goddess from the moment he saw me.

That I retained my looks, he said, was only further proof of my divinity. But if we continued, I couldn't stay young forever because it would raise too many questions.

I'd begun to form a plan for us to leave the city as I'd done in the past, perhaps traveling across Europe until I could return. It would've worked too, but life didn't let us get that far.

The first tremor came in 1879—a subtle shake in René's right hand made him drop his paintbrush.

"Merde." I found him retrieving the brush, paint spattered on his white shirt, a glob of royal blue marring the center of his painting.

"What happened?"

"Nothing," René said, staring at the blob. "Clumsy, I guess."

He wasn't clumsy. René was one of the most precise men I'd met, from setting up his paints to lining his shoes in the closet. "Clumsy" was the last word I'd use for him.

But clumsy he became.

Dropping paintbrushes.

Knocking over glasses.

Making mistakes on pieces.

At first, it happened only once a week.

Then once a day.

Eventually, sharp spasms shot through his hand consistently, smearing paint and destroying hours of work.

We consulted with doctors, healers, and eventually quacks, anyone who promised a cure, but none came. Tonics, elixirs—anything that anyone could sell, René would buy them, downing one after another and watching and flexing his hand.

Nothing worked; if anything, it grew worse.

It took a toll on him. My brilliant René, once active and joyful, began to spend his days in bed, staring out the window, wrapped in heavy sheets, binding himself to still his quaking body.

I did my best to distract him. I kept him company. I read to him and brought books and other entertainment, but he remained unmoved.

"Maybe you can switch mediums?" I suggested one day in early September.

"What?" His tone should have warned me off.

"Make art in another way. I know you need to create."

René sneered. "How, Marguerite? I am a painter, but I can barely hold a pencil. Should I cut shapes from paper?" He snorted. "Perhaps I take up sculpting? I'm sure I'd be great with a chisel."

He turned his back and didn't speak to me the rest of the day.

I didn't know what else to do, when suddenly the tremors improved.

I thought it was a miracle. After months of being unable to grip the brush, René was back at his easel, painting like a man possessed, and his mood improved. His work was different from before—big round shapes, clashing colors, and odd themes. I didn't critique or comment because he was creating again, even if his muse seemed to have changed.

All was well until he started disappearing. Though he could paint again, I found him less in the studio and less in the house—staying out all night and not returning home for days. When he did return, the slightest comment could set him off.

And then the money went missing.

At first, small increments, then hundreds, then thousands of francs, vanished without explanation.

I suspected another woman but found the answer at the bottom of his coat pocket.

An opium vial stained blue.

I didn't do anything at first.

Being with René—a René who could paint—was better than being without him, but that René slowly shifted, his sweetness souring, tension threading through our every interaction. With each passing day, he grew more irritable and violent, smashing wine bottles and slashing at his canvases. I wondered if one day that anger would be focused on me.

"There's not a problem. I'm creating. It's the process," he'd bark and scream.

He grew skinny, his face haggard, eyes heavy lidded, at times zombielike, others manic. He continued the cycle, sleeping through the day, growing angry, and disappearing.

The final time, he was gone for a week, along with one thousand francs I'd hidden in the house for emergencies. After the fourth day, I was sure I would receive word of him dead in an alley, and half hoped I would, exhausted by his ups and downs. But I kept checking our familiar cafés and other haunts, hoping someone had seen him.

At the end of the week, I discovered him comatose in his studio, skin waxy, thinner than he'd been before. Wine bottles and blue opium vials littered the floor, and candles and soot-stained opium pipes lay prominently on the table. The room stank of sweat, smoke, and oil paint, half-finished canvases on three easels—sharp-sided figures with gnashing teeth.

I collected the bottles and cleaned the entire place, throwing the windows wide and waiting for him to wake up.

He did so slowly, groggily, blinking at the bright light with unfocused eyes. He started to smile, his old one, and for a second, I thought it would all be okay.

And it was.

Until he started riffling through the covers with his left hand, his motions frantic as he ripped the sheets back.

My heart sank.

I sat beside him. "René, you have to stop this."

"Stop what?" he said, avoiding my eyes, still searching.

I gripped his hand. "You know what I mean."

He snatched his hand back, getting to his feet, wobbling. "Who are you to know?" he spat.

"René! I'm only trying to help!"

He yanked the covers from the bed and pushed the mattress to the floor. "Do you think I don't know how you taunt me? Do you think I haven't noticed?" He dropped to his knees, scouring under the cracks of the bed. Finding nothing, he stood, knocking into me as he rambled through the table's drawers, searching for his stash. "Where is it? You can't hide it from me!"

He wouldn't find it. I'd already disposed of it.

"René, calm down, lay back. Rest and let it pass. You can paint later." I wrapped my arms around him, soothing. I'd seen him like this, before he disappeared.

He needed the opium. It had hooked itself into him.

He fought against me, thin but still strong. "You're trying to trick me—you, you witch!"

He shoved me, and I fell to the floor, knocking my head on the edge of the bed. Tiny white spots danced before my eyes. I pressed my fingers to the side of my head, and they came away with blood.

René kept searching, muttering, turning over the table, and slamming books around.

"They told me I couldn't trust you. I knew it. You're a witch, Marguerite! A damned witch!"

"René, stop!"

"Tell me the truth!" He came over, grabbing me by the shoulders. The smell of his unwashed body rose, cloying, as his fingers dug into my shoulders. I knew I could do nothing to stop him. "You're the same, the exact same as the day I painted you. How are you unchanged, while I have this?" he asked, waving his palsied right hand. "Have you bewitched yourself?" His eyes glossy with unwept tears. "Or cursed me? Tell me!"

"René, it's not that. I made a deal—"

"A deal with who? Satan?" His eyes grew wide, and he shook me even harder. "Who is your master, you lying bitch?"

"René, you're hurting me!"

"You, you damned whore of Satan." He grabbed my face, fingers squeezing into my jaw, his nails cutting into my skin. "You are still young and perfect while my arm wastes away!"

"Stop it!"

"They told me. They told me you're sucking me dry for your youth."

Spittle formed at the corner of his mouth; his irises disappeared, and his eyes went black.

My René was gone.

He launched himself at me, hands on my throat, squeezing, his ragged nails tearing through my skin. I sagged to the floor, scrambling for anything to defend myself. When my hand connected with a thick wooden palette, I grabbed it and thrust it toward him.

The first blow glanced him, but the second one connected with his temple with a sick thump, and he slowed, blinking once before he collapsed forward, crumpling on top of me.

I heaved beneath him, hands shaking as I pushed up, shoving him off, oil paint smearing us both, the lead white mixing with the red of his blood.

He breathed, but only just.

I gathered myself, the room in a state, and backed away.

No matter how much I loved him, there was no coming back from this. Never in my life would I forget the emptiness in his face or the pain of my lungs yearning for breath. He was unrecognizable.

Nothing good would be found in the bottom of that vial or with René ever again.

After more than half a century, my time in Paris had come to an end.

# A VISIT FROM DEATH

Death found Nella in her room, in the hour between the deepest night and the first glimmer of morning. She was huddled in the sheets, face still red from René's blows. He bent quietly over her. He hadn't planned on visiting that night, intending their next meeting to take place a few years off, but given the night's events, he had to see her.

He straightened his human form. He'd thought perhaps she'd finally seen the truth and would be ready to end their deal.

What *he* hadn't been ready for was the sight of her.

Large purple bruises bloomed across her light-brown throat and a spate of scratches marred her jaw, sparking a black feeling in the center of his being. He didn't have a word for the feeling, but he was glad the man who'd done this would soon be collected, his time on earth nearly up. He thought about collecting him sooner in punishment for harming her, but that was not the way of things.

Nella didn't acknowledge Death as he sank onto the bed. She stared steadily at the wall, the silence thick between them.

"You *would* choose tonight," she said, tone bitter.

"Given the events, I thought I'd check in—see if your position has changed." He almost said, *See if you're well.* But how could she be well?

"Should I always expect these visits when something terrible happens to me? That you'll come here, goading and gloating? That you desire a front-row seat to my suffering?"

"Do you see me gloating?" He stared, daring her to look away first. "This brings me no joy. It only proves my belief. You thought him good—one of the redeemable ones—and look what he was capable of."

"Did you know it would come to this?" she asked quietly. "When it began?"

"That he would hurt you?" He leaned his head against the bed frame. "You know what I think. They will always hurt you in the end."

"What's wrong with him?" Nella asked, wiping her face against the sheets.

"He has a disease. It will eat at him, consuming him steadily. His brother is similarly afflicted. But he'll find his end before the disease takes him."

"So that's what will kill him? The vials?" she asked.

"The vials," Death confirmed.

They were quiet as the dark-blue sky eased into light. It was another day for both of them.

"Do you still believe in the goodness of man? Believe their lives are worth your suffering?"

"It's not always like this," Nella said.

"The longer you go on, the more of this you will face." Death turned to her. "I can make it simple. Say the word, and I can take away all your pain. All of this will cease to exist. I can . . . I can take you with me, into a better world."

Was there truly a better world than this one out there? Why wasn't it enough to ask *this one* to change? She glanced at the papers on the table, copies of all her published pieces from the past several decades, all the stories she'd been collecting, still collecting, the ones that had brought her a measure of joy and peace. Were they enough? Would they outweigh the actions of one man?

She swallowed, her throat constricting painfully. "I know what you came here for, but I can't give it to you—not tonight."

Death studied her as if he could see into her soul. "Not tonight then, but one day."

"Why are you so convinced that I'll lose? Has my work shown you nothing?"

"Your work has shown me pockets of potential, but humans can only wound, Nella. They destroy what they touch, only building it again for future destruction. It's in their nature—and one day, your love for them will destroy you."

She closed her eyes, probably wishing she could close her ears to the truth of his words. "I know you don't believe it, but there will always be someone worth saving."

"That may very well be true," Death conceded, "but perhaps you'll grow tired of the sacrifice."

"Well, that day is *not* today," she said with finality.

Death rose, pausing only to collect the newest pages spread across her desk, the ink still fresh, and slipped away, leaving as the first rays of light spilled across her sheets.

One day . . . he would be right.

# PRESENT DAY

Savannah, June

# Sixteen

Sebastian settles next to me, placing a cup of peppermint tea in my hands—the heat soothing. I sip gratefully, my throat raw from talking for hours.

"You've got to be tired," he says, glancing at his watch. "It's half past one in the morning. We can always stop if you want."

"I am exhausted, but I've tried to bury all these memories for so long that now it's—it's like they're all sprouting up at once, waiting for their turn to be shared. I'm willing to keep going if you are."

"Are they all bad, like your last time seeing René?"

I shake my head. "There's plenty of bad. It still hurts sometimes. Feels almost as fresh as it did then."

"I imagine it's like ripping off a million and one Band-Aids."

I laugh despite my melancholy. "But other parts, they don't hurt at all. And then there are the good things I've forgotten. I don't think I could have done this without you."

I take another sip, grateful for this rare moment. However alone I was the night I left René, I'm not alone now.

"One last time: Do you want to stop?"

"Why stop? The story will be over soon enough." My guilt twinges. *And so will everything else . . . Death will be angry at me for breaking his rules . . . and for showing my whole self to someone again.*

He sweeps a springy curl from my forehead and stares into my eyes. "The things you've seen are remarkable. I still can't believe it. The rational part of my brain wants to reject it, but another part of me, the details you know . . . only someone who's lived it could know so much."

"I've seen more than I should." I rest my head on his shoulder.

"Where did you go after Paris?"

I sit up, and my mind toggles through that decade, the memories coming in flashes. "I wandered for a while, first to Africa, Freetown in Sierra Leone, working in orphanages and hospitals with the Krio people, then to Algeria as the personal secretary of a merchant family, and afterward, I found my way to what is now known as Turkey as a correspondent for a British newspaper."

I lean over to pluck a silky red shawl from the trunk—a dupatta, luxuriously embroidered in gold with birds, leaves, and flowers.

Another gift, from another love.

It's lain here, heavy with meaning, only a memento, for decades. Even though these memories cut me to the bone, the pain rising raw and fresh, a bit of joy peeks through too, as I remember the day I received it.

Sebastian adjusts his glasses. "I think I already know the answer to this question, but . . . Why didn't you return to America?"

"Newspapers reported on the plight of us. It was terrifying, what befell Black communities at the time. I sent money, but I couldn't send myself. I simply wasn't ready. The ghosts still felt too real." I say these things, and my heart twists with a familiar guilt. Could I have done more here at home? Should I have returned and tried to help?

But I know the truth. My heart was shattered. If I'd tried at that point to wrestle with the past, I wouldn't have survived.

"I wanted to find a place where I could lose myself in nothing but words, so in time, I found my way to London at the turn of the century, years before the First World War began."

# PART IV: LONDON

## The Dupatta—1901

# Seventeen

I wandered until I could no longer feel the pain of René shadowing me from place to place. I'd settled in London, writing under a male pseudonym for the *Rivington Chronicle* while attending lectures at University College London, trying to use the long years of immortality to expand my understanding of the world. I bustled in the door, the cold gusting as I made my way to the back of the hall, thankful to be out of the weather. Even after a year in London, I still hadn't grown used to the constant dampness crawling into my bones, so different from the warmth of Freetown, Algiers, and Constantinople.

I supposed that was what I'd asked for. London felt like a world away from my other life, with few reminders of René and the years I'd spent in France. I avoided art museums and galleries for a time, but the pull of beautiful things always won. Even the blustery and gray city had its own grim beauty. It was as good a place as any, and the bleak weather matched my mood.

I slid into a corner seat in the hall and opened my journal, ready to take notes. London felt like the center of the world, with access to information through lectures and classes and plentiful papers and cultural institutions. Instead of traveling the world over, I could hear from many experts on things I couldn't conceive of knowing otherwise. I navigated barriers—some talks closed to women and some due to my race—but most of the time, it was nothing a few well-placed guineas couldn't fix. My banker in Paris knew me only by an account number, so my change in identity—I'd adopted "Arden Bell" as my alias on newly forged documents when I arrived—was no issue.

Still, London's rigid social order quickly reminded me of where I fell. While my skin didn't draw the same reaction it had in my time in Savannah and New Orleans and Paris, it still marked me as different, leaving me to navigate yet another societal in-between where the rules were blurry and constantly rewritten.

I watched the students file into the room, the attending women piling into our designated section. A woman named Barbara Hale came up almost immediately, beaming, her pale hair swept back in a bouffant. "Arden! So glad you could make it."

"You extended the opportunity so graciously," I said, happy to see a familiar face. "How could I not?"

"I'm simply tickled that you could come. We have several speakers and then refreshments. I do hope you find learning about our cause interesting." She smiled at me like she always did, her eyes finding my curls as if I were a peacock that had flown in from some faraway place.

"I surely hope so," I said. I thought I could write something interesting about the organization for the *Englishwoman's Review* or another publication. Death wasn't the only being who needed reminding of what good humans were capable of.

Barbara beamed and fluttered away to greet more guests as they poured in. We'd met at a literature course I'd audited. I could attend as long as I didn't matriculate, and provided I wasn't "a distraction" as a tiny fly in the milk.

I'd met Barbara in the female commons room as she campaigned to get as many women as possible to register to vote in Britain, raising money and awareness for her cause. She'd been a good contact, also involved at Girton College in Cambridge, the first university-level institution for women in the UK.

"The more we make our presence known, the better," a woman shouted. "Deeds, not words, ladies."

Thunderous applause filled the room as they parroted the slogan of the suffragette movement.

A few handed out pamphlets detailing the rights of women to own property, and organizers talked about other issues like the care of orphans and improvements in housing, while others sent around a collection plate to gather money to bail out women who'd been jailed at recent protests.

It was easy to get swept up in their fervor about rights and freedoms as I blended into the back, trying not to be seen and wondering if they'd included me in their demands to the men of the government. As the night wore on, I couldn't help but notice some speakers describing a London that applied only to them, wealthy and middle-class women who sought enfranchisement in the political sphere.

I wondered if they'd even considered what the world was like for those who didn't share their station or skin color. If I'd had the courage to stand and ask, I wondered what they might say. Then Barbara announced the final speaker for the night.

"Before I get you over to the refreshments, we have a late addition to the agenda. Rohan Naoroji is a representative from the East India Association who will speak about the aims of his organization and provide a sneak peek at his upcoming lecture series. We must all better ourselves, ladies. We must remain one step ahead of them at all times."

A murmur rumbled through the audience as a handsome Indian man strode to the small podium positioned at the front of the room. The women straightened, and many sat on the edge of their seats.

Tall, with umber-brown skin and a dark beard, he stood out from the crowd. I'd come to know that the white hat fixed on his black wavy hair was called a turban. It matched the bright-white fabric of the shirt skimming his body, so different from the dark and neutral-colored jackets and gowns worn by most in the room. We appeared nearly the same age, in our mid-twenties, even though I was well over 140 years old at that time.

"Ms. Hale, thank you for your kind welcome and opportunity to present to you tonight." He spoke with a strong British accent, only the whisper of another language in his consonants. "I'm here as a representative of the East India Association, started in 1866 by my uncle, Dadabhai Naoroji. Our organization aims to represent the interest of Indians in Britain and India, and share the realities of living in India under British rule."

With that, he dived into a brief history lesson of Indians in Britain, which prompted a memory of my readings of Dean Mahomet all those years ago in New Orleans.

Rohan continued, "Our sailors with the East India Company built up the British maritime presence, giving rise to this empire, yet we labor under the worst conditions, often for eight or nine shillings per week, unable to unionize. In the same way Britain rules over Ireland, so, too, it rules over India, allowing few opportunities in civil service for native-born Indians in our own country. Much like you, we believe in improving the position of women in this society and abroad. As I have listened to you tonight, seeking justice and freedom for yourselves, you must also acknowledge the desire of others of varied backgrounds, ethnicities, and hues for the same goal."

Some attendees shifted uncomfortably—maybe at his gender, maybe at his color, maybe at both—but they couldn't deny his points.

As he talked, I realized how little I knew about these groups of people. I'd seen them, true enough, often encountering Indians and other East and South Asians as they'd made their way to work in dockyards as lascars or to private homes to tend to children as ayahs, but I hadn't had any meaningful contact. Perhaps there was a story there . . . of different people making their way in a strange land, all united in the pursuit of opportunity.

He wrapped up, his narrative turning personal, each attendee enthralled by his words.

"I traveled here as a small child for education and opportunity. I have seen the advantages that the British Empire has to offer. As the son of a cotton merchant, I was fortunate to claim many of them, but now, I also work to help others. I hope that with continued connection and understanding, I have helped broaden your perspective. I invite you to learn more in our regular meetings in Winchester. By identifying what connects us, I hope we will all reach our eventual goals."

Recognition flared in me. Here was a man who wanted better for himself and his people, and was taking steps to make it possible.

Barbara clapped as he stepped back from the lectern. "My! You've certainly given us all something to think about, Mr. Naoroji. Thank you again for a wonderful evening," she said before giving us a few more announcements and then dismissing us to the food.

I gathered my things as the crowd trickled out, my thoughts still on his speech. I had furiously copied down notes and ideas from his speech. I was debating whether I should thank him when I found him at my side.

"I couldn't help but notice you," he said. "I'm Rohan Naoroji. And I am pleased to make your acquaintance." His name lingered on his lips, as if he'd managed to lace it with music. He smelled of cinnamon, sandalwood, and other fragrances I couldn't name. "There aren't many here who look like ourselves," he said, his brown skin a touch darker than mine. "Miss . . ."

"Bell. Arden Bell," I said, shaking his hand.

"Well, Arden. I saw you with Barbara. Are you one of her students?"

"No, I attend lectures here and write." I lifted my notebook.

"A writer?" He rubbed his dark beard. "Maybe I should've been more careful with my words."

I laughed. "I'll only report the good things."

"So, now I know what you do," he said, his eyes crinkling as he smiled. "But who *are* you?"

How unusual, I thought, to inquire about a person that way. How perceptive and curious. And that was how the first interview began, his words cracking open a dam I'd been holding up for so long. I detailed all that had enthralled me for the past few months, from the death of

Queen Victoria and the ascension of King Edward to the throne, to the architecture and art on display at the Glasgow International Exhibition and everything in between. I hadn't let anyone close enough to me to speak freely in years, and yet this stranger had excavated what I'd hidden away with a simple question imbued with tenderness.

The conversation flowed as the crowd streamed around us. No sooner had I told him of my work with the repatriated to Africa than he followed up with a question about the clashes among the different ethnic groups who made their home in Sierra Leone.

His intellect was astonishing.

"You've seen so much of the world for such a young, beautiful lady," he observed.

"I've found there is always more left to see."

"And you have been in some dangerous places," he added. "Were you not afraid?"

I'd been *born* into danger. Death had given not only an escape but a guarantee that I couldn't die, even if I could still be hurt. Still, I wanted to answer as honestly as I could. "At times . . ."

"'Thus fear of danger is ten thousand times more terrifying than danger itself when apparent to the eyes; and we find the burden of anxiety greater, by much, than the evil which we are anxious about . . .'"

My eyes widened. "*Robinson Crusoe* . . ."

"You know it?"

"Of course."

My curiosity kindled from a tiny candle flame to a roaring fire. Soon, only Rohan and I were left by the seats, deep in a conversation about our travels and studies. He quoted more books we'd both read and discussed the latest headlines in the newspaper about England's pursuits abroad. He seemed to love when I disagreed with him.

Barbara made her way back to us. "Arden, would you like me to have some refreshments wrapped up for you both?"

Rohan looked about us, startled, surprised at how much time had passed. He stepped back. "I should let you get back to your evening.

Though, if I may be so bold, there's another talk tomorrow afternoon with more representatives from the East India Association. Perhaps afterward, we could share more, possibly a meal?"

It took only a moment to think it through. I would not take an interest in Rohan's heart. My own was too broken. But his mind . . . that was something else. "I'd be delighted to—in a professional way, of course."

He smiled, teeth strong and white. "Then I shall look forward to it," he said before giving me the address.

I said my goodbyes and departed into the deepening night. Though the chill and dense fog crept in, the flame of a new connection kept me warm on the short trip home. Maybe a true friend was what I needed to pass the time.

∼

The atmosphere of the meeting was miles different from the lecture I'd attended the night before, the diversity notable from the start: Men and women of all hues, ethnicities, and dress made up the audience. They spoke on themes similar to those from the previous day's program, espousing the ideals of opportunity and freedom. A petite woman dressed in a yellow sari spoke of the need to educate young girls, while another man spoke of the need to move the civil service tests to India rather than London, thus decentralizing power. Each person spoke eloquently about the world and what action was needed to make change possible.

Rohan presided over it all with aplomb. He called the speakers up and then, after about an hour and a half, opened the floor for questions.

He called on folks from the audience. "Ah! Mr. Boudreaux. Good to see you again. What's your question."

My head snapped up at the name. *Boudreaux?* I thought of Jacques, though it had been decades since he'd last entered my mind. So much time had passed, and we were so far from the American South. Surely this man was no relation. I craned my neck to see.

A young man with blond hair and broad shoulders stood.

"With cotton production still down in the US, what opportunities can you see for American investment?"

It was a fine question, but I couldn't even hear the answer; I was more focused on the speaker. Likely in his late teens or early twenties, he spoke in a firm and smooth voice, his accent distinctly American. If he was related to Jacques, he appeared young enough to be his great-great-grandson.

I was stunned, thrown into both the past and denial. Boudreaux was a common enough name. Wasn't it? Jacques's family plantation produced sugarcane, not cotton. Surely this was merely a coincidence.

And yet, what were the chances he'd be here if he *was* related to Jacques?

Was the world really that small?

At the end of my long life, would it all lead me back to the very beginning?

The meeting ended, and everyone rose to their feet, the chatter in the room rising. As I peered closer at the young Mr. Boudreaux, I couldn't help but notice the similarities to Jacques—the way he held himself and moved across the room felt familiar. There was no question when I saw him from the front: His face and storm-blue eyes matched my long-ago lover's.

I hovered closer, not brave enough to approach, for what would I say? *Hello, young man! Do you have a great-grandfather named Jacques?* Madness.

The smart move would be to stay back and away, not allowing a past life to collide with this one. Rohan stood near the lectern, speaking with the man about the civil service test. I could've waited for him, pretending to have never seen the boy, and been on my way.

But a feeling held me in place, a ping of intuition I couldn't ignore.

When young Mr. Boudreaux glanced about the room, his smile slipped as if he were wearing a mask—something was off. He stood near an alcove with another short, young white-skinned man, a cluster of acne marching up the smaller boy's cheeks, his hair thick with pomade, eyes scanning the crowd.

I moved closer as if drawn forward, their conversation floating back to me. I feigned interest in a pamphlet, ears on high alert.

"So, tell me about the plan."

*Plan?* I stopped, careful to stay several steps back, then sat behind them, eavesdropping. My curiosity quickly evolved from interest into alarm.

The Boudreaux boy laughed, his manner shockingly familiar. He leaned closer, flicking his friend playfully on the shoulder. "My father says it will be simple. No one has business sense like us Americans, right? The savages will never see it coming."

*Savages?* My stomach wobbled at the smirk on his face. *Who wouldn't see what coming?*

"Are you all right?"

I jumped.

Rohan gazed down at me, concerned.

"I'm fine, thank you," I said, fanning myself with the pamphlet. I glanced back, but the Boudreaux boy was already making his way down the hall, friend in tow.

"I wanted to ask—that boy there, who asked the question about Americans and cotton. Do you know him?"

"That's Benjamin Boudreaux, an American here for schooling. His father, Bartholomew, is working on a deal with my uncle's trading house. Why?"

"I . . . um . . . believe I knew some of his family . . . once upon a time."

Rohan brightened. "What a coincidence. Shall we make introductions?"

"No!" I said, my gut queasy. How would I even go about explaining? "I mean—it's not necessary. He's halfway out the door, and it is such a small world, you know. I'm sure I'll run across him at some point. We should get going before it's dark out."

"Let's be off, then," Rohan said, extending his arm. I took it, and we headed in the opposite direction, but my mind was still thinking of the blond boy with links to my past.

∼

"What is that?" I asked as he spooned powder into a cup.

"We call it chai, while you may call it tea." He filled the cup, the steaming liquid swirling, specks of spices throughout, and handed it to me. We were in a quaint Indian tea shop on Brick Lane, not far from where he lived, the atmosphere cozy in a way that I didn't know I longed for, the patrons of all hues. We blended in, taking a table in the corner. It was a relief not to stick out for once. The feeling reminded me of Freetown and Constantinople.

"So, tell me about yourself." I leaned back comfortably and blew on the hot cup, the scents of cinnamon, cloves, and honey in the chai rising.

"I daresay there isn't much to share," he said. "I work in my uncle's trading company. I support the East India Association with talks and advocate for new arrivals. My father died when I was young, and his brother took me in, giving me a role in the business."

I sipped the fragrant, delicious liquid. "It must be a powerful feeling, having a family to support you. I've been on my own since I was young." That bit of truth felt safe to share.

"I am lucky. My uncle's been a great mentor. He has enough ambition for himself and all of India. He talks of running for Parliament here and also back home. He travels between the two often. I enjoy the work and supporting the cause, so my life is now the business."

"And what exactly is your business?" Knowing he worked with Jacques's family piqued my interest. Living as long as I had, I was beginning to understand the threads of my former lives were bound to cross at some point. Could the plan Benjamin referred to have something to do with Rohan and his family business? It was too early to ask those sorts of questions.

"Agriculture and some industry. Our main export is cotton, with other crops from Gujarat shipped here for processing."

"Cotton?" I kept my tone neutral, my mind slipping back to when Miss Wilcox married Master Carter and I transitioned to outside work. I still remembered the bite of the cotton boll, the endless sorting of the white fluff into baskets, and the scratchy hairs and seed coverings that tore at your hands. I wondered if it was any different in India than at home.

When I left the plantation, cotton production had been in its infancy, all pulled by hand. Thanks to Eli Whitney and his cotton gin, cotton production exploded, and I'd seen huge bales coming through the port of New Orleans for processing. Still, the white fiber demanded a heavy price in human lives.

"It's labor intensive, for sure. Many people in nearby towns work with us as growers. We're expanding—buying more land and exporting to other markets like America and China, setting up the shipping lanes here—hence the deal with Benjamin's father."

I turned to Rohan. "Do you like them? The Boudreaux family?"

He shrugged, the motion fluid. "It is not a matter of like but more of business."

"Do you trust them then?"

"Trust?" His brows lowered.

"I overheard a conversation perhaps not intended for me. It may be nothing." I shook my head. "It isn't my place."

"No, please, continue."

I let out a slow breath, working up the courage. "Benjamin mentioned something about a plan to his friend at the lecture. Boasted that it would be easy to trick you. Given what you said about the deal . . ."

Rohan sat back, seemingly confused but trying to remain composed. "I'm glad you trusted me enough to tell me," he said, his voice sincere.

"Here we are!" the owner said, interrupting us as he popped a plate onto our table, the scent of heavy spices floating toward us from the crispy balls stuffed with potatoes and chickpeas, heavily doused with sauce.

"Come. No more talk of business." Rohan plucked a hollow ball from the plate. "It's called pani puri. Try some."

Heat, spice, and tamarind exploded in my mouth.

"Now, how is that for food?" he said, grinning.

"Oh my goodness," I said, the flavors reminding me of my travels through Freetown, Constantinople, and Algiers: a tremendous contrast to the subtler tastes of standard British fare. "The best thing I've had since I've been here."

A pleasant silence stretched between us as we devoured the dish. Though this was all a new experience, I felt more at home than I had in ages. I'd forgotten what it was like to relax.

"So, you mentioned your uncle's plans for you. Do you have any for yourself?"

He bit into his last fritter, bliss blossoming over his face as he considered the question. "It's been the plan since birth: study, marry, and work in the family business, supporting my uncle's trading house, and have children."

I marveled at his plans for a long moment, part of me wishing I could have something as neat and tidy. "And you're okay with that?"

"Of course. Family is everything, and this is my duty. Besides, it puts me at ease. I have friends who flounder about, wondering what to do. Should they study law? Medicine? Strike out someplace new or stay where they are? For me, it's simpler. Help grow my uncle's business. Leave a legacy."

The word "legacy" haunted me, conjuring Death's words from the day we'd made our bet: *"You shall have no descendants. No family. No tangible legacy on this earth. Only the words you write for me."*

Rohan made it all seem so simple; he was a captain charting his voyage to a well-known port, his arrival assured. As I took another nibble of pani puri, I thought about all the pieces I'd anonymously written and all the anonymous donations I'd given. The price of the bet finally crystallized inside me as solidly as Rohan's destiny—total anonymity.

"Could you show me a bit of the business?" I interrupted to change the topic of conversation.

"Are you asking to see me again, Arden?" His mustache twitched as he fought away a smile.

"Is *that* what you heard? Hmm. Interesting." I tried not to like him. I had not loved anyone in so long, and I was afraid to open to the possibility. But the more we talked, the more at ease I was in his company.

"In any case," he said, "I accept. I'll arrange a visit to our offices on Cumberland Street, and we'll make a day of it."

"I'm looking forward to it."

We stepped back outside as the sun kissed the horizon, coloring the gray sky a pale pink and casting long shadows. The last of a summer breeze found its way through my skirts. My carriage and footman waited on the corner, tucked out of sight. I wasn't sure I wanted him to know that I had one of my own. I'd become skillful at hiding my wealth.

"I thank you for the food and the trip," I said.

"Surely you don't think I can leave you here. I insist on making sure you make it home properly to your family."

I couldn't tell him that I had no family, that I lived in a mews house in Kensington by myself.

"My footman is here." I motioned toward the carriage. A small shock registered on his face.

"Allow me to escort you like a proper gentleman does." He led me by the small of my back.

"Would you call yourself a 'proper gentleman,' then?"

"I think you'll find I'm among the very best." Rohan stopped under the shade of the carriage roof and waited, suspended in that time of needing to go but wanting to stay, unwilling to break the thread of magic that laced the moment. "Will you permit me one indulgence?"

I worried my lower lip, and my senses filled with the scent of apples. My past always seemed to be chasing my present. "Yes."

He placed his hand on my shoulder, and I didn't shrink from him. Instead, curious, I silently tilted my chin toward him. He brushed his lips across my cheek, the movement soft, his touch gentle. I'd thought a kiss might feel like a betrayal to René, but instead, it only reminded me of how long I'd been in solitude.

He stepped back, smiling. "Until next time."

"Until next time," I repeated.

I ducked into my carriage, purse swinging in my hand, a lightness to my heart, anticipating our next encounter.

# Eighteeen

As promised, Rohan arranged for us to meet the following Saturday. A cornflower-blue morning stretched overhead into infinity, the last warmth of September clinging on and brimming with the possibility of adventure.

"This is one of our processing plants," he said over the noise, the machines pounding as bits of cotton fiber floated in the air. He led a tour through the spinning room as the cotton was twisted into thread and bound in great sheets. I had, of course, seen the bolts of fabric in the shops, but I had yet to learn the scale of industrialization that had machines turning and twisting fibers into great sheets of cloth.

Men worked the machines as they spun at a roar, making it hard to hear. They fed the insatiable beasts, sweat dripping from their thin limbs. It was a welcome respite when we escaped to the storehouse, which held the bolts of finished fabric. The work was hard, but it was as honorable as any other work, not demeaning like my experience at home.

As we walked farther from the din, Rohan explained: "With the American Civil War, Britain could not get the cotton it needed. While my grandfather was very much in favor of your North winning the war, many cotton growers in India wished it would have gone on longer. The war and the end of slavery raised the price of cotton, and the British tried to keep a stranglehold on the cotton mill industry. The British buy Indian cotton, pence for the pound, only to sell it back to us once it's refined. They prevent our creation of mills, driving down competition and keeping the lion's share for themselves. So that is why we are here—attempting to do it ourselves."

"That's admirable. Having control over the process."

He nodded and then hesitated. "You must forgive me if I'm rude, but are your interests in cotton production personal?"

I understood the implication. It was his way of asking, *Have you, or any member of your family, ever worked in the fields?*

"I've . . . engaged . . . with cotton production in the past. It was a painful period. I'm glad to be free of it and that others back home are also free. Your business is nothing like that."

He gazed over the tall machinery and the workers bending over the mechanical rows as the bobbins spun. "These people are paid, and we do our best to care for them. That doesn't make the work less hard, or the overall systems fairer. We also do not employ children."

The truth burned: The work needed to be done, and profits needed to be made. Rohan was doing the best he could. At least, his people were looked after. Likely at a cost to his bottom line.

"Well, if you've gathered what you needed, should I take you back?"

"The time went too quickly," I admitted.

Rohan seemed delighted by my admission, even if a bit flustered. "If you're not otherwise engaged, there's a gathering tonight. My uncle is having a function as they finalize a new deal with the Americans. Would you like to come as my guest? There'll be many people there, including friends of the association, professors from the university, and some merchant families." He hesitated. "I think it would be lovely if you came."

"But I—I've only known you for a few days," I said, despite the flattery I felt from his invitation.

"What does that matter?" Rohan asked, his hand brushing alongside mine. "If I'm having a celebration, it could only be better if you were there." His rich brown eyes were shrewd, with a charming sparkle we both knew was irresistible.

"If that's the case, we must leave soon so I can prepare. I'll have to wear something dazzling for such an event."

He drew me closer, his words only loud enough for me to hear. "You should have no concern there. You dazzle me just as you are."

# Nineteen

At the party, professors and administration folk buzzed around tables of food bursting with savory meat, decadent vegetables, and a plethora of colorful sweets. I plucked a skewer spiced with coriander, cumin, and turmeric, then piled several gulab jamun—balls filled with milk solids and soaked in rosewater syrup until they swelled—into a tiny pyramid on my plate. A jubilant, festive mood ran through the party as the musicians played and the guests formed a circle, taking turns dancing through the middle. Others clapped in time to the music.

I recognized a few people and made light conversation but mostly hung back and observed. Rohan's uncle Dadabhai reigned over it all, greeting guests and encouraging them to eat as they lined up to pay homage to him. He looked stately, like a raj from one of the Indian provinces, with his well-oiled beard and vibrant vest beneath his tailored coat.

I spotted Benjamin first, half a head taller than the man who must have been his father, the resemblance uncanny. Bartholomew, a man in his forties, a touch of gray at his temples, stood before his son, surveying the party, his suit impeccable. Benjamin had his father's looks, but both lacked Jacques's warm charm. There was a tightness in his father's mouth, and his dark-blue eyes glinted like ice. It was like being in a hall of mirrors, the familiar distorted into the unrecognizable. The ghosts of my previous lives had never shown up like this, and I wondered if Death was playing some ultimate trick on me.

I faded behind a wooden lattice as they passed, taking a place far from the main group. It was silly to hide. There was no way they could know who I was or recognize me. Jacques would have had no cause to bring me up. I would have become a relic from his past. Still, I stayed in place as they stopped on the opposite side of the trellis, clapping along with everyone else.

"How much longer, Father? The food and music are horrible."

"One day, I hope you'll get the idea of discretion through that fool head of yours." Bartholomew glanced about.

Benjamin shrank back as he picked up a gulab jamun and stuffed it in his mouth. Only I was close enough to see him wince before he forced a smile and swallowed it down.

I skirted the pillar and waded through the crowd while searching for Rohan. He was in a circle of friends, holding court and in the middle of a joke. It must have landed, since raucous laughter broke out, and they clapped each other on the back. He caught my eye and excused himself.

"Enjoying the party?" he asked.

"Quite. I don't remember the last time I enjoyed myself this much. And you?"

"It's been difficult." He smoothed his beautiful fingers along his facial hair.

"Oh?"

"I'm having difficulty focusing when all I can see is you."

I wanted to enjoy the pleasure his words elicited, but made the mistake of glancing at Bartholomew, whose eyes were on me, wide open as if he'd seen a ghost. He seemed to take an involuntary step toward me, the puzzle evident on his face. I didn't need my gut to know that the ghost was me.

"Excuse me, Rohan, I need to adjust my dress," I said, quickly turning on my heel.

"Okay, I—"

I didn't hear the rest of what he said as I left his side, heading in the opposite direction of Bartholomew, joining the crowd. He wove through the crowd at the same rate. I could see Benjamin not far behind from the corner of my eye.

I was near the door when a sharp tug came at my elbow.

"Who are you?" Bartholomew demanded, his expression dark as his eyes swept my face.

"Excuse me?" I jerked my elbow back. "What business is it of yours?"

"I'll mind that," he said as he invaded my space. "Who are you?"

"I'm a university student. And I am a guest here. Who are *you*?" I backed toward the door. There were too many people staring, too many witnesses for something I could not explain.

His eyes bored into me. "My grandfather kept a miniature of a woman hidden in his desk. As a child, I stared at it constantly. Yet he would never speak of her. You look exactly as she—" He covered his mouth with disbelief. "*Exactly* as she."

"Is there a problem here?" Rohan and his uncle cut through the crowd, attempting to calm the situation.

Bartholomew relaxed his face, patching on a smile, transitioning alarmingly from anger to ease.

"Of course not. I merely thought her an acquaintance." He glanced at me, but darkness lingered there. I moved closer to Rohan.

Rohan's uncle frowned. "You will not mishandle a guest of mine in my house, sir. Our family and conglomeration only have members of the most upright character!"

Bartholomew blanched. "I'm sorry, sir. All a misunderstanding." He glanced about; guests stared at us in confusion. "We'll take our leave. Come on, Benjamin," he muttered.

They hustled out of the party as the murmurs rose. Thankfully, the musicians played their instruments, filling the silence and restarting the conversation.

"What was all that?" Rohan glanced between me and the Boudreaux family, hastily retreating.

"As he said, it was truly a misunderstanding. Please, you have guests. I must take my leave."

Rohan's uncle acknowledged me apologetically before returning to his nephew. "Come, my boy, I have others to introduce you to."

I felt Rohan's eyes boring questions at my back as I left, his uncle guiding him deeper into the crowd. Before I started for home, I waited outside to ensure that Benjamin and his father hadn't lingered. I'd learned long ago the trouble that men worked in the shadows.

~

Deep into the night, sudden sharp cracks against my window woke me. I sat up, instantly alert. It had taken me ages to fall asleep, the night's events replaying in my mind. I kept seeing Bartholomew's face as he questioned me—his anger. Two more objects thwacked the window frame. Had he somehow followed me?

I threw back the covers and carefully drew the curtains to spot the source of the noise. Rohan stood in my courtyard with a small clutch of pebbles, white moonlight casting a halo around him.

I unlatched the window, letting in the cool evening breeze. "What are you doing here?"

"I knocked, but no one answered," he said sheepishly, his face endearing under the soft glow. "Forgive me for this forwardness. I don't know what has come over me."

"It's after *midnight*." As bewildered as I was by his visit, I had to admit a part of me was thrilled.

"I wanted to check on you after the party. I've only managed to slip away. I thought I'd see if you were up."

"By damaging the side of my house?"

He ducked his head. "If it makes a difference, I chose the smallest pebbles."

"You shouldn't be here, Rohan." As I spoke the words, I smiled.

"You are all I can think about."

But for how long? Letting someone into my heart—again—felt like a fool's errand. Who would see me, who would think of me beyond Death? What could I offer, except a few good years? Rohan was a family man. Jacques had been one, too. He'd wanted me to carry his children. Having faced his descendant, I was glad it had never been a choice. And yet, Jacques had carried his memory of me, over generations, despite our distance. Maybe I didn't need crowds of people to know me.

Maybe I just needed one.

"Come up, you'll catch a chill. I'll put on the kettle." I shrugged on a thin silk robe and hurried down the stairs to open the door. Rohan was still dressed in his party clothes, a little timid and unsure, but there nonetheless.

We settled into my receiving room, him sitting on one couch and I on the other, the air thick and electric. I lit a lamp, aware I was in my nightclothes and of the precise distance he sat across from me.

"I appreciate the concern, Rohan, but I'm fine. There was no harm done."

"Oh, but there was. I'd thought you'd like to know the result of your encounter and your keen observation."

I put the kettle on and brought him a cup of tea. "It isn't chai, but I hope it'll do."

He tipped his head in appreciation and blew on the hot liquid before taking a sip. He set the cup down. "After the scene Boudreaux caused, I told my uncle of your misgivings, and what you'd overheard. No sooner had we discussed it than another investor approached my uncle and told him of a double deal the Boudreaux family planned. They meant to nullify the land deal, which would undercut all our shares and cause their price to fall. They would bet on the short, thereby raking in the funds. That would have left us in ruins, and the land in foreign hands."

I gasped. I hadn't imagined the scale of the betrayal. "Could they do that to you?"

"Lesser men have tried greater." He reached out for my hand. "The point is, because of you, my uncle believed what he was told. We were able to pull out of the agreement before it was signed, thanks to you."

"Based on what you said, it would've been discovered eventually."

"Your modesty is heartwarming. But maybe, just maybe, I'm giving you the credit you deserve."

Our thumbs brushed together for a moment before he drew away. "I am glad your family's business is safe."

"I have something for you—a gift. In thanks."

I hadn't noticed he'd brought in a small bundle. He offered it to me and I was too eager to open it, revealing a glorious dupatta—a long red shawl stitched with golden thread depicting birds, vines, and flowers, with intricate beading along the edge. The whisper-soft fabric rippled in the breeze from the open window, swirling around us.

"It's beautiful," I said, clutching it against my heart.

"Not as beautiful as you."

"You are too charming." I playfully poked his chest, tempted to linger. I shook my head to dispel the snap of desire. "It's the middle of the night. Where did you buy this?"

"I got it on Brick Lane, just after our dinner there. I had been saving it. Then I thought, 'Why wait?' I felt drawn to it, as it appears I feel drawn to you."

"Rohan," I said gently. "You are so kind, but does . . . does your uncle know that you're here?"

He pressed his lips together, his expression rueful. The answer was clear. I stood, and he followed, slowing as we reached the door. I held it for him.

"Thank you for the gift. I hope you have a good night."

He closed the distance between us. "You were brave enough to tell me the truth about the Boudreaux family, now I must do the same. The truth is, being with you is the first thing I have ever wanted for myself, outside of my family duties. When I saw you across the lecture hall, something came alive in here." He gripped the place over his heart. "I believe it to be love. I am no longer consumed solely by my duty and responsibility. Instead, I think of my brief moments with you, and the simplicity of, well, *being*, and I imagine I could have thousands of those moments with you."

"Rohan," I pleaded. Thank goodness for my solid door. I had something sturdy to keep me upright.

"Please, Arden, let me finish. I know of my uncle's plans. But when I'm with you, I think of more."

I told myself to return to bed, but instead I reached for him. He wrapped his arms around me, his heart thundering through the thin fabric of his shirt. The dupatta tangled between us.

"I can't promise you anything." *Especially forever,* I thought darkly. *No one can ever stay long enough for that.*

"All I'm asking of you is your company."

The honesty of his words lay between us. He wanted time free of duty, and I wanted time to be known, fully known, by someone existing on this earth. Would it be so terrible if we were to comfort each other for a little while?

I said slowly, "Could we do simply that, then? Enjoy time together? Without promises or expectations?"

"You wouldn't think me callous?"

"I'd think you are brave enough to ask for what you want and strong enough to share your feelings with me." I traced the fine stitching on his chest with my fingertip. "You are also one of the most brilliant minds I have ever known."

I shut the door behind him, then led him upstairs. That night we did more than lie together, enjoying each other's warmth and company—forgetting our duty to the world and focusing on only each other.

# Twenty

Our time together stretched for years as we made a life in Whitechapel, supporting others and their independence movements, helping with time and money.

Rohan took on more and more leadership within the association and trading house. His uncle was aware of me, and while he didn't approve, he didn't ask Rohan to change our relationship either.

I spent the time writing, documenting, and preparing for a meeting with Death. The population of the city continued to explode, and immigrants from Africa, the Caribbean, India, and all the British colonies trickled into London seeking jobs and opportunities. I'd been able to put my money to good use, funding aid for the new arrivals, and our home for orphans was almost ready.

I recorded the stories of their lives and migration to London, all hopeful, all seeking a better life. I interviewed lascars as they awaited return ships from England, detailing their hard work in steam engine rooms of blistering heat. I interviewed Black maids and ayahs, Indian nannies who cared for the children of the rich. Their lives found their way into what was rapidly growing into a book. It was a time of invention and advancement, technology accelerating the reach of commerce and comfort for the first time down to not just the noble class, but the working person.

I was content in Rohan's companionship, his intellect tethering us to each other. Each day I wrote pieces for *The Daily Telegraph* and

*The Times*, hoping they would be enough for Death. Each night, in the soft cocoon of our room, Rohan read to me, interpreting some of the important texts of Hinduism—books and stories I hadn't known existed. They opened my mind to a new way of viewing the universe and my place in it. A way I would never otherwise have experienced.

One rainy evening, lost in a sea of bedsheets, our room alight with candle flame, he read from the Ramayana: "'Ever since I have been separated from you, Sita, everything to me has become its very reverse. The fresh and tender leaves on the trees look like tongues of fire; nights appear as dreadful as the night of final dissolution and the moon scorches like the sun. Beds of lotuses are like so many spears planted on the ground, while rain-clouds pour boiling oil as it were. Those that were friendly before, have now become tormenting; the cool, soft and fragrant breezes are now like the hissing serpent. One's agony is assuaged to some extent even by speaking of it, but to whom shall I speak about it? For there is no one who will understand. The reality about the chord of love that binds you and me, dear, is known to my heart alone; and my heart ever abides with you. Know this to be the essence of my love.'"

He caressed my face with each word and took my breath away. What beauty, what wonder we are capable of when we consider our lives in relation to others, in relation to the divine. Because of Rohan, my mind was alight with possibilities; new pathways opened in my soul.

We kissed then, intertwining our bodies and our souls in a way I had never known before.

∼

Rohan came to me at Christmas in 1914 with the latest news. The winds of World War I that had begun to blow across Europe in July were steadily becoming stronger.

And I had unexpected news of my own.

He sat across from me, the bed creaking under him, and sighed. "My uncle says he wants to shut down the trading house."

"Shut it down?" I couldn't believe what I was hearing. "After all you've done? Why?"

"He is scared of the day the war reaches here. He wants to return home to Bombay."

The silence hung between us.

I'd read in the papers about the assassination of Archduke Franz Ferdinand over the summer and the cascade it had set off in continental Europe. No one thought it would touch England at the time. I hadn't ever considered leaving London in preparation.

"And what do you want?" I pressed a hand against my stomach, now anxious about my own news. I already knew his feelings on family and duty. I didn't want to force his decision. If he wanted to go to India, I would not stop him.

"I want to stay with you and continue our work. I want to honor my family and do what is right." He leaned forward, resting his head in his hands. "I want both. But it is impossible."

I took his hand in mine. "You have to follow your heart. There's no other way."

"We would not fit there," he said, "but I can't leave you, Arden. I will go and settle my uncle, then I will return to you. It will be three months in total. A month's journey on either end. I'll leave in one week." He put his head in my lap. "Will you wait for me?"

Part of his words stung. We would not fit in Bombay. One would think I'd get used to not *fitting* somewhere.

"You'll be back in plenty of time to open the orphanage," I assured him. "I'll miss you, but I know this is temporary."

He exhaled, a look of relief on his face. "You are an angel. Somehow I will manage it. I will give us the best of both worlds."

I bent forward to kiss his temple.

Us. *We.* I wanted to believe that existed. Never more so than earlier that day, when I'd received word that that exclusive group would soon include one more person.

Two months earlier, I had found that my cycles, always right on time, had been absent. Death had promised that I wouldn't suffer illness, but I had gone to a doctor in fear for what it could mean.

Pregnancy was the last thing I expected. I couldn't puzzle how or why. It violated one of Death's most important stipulations. But the news filled my heart, unlocking something I hadn't known was closed.

But even with the new possibility, I knew to be cautious, for it was early still, and with my track record with Death, I couldn't take anything for granted. Rohan could go on the trip without worrying about me, and when he returned, we'd start the next phase of everything together.

~

Rohan left a week later, standing at the back of the boat, waving until the ship was too far out in the harbor and he faded to a dot. By those days, steamships had improved travel speed, but the journey from London to Bombay would still be a month, and with the growing war, the sea voyages were perilous. I'd kept my fears to myself: no need to let them take root in both our imaginations. I focused on understanding this pregnancy, and I focused on the children's home and the final designs. We'd have space for fifty orphans. I'd anonymously bought and donated an additional lot next door so there would be more room to grow in the future.

I'd seen two physicians about my state to be sure, then clung tight to this flicker of hope. I ignored thoughts about what it would be like to welcome a child, only for me to never age alongside them. I ignored thoughts about what this meant about my deal with Death. I ignored worries about what was to come.

German bombs rained down on London, and life screeched to a halt. The orphanage plans, my writing, even preparations for a baby—all of them faded beneath the wail of air raid sirens. Days and nights blurred as I huddled in underground shelters, waiting for word from Rohan. I took up knitting to steady my nerves and keep my hands busy while the city fought to hold itself together.

Rohan had been gone two months without word. I'd written him letters while bombs burst in the skies above London.

On a gray, cloudless morning, I spotted Gopal, Rohan's assistant, on the street after curfew. The heavy iron gate swung free, opening to my square garden, crowded with the thick green hedge that climbed up the walls, forming a private oasis. I knew the news she carried as soon as she stepped on the path.

I opened the door, and a single tear skated down Gopal's cheek. "Arden, there's been an accident!"

My own tears had welled up, and I instinctively knew what she was going to say.

*Rohan.*

Time stopped, clearly delineated into the period before and after that moment, one where I was happy, and the other where the bottom had dropped out of my world.

Rohan's steamer had reportedly caught fire off the coast of Bombay on its way back to London—all hands lost.

*He was on his way back to us,* I thought as I cradled the small bump pushing beneath my nightgown. *He was coming home.*

My mind cycled through my hopes.

*Perhaps he managed to swim away?*

*Maybe he is in a hospital somewhere.*

If I pretended well enough, I could tell myself that Rohan was still alive. I kept everything in our house the same, almost like a shrine, because surely he'd return. I cleared the gate of flowers that people left as condolences. I kept the curtains drawn. I refused visitors. If I kept everyone away, no one would say they were sorry, and I could pretend he was still out to sea, on his way home to us.

Only . . . there wasn't an "us" for much longer after that.

The bleeding started a week after Rohan's death.

I didn't remember fainting.

I just remembered waking up in the hospital ward and hoping I could close my eyes, never to see light again. Death would finally get what he wanted and I wanted to disappear.

So, I did.

I settled my estate, and as soon as I could, I booked passage on a ship leaving from Liverpool to disappear into my next life abroad.

# A VISIT FROM DEATH

Nella appeared shrunken as she stood rigidly in the graveyard, her black dress swallowing her slender frame, eyes on the plain wooden coffin. She'd put the remains of the baby inside, along with all the items she'd knitted during the bombings.

Death hadn't sent an invitation to meet, for there was no need. He'd known where she would be.

He waited in the in-between as the ceremony proceeded. It was only Nella and a priest. Out past curfew. There was no task for him there, for he'd already carried this child's soul away. He'd felt regret for the first time, the feeling coalescing in his chest. While the war raged across Europe, he'd been busy, taken his eye off her. So many dead to collect. He hadn't even had the time to read her articles. The papers still sat in his cloak pocket.

The priest crossed himself, and they laid the dirt on top, one shovelful at a time, until nothing was left but a mound and a marker with the name "Baby Naoroji."

Nella stayed long after the priest had gone, despite his warning about the coming airstrikes, staring at the headstone. She remained rooted to that spot, as if she could wait until the end of time.

Death appeared then, quietly, reflective, understanding a bit of what the loss meant to her. Nella had written of Rohan, of his light, his intellect, of how he'd helped people despite the risk to his own health and safety. Rohan's death and the loss of that impossible child were among the heaviest burdens she'd borne. Even Death, somehow, felt this despite all the reaping he had done.

He hadn't meant to let this happen. Their bet was meant to erase Nella's ability to have a legacy beyond her words for him. But it *had* happened. He had been occupied. And while part of the world had been tearing itself apart, her will and love only grew stronger than ever.

"You knew this was coming," she said, her eyes fixed on the marker. Her voice was a dead thing.

"The end always comes. For everyone. Nothing you could have done would have prevented it. And you know as well as I do, this shouldn't have happened in the first place."

Nella was silent for a long time, her thoughts clearly at war. This was the closest she'd ever been to giving in. He could sense it. He supposed he should feel victorious that she'd come closer to his way of thinking, and that this work would end soon.

"You mean, it'll come for everyone except me."

"For as long as you keep this up—yes."

She turned to face Death now, her eyes burning in the dark like the candle she held. "Then why did it happen? Why allow me a taste of this feeling, only to rip it away? Did you think it would help you win? That you'd break me?"

The sharpness in her voice wasn't of pain, but rather anger forged by the fires of loss and anguish.

"I wasn't—" he started to say, but she reached into her pocket, pulled out a copy of her diary, and shoved it into his chest: no elaborate stories, pleas, or evidence.

"Read."

Death stared at the book. "You still believe, then?" Strangely, he was not deflated at the news. He even felt the tiniest ping of satisfaction that their work would continue.

"Rohan was beautiful, and our child would've been too," Nella said, eyes still on the grave. "Our time was beautiful. He'd hate it if I'd forgotten that."

Death placed a hand on her shoulder, and she allowed it. They stayed like that for a bit as the wind whistled around them and the skies started to light up with German bombs. He would keep her safe here. Nothing would touch her.

When dawn came, he left without a word, for what was there to say? He watched her from a distance, wanting to be sure she'd return to the house without incident. He needed to collect the night's dead eventually, but they would wait their turn.

Nella stayed at the grave well into the morning, looking as if she wished there were room for her too.

Her last words before leaving were whispered so softly that even he could barely hear, with her hand on the cold, hard stone. "'The reality about the chord of love that binds you and me, dear, is known to my heart alone; and my heart ever abides with you.'"

# PRESENT DAY

## Savannah, June

# Twenty-One

"So much loss," Sebastian says, shaking his head.

We're still on the couch, leaning into each other, his left arm wrapped around my shoulders, my feet tucked under me. His touch is comforting, but the past weighs on me. *When will I learn?*

"I understand your time with Rohan was short," he said, "but I mean, the impact. Did you blame Death? Did you ever think he took them both to force your hand? To win the bet?"

This idea had gone round and round in my mind over the years—the bits I'd gathered from my conversations with Death, my studies in religion, philosophy, and the occult, and my general understanding of the cycle of life—all to make sense of my life and my experience.

I start slowly: "Everybody seems to have a time, preordained from the moment they draw their first breath. There's no use hiding from it, as it's the one guarantee in life. Someday, you will face death. The task left is for the living, to figure out how they will go on and continue to have hope and to dream, despite this." Death had never said this explicitly, but I'd pieced it together. It seemed he could only collect souls at their allotted times and would do so for eternity. This was his fate. His one possible escape was the only other power he possessed: the destruction of all.

"So, how did you go on?"

"You know, you should give interviews a try. You're good at them. I bet you could get a few published."

"I am certain now that a compliment from you is hard earned." He flashes a wry smile. "When you're ready."

I clear my throat. The steady light of the recorder shines like a sentinel, capturing my words. I pull the embroidered gloves from the trunk, stroking them lightly, turning my thoughts to Adam.

# PART V: NEW YORK

## The Gloves—1918

# Twenty-Two

New York provided a refuge after Rohan—it was a blank slate, devoid of memories everywhere I turned—a place I could blend in while I tried to piece myself back together. A soft welcome home. It had been more than a century since I'd set foot on American soil, spending so many years in Europe, Africa, and Turkey. I hadn't imagined how strange it'd feel to see the descendants of enslaved people now free. Some thriving and some struggling, but all free from chains.

As it turned out, I was one of the struggling. With the war, my investments tanked, and I had had too many expenditures supporting Rohan's work, all our charitable commitments, and the expense of the orphanage. I was nearly wiped out. After booking my ticket on a steamship in April 1915, I had just enough money left to rent an apartment on West 135th Street, on the edge of what would come to be Black Harlem.

I drifted in those first few years in New York, living only to work and sleep. Anytime I stopped, the thoughts and memories would haunt me, the grief dragging me down. I survived by keeping myself carefully numb. I had lost first William and René, now Rohan and a child I'd never realized I'd desired. I could feel my resolve against Death, my will to win his bet, weakening.

I took a job translating, astounding little grandmothers, newly arrived from Ellis Island, when I could speak perfect Polish, Yiddish,

Italian, or German. I also worked as a private secretary for wealthy women in Manhattan and, eventually, copyediting for *The New York Age*. I kept my hands busy, and in doing so, years passed.

By the time I met with Death in 1918 in Central Park, I'd regained a tenth of my former wealth. We walked along the promenade as I shared my pieces interviewing the new arrivals to Ellis Island, recording the kind of immigrant stories I'd written about in London, using my gift of language. I also documented the growth of the city as it built bridges. I shared the opening of another subway line, human ingenuity at its finest. He clutched old issues of *The New York Globe* and articles I'd written under the name Tessa Thorpe.

"My dear Nella," he said, flicking through the pages, "humans building monuments to themselves is nothing new to me, but the foundation of it all is destruction, disrespect, and great inequity. Take this park here," he'd said as we walked along the path, shaded by trees. "This used to be home to a thriving settlement of Negroes, their land seized and their homes displaced, all in the name of progress." He shook his head. "All human advancement comes at someone else's expense."

"Do you feel the same way about a bird eating an insect? Or a beaver who builds a dam, flooding the ant colony?" I countered, unsettled by his point. "The world is filled with life and death. Do you begrudge the lion for killing the gazelle, for it must live? Or me, the fish I may dine on at dinner? All life comes at a cost."

"But must it? Some things are a necessity, like eating. Displacing one another due to hatred and intolerance doesn't seem so," he said, my papers still in his hands. "Not far from here, people starve in tenements. Some humans have enough money to feed, house, and clothe them all, yet they do not, their wealth a testament to capitalism and greed."

"Some do good," I countered. "John D. Rockefeller, Madam C. J. Walker, and Andrew Carnegie spring to mind."

Death laughed. "As well they should, as most of their wealth comes at others' expense. What you call good, I call easing a guilty conscience or avoiding another labor strike."

"Motivations aside, they still did it. They have, just like me, done good in the past and will continue to do so in the future."

"Well, it's a shame that you are one of the too few."

"You know, that's the first time you've admitted that there's even one human worthy of your mercy. Could it be that I'm winning this war?"

"Perhaps, half a millennium from now, you will have convinced me." His lips twisted in what I hoped was a smile.

"You have to admit the human condition is better than it was thirty years ago. Imagine how much better it will be in thirty more."

Death nodded. "There's that naive optimism."

"It's faith."

He turned to me. "What of Jim Crow? The lynchings? All I see is continued hatred aimed at people like yourself. How can you defend a system so corrupt?"

"My task has been to prove people are worth saving, not solving all the ills of the world."

"Pity you can't do both."

We continued to walk in silence. If I could have snapped my fingers and made the world kinder and less selfish, I would have. I saw the same evils Death did. But I still believed that the instances of good could outweigh the bad.

"And I must add," Death said, interrupting my thoughts, "though I find your writing as eloquent as always, these vignettes won't suffice in the next go-round."

"What do you mean?" He'd never commented on my choice of topic before.

"These stories are all well and good, but the more humans there are, the more my job will grow. I'm craving something different—something inspired. I want something new if you're to keep this up."

"Vague as ever."

"I'm sure you'll rise to the occasion. You always do." He smiled, truly smiled, as he disappeared.

Death wanted something new. Over the years, I'd constantly searched for it, never sure when he would call for his proof, writing about the National Association for the Advancement of Colored People and its programs, the reforms after the Triangle Shirtwaist Factory disaster, and breakthroughs in medicine, like antiseptics, saving lives and making less work for him. All laudable things, but I knew he'd want more even as I'd written them. What would be good enough, new enough, to impress him? What would be sublime?

As the wave of Spanish flu swept the globe in 1918 and millions died, I couldn't help but think this was a small taste of his plan. Despite all I had been through, I still wanted to keep my part of the deal, but by 1920, I'd felt the pressure. My fortunes returned as I learned the benefit of buying stocks in companies that provided what people needed—things like food, homes, energy—and I taught other Black women through creating my own little salon in my living room.

When I happened to buy stock in 1919 in a little soda company from Atlanta that I'd liked, my wealth exploded.

The next year, I moved into one of the newer apartments in Harlem, built to accommodate the swelling Black population. The Great Migration was drawing thousands of people from the rural South searching for work and opportunity, packing into the tenements as they searched for jobs on the docks or in factories. It was a vibrant community of established shopkeepers living next to washerwomen or women of the evening alongside working men on their way to the shore, all crammed in square blocks, bounded by their Blackness.

I used my wealth to help, but after London, I'd learned to be more discerning in my investments and monetary status, ensuring I'd never be left in those financial straits again and also to blend in better. The sting of letting all those orphans down still burned. The orphanage project had eventually been completed, but it was years after I'd hoped. The war, Rohan, our child. Too much loss had disrupted my plans.

I found people far too curious about my being a Negro woman with means, the very idea breeding jealousy and contempt. So I kept a low profile dictated by the racial strictures of the time and donated anonymously, also giving my time where I could, helping in soup kitchens, keeping my learnings with Rohan firmly in mind. Volunteering and writing kept me busy as I searched for evidence worthy of Death's new challenge.

I stared out the window, listening to the noise of the city, trying to write a new piece to submit. I kept coming up blank—all my ideas felt trite. What would Death care about architecture in New York? Or about improvements to the subway? I'd just snatched the paper from my typewriter when a knock came.

A woman stood at my door in a finely tailored ankle-length plum dress that complemented her rich brown skin. Her Eton crop hairstyle glistened with oil, and a dainty necklace draped across her collarbone. She smiled shyly and carried a white pamphlet in her hands. "Hi there! I saw you're new to the building and wanted to introduce myself. I'm Willa. Please forgive me if I'm intruding." I nodded politely. I'd seen her in the building; she was friendly.

"I'm Tessa. Tessa Thorpe."

"I'm the secretary for a mutual aid society here, and we're having a fundraiser."

"How wonderful. I'd be happy to donate. Let me go get my pocketbook," I said, stepping away.

She came in a short distance, stopping by my desk. "What's all this?" She pointed to the stacks of papers.

"I'm a writer."

"A writer!" Willa beamed. "I've never met a woman writer before—not in person, anyway. Have you published anything?"

*Every writer's favorite question*, I thought.

"A few things abroad, little articles, things like that. I'm currently writing for *The New York Age*."

"Well, that's amazing!" she said, impressed. "Maybe our fundraiser this weekend would make for a good story. There will be an auction to help fund a community center." She handed me the pamphlet with the time and address for that upcoming Saturday. "It's an open event, so if you know anyone else interested in the cause, please bring them."

I nodded. I didn't have anyone to ask. I didn't have friends or family, and most of my contacts were related to the newspaper office, where I only stayed long enough to file my copy or meet with my editor. I was warmed from the interaction with Willa, enough to ensure my anonymous donation would cover their entire request.

The spring turned to summer, and Willa always made sure to speak whenever she saw me, and over the months that followed we chatted about mundane things—the weather, if I was going to a particular show, the neighbors' chitchat—but I liked having someone, anyone, to talk to.

The September leaves found their way into the apartment building foyer. The next time she approached me, I was collecting my mail.

"I hoped I'd run into you, Tessa," she said, unlocking her box. "You popped into my mind the other day, and I wondered if you would like to have dinner tomorrow night? With my husband, Nathan, and me. I rarely see you with friends, and you never got a proper welcome to the building."

"Rarely" was a kind way of saying I had no friends. None but her. I was flattered but knew better than to get too close to someone. "I don't want you to go to the trouble."

"What trouble?" she said, throwing her arms in the air. "No trouble at all. It'll be fun."

"I'm not sure."

"Tessa, you have to eat. I'm cooking. Come on over." She made it seem so simple, harmless. I had no plans other than a bologna sandwich—maybe with mustard, if I was feeling fancy. Perhaps one dinner with the neighbors couldn't hurt. I'd spent so many nights alone at my little round kitchen table, a single candle, a single plate, while I ate and watched the city street as life scurried down below. The loneliness of eternity could be summed up in dinners alone by the window.

When I arrived, I was touched by all the effort she'd put in. Her apartment was modest and warm: Black-and-white photos of her family that she'd carried from Alabama covered the walls, a tipsy sofa was adorned with tufted pillows, knickknacks covered every available surface, and a lovely table displayed the best china she had to offer. The chicken she fried reminded me of Georgia, and the peach cobbler she'd made from late-season peaches felt like a slice of summer.

The conversation was spirited. I got to transform into what I appeared to be—a young twentysomething with my whole future ahead of me rather than several lifetimes behind me. We discussed the blouse dresses and cloche hats in the windows of the Bonwit Teller and Macy's department stores, wishing we could browse and try on the latest fashions. Then there were Willa's plans for the next fundraiser, and her interest in the articles I'd written. It was a welcome break from solitude and thinking about Death's next visit.

Nathan was a wonderful partner to her, quiet and contemplative, his full beard hiding most of his handsome brown face. He worked in his father's pharmacy, the only colored-owned one nearby. They'd made a comfortable life for themselves.

The dinners became a regular thing—nice, lighthearted affairs, talking about the news and books and playing records on the gramophone. I knew the dangers of getting too close, but it was nice to pretend to be carefree, and it was nice to have friends. I resolved that if I found myself too greatly entangled, I could always move.

"You know, Tessa," Willa said one Friday night, "there's a dance at the Marshall hotel next week and Bojangles will be there. Nathan's good friend Fess is the bandleader. You should come with us. I may have someone in mind for you."

"No!" I covered my face, my knife clattering to my plate.

Willa and Nathan froze as the noise cut through the soft jazz record playing.

I avoided their eyes as I retrieved my errant knife. I had promised myself: no more love. I didn't have any space in my heart or life for that. Not after William. Not after René. Not after Rohan. Not after the baby.

"I'm not up for meeting anyone new." I tried to brush off my outburst with a smile, but Willa didn't seem to buy it.

"I just thought—you never go out. You're always bent over that typewriter up in that window. You deserve a good time."

I'd hurt her feelings. The silence drew out as we picked at our peas. "I'm sorry. I just . . . have been suffering from a broken heart." Four times over. But the half truth felt good. Something in my friend's reaction made me relent. "You're right. I do deserve a good time. Yes, I'll go."

Willa clapped her hands, barely containing her excitement for me. "How wonderful!" With that, all the tension melted away, the conversation resuming easily, for which I was glad. I had no need for dates, but I appreciated a friend.

"Should be a good time," Nathan said. "Finally, a place where we can go. Not one only catering to only white folk who want to come uptown for some color." He detailed all that he'd heard from his friend about the new "black and tan" establishments opening for Black clientele to enjoy live jazz music.

As the conversation turned to the excitement of going out, I realized I still had one problem.

I needed a dress.

~

To solve my problem, I went to Ms. Martin's dress shop, where all my dresses were made. I worked with Gertrude, a tiny light-skinned Black woman with gray hair streaking through her dark curls, who helped me select the fabric and pattern—a cream cotton dress with a high neck and a soft sage folded into the pleated edging. Other women may have worn more eye-catching colors, but I stuck with muted neutrals, best suited for blending in. Gertrude confirmed my measurements and promised she'd have it ready on time.

With my errand done, I had nowhere to be, so I walked down the street, window-shopping, mindful of my purse. It was a respectable area of town, but you couldn't be too sure.

A cold wind swept through, the day blustery, but I enjoyed the fresh, crisp air after being inside. New York was a mix, a few blocks determining the difference between an Italian, Jewish, or Black neighborhood.

I continued to walk and found myself on Ladies' Mile, admiring the wares on offer. Of all the cities I'd been in, New York was the one most on the rise. The stores displayed their goods, and you could buy anything you could think of.

I lingered at one window and admired a set of silk gloves trimmed in green on display, with elaborately trailing embroidered flowers. I had no use for them, but they were lovely—something for beauty's sake.

A knock startled me.

A hand rapped on the glass above my head.

I flinched, expecting trouble. I'd been in New York long enough to know that the people of this city had no problem expressing how they felt, good, bad, or ugly.

The shopkeeper waved from inside, a pale man with black wavy hair, grinning, motioning me to come inside.

I shook my head no, but he gestured again, smiling. I stepped back and scanned inside the shop. No signs barring my entry were on the windows, but that didn't mean it was friendly to "coloreds," as we were called then.

*Come in,* he mouthed, grinning again, almost like a dare.

I wasn't sure why I went in—I would've kept walking in any other instance, but he'd made me smile despite myself, so I entered through the front door.

The tiny bell chimed through the empty shop. The light was dim, just the sunshine coming through the large display windows as the shopkeeper stood in the middle of the floor. He was less pale up close, his skin faintly tan, with a scattering of reddish freckles across his nose.

"Am I allowed in here?" I glanced around as I looked for white women, often upset at the presence of Black customers.

"You could be anywhere you like. Why not here?"

"This store may not cater to a particular type of clientele. Can't be too careful." Nerves fluttered in my stomach, increasing as I glanced around, taking in the expensive wares. The man's outfit was exquisite, matching the quality of the merchandise. The store's wooden fixtures gleamed handsomely, indicating clientele of the noncolored type.

"Normally, you'd be right, but I have the run of the place today. The owner's down with the flu." He made a swift bow, and I blushed. This person was eccentric. I'd never met an American white man of this era who'd been so friendly. "May I interest you in that set of gloves today, miss?"

"I was just browsing. I already have a set," I said.

"Yes, and while they are lovely indeed, I don't believe you can't also have these too." He fished them out of the display. "They are silk, edged in silk brocade and embroidery." He lifted them to the light, his hands smoothing the fabric. "Just in on the last shipment from Paris. You'd be one of the first to own gloves in this style." He tilted them for a better view.

I flashed him a warm smile. "As nice as they are, maybe another time."

"What time?" he asked point-blank, startling me.

"What time for what?"

"When's another time?" He gestured to the gloves. "You obviously like them. They're beautiful and won't be here long. You look like you can afford it. So, get them!"

"But it's not practical."

"What is? If you want practical, you could dress in a potato sack. It's obvious you have taste. Why not indulge yourself?" His confidence and earnest demeanor were disarming.

"But I don't have an occasion fancy enough to wear them." Socialites wore gloves like these—the daughter or niece of an Aster, Roosevelt, or Vanderbilt. *Maybe* they could work for the dance, accentuating Gertrude's designs, but surely they were too fine for a regular dance.

"Make one. Better yet," he said, motioning me to the back glass case, "finery such as that is begging for an added piece. Perhaps a brooch for your throat to draw attention to your lovely skin?"

"You must think me an easy mark."

"Not at all. You are a woman of means in search of beauty, which you rightly deserve. As soon as I saw you, I knew I had just the thing." He spoke earnestly, his eyes assessing but not invasive in the way I sometimes felt from men. No lust lurked there. Only warmth and friendly curiosity.

He pointed at a small set of jewelry, emeralds in gold, with a matching necklace, the tag within sight. "See those, they would be perfect! You must have them."

"It is very costly."

"You won't regret the price. You'll only regret not taking the chance and buying these pieces that light up your eyes . . . if you'll forgive my impertinence."

"These *would* be perfect together," I said.

I *could* afford it all. I wasn't used to splurging on myself this way. I had immortality. It felt selfish to want more.

"I agree." He pulled them from the case. "Why be ordinary when you could be *extraordinary*?"

Why not, indeed?

"It's all rather sudden."

"That's what life is." He winked. "All sudden and then it's over. Best to get the dress, have the wine, and have a grand time."

A laugh burst from me. I felt lighter than I had in so long. "I didn't even come in here for this."

"But you're leaving all the better for it. I promise!"

I'd been sold by shopkeepers before, but this was something else—no room for guilt, only glee. "Fine. I'll take it all."

He beamed at me and wrapped each item carefully, folding the paper into crisp corners before he handed me the bundle, nodding in satisfaction. "I know you didn't expect to find yourself here today, but I bet you'll be glad you did."

"I already am."

"You know, if you're free, I'd—"

The jangle of the bell cut him off as an older white gentleman with a waxed mustache came in. The customer's head tilted imperiously back as if his neck had grown stiff from staring down his nose at people.

"Hello, Mr. Simons, right with you," the young salesman said, dipping his head in a subservient manner I hadn't seen from him yet. It was as if a mask had slipped, and I had been privy to his true self. "Have a good day, miss. I hope you can return to this fine establishment soon."

"Maybe once my purse has some time to recover," I said, taking my leave, purchases clasped in my hand.

I mused over the shopkeeper's words as I walked back home.

*Extraordinary.*

That's what Death would be interested in—the extraordinary. I just needed to find the right topic. I sped home with not only the gloves and the jewelry but also with a burst of inspiration, the kind where it feels like you've created magic, and it leaks from every bit of you. I went through all my books, searching for topics for the rest of the day, staying up well into the evening, sure I could find the perfect thing.

In the early morning, I was still hard at work, energized by creativity, with my gloves and jewelry beside me. I sensed that I was on the verge of a breakthrough. All I needed to do was persist and stay attentive; inspiration would come.

# Twenty-Three

The glowing marquee of the Marshall Hotel dusted well-dressed Black folks in warm light, their skin glistening, the ladies' beaded flapper gowns sparkling, and the men's top hats as shiny as oil slicks, all eagerly awaiting the doors to open and the night to begin. The night held the promise of jazz music, illegal spirits, and feet gloriously sore from dancing. I stood with Nathan and Willa, eager butterflies flitting in my stomach as I adjusted and readjusted my new dress and gloves and jewelry.

As the line moved, a tide of bodies flooded the ballroom, gradually settling into a sea of draped tables and elegant chairs. I realized how long it had been since I'd belonged to something. The salons of Paris were the last time I'd sat in the presence of live music, listening as orchestras and composers tested their pieces before intimate crowds.

Nathan's friend, the bandleader, had reserved us front-row seats for the night's festivities. The jazz music poured over me, the ingenuity of it electrifying. Invitations to dance came fast and furious alongside the sidecars and hanky pankies. The buzz of the prohibited alcohol flowed through my veins, allowing me to lose myself in the sway of the dancing bodies and the feeling of a man guiding me along the rhythm.

"You're beautiful," a man whispered in my ear, and I let myself feel that way that night.

The dance ended promptly at ten o'clock, and with it, the sadness of the quiet settling through the space that had once been vibrant with music and revelry.

"That was wonderful! Thanks for the invitation," I said to Willa as we headed back, arm in arm, along West 135th to our apartment building. Nathan followed a few steps behind. The gas streetlights lit the path.

"I'm just so glad you could come," Willa gushed. "It was amazing to be out on the town."

"I haven't had a night like this in ages."

"I did notice that *you* were never short of attention," Willa said appraisingly. "Green is your color."

"Well, I guess that shopkeeper was right. The gloves were a worthy investment then." I stretched my hands up, letting the streetlights bathe them in light.

"I'm surprised, Nella. *You* fell for a salesman's patter?" Nathan said, unbuttoning his collared shirt. "You always seem so sure and confident. I didn't think anyone could get anything over on you."

"You'd be surprised," I said, thinking of the winding road of my past. "Anyway, he was right in the end. We only regret the things we end up *not* doing."

And I regretted nothing. It had been a lovely evening, and it had been nice to go all out, dressed to the nines. Alcohol still buzzed through me as I tried to hold on to the magic of the night. As we turned on 142nd, the streets hummed with a well-dressed crowd leaving another venue. We greeted each other, passing through the large group until a familiar face made me pause.

I stopped right then and tapped the man on the shoulder.

He turned on his heel. "Ah, my favorite customer." His skin was golden under the flickering gaslight, his smile steady and sure.

"Speak of the devil, and he shall appear."

"I'm no devil," he said seriously, then reconsidered, "though it depends on who you've been talking to. You've been speaking of me? I'm flattered."

"Only to tell my friends of these gloves you goaded me into. What are you doing all the way up here?"

He stopped and tapped his chin, squinting up toward the streetlamp. "Well, see, that's a very philosophical question. What is 'here,' anyway? What's life's purpose? One for the ancients, really."

"Stop it. You know what I mean. Why are you this far north?" Meaning, in the colored section of town.

"If there's action, I'm there." He smiled widely, glancing at me, then my friends. "Why are you here on this fine evening?"

"We've just left a dance at the Marshall Hotel. Willa, Nathan, this is the shopkeeper I met the other day. His name is . . ."

"Adam, Adam Herriman. Now, I know everyone's name but yours. How can that be?"

"Tessa Thorpe."

He tipped his hat in my direction. "Glad to make your acquaintance, Tessa." He noticed my gloves. "I see you found an occasion."

I admired my right hand. "They weren't doing much good in the box."

Adam grinned. "I told you you'd like them. I decided to use the color combination as inspiration."

"Inspiration?" I asked. "For what?"

"For my clothing line."

"Clothing line?" Willa arched her brow with interest. "I thought you were a shopkeeper."

"In truth"—Adam leaned in conspiratorially, biting his lip until he had all our undivided attention—"I'm a spy."

"A spy?" Willa's hands flew to her mouth.

Adam nodded seriously. "Yep. I'm observing the way they do business so my mother and I can start our own shop—for the race."

"'For the race'? What are you talking about?" Nathan frowned, eyeing Adam up and down impatiently. But there was no threat.

Adam laughed again. "Don't tell me I've fooled you too." He pointed to his hair, much curlier without the pomade. "I look white, but I'm as colored as can be."

Out of his shopkeeper's uniform, with his wavy hair loose, I could see it. It was remarkable, his ability to shift. Now, standing amid a group of Negroes, he was one of us.

"Isn't that dangerous?" Willa asked, eyes wide.

"I didn't make the rules." Adam laughed. "I just play by them. They had an opening. They're one of the finest shops in the city. I thought I'd apply. The ad didn't say 'No colored,' just implied." He seemed to brush it off. "It's their fault, if you ask me."

"Are you worried they'll know?"

"Shoot, no. These people only see what they believe. Walk with the confidence of a white man, and you can be one. They don't pay enough attention."

"What will they do if they find out?" The fear of violence flashed in my mind.

"Seems like tomorrow's problem. Besides, I can do what's needed. All I told them was that my grandfather was a tailor, and he was. That part was true, and *he* was white. What I *didn't* mention was that he was with my grandmother, who was Black. Ma and I made our way here from New Orleans after Dad died, making a name for ourselves."

"Nouvelle-Orléans." The old name of the city slipped out. It'd been so long since I'd thought of that place, still wondering what it might look like now. "So, you're passing?" I'd done my fair share over the lifetimes, allowing people to believe I was whatever sort of exotic bird they fancied—Sicilian, Algerian, Moorish, a traveler, and the like. I didn't correct their assumptions, the cloak of ignorance keeping me temporarily safe.

"Don't laugh. They call me 'the Greek.' Can you believe it?" He ran a hand through his short curls. Now that he said it, I could see it, remembering the time I took a boat through the Mediterranean Sea to Mykonos.

"Did you say it first? Pretending to be Greek?"

He flashed us a smug grin. "Nope, my old pal Don did, and Don's quite dense. He would rather believe me to be a descendant of Zeus than of the Negro race. No matter, I'm doing whatever it takes to achieve my goal. You're in the presence of one of the finest tailors in New York—and if not overstating things, maybe these United States—who just so happens to be colored."

"Are you really that good?" I asked, intrigued.

"The best. I'll show you sometime." He tipped his head, a twinkle in his eyes, before blending back into the post-party crowd. "See you soon, Tessa Thorpe!"

"What an odd man!" Willa exclaimed as we continued our way.

"That's a dangerous business he's playing at." Nathan shot me a warning look. "I don't know if it's a good idea to mingle with the likes of him."

"Don't worry, I know," I replied.

And I did. In that simple conversation, I'd found my next topic, and it felt like coming back to life. I knew what extraordinary thing Death could be interested in.

And Adam, if he was as good as he said, could be the key.

# Twenty-Four

The opportunity to create something for Death came a few days later.

I hurried to answer the door. Adam stood there, carrying a big box. "Top of the morning," he said in greeting.

"Adam! I wasn't expecting you until next week." I'd returned to his store the day after we met on the street and told him my plan.

"You inspired me. I was up all night. I couldn't sleep." He hefted the box inside and lifted the top with his free hand. Ivory silk billowed from within.

"It's gorgeous! I—I mean, why'd you bring it here?"

"I can't finish it without your final fitting."

"I would've come to the studio. You didn't have to drag it uptown."

"I couldn't wait. The dress was like fire in my blood; I had to get it out." Adam unwrapped the garment, holding it up to the sunshine, the light sparkling on the clear beads that trimmed the waist. I hadn't seen anything like it before. "Will you try it on?" he asked.

"I'd love to." For modesty's sake, I retreated into my room, stripping down to my thin chemise and drawers and wrapping myself in a robe. Was this ridiculous? I'd met him only a week ago, yet here I was, down to my undergarments. I felt completely safe, having discerned that Adam had no romantic interest in me—in fact, none of that interest in women of any kind.

He dutifully turned around as I slipped the dress on. He laced up the back, pulling on the built-in corset. He was not distracted by my robe at all. His focus was solely on the dress and its fit.

The dress was a vision, the color complementing my skin tone. The white silk rippled from my waist, gathering in a full skirt with emerald-green trim and ruffles. He stood back to assess every detail critically. "All you need are the gloves and a few tweaks here and there."

I pressed a hand to my chest. I'd worn beautiful garments before. Some from the greatest French couture houses, but nothing quite compared to what he'd made for me. "I must say, Adam, you are, in fact, the most wonderful tailor in New York."

"In the *world*, but we'll leave it there for now." He smiled, bending to pin the hem, his touch professional and efficient. It was refreshing that he wanted nothing from me but to be beautiful.

A knock interrupted us, but he kept working.

I opened the door, and Willa clapped her hands over her mouth in giddy surprise. "Tessa! You look amazing!"

"Thank you." I warmed under her admiration. The dress hugged my every curve, making me feel powerful—strong.

"It is like nothing I've ever seen! It's divine," she gushed, circling to look at it. "It's—oh!" she said, turning bashful when she noticed Adam. "I didn't see you there."

The tailor waved cheerfully. "Glad you approve of my work."

"This is your dress?" Her eyes bulged, glancing between the dress and Adam. "You *weren't* joking the other night, were you?"

"Nope. Happy you can appreciate it." His eyes twinkled. "This dress deserves a night on the town. I know a happening spot; they play it all—jazz and blues—and we'll have a time. You can meet my friend Pierre."

Perhaps it was Adam's innocent, radiant hope. Perhaps it was the dress. But it was so lovely to say yes. It was so lovely to have the desire to want to go out.

"Well then," Adam said, "let's hurry and adjust the length of this skirt so I can introduce you to the crew."

I marveled as he labored. Maybe this could work. Maybe with his help, I could be ready for Death and give him something brand new.

# A VISIT FROM DEATH

Death sat nestled into a high-back velvet chair in the private section of the dining room, swirling a brandy snifter. The chandelier winked overhead, each crystal a blazing star, casting sparkles throughout the room.

An odd mood descended upon him as he waited for Nella. He drained the brandy snifter and motioned for another one. The waiter topped it off and he downed that one too. The liquid burned inside his body, making it hot.

He'd almost done it, wiping the world clean, all bets aside. It's what they deserved after the horror of World War I: millions more souls for him to collect, leaving blasted bodies strewn across Europe, men cut down like marionettes, and for what?

So he had allowed influenza to creep forward, leaping from port to port, town to town, house to house, and bed to bed, with entire families gone in mere days. The young soldiers stacked up like driftwood in the barracks, small children languishing in their government schools, their elders dying in their villages, all victims of the purple fever, their faces bluish black as their bodies starved for oxygen, red, wet lungs so engorged with liquid that the people drowned, struggling to draw air.

He could have let it rage on, claiming every soul . . . when he'd stopped.

It had been a small thing as he gathered people in Vienna, collecting the soul of a young mother as her young daughter clung to her body. Wonderful pots had lined the room, created by the mother's deft hand.

She was no one famous. Her name was of no importance.

She was just a woman with a talent.

And still he lamented that no more of her art would ever be made. A shame. It was the first time such a thought had flittered into his mind. He'd shaken it off, leaving the daughter weeping over the body, knowing he'd be back for her soon, but the thought crept in still, catching him unaware.

Death had been having the oddest sensations of late as he collected the souls. Some were business as usual, while other deaths lingered. The faces of the dead came to him, burdening him. It wasn't just the moments of their passing, but other memories as well. Births. Loves. Dreams fulfilled. Happiness. Bits of goodness had attached themselves to him and stuck. He could feel them now, see them for what they were—the sensation.

It unsettled him.

He'd stopped the influenza because, after all, he'd made a deal with Nella not to take them *all* before he officially won. He'd known he'd cheated, and there was something unacceptable about that.

He was a being of his word.

That was what he told himself, at least.

Almost as if *she* had the power to wink into existence, Nella slid into the seat across from him, radiant, wearing a silken white dress and the emerald ring he'd left beside her washbasin.

"You look lovely, Nella. Quite expensive," Death said, taking in her attire and her disposition. When he'd last seen her, she'd been shattered and hollowed by the loss of her child. A child he'd been responsible for because of these wretched, brutal humans. He was beginning to think he'd never see her smile again, but something in Nella glittered brighter than the beads of her dress.

Death motioned to the waiter for a glass of champagne, as he had already guessed she'd be in a celebratory mood.

"I appreciate the compliment," she said. "I believe New York agrees with me. It appears you may need some of what the city offers yourself."

Death glanced at his pale, pallid hands. This was not the most handsome form, with thinning brown hair, poor sight, and jumbled front teeth.

It was fitting, though. The rough look of the man matched how Death felt. "This one was stabbed to death by his partner for embezzlement." He shrugged indifferently, when deep down he wanted to argue. "But, humans, what can you say?"

Nella fixed him with a gaze. "Seems a poor choice by two *individual* humans."

"Still fighting for the underdog."

"I'm still fighting for what's *right*." Nella picked up her glass from the stem, pearls of condensation dripping down. "Have you come around to my way of thinking yet?"

"Using my words? Nice try, Nella. But it's true, my work hasn't gotten any easier or better. If anything, it's become more difficult." Death shook his head and tried to shake off the clinging thoughts of the souls he'd reaped. He did not like the feeling. Nor the feeling that he could not look away from her. "I must say—you're radiant. Is it love again?"

"Living all these years, I've discovered there are innumerable ways to define love. Each time it's different. And it does help to pass the time," she said neutrally.

"Ah yes, time." Death sighed and swirled his glass, downing the drink quickly, the loose feeling intensifying. "It certainly passes, doesn't it? Almost a hundred thirty-six years, by my count. Quite the history between you and me."

"Are you feeling nostalgic?"

Death glanced at her and then away. In reality, he was. But it was more than nostalgia. Despite all he'd thrown at her, she still had the capacity for joy. Even though they were at odds, he was awestruck by her. The way she found strength despite the challenges. One might call it inspiring.

"I suppose. But we digress." He set his glass down, preparing himself. He already knew what she'd say, but their game necessitated this meeting. Like actors on a stage, they both had their parts. Someday soon, one of them would have to break. He'd always been sure it'd be her.

"What did you bring today?" he said expectantly. "A poem? Another book, perhaps? I've read your articles in *The New York Globe*. Fair effort."

"Am I that predictable?" She motioned to another waiter for—what? "I thought I'd bring something a bit more visual."

Five women entered the dining room upon her signal, draped exquisitely in silks, satins, and crepes. As they strutted, they sent the room into a tizzy. The women circled the room twice. Pearls, gems, and beads danced in the chandelier's light before they exited the way they came. The last one held up a single card, handing it to the head waiter as she left.

Pandemonium ensued as two gentlemen jumped up, jockeying for the view, while several women fanned themselves. The murmurs became a roar as gossip flowed about the dresses and where they were from.

Nella smiled, the impact clear.

Death swished his snifter in his decrepit hand. While the dresses were visually appealing, he didn't think anything she could've brought would've lifted his spirits. Then another waiter came forward with a box holding one dress.

"Here is the best one. It's the first one that Adam made for me." Nella gently removed the dress from its wrapping.

Death stroked the fabric, the uncomfortable feeling floating up again. "Charming, Nella," he said softly. "Creating something as fine as this must have taken a skilled hand."

Something as beautiful as this would not last forever.

A new thought slithered in the tumult of his mind: *But does it have to?* He knew fabric would fade. The threads would disintegrate, eventually leaving the glorious garment for rags. *But is it better? Better to have a beautiful thing for even a short while rather than not at all?*

"The tailor is an artist," she said proudly. "The creation of beautiful things, once reserved for the elite of society, can be made and had by all. This is innovation. One of the key traits of humans."

"Innovation?" he said, frowning. "Perhaps. I remember when humans wore nothing. Naked as they were born. What you call innovation, I see as the binding of people into particular roles in society."

"I disagree. Clothes can become your armor or your passport into a different realm. You can choose who you are."

"But does it matter?" Death countered, ready as always. "Did your new dress help you hail a cab on the way here? Did it stop diners in the luncheonette from scowling at your presence?"

"You've been watching me," she says, spitting the words. "We made a deal. I have a task. You've got to stop intruding in my life and leave me to it, especially when you only seek evidence to accuse me." She snatched the gown back, the beads brilliant under the lights. "I can't control what any of those people do. All I can do is present you with the evidence you require. Yet you never name what you're after—what will be enough for you?"

"I'm waiting for you to understand, as I know, that none of it is worth it, and it never will be."

"It's all worth it. Every bit." She breathed through her nose, calming herself. "Look, the work in front of you and on those women is exquisite, made by the hands of a genius. Surely humans capable of creating such beauty are worthy of saving."

Death pointed to the garment. "What of the work to make this satin and silk? The laborers who spend time in the field gathering silk or sprigs of cotton? Or have you forgotten them? Many die in pursuit of the raw materials for this luxurious fabric. Are their lives less important?"

She would not be baited. "All life has value, and there are many types of work in this world. Inequity is part of it, but as you have likely seen, societies change. This one has changed since I was born. People must now be compensated for their labor. It's a step in the right direction."

He gave her a look. "Nella, really? Compensated? At a fair rate?"

Nella couldn't argue that point. "It's not what it should be, but the argument is whether humans are worth saving. Through the work of myself and others, conditions are getting better. Humans can improve, and they've shown it over time."

"But only after they've gotten worse," he pointed out. Did she not know that he was not some idle being, that he held the fate of every individual on earth in his hands? "Millions died over the condition of servitude. Millions more died in the Great War. Is that progress?"

"Humans fought for what was right. Not more land, but the freedom of some of its people. Some things are worth dying for—worth fighting for."

"Perhaps." Death sipped from his glass, thinking. He'd missed this, sparring with her . . . being seen by her . . . but he must not forget his purpose. "Do you still consider this life worth fighting for? I'll admit you're much better situated than at other times we've met."

Nella stiffened, afraid, like she was bracing for a wave. "Each of those other times, you had just taken someone from me."

"It's the game, Nella," he said, her name a caress. "You will outlive anyone you love. Will you blame me for them all?"

"Not all of them," she admits. "I sometimes wonder if I did die that day, and this is my personal purgatory of loneliness and loss."

"I can promise you, this isn't hell. Dante wasn't even close. There aren't any levels, only unceasing, endless pain."

She shivered, leaning slightly away from him. He regretted his words. Most of them.

"But let us not talk of such things." He could fix this. "Tell me—how is your writing coming?"

"I've just been given a lead travel column, so there'll be more articles in the future."

Death raised his glass. "I look forward to it."

"Do you read them too? The things I've published?"

"Why does that surprise you? They sustain me between our meetings." And they did. He read snippets in the quiet moments whenever his own loneliness became too great. It had become a weakness, as had their sessions. He felt too eager for them.

Perhaps what she needed was more time. Time would remind them both of the inevitable outcome. No one could bear the weight of a bargain for eternity. And he had a duty awaiting.

He stood somberly. "I must go."

Nella blanched at his abrupt words. He slipped away, leaving her at the table with only the dress for company, back to his lonesome work, already looking forward to the next time they would meet.

# Twenty-Five

I walked away from that meeting thinking I'd won.

In a way, I had.

My entire life changed over the coming years, the dull gray of isolation blooming into full color. I had friends. I had connections. Willa and Nathan had a healthy, chunky baby boy named Nathan Jr., a regular visitor at my apartment, where I became an honorary aunt and got to experience the joys of helping to raise a child. I spent my days writing articles and evenings out with Adam as we explored all that Harlem's nightlife had to offer.

As promised, Adam introduced me to a whole new world. We were regulars at the Savoy Ballroom—there for its opening night in March 1926, when it opened on Lenox Avenue, just down the street.

I hadn't seen anything like it, with its pink interior, mirrored walls, marble staircase, and myriad-colored lights giving it a futuristic glow. Couples spun across the packed dance floor as hundreds were turned away from the red-and-gold sign due to its limited capacity. The best part was the diversity of the place, as both Blacks and whites frequented it, enjoying the music that poured from the bandstand. We'd crowd the "Cats' Corner" as some of the best dancers I'd ever seen did swing and the Lindy hop. It was among our favorite spots.

I was there for Ella Fitzgerald's debut on that stage, when she was just a teenager, right after she won the talent competition at the Apollo. We danced to Duke Ellington. I watched Count Basie and his band battle Chick Webb and his orchestra. You'd walk in, the drums going, horns blaring, the whole place moving with the beat as the dueling bands played.

Living in Harlem at that time, I didn't just see famous Black stars like boxers Jack Johnson and Joe Louis and entertainers like Cab Calloway and Louis Armstrong, but white ones as well, from Fred Astaire and Greta Garbo to Orson Welles, Lana Turner, and Clark Gable. Everyone came to see the fabulous dancers and have the time of their lives. Harlem was glamorous in that way. Someone said they "wouldn't leave Harlem to go to heaven." Even though segregation still reigned, and people could not dine at Chow's or Woolworth's, we'd made the best of it uptown in our refuge.

To keep up with the demand for his fashions, Adam quit his shopkeeper role and spent all his time in a new atelier with the help of three seamstresses. I helped introduce him to elite clientele and spread the word about what he could do with expert patronage. Our scheme was destined for greatness, as he had already earned back twice my investment. His mother had been able to step back from sewing and now managed the other seamstresses. When I wasn't writing, I spent the afternoons in the studio watching as Adam created his gorgeous designs, shifting silks and satins into works of art, beauty forming at the tip of his needle. Whereas I used my words to conjure, he used his hands. More than just a brilliant designer, Adam transformed into my dearest friend and trusted partner.

As his acclaim grew, Adam had friends across all sets: writers, dancers, jazz musicians, artists, the toast of Black society. I didn't know it then, but this was the start of the Black Renaissance, now known as the Harlem Renaissance. An empowering shift to what I thought possible for the community, challenging notions of what we were capable of and where we'd begun in this country. I went to literary salons with Nella Larsen, Langston Hughes, and Zora Neale Hurston, learned to write better poetry with Countee Cullen, stayed out too late at the Paradise, saw Billie Holiday live onstage, and hung out in her dressing room as Adam completed her fitting.

Despite what the world said, we were using our voices and working to define and share what it meant to be Black. How could we be inferior if we created first-class art? Our books, music, paintings, poems, and plays displayed the breadth of our spirit and the depth of our souls.

The best part of all was having the freedom to create.

With only the truth of our words and the stories we wanted to share, we explored the world around us in all forms of art, sharing our experiences. We breathed, fought, lived, and died like anyone, and we would record and share what it meant to be us in America. I worked with W. E. B. du Bois, contributing to *The Crisis*, submitting requested pieces to Jessie Redmon Fauset, the visionary literary editor and one of the most incisive women I have ever met. Along with that came another type of freedom I'd never thought possible.

History had a funny way of sanitizing things, leaving out the details the world wished it would forget. Having lived through it, I found the process fascinating, especially how modern society pretended the past was as conservative as some fictive history would wish it to be. Same-sex relationships, cross-dressing, and gender fluidity had existed for as long as I had, and centuries longer, perhaps since the beginning of time.

In Harlem, I found a community of others who loved or had loved like I had. Adam had always loved men and made no apologies for it. I never took another lover in New York, keeping my vow of celibacy, but I accompanied Adam as he attended different parties and circles.

Before we knew it, a creative gay and lesbian community had sprouted in Harlem, a kind of open secret. It was a profound experience of found family—the community coming together, often after they'd been cast out by their families, to make ones of their own. So many of us had fled the South, me of course, long before, but in search of something better—a new opportunity and the chance to be ourselves. You could see Jimmie Daniels onstage at the Hot Cha, listen to Gladys Bentley entertain at the Clam House, catch Ma Rainey onstage, or swing by A'Lelia Walker's place on West 136th Street, known as the Dark Tower, for one of her private get-togethers. It wasn't only about the physical relationships but also about the space to be—to exist as one's authentic self.

Simply put, we thrived despite what society would say about being Black, gay, or both, focusing on creation instead. The sensation of being stared at had grown familiar ever since I started funding Adam's work. People sometimes stopped me in the street, demanding to know my tailor. I'd learned to smile coyly, leaving a card with only his initials and contact information, which was a simple tactic that had great effect. A niece of the Roosevelts' had commissioned Adam to design her fall wardrobe, guaranteeing his studio's continued success.

It was the best time. I'd wanted a family for so long and had finally found one—made up of Willa, Adam, and both Nathans. But the thoughts whispered at the back of my mind. How long *could* it last?

Adam knew the secret of my money, but not my long life. He was a true friend. He'd had loves over the years, some you might know, some about whom you've read, but it's not my place or truth to tell. We made a life in that apartment—me with my stories, him with his designs. I knew it wouldn't last forever, but just like with Rohan, I pretended it would never end. Believed in all except my arrangement with Death.

In reality, it was the only thing I could rely on.

Things ground to a halt when the New York stock market crashed in '29, and the Great Depression slammed the country. I weathered it well, my Parisian banker having minimized my risk by investing heavily in gold and other precious metals. So I became an anonymous patron of sorts, helping when a fellow writer or musician couldn't cover their rent or pay school fees. We weathered our time together through the end of the Great Depression, the years passing through Pearl Harbor and the start of World War II. I watched the newsreels, knowing what it all meant—more death.

Death gave me no clue as we met through the years, me sharing my writing and plays for his enjoyment. I never knew when the other shoe would drop, when he'd snatch someone away.

"There's no use in letting you know, Nella," he said at one of our meetings. "For that's the only promise I can give you in life."

"I think you delight in it."

"I don't, but it is a helpful reminder of what is at stake. In the end, there is only death and loneliness. The sooner you find that out, the better it is for both of us."

I put that bleak thought out of my head, watching over Willa, Nathan, and Junior for every cold and every injury. They continued to flourish. I did the same for Adam, but he, too, remained in perfect health.

Until he didn't.

The signs were subtle at first. He started complaining of bone and eye pain. I thought at first it was from him working too hard and often late at night. He complained of blurry vision and headaches that would drive him to his bed for hours at a time.

I deluded myself for months, much like I had with René. Adam was only in his late forties. He had headaches, but who didn't? Surely he'd get better.

I told myself that every day, even as things grew worse. He lost his appetite and complained of an upset stomach, and he shrank, his form turning skeletal, his cheeks hollow.

Adam was Adam through it all, even after the doctor confirmed his diagnosis of leukemia, the cancer in his blood.

I shut the door behind the doctor and went over to Adam, lying on his bed as he gazed out the window. His hair was patchy, and a rash covered his hands.

"You'll still tell me I'm beautiful, won't you, love?" he asked weakly but with his usual charm.

I touched his cheek. "How can I tell you something you already know?"

He snorted. "You're right about that. I always was a looker. Everyone loved a fella with freckles." We listened to the car horns and radios playing from the apartments nearby. "It's been a nice ride, though I had hoped for longer."

"Don't say that. You'll get longer, I swear it. Just see." And he had to get better. I couldn't imagine my life any other way. Our friendship was the flame that kept me going.

"Now who's the optimist?" he said, his smile tired. He shook his head. "No, Tessa," he said quietly. "I can feel it. It's okay. Truly."

He sighed, the movement taking strength from him. "I always had a fire inside of me, you know. Like I had to get it all out, live life to the fullest. Even if others thought I was odd or too much or peculiar."

"You certainly have lived a life," I said. He had been a fashion designer to the stars, and my best friend. I knew what was to come; I only had my time with him now.

"I sure did, with my best girl at my side." He squeezed my hand.

I prayed to God.

I prayed to Death.

I asked them both to save Adam.

Begged and pleaded.

But there was no respite. I threw everything into his treatment, but he'd developed the disease before effective treatment became available. Winter crept in, and Adam caught a cold he couldn't fight. He went to his bed, fever climbing steadily higher, until he couldn't hold anything down, breathing labored. It was clear that he was at his end.

On the edge of the sixth morning, Death arrived while I sat with Adam. As he always did, Death appeared at my side. He was as I had seen him at first, his expression remorseful.

I choked back a sob, the weight of the past days sagging upon me. I had kept hoping—believing that if I just held on, Adam would live.

I pounded his chest with my fists. "Save him. He's my dearest friend. You saw what he's made. What he's capable of!"

Death eased into the open chair and sighed. "Nella . . ."

"*Why* can't you save him? You've seen his work. You know he's worthy. He is so young . . ."

Death shook his head sadly. "I changed everything for you once. I can't do it again."

"Can't or won't?"

"Can't."

"You mean there's someone else in charge? Who can I speak to? If there's anything I can do, I'll do it." If Adam had taught me anything, it was not to take no for an answer.

"Nella," Death said. "Look at him."

Adam stirred in the bed, head thrown back, sweating, body tense. Agony racked his body. I squeezed my eyes tight against the truth. "Then fix him."

"Death isn't always a punishment. Sometimes it is a release."

I sniffed, throat tight and swollen. "You're just taking him because he's mine."

"No. I'm taking him because it's his time."

"I don't believe that! It doesn't have to end this way!"

Death shook his head. "Nella . . . it will *always* end this way. " He sat on the bed next to Adam, gazing at him. "I, too, am exhausted. I know what this young man can do, and I've seen the things he can create. Sometimes I wish . . ."

"Wish what?" I let the words ease out, careful and unsure. I'd never seen Death like this before.

"Most are bad, like I've always believed . . . but there are some . . . every once in a while . . . who can make me think . . . for a second, that some good can be found in the world."

"So stop."

He shook his head. "I wish I could. But that is the inescapable loop we're trapped in until one of us breaks. This is how it will always be between us." He gazed at Adam, whose breathing was growing ever more difficult.

"You thought not falling in love would save you pain, but there is always pain as long as someone holds space in your heart. Your love for him is no different than that of a lover. The passion of friendship of equal value. I . . . don't wish it for you, but that is the way that it must be . . . Unless you would give all this up. Give in and agree that nothing is worth this pain."

I thought back to all Adam and I had experienced together, all that Adam had created. Despite what Death had done, I couldn't give in. Adam wouldn't want me to.

Hot tears dripped down my cheeks at the futility of it all. I wanted to hate Death, but I knew the truth of what he said. As long as there was life, there would always be death. They existed hand in hand.

I don't know who reached out first, but Death drew his arm around me as I sobbed. His arms contained an otherworldly sense of strength, as if I could never fall again. I wanted to push him away, but he'd be taking Adam if he left, and I needed more time. His jacket smelled of salt and blood and sweat: the perfume of the dying. He sat quietly through my grief, as if, for once, he was reluctant to do this task. A tiny part of me was glad that he stayed, because he was there despite all the pain.

I sat there, staring at Adam as he struggled. A strange calm settled over me. "Is it good where he's going?"

"The best." He seemed sincere. He brushed his fingers along Adam's head, and a golden glow flew from his skull like a falling star. His soul separated from his body, golden, glimmering, and translucent. Adam smiled sadly before his mouth slackened.

I nodded, understanding.

His time was up.

Adam stood beside Death, and they winked out like someone had snuffed a candle, leaving me alone in the dark.

I didn't even have the energy left to cry.

I lay on the floor beside Adam's bed, holding his hand, staying there until long after he had gone cold.

# PRESENT DAY

## Savannah, June

# Twenty-Six

I wipe my eyes, drained.

As the hours press on and I tell more and more of my story, I worry about Death growing closer, angered by my willful breaking of his rules. "You'd think I'd be used to it by now," I say bitterly. "Besides Death, loneliness is my one constant in my life." I sag into Sebastian, grateful he's still by my side.

"When Adam died, it was almost like waking up from a dream. As long as we were together, supporting each other, going to ballrooms, and hanging with his friends, I could pretend it would never end."

The tears well up again, and I snatch another tissue, the injustice feeling brand new. I rub my face, my skin feeling raw.

"I was so close, Sebastian—so close to living a life out loud, sharing that with someone who could see the real me. Adam didn't know everything about my past, but when he looked at me, I knew he saw me. And once he died, I saw how vulnerable I'd left myself. What would I do when Willa got old? Nathan? *Junior?* Staying with them was just pain waiting to happen. They'd started to notice that I didn't age, that I never got ill."

Sebastian holds my hand.

There isn't anything to say.

"What happened with Willa? Did she live?"

"I kept track of her for a while after I'd left the city. I slowly faded from their lives, existing only in letters." I glance at the trunk, where many of Willa's responses to my letters are wrapped in ribbon. "Willa and Nathan had two more sons, and Willa lived to be eighty-seven, dying six weeks after Nathan in 1982 from what I can only assume to be a broken heart."

"What did you do after New York?"

"I did what I always do—get a new name and go as far away as possible."

"Where specifically?"

"Back to Europe. London and later Paris."

Sebastian flips through his notes. "And when was this?"

"In 1943."

Sebastian pauses, dumbfounded. "But . . . wasn't Europe *at war* in 1943? You mean to tell me that you left New York and went *to* war-torn Europe?"

I sigh, rung out. "The soldiers were doing it."

"What did you think would happen?"

"I don't know," I say, crumpling my tissue in my lap. "It made sense at the time." And it did. It was far away from my problems, and if I'm honest, I was probably trying to tempt fate. I didn't know if I'd survive a Luftwaffe drop, but I honestly wouldn't have been mad. I was not in a good headspace. "I guess I wanted to go somewhere where my problems would seem small in comparison. With so much destruction, I could go there and be of some help. Or at least tell their stories.

"Look, all that matters is that I closed that chapter of my life. After Adam died, I didn't care what happened to me, like something had broken on the inside. It was easier to let go, to float, Death almost having won our challenge."

"I know a little of what that's like," Sebastian says quietly, eyes downcast.

I turn to him. In all his listening, Sebastian hasn't volunteered much about himself. He has kept asking questions, taking notes—bearing witness to my pain.

A twinge plucks at my consciousness. I've been selfish, recounting my life and loves, and haven't taken time to delve into his. I wait, letting the silence build, allowing space for his story to come through—his own loss. By the look on his face, it must have been a great one.

"Who was it?"

"Her name was Patricia, named for her grandmother. She went by Tricia, but I called her Pattie Cake. She hated it." He lifts from the couch, digs into his pocket, and pulls out his black leather wallet. He flips it open and hands it to me.

A pretty woman with clear, tawny skin, almond eyes, and long black Senegalese twists smiles up from the photo, a red-and-white stole on her black graduation robes, diploma in hand.

"We met in our master's program at Vanderbilt during a seminar. The only open seat was next to her, and I was so aware of her that I didn't remember a word Dr. Lee said. I was completely distracted by her presence. She had that ability to light up a room. And it wasn't just that she was beautiful. It was that she was brilliant. She was dynamic, singularly unique. She had been a teacher and returned to school to learn how to effect change. I felt flattered when she asked if I wanted to study and work on a presentation together."

"Come on, Sebastian." I gently elbow him. "You haven't exactly been hit with the ugly stick."

He chuckles softly. "I get that. But right away, I felt she could make life better—a person just for me."

"It sounds wonderful." I'm sincere when I say this. I know the feeling he's describing well. As much as love can hurt, it's glorious when it's new and surrounding you. I glance at the picture again and can see what he means.

She's radiant.

I also know that something did not go to plan. He's using the past tense. She is no longer in this world.

"My friends would slap me on the back and tell me how lucky I was, that she was the total package. It was more than she was beautiful—she had a beautiful soul. She volunteered with her sorority, mentoring young girls. Like your Adam, she saw me. Not only me but the man I could become. With her, I felt like Superman, like the strongest man in the world."

Tears flow down his face as he gazes at a spot above the coffee table, in the present but seeing the past, unearthing his pain and sharing it with me.

I squeeze his hand, hoping I can do for him what he's doing for me. Sharing the burden—lifting the weight of the pain that has kept you alone and apart for so long. Finding ease, knowing that you're not the only person to whom life has been unkind.

He clears his throat and continues, "It all started with a stomachache. We were on vacation in Punta Cana, celebrating the end of our master's program and the start of our PhD programs, when she started having cramps. Her cycle was on then, so we thought nothing of it. Honestly, I wasn't focused because I was too nervous planning my proposal."

He squeezes my hand and releases it, running his hands over his pant legs, jittery, slightly rocking back and forth, living in the memory. I sit back and picture it as he describes the scene. He takes a deep breath and continues.

"It was perfect. She'd told me years ago how much she liked the ocean—its enormity, that it had existed before anything else. She said that the water held time. I thought it would be the perfect place to confess my love, sure of the timelessness. So, as a surprise, I flew her parents and sister down, along with her eighty-one-year-old grandmother. Big Pat had just had a knee replacement and could hardly walk in the sand, but she was there for her grandbaby.

"After an early dinner, I invited her for a walk on the beach to see the sunset. She almost said no, but I insisted, saying who knew how many more sunsets she would see in Mexico." He pauses for a moment. "I'll never forget that, especially when I realized how true it was later." He clears his throat again.

"So, she came with me, walking slower than usual. We hiked up a small hill of sand, and on the other side was a stand of palm trees. Her family was standing just underneath. I went all out, flowers and candles, the 'Marry Me' in big white letters, lit up against the reddish sky. It was perfect. It was honestly one of the best days of my life."

A small smile lights his face as the memory plays.

"If that was the best day of my life, the worst one came three weeks later. It was in the middle of August, right before classes started for the semester. I had come back from errands and noticed she wasn't home. It wasn't strange—she was into fitness and often went for long runs. I didn't even worry until it got late at night, and I hadn't heard a thing. I called her parents and her best friend Meghan to check on her, but no one had heard from her. I was in the middle of calling her sister when the police knocked on the door."

All the air in my lungs flew out at once, making me lightheaded, tears pricking at the back of my eyeballs. "I'm so sorry," I whisper.

His expression's so heartbreakingly mournful that "sorry" doesn't seem adequate. I squeeze his hand and hope that he knows that he isn't alone. "I, um—rushed to the hospital. Another runner saw her go down, where she cracked her head on the pavement, and called 911. They'd had to do surgery to relieve the pressure, and she was in a coma when we went in. When I finally saw her, her face was all bruised, and they had shaved off part of her braids."

"Did she ever wake up?"

"She did. She woke up two days later. She was even herself—making jokes about a new hairstyle and how she would take up yoga instead. As scary as the hospital stay had been, she was still here, and I would take care of her. I looked forward to helping her, when the other test results came back."

I swallow.

"Turns out the reason she fell was from pain. She had lemon-size blockages in her intestines. They tested them. It was stage II colon cancer. It had already spread. According to the doctor, we had to prepare for another surgery and prep for chemotherapy right then if we wanted to stop it."

"I'm so sorry."

He nods, biting his lip. "It just came out of nowhere. Here she was, this young, vibrant spirit. She was one of the healthiest people I knew, but in retrospect, there were signs. The cramping, changes in bowel habits, and she had started losing weight. We thought it was due to her workouts. Once the news came, there was nothing we could do. That next day, she had surgery removing thirty percent of her bowels and started chemotherapy right after.

"She got so tiny during the treatment. I begged her to marry me early on, but she said she would when she beat it—cancer wouldn't take away our special day. The treatments went on, and it seemed to be better for a bit. By the following year, we had picked a day, June fourth, to get married, when the report came back that they had found the cancer had metastasized to her liver.

"We postponed the wedding, but they couldn't do anything once it had traveled to her liver. She just deteriorated so quickly. Watching the light slip out of her was the most painful thing I've experienced. She was convinced she could beat it right up to the end. She prayed daily and started an all-vegan diet, but nothing we did made it any better.

"It wasn't until they recommended hospice that she finally agreed to marry me. We got married—in that little room, with the monitors beeping, her parents, sister, Big Pat, her line sisters, and all the nurses on the floor in attendance. Her mother had come in and done her hair, and her sister helped her into a white dress. She was so small; I remember how it hung off her body—how they arranged the fabric to hide her chest port. It was beautiful. There wasn't a dry eye in the room, including the priest. We exchanged those rings, and I wished with all my soul that some miracle could save her.

"She got to be my wife for two weeks while I cared for her at home in our little apartment. I kept her company as she slept, gave her meds to stave off the pain, and witnessed the end of her beautiful life."

Muffled early-morning sounds filter in from outside, reminding us that life is still going on around us despite our mutual foray into the past.

I take his hand back in mine and pull him close, hoping he can feel my heart break for them and their life together. He squeezes me, my head fitting into the space under his chin, his spicy aftershave surrounding me. We stay that way for a while, clinging to each other in our respective seas of pain. His eyes glitter with unshed tears when we break apart, sparkling like tiny stars.

He coughs and wipes his eyes with a tissue. "So, I get what you mean about being numb. I wasn't that at first. First, I was angry—mad at God, fate, and the universe for what they had taken from me. The wound ripped open every time I came home and she wasn't there. After the anger came the darkness. I hadn't started my PhD program, having deferred my acceptance to care for Pattie, so I had nothing to do and nowhere to be. I just existed in my dark and dirty apartment, sleeping away the day, waiting for the pain to stop."

"Did it?"

He shakes his head. "It never did. Until I lost Pattie, I didn't know a human could live with that amount of crushing pain. It felt like I would never be happy and never know love again."

"But what happened?"

"Big Pat happened. She pulled me out. One day, about six months after the funeral, she knocked on my door. She had left her assisted-living facility, called an Uber, and made her way across town because she said she had a message for me. She said she'd had a dream the night before that Pattie had told her to find me. She said I had to live for both of us to make our dreams come true. I just fell to the floor, crying like a baby, as her grandmother comforted me. I don't know how to describe it, but it was like Tricia was in the room with us. For the first time in that whole episode, I felt a brush of peace—like the burden had lifted for a moment. It was as if to tell me that was enough. That I needed to get back to work and have a life."

"And that worked?" I marvel at the concept. I've had no one to pull me back from the edge. How nice it would have been to have a support system, anyone at all.

"It did . . . The thing is, the night before, I was having some dark thoughts. Thoughts about how this pain wasn't worth it. That life seemed to have no point. Big Pat showing up the next day seemed like a sign.

"So I got up. I cleaned the apartment and moved out. I found a smaller place with fewer memories and started living again. That's when the numbness started. I would get up, go to class, and then come home, living like a robot, the same day over and over. Big Pat would call and make sure I ate. She was my lifeline at the time. Pattie's parents were deep in their grief; they had no room for me. I understood, though. Every time they saw me, it had to be similar to what you went through—a potential future, the hope of grandchildren and family memories, crushed."

"Are you still in touch with Big Pat?"

Sebastian cracks a grin despite the mood. "Sure am—visit whenever I can. She's giving the orderlies hell at ninety-two."

"You're a good man, Sebastian." There is something so sweet and pure about him checking up on her. He has a kindness that life hasn't taken from him yet.

I lie back in his arms, tired but safe. He has known loss, too, experienced the darkness that comes with being alone, and has managed to come out on the other side. He sat on my couch, listening to my story, allowing me to relive it one last time, dredging up all the sour and sweet memories.

I picture the stack of postcards sitting in my trunk, waiting for their tale to be told.

I'm glad to tell him.

I'm glad I'm not alone.

Especially as the next memories might have been the most bittersweet of all.

# PART VI: MONTGOMERY

## THE POSTCARDS—1955

# Twenty-Seven

I reviewed the notes as the plane's two propeller engines roared around me, trying to get an angle on the story—a planned bus boycott in Montgomery, Alabama, starting Monday, December 5, 1955. The protest was in response to a Black woman being arrested the Thursday before for not giving up her seat. All I had was a name: Jo Ann Robinson, with the Women's Political Council, based in Montgomery.

It wasn't my usual beat—it'd normally go to Mattie Smith Colin, one of the other writers on *The Chicago Defender*'s staff, but she was still busy covering Mamie Till and the aftereffects of her son Emmett Till's murder. She'd been the one to interview Mamie when Emmett's body arrived in Chicago for his widely publicized second and final burial.

I'd been covering the international wire for *The Chicago Defender* since returning from Europe in '53 as Jimi Ireland, a young and ambitious reporter with international experience and a talent for languages. In my last act as Tessa Thorpe, I'd written several letters of introduction and recommendation to other Black newspapers across the nation, along with samples of "Jimi's" work. These letters, combined with the skills of an excellent and expensive forger, and a short new pixie haircut, helped me secure the new role and leave my life as Tessa Thorpe behind.

I could've retired to a house in the country—but then I'd be alone with my thoughts. Working and writing was far better for me. I'd been around various newspapers and news outfits for close to sixty years, and

I liked the work—the act of losing yourself in someone else's story a helpful way of forgetting your own.

At first glance, I hadn't seen much of a story there—not enough to travel halfway across the country for a one-day boycott—but I was intrigued. I imagined that the type of people who participated in this fight would be the redeeming type. Once John Sengstacke, my editor at *The Chicago Defender*, had given me the story, I'd booked the next flight out, connecting in Atlanta, stopping only to collect everything I could on Alabama from our research department.

I stepped outside, the thick morning heat sliding across my skin like a warm glove. Despite the winter, the South still never seemed to freeze. The coos of mourning doves and harsh caws of crows mingled with the hum of propellers and the roar of landing airplanes as I descended the short steps. I hadn't been back to the South since I'd left New Orleans all those years ago, and the thought made my stomach queasy. It wasn't like living in New York or Chicago had been smooth. Racial covenants, racism, discrimination—I'd experienced it all firsthand and had sat in the colored section in the front of the plane for the past two hours, living the segregation in travel that these people were trying to fight. I made the trip because I wanted to know what had inspired them to action in the face of violence.

I didn't have long to wait, as my driver, Henry, gave me the scoop as soon as I hailed his cab. A former navy man, he helped me with my bags, jumping right into conversation and giving me his opinion of the planned boycott. His dark skin glistened with sweat as the scorching Alabama sun blazed through the car windows. "It's about time they did something. It's a shame how those drivers treat us. The whole city."

I scribbled in my notebook to keep up. "What have they been doing?"

Henry snorted. "Bunch of different things built up over time. Some drivers are all right, but some are downright mean. We have to get on the front to pay, and then we have to get off again to get on through the back, the first ten rows reserved for whites. Sometimes the drivers take your money and drive off before you can return to the bus. Plus, if the bus is full, you can't ever sit in those reserved seats, no matter if no whites are on. And don't get me started on when it rains; the bus will drive right by, leaving you soaking and late for work." Henry sneered. "Injustice after injustice."

"Is that why you drive the cab?"

He nodded. "In here, I'm my own man. I get to choose who I take where."

"How long have you been driving the cab?"

"Five years now. The rate is forty cents, while the bus is just a dime. I expect I'll be busier if this boycott goes through."

"Is everyone for it?"

He met my eyes in the rearview mirror. "It's a mix. Some people are sick and tired of being sick and tired. Others think this is just the way things are."

"How about you?"

He flicked the picture hanging from his visor—a snapshot of him, his wife, and two little girls, around seven and three. The older one had his wide, gap-toothed smile. "You see these girls here? I got to believe the world will be a better, kinder place for them than it was for me. They got just as much right to things as anybody else."

The quiet assurance in his voice filled me. Progress wasn't just for yourself. It was for whatever future you wished there would be. "Do you think it'll work? The boycott, I mean?"

He drummed his fingers on the steering wheel. "They arrested a little girl back in March, just fifteen, for the same thing. This feels different. I know Ms. Parks. The people are riled up."

"I certainly hope it brings the change you want."

"We won't know if we don't try," he said as he pulled to the curb, stopping at the Ben Moore Hotel, a four-story brick building on the corner of High Street, the only hotel for colored people in the city. A sign reading MALDEN BROTHERS BARBERSHOP hung over the doorway to my right.

Henry hopped out and helped me with my luggage. "I hope you get everything you need for the article." He handed me a card. "Call me if you ever need a lift. I'd be happy to oblige." He tipped his hat and sped away.

Thunder rumbled as heavy, gray clouds streaked the sky, threatening rain. With an eye on the weather, I hurried inside, glad to know the interview spot wasn't far. The owner's wife checked me in and showed me a tidy room on the third floor, above the barbershop and right under the Afro Club, the rooftop garden restaurant. I didn't know it then, but the Ben Moore Hotel was like Civil Rights Central, where leaders came to plan, and even where Martin Luther King Jr. got his hair cut, since the church he pastored, Dexter Avenue Baptist Church, was right across the way and where I was headed next.

Thankfully, the gray skies withheld their torrent, and five minutes later, I arrived at the two-story redbrick church, a certified hive of activity.

Two rows of white wooden steps rose to the main sanctuary, but the basement was where the action was, the door scarcely having time to shut as people streamed in and out. I knew some form of organization would be involved, given the announcements that had gone out, reaching *The Defender* in Chicago, but this was another level. What I had imagined to be the grassroots effort of a few was the collective labor of many, run with military precision, the execution and efficiency palpable. Tables were arranged in rows, one with leaflets, others with phones ringing off the hook.

Within seconds, I was pointed to Jo Ann Robinson, a petite woman with short curls, a warm presence, and a refined demeanor, her brown skin expertly powdered against the heat and humidity. She stood and shook my hand, her assertiveness and open manner making me like her at once. "You got here so fast. I can't believe the news made it to Chicago already."

"It's all thanks to you, from what I hear. You want to tell me about it?"

She nodded, brown curls bouncing. She glanced at her watch. "We have another Montgomery Improvement Association meeting in a bit, but I have to make time, especially after you've come all this way."

In that hive of activity, I got lost in her story as she detailed the work of the Women's Political Council and how, as president, the idea had started months ago. "I had the idea back when they arrested Claudette Colvin, a local fifteen-year-old, in March. We had already been working with other groups and leaders like E. D. Nixon, the head of the Progressive Democratic Association and a leader of the Brotherhood of Sleeping Car Porters, and the Citizens' Steering Committee, who had met with bus company representatives, to no avail. When they arrested Rosa, carting her off to jail, something just broke. I remembered how I had been treated by a driver, screaming at me because I happened to sit in a reserved seat. I'm a teacher at Alabama State University and, more importantly, a human being; no one should be treated like that. So, Thursday night, I talked to Freddy from *The Montgomery Advertiser* about it and knew we had to do something. I drew up these flyers and got the word out."

She gestured around the room. "I can't believe all we've done in two days. As you can see, it's going even better than I could have planned. We met with the ministers this morning and started all this this afternoon. It's truly amazing." The joy lit out of her like a candle, incandescent in its warmth, spilling over into me. She was a fixer, not content to let injustice be. The more we talked, the more inspired I became. I understood why John had thought this was more than a one-day thing. These people were not just fighting to sit on a bus. They were fighting for their dignity and their fundamental rights. I couldn't have conceived of anything like this movement happening.

She glanced at her watch. "I'm sorry. I've got to attend the next meeting. You're staying, right?"

"I had planned to. How can I help?"

"We need to make sure everyone has rides for Monday." She pointed to the table farthest away, a lone woman hovering over it on a phone.

"Gabrielle's coordinating those that might need rides and getting the word out. I'm sure she'd love some help."

We said our goodbyes, and I crossed the room and was approaching the table, ready to offer my services, when Gabrielle smiled up at me. The kindness in the beautiful woman's bright-brown eyes startled me, making my heart quicken. The surprise of it made me blush. Up close, she radiated, her looks what one would expect in a magazine nowadays. She was model tall, her sienna skin flawless and smooth, her simple blue dress molded to her form, an inner grace to each movement.

My jacket felt too hot and too tight all at once. My curiosity was piqued.

Gabrielle's eyes flicked over me as she held a finger up, finishing her call. "It's all right, Mavis. I've got a driver going in your direction most mornings. It'll be early, though, around six. Is that all right?" She listened, a broad smile illuminating her face. "Fred will be over first thing. Call me back if you run into any other trouble." She hung up the phone, turning her attention back to me.

"Well, aren't you a bunny." Her eyes traveled up and down the full length of my body with such open admiration that I almost gasped.

"I'm Jimi," I said, flustered, pointing vaguely in the direction I'd come from. "Jo Ann said you needed some help."

Her presence rattled me, and I couldn't figure out why.

"Sure do," she said, reaching for my hand with both of hers and holding it in some approximation of a handshake. "I'm Gabby, and I'll be glad for any help you have to give," she said as the phone rang again.

She plucked it off the cradle as I tugged off my jacket, grateful for the slight relief. My temperature was still climbing, and I had to marvel at my seemingly endless capacity to feel so unmoored, still, by this kind of youthful attraction. It seemed no matter how many years passed, no matter how many times I tried to lock this part of myself away, some part of me was undeniably, painfully connected to the world around me.

*Watch me,* Gabby mouthed, the phone nestled in the soft bend of her neck. "Dexter Avenue Baptist Church, Gabby speaking, how can we help?" Efficiently, she recorded the caller's name, destination, desired time of arrival, and phone number in the book and location, promising a callback.

"We've been getting calls like that all afternoon," she said, running down the list of drivers for the callback. "We've got to build up the pool of drivers and coordinate, so when all of this happens, folk can still get to work. How well do you know the area?"

"Not well at all. I'm down from Chicago, writing the piece on the WPC for *The Chicago Defender*."

Gabby beamed, pausing her search. I never tired of this reaction to my profession. "A writer! I love to read. It's my favorite thing to do when I'm not teaching. There's nothing quite so alluring as a talented pen," she said wistfully. Then she turned the full force of her attention on me. "Tell me what it's like. What exactly do you do for *The Chicago Defender*?"

It didn't matter what she'd asked me; I would've told her anything just to keep those eyes focused on me.

"I've been there a little over a year," I said, stumbling. "I cover the international wire, mostly."

"International! But you're so young!" Her eyes lit with interest. "You must've traveled to get a beat like that."

"I have," I confirmed.

"*And* you speak other languages? So, you're skilled with the pen and the tongue," she said, and at this her voice dipped low. I nodded, momentarily stunned when she unconsciously caught her bottom lip between her teeth.

Her brazenness felt like ice melting down my spine on a hot summer day. Who was this young woman? I'd known her a handful of minutes; in the growing ocean of my life, it was but a drop of water's worth of time. We didn't know each other at all, and yet there was recognition between us. I'd felt it before. After all this time, I'd learned to recognize it—this mixture of desire and fear.

"You know," she said, leaning in conspiratorially, bringing with her a rush of rose-scented perfume and the sweet musk of her pomade, "I teach English at Booker T. Washington High School. Maybe you'll come to talk to my students if you've got time. We've got a student paper, *The Washingtonian*. They'd love to hear from a working writer and reporter. You can tell them about your travels."

"I'd love to," I said, a frothy feeling expanding in my chest, surprised at how swiftly my body and mind had responded to this woman. It wasn't love. Not yet, but it was a prelude and a promise. It was something inside and outside of me telling me to listen. To follow.

The phone rang again, and we were off to work. The volume of calls increased throughout the evening. Gabby took a few more calls to demonstrate the routine and let me handle the rest.

I spoke with maids from outside the city arranging to get to their employers' homes, elders arranging to get to Tom Johnson's, a local Black pharmacist who had a parking lot to use, and also the names of drivers who could volunteer their time. Gabby handled calling back and confirming rides, making our two-person system effortless and efficient. The calls kept coming as we built up the complicated transportation web, coordinating pickups and drop-offs to ensure no one had to take the bus on Monday.

Two hours in, a woman named Martha dropped by with a plate of biscuits and fried chicken. I munched the food down gratefully, so absorbed in work and in Gabby that I'd forgotten to eat. It reminded me of my time with Eulalie, when the affluent personnes de couleur came together to secure their advance, and my time in London, helping with the orphanage, the intoxicating pull of helping others. Wherever women came together for a greater cause, change was made.

Time continued to fly, and we worked until six, well into the winter night. I sagged into the seat after taking the last call for the night.

"You did good, Jimi. I couldn't have done it without you," Gabby said, tidying up. "Are you up for coming back tomorrow afternoon after church service?"

My skin tingled at the warmth of her praise. I might've imagined it, but her gaze lingered, flicking over me, and the heat rose in my cheeks. It didn't make sense, as there were other leads I could be following, but I liked working with her, feeling truly useful for the first time in a long while. More than that, I liked *her*. I wanted to talk to her, learn about her.

"I'd be happy to."

"Great, see you tomorrow," she said, beaming her smile bright, letting me know I'd made the right decision.

The next day, I attended the morning service, listening to the sermon and gathering bits for the story, immersed in the activity around me. I'd attended various churches throughout my life, more because of local customs than anything else. The pact with Death had loosened the grip of my mother's religion on my soul, making me question the meaning of existence. My extended life was a testament to the presence of a higher power, but as Death explained it, and the way my exposure to Hinduism, Islam, and Buddhism had shaped my understanding of it, how one treated people mattered more than one's religious denomination or attendance at formal worship.

Church members came to help, and ministers came by to organize. Everyone was motivated by the boycott's success. Though I was an outsider, they drew me in, making me feel like a cog in a machine that was working its way to justice.

The best part of all was Gabby.

"All right then, favorite book?" I asked between calls.

She squinched her nose in a way that I'd come to know was her thinking face. "That's not fair. How can you make me choose?" she said, shaking her head. "My favorite is whichever one I'm reading now."

"So, which one?"

"Why in the world would you think I'm only reading one? I'm in the middle of *Go Tell It on the Mountain* by James Baldwin, *The Invisible Man* by Ralph Ellison, and rereading *Their Eyes Were Watching God* by Zora Neale Hurston."

"Three books at once?" I said, entering the last address. "How do you keep them all straight?"

Gabby shrugged, eyes twinkling. "I read by what I need. Zora's great when you want to remember who you are and seek a life with love. I call it my book therapy."

"Zora is great, indeed." I hid my smile at my friend's name. I wondered how she was doing. I hadn't seen her in years, not since those early days when she and Langston Hughes had gathered, working on stories. I knew she was still alive, but there was no point in trying to see her, as how could I explain appearing the same more than thirty years later?

Time felt liquid as I worked with Gabby, the hours fleeting. I craved more. That evening, I discovered that she was a widow with a five-year-old son named Winston. That she ate slices of cake upside down to leave the frosting for last. She hated heels and preferred to walk around the room only in stockings to feel closer to the earth. And she'd lost many family members in a fire set by the local KKK chapter, which had fueled her desire to do her part to change the American South and beyond.

I'd marveled at the number of folk doing the same I'd learned about—stretching themselves beyond every limit to try and make their part of the world a little bit better. If not for themselves, then for others. It took no effort at all to conjure thoughts of the great many people who would do the opposite, but somehow that only made Gabby's efforts shine more brightly. Here she was, using her spare time and energy for a cause bigger than herself. I'd used my words . . . but I'd always had to think about Death.

We worked late into the night, taking phone calls and planning for a rally at the Holt Street Church the next evening.

Emotions ran high, and the Montgomery Improvement Association (MIA) and Women's Political Council (WPC) leaders and ministers hoped to check in on the boycott's effectiveness and help keep the masses under control. The slightest spark of violence could ignite all the work and planning into a conflagration.

I hung up the phone and sighed, exhaustion and exhilaration tugging at my bones. I watched Gabby on her last call of the evening, her stocking feet stretched across her desk and her red lipstick a little smudged along her mouth, as if she'd been kissed. The gorgeous huskiness of her voice, deepened by overuse, made me think of Eartha Kitt's music, and I closed my eyes.

The warmth of hands on my shoulders made my eyes snap open. I gazed up to find Gabby staring down at me, her mouth a perfect rose and the dim overhead lights leaving angelic balls of light across her brown skin.

"You have a birthmark near your collarbone." She rested the pad of her thumb there, her touch brief but electric, sending a pulse through me. "At least you don't wear your heart on your sleeve."

The joke tore from me a laugh I didn't know I was capable of, shaking something loose within me. We both followed the way her fingers gingerly traced my collarbone to the neck bow on my blouse, like she needed an excuse to make physical contact. We stayed in that moment, bound by a connection bigger than ourselves that tightened the longer we were together. She stopped laughing first and gazed into my eyes, and I couldn't remember another time when I was as happy to just exist.

A door slammed at the front of the room, startling us both and disrupting the energy between us.

I jumped up. How much longer could I surrender to these feelings? "I should go."

"Did I do something wrong?" Her eyes pleaded with me for honesty.

I took her hand and squeezed it. "No, nothing at all. I'll see you tomorrow." I bade Gabby good night, pushing down my desire and tangled-up feelings about wanting to let the question of *what if* slide between us despite knowing how it would all end. The faces of William, René, Rohan, and Adam flashed through my brain. I walked back to my hotel buoyant and hopeful and nervous and electrified, all in one. It had been good work, hard work, just the type of thing that would serve as proof of humanity's goodness, and the time with Gabby filled up the cracks left behind by lost loves. I knew that this all was for Death, but at that moment, in the quiet street with only the sounds of crickets for company, it was for me too.

I had forgotten that I couldn't just look for what was wonderful in humanity. I had to feel the wonder myself. I walked up the stairs, comforted but praying for the boycott's success. I'd write and file another story tonight. Only in the morning would we know if all our work and the boycott would be successful.

# Twenty-Eight

Monday morning dawned, and I lit out of my hotel room first thing, returning to the church and finding Jo Ann. The news of the boycott had leaked over the weekend, and *The Montgomery Advertiser* led with bold headlines: **Extra Police Set for Patrol Work in Trolley Boycott**. Fear settled in my stomach, the mix bitter and noxious, for the safety of the boycotters and the movement. Far from the boycott being a secret, the white citizens of Montgomery were now aware of the plan, and the police had become involved. I handed the paper to Jo Ann. "Are you worried about it?"

Jo Ann scanned the article before snapping it shut. "Nope. It works out even better for us. Maybe it got out further to those who didn't know about it. Now they know we're serious."

And she was right. They were serious.

The first yellow buses trundled by, empty of riders, as they took their usual routes, trailed by motorcycle police escorts. The thought was to prevent any interference from protesters, but their presence aided our cause, as it scared off anyone thinking of riding.

The word spread like wildfire, and the Black citizens of Montgomery heeded the call. On foot, by car, and some by cabs running fares of a dime, the population stayed off the bus. With over 75 percent of the riders being Black, mostly maids and other workers heading into town for their jobs in the morning and back home in the afternoon, this boycott would demolish the bus company's bottom line.

I didn't see Gabby that morning, as she had school to teach, and part of me felt disappointed without her presence, so I recorded stories. I interviewed the people walking, gathering their hopes and chronicling their ambitions for the boycott.

"Why are you walking all this way?" I asked Tucker Mallett as he shuffled, stooped with old age, gray running through his short hair and leaning heavily on his cane.

He paused, dabbing his head with a handkerchief, thinking. "Because I'm a human. I had seven children, all of them grown. I pay my fare and should be able to sit where I please. I'll walk in the rain, the snow, whatever I must do if I have to."

"What do you hope will happen at the end of this?"

"That we get what we were promised: life, liberty, and the pursuit of happiness."

Most of my interviews went the same way. People were excited, defiant, and determined to improve their lives.

All day long, the buses ran empty.

All day long, the phones rang, relating the news.

People had stayed off the buses, and only one arrest was made. They had done it! The joy carried with me as I made my way to the Holt Street Church that evening along with two thousand other Black people, jubilant over the day and their success. The packed sanctuary was filled almost to the rafters, and the rest of the crowd poured outside, listening to the speaker. Small clutches of police officers stood at the edges, surveilling the activities for "our safety." Again, they weren't needed, as people carried themselves proudly.

I was standing off to the side, scribbling notes, when someone tapped my shoulder.

"Jimi, did you see?" Gabby wrapped me up in a hug, her embrace strong and warm and lasting a second longer than was appropriate. Her perfume engulfed me. "I don't know about you, but it's like I can feel it working. I can feel the presence of God on our side."

Even as the ministers came to the pulpit, reporting the success, I couldn't stop thinking about that hug or her hands on my shoulders from the day before. I knew I shouldn't read too much into it. It was the Deep South in 1955. A hug was just a hug and wasn't anything more.

Except I had many reasons to believe it was. With every passing hour, I hoped that I wasn't misinterpreting her signals; I was increasingly desperate to come right out and ask.

Instead, I focused on the events, writing them all down for the article later, the energy infectious, vibrating with the vigor of two thousand souls. When a minister asked if we should continue the boycott, the "Yes!" rolled through the building, echoing up into the atmosphere, the sound of a people united.

The one-day boycott had been a success and would continue. I got on the phone with my editor John and extended the trip. He wanted me to stay on the story for as long as it took.

We dug in from there.

In the months ahead, I would forget to be an observer, caught up in all the volunteering and organizing, often working alongside Gabby for long hours into the evening. When she wasn't running the phone trees, other meetings took up her time. Some she brought me to, always managing to save me a seat. Her energy and commitment to helping others reminded me of Rohan, who had been gone just over forty years by then. Gabby was a helper, expressing her love for the world through service.

Gabby and I attended an ice cream social after the meeting on Monday night. We walked a little way, quietly, eating the sugary, sweet treats and enjoying the crisp evening air.

"Did you ever think it would get this far?" I asked, taking another spoonful of my rocky road.

"No, but I'd hoped so. It's good we're still going—not giving up the fight."

"It is," I said, "but it's a shame we have to fight at all."

"That's true, but what else would we do? Imagine the free time," Gabby said, laughing.

"I don't know, have a life?" I said. "Who knows what life would be if you could thrive instead of merely survive?"

"I don't know, Jimi. That's a rich fantasy I can't afford to have."

I stopped short, the ice cream pooling in my bowl. "I'm surprised at you, Gabby. Imagination is free. Come on now, you must know what you'd want if you could have anything."

"Anything?" Her eyes were full of a ferocious longing. It wasn't the first time I'd wanted to share my gift. But in that moment, oh, how I wished I could.

"Anything."

For a second we stood there, eyes locked, the fantasy of what "anything" could mean filling the space between us. She was the first to break, resuming our stroll down the block.

"I have to be practical," she said with a little laugh that was more sound than feeling.

"Practical?" I wrinkled my nose. "What fun is that?" I didn't know why I was pushing it so, but at that moment, it became vitally important for me to understand what she wanted. Not for her students or for the people involved in the boycott, but for herself.

She hesitated. "Okay, I'll tell you but you can't laugh."

"Why would I laugh?"

"Because it's impossible," she said, exasperated.

"Only if you never do it," I said.

"Hmm," she said thoughtfully. "That is true. Well, if I could do anything . . . I've always dreamed of being in the movies."

"The movies? Like an actress?"

She nodded fervently. "I love them. Acting, too, the whole pretending that you're someone else."

I hadn't expected that. I knew from experience that being someone else was overrated, but I was curious. "Why not simply be you?"

She grinned. "Don't you see, Jimi? That's the beauty of it. I'd get to be me *and* anyone else I wanted. I've always liked acting. Playing with my sisters outside after church. Pirates, fairies, goblins, anything we wanted, and it didn't matter that we were little Black girls in Bessemer, Alabama. We were whoever our minds could be. I went to school to be a teacher because it's respectable, but I went to the theater and plays. We'd put on Shakespeare—*Taming of the Shrew, Macbeth, Hamlet.* One time, I was Ophelia." She gazed into the distance, the ice cream dripping off her spoon, the memory playing. "I can hear the applause now. Much better than what we typically get around here," she said, gesturing as an empty bus trundled by, lumbering into the distance.

"I'm sure you could do a play here once all this is over."

"I guess I could," she said, "but if we're talking about dreams, being in movies would be the biggest one I could get."

"Well, you're pretty enough to do it—talented too. I can see it in the way you command a room." I squinted down at my bowl. "I could see you lighting that screen, the audience caught up in your glow. Lost in your storytelling."

Gabby blushed. "You writers with your flattering words."

"So that's it then. You become a Hollywood actress and grace the silver screen. What else?"

"Oh, why, after a fabulous career with an Academy Award or two, I'd travel the world, seeing all there is to see." She paused, a distant look in her eye as if gazing into the future. "Did you know I've only been to two places? Georgia and Alabama. I read all these books about all different cities—even countries—but I've never gotten the chance to see them. I want to do more than just read about it. I want to experience it."

Desire bloomed like a rare orchid within me. I could imagine traveling with her, experiencing the world once more and through her eager eyes. I could afford it, but would she want to go with me if she knew how I felt?

I licked my lips, sweet from the ice cream. "Where would you go if you could?"

"I can show you better than I can tell you." I held her bowl while she dug into her purse and came up quickly with a bundle of postcards, tied with a string.

I fanned them out, then flipped through the stack. They were old, one side blank for addressing, the other brilliantly colored, depicting vibrant scenes from the locations—a man surfing on the ocean, a food stall at a market in the afternoon, and a woman dancing in the street—all moments of beauty captured on the cards. They were from all over—from Havana, Bangkok, Cairo, and Casablanca to Manila and Honolulu, Hawaii—over fifty in total.

"You want to go to all of them?"

"As many as I could," she said, laughing.

"How'd you get these?"

"My mother used to clean for this woman. She had this box of postcards and things she had collected to display. I'd look at it every chance I'd get. My mom asked for the box when she died."

She picked one up from the pile and brushed her shoulder against mine. "I could always imagine a different life with these. Imagine seeing the Great Wall of China or dancing in the streets of Buenos Aires. I'd want to see the whole world and live it myself."

There it was again. That undeniable feeling. It was beyond friendship. Dangerously so. I knew what it meant to love a woman and the challenges we could face. That didn't make my feelings any easier.

"Well, that's only two things," I said, enumerating with my free fingers. "Become a famous actress and then travel the world. Seems simple enough."

She snorted, taking back her ice cream bowl. "So, it's that easy?"

"You're better off than most. At least you have a dream."

"A dream can be like this here ice cream. Nice and safe tucked back in the freezer, or a big melting mess if you take it out and try to have it all."

"True, but you'd never know how sweet it is until you taste it." I hadn't expected my voice to sound so husky or to find myself focusing on her full lips. "Sometimes the mess is worth it."

A moment passed between us, electric, the air razor edged. *Have I said too much? Am I wrong about her after all?*

"How about you?" she said, coughing to clear the air. "What do you dream?"

I put some space between us in case I'd stepped too far. "If I were honest, I suppose what I'm doing. Writing for *The Defender*."

"It is mighty prestigious," Gabby said, her voice returning to normal, "but something tells me that this isn't all you want to do."

"It's enough for now. Truly."

We sat in companionable silence, our bowls completely empty, the long shadows of night creeping in.

"Do you want a ride back to your hotel?"

I nodded, wanting to leave but also wanting to stay in her presence just a little longer. We disposed of our bowls and climbed into her car. We didn't talk during the short drive. She parked just away from the hotel before shutting off the engine, but neither of us made a move to get out of the car. We sat, the air thick with things unsaid.

"Did I ever tell you about my husband, Edgar?" she asked, her voice loud in the silence.

I shook my head, keeping myself still. She hadn't mentioned anything, almost seeming to go out of her way not to talk about him, so I hadn't pressed. It was easy to let people keep their secrets when I had so many of my own. But when it came to Gabby, I wanted to know everything.

"Edgar was a good guy." She smiled at his memory, still gazing out the window. "Sweet, mannerable. I'd never thought I'd find one. I never liked boys until I met him. Give me a book or a boy, and I'll choose the book any day." She laughed. "But Edgar wasn't like the others. Not loud, all flash. Real gentle.

"When he died . . ." She inhaled shakily. "I thought my world had fallen apart. It was pneumonia. It's so odd how something so invisible could take him like that, attack him from inside—strong and healthy one second, gone the next. It was cruel, and on top of it, I had our son to raise. I threw myself into my work and thought it'd be enough."

*You have no idea how deeply I can relate to you.* My heart hurt, knowing exactly how cruel Death could be.

"He was like my best friend," she continued. "Even though I loved him, I always knew that it wasn't as deep as it could be. Something was missing."

She adjusted her grip on the wheel, staring straight ahead. I focused on the keyhole to the glove box, trying to control my breathing, hope catching in my chest. She turned to me then, her eyes bright with unshed tears. "I just didn't know what was missing."

Sweat gathered at the nape of my neck. I held still, afraid that even the smallest disruption might halt her story. And this was one I needed to hear.

"I don't know how to say this," Gabby whispered. She trembled at the risk she was taking.

"Try. I'm here."

"I like you, Jimi, but I don't know what to do with it. Outside of Winston, you're the best part of my day. If I'm reading a book, I'm taking notes for your thoughts. When you leave at the end of the day, I can't help wishing you would stay longer. But I worry that I scare you."

"Scare me? What would give you that impression?"

She smiled and slowly trailed her fingers down my arm. "You tend to jump whenever you see me."

"I don't do that." I crinkled my nose because I couldn't deny it. "Perhaps it's because I am scared."

"Of what?" Gabby seemed magnetized to me, our faces gravitating toward each other.

"Of this."

She leaned in. We kissed, her lips warm and soft, sticky sweet, the sensation satisfying. Her tongue parted my lips, bolder than I anticipated. I adjusted in my seat to better hold her, biting her bottom lip in soft nibbles. Our noses touched. I lost myself in the feeling, sinking into her touch and losing all sense of time.

She broke the kiss first, leaning back and leaving me gasping for air. "So was that scary?" she asked, her voice husky in the small space.

Yes. No. "It is a fear worth conquering."

She sighed, studying herself in the rearview mirror, rubbing her fingers alongside her cheeks as if they could erase the small signs of aging, signs sometimes I craved to see on my own face: a road map of a life well lived. "I'm far too old for you."

"I'm mature for my age," I promised.

She traced letters on my forearm, the sensation skittering pleasure through me. "I have long known who I *really* am, even before I married my husband. I've never acted upon it, but it is exactly how I imagined it, especially after first seeing you."

The confession felt so tender, I hoped I could protect her for as long as possible. "I've been with different kinds of lovers in the past. It has taught me about my own pleasure. My own desires."

She frowned. "I sense a 'but' coming."

I intertwined my hands with hers, marveling at the ease and the rightness of us touching. "The ending of my last relationship was rough, to say the least, and I didn't want to start something again, only to end in tragedy."

Gabby had this way of smiling that would chase away any dark cloud. "All endings are tragic when you think about it. But the beginnings are pretty damn worth it, don't you think?"

"Do you care what others think or say?" I asked her.

"Doesn't everyone?" She worried her lip. "Life would be much better if people could live their truth. But the way things are, it's easier to lie and not be fodder for the gossip mill, or worse."

We stayed like that for a bit, holding hands in her car. A relationship like ours would have its challenges anywhere, but especially in Alabama in 1955. It could also be dangerous, but I didn't say this aloud. She knew what I knew. Now that I had tasted her, I didn't think I could go back to the way it was. And this love already felt different. I'd dived headfirst into love before, and this was no exception.

What would it be like to live here, to share her life? Slow Sunday mornings, reading our respective books or enjoying a meal we'd made together, and discussing our work and the day. Playing with her son, Winston, at the park and helping him get ready for bedtime. Experiencing again what it might be like to be in a child's life. I thought of Nathan Jr. from time to time, wondering how old he might be now when the years blend. All that talk of dreams and love felt like the most faraway wish. It was so easy to believe that maybe, for once, my deepest desires could come true.

But then reality set in. Beyond the discrimination we'd face, there were the constraints of my deal with Death. Loving her would mean losing her as I'd lost the others. And yet, despite every visit with my oldest friend—though he'd likely hate being referred to as such—I couldn't imagine my long life without the people who had touched my heart. Perhaps that was why, despite everything I'd come to know, I always made the foolish choice. The hopelessly romantic choice.

I knew what this would mean—what I was opening myself up for. But I didn't care. She helped me remember how to dream in that moment.

Gabby looked at me. "What happens now?"

I kissed her. "Whatever we like."

# Twenty-Nine

And we did what we liked, as much as possible, during those times. I learned that one benefit of being two women in a relationship in a world that considered such things unnatural was that we could use the trappings of femininity to our advantage and avoid much scrutiny. I moved into her house discreetly, as Gabby's "roommate," building the life I had dreamed of. Each night, we found the softest parts of each other. I felt a yearning for her touch that I'd never experienced before. My whole body hummed as we'd collapse into sleep, bodies sweaty, curled around each other.

Each day, I watched Winston while she was at school, and we continued our work as the boycotts dragged on. I wrote about it all, writing articles for both *The Defender* and *The Montgomery Advertiser*, depicting the developments with the boycotts, the failed negotiations among the city board with the mayor and the police commissioner, and the fundraising efforts to pay for gas, new station wagons to add to the car pool, and legal fees and fines.

I was there moments after the bomb exploded at Dr. Martin Luther King Jr.'s house. Glass glittered in the street, the porch of his house destroyed; his wife Coretta, his daughter Yolanda, and a neighbor were in the house at the time. If not for his calm and caution that night in the aftermath, the crowd would have turned into a mob, setting the city alight.

I covered the growth of the White Citizens' Councils, the news stories, and the pushback we faced on all sides. As the months stretched on, the violence increased, young men attacking people or throwing objects at us from their cars.

One night in February 1956, I experienced it firsthand. While I walked home, a car whipped by, the occupants pounding on the roof, hooting at me, their shrill voices tearing through the night air. I bolted, green glass bottles exploding by my feet, leaving streaks of urine across the pavement. If their aim had been better, one of those bottles would have met my head. I ran the narrow way between two houses and managed to escape.

The harassment only picked up from there.

I was there to make bail when Gabby was arrested in April for being part of the movement.

Despite all the fear and intimidation, we persisted, strengthening the car pool network and commitment despite the threat of arrest. My work and that of other journalists continued to bring attention to our cause and to our need for more funds and resources.

Finally, word came in late December 1956, nearly thirteen months after the start of the boycott, as we all sat in the church basement. Jo Ann took the call, shushing us all. The entire room froze as the shock washed over her face.

"We did it!" Tears streaked down her face. "They ruled in our favor. It's over. It's all over." She jumped up, hands lifted in praise, and we joined her, exuberant. The feeling of indescribable cheer and joy poured out of each of us from the fact that it had been worth it. While we had been making our case in the streets, the case had also been continuing through the courts in *Browder v. Gayle*. In June 1956, a district court had found in our favor, deeming segregating buses unconstitutional since the practice violated the Equal Protection Clause of the Fourteenth Amendment. The state and city had appealed to the Supreme Court, which affirmed the ruling and the decision; the official notice was delivered to Mayor Gayle on December 20, 1956.

We all rode the yellow bus the next day, each paying our dime and climbing aboard. I sat next to Gabby, near the front, two rows from the driver, my heart beating fast as we watched Montgomery roll by. I pressed my hand into the seat, her pinkie finger looped with mine, out of sight. We rode around town without a particular destination, relishing the fact that we'd achieved our goal.

I turned to her as she watched out the window, her thinking expression in place as the bus rumbled on. "A penny for your thoughts?"

"Life," she said, turning back to me. "A year ago, I couldn't have imagined this—riding on this bus . . . you. It just makes me think of what's possible in the future. What can be true for Winston? He's a little boy now, but think of the world he can grow up in."

"So, what do we fight for next?"

She sneaked her hand into mine. "We do the work, *and* we fight for our dreams."

"Are you saying what I think you're saying?"

She nodded. "We only have this life, as you said. We might as well get busy living it."

We continued volunteering our time and money to the Civil Rights Movement, culminating in the Civil Rights Act of 1964 and the Voting Rights Act of 1965. We lived through it all, and Montgomery was just one of the sparks of the massive changes that swept through the country.

We left the South soon after that, renting a two-bedroom apartment in Los Angeles and making our lives there as she pursued her dreams. She got small parts at first until making her big break in *The Last Dance at Midnight* in 1971.

While Gabby pursued her acting dreams, I earned a role of my own, one I'd never thought possible—the role of mom.

I never thought I'd have the chance again, and Winston made every bit of it pure joy. I was his "Aunt Jimi," and he was my best bud. An active boy, Winston was all knobby knees, taller than us both, and his growth reminded me of how much I stayed the same. He never questioned it, though, and together we navigated middle school, high school, and college, him choosing Savannah State. Living with them made it easy to find evidence for Death. I would file stories, still writing as Jimi, mainly about travels as the three of us journeyed according to the postcards. I wrote about our trips and the seemingly unending changes that continued to sweep across the world, one of the biggest in our life being the rise of Gabby's career.

By 1978, Gabby had regular guest spots on everything from *The Jeffersons* to *Good Times*. She became increasingly recognized, and we were swept into the fashionable set. It was like my time in 1920s Harlem as she mingled in parties with the stars of the time—Ruby Dee and Ossie Davis, whom we'd met at the March on Washington, plus Alice Walker, Sidney Poitier, and Billy Dee Williams, whom she'd played opposite in their last film. I slipped into the background, happy to let her shine. But I won't lie—there were moments when being seen felt suffocating.

We were at an industry party that October, celebrating the film release of *The Wiz*, when a woman shrieked near me.

I turned, clutching my chest, imagining some danger, to find a brunette with thick winged eyeliner and tight bell-bottoms jumping and down. She shouted over the pulsing disco music, "Oh my God! It's her! *The* Gabby Reynolds! How do you know her?"

"I'm her assistant." The lie cut me the way it always did. I was more than that, but the role gave people a place for me in her life, explaining my presence and protectiveness.

The woman's eyes filled with interest. I could see she thought this was her chance. For what, I wasn't sure. But the '70s had taught me everyone wanted their fifteen minutes of fame. "Maybe I'll give you a headshot?"

"Maybe," I said, rattling my empty glass. "Going to get another drink."

"I can get it for you," she said, but I'd already slipped off, snaking between the sweaty bodies, the packed space stifling.

I searched for Gabby and found her at the center of a cluster, enthralling them, her allure magnetic. I didn't need or want the spotlight. Our life worked.

I got a refill and calculated how long we needed to stay for her to schmooze. We had no time constraints, as Winston was fully grown and living in Atlanta by now, working in finance and doing the books for Gabby and me. After the party, it'd be a quiet evening of reading books or any upcoming scripts from her agent.

I'd just taken the first sip when my skin hummed, alert. A shadowy energy filled the room. I swallowed the harsh bite of the martini and readied myself. I gripped the lip of the bar for support.

Death stood at my side, dressed in all black, his vest opened to almost his navel. In his regular form, with his brown skin glistening under the flashing party lights, we blended into the crowd, the music pulsing, bodies swaying around us. The noise of the room dissipated.

"What are you doing here?" I asked, harsher than I'd intended.

"Don't worry," he said, seeing my face. "Not an official visit. Just in the neighborhood."

"You just happened to be in this nightclub on a Saturday night?"

He shrugged elegantly. "It's a nightclub on Saturday night. Someone in a bathroom downstairs is going to realize that ingesting large amounts of liquor and cocaine is a *very* bad idea. He motioned for a beer, scanning the crowd. "Fear not, Nella. Your Gabby will be here for many years to come."

"How long will that even be?"

"How long is long enough?"

It took everything I had not to run from the bar, dragging her with me.

Death took no notice as his drink arrived. He brought the glass to his lips, murmured something I couldn't hear, then drained it in one long swallow.

Over the last few visits, Death had been drinking more. It brought back painful memories of René slipping to a place I could not reach him. That couldn't happen to Death, could it? "Are you all right?"

"Why wouldn't I be?"

"I don't know. You're not acting like yourself."

"You're an expert on Death." The statement caught me off guard. "Tell me, Nella, what do you see when you look at me?"

"I'm not sure." I always avoided looking too directly at him, but I couldn't deny this. His mood was erratic, his eyes tired. I didn't know what he had done in the intervening years except work without reprieve, but how lonely that must have been. Despite all that was at stake and everything he had taken from me, I felt sorry for him. What did he want me to say?

"Forget it," he said. "I've been preoccupied. The number of souls I gather daily in Afghanistan and Cambodia is staggering." He motioned for a refill. "Famine, war, disease . . . the work never ends. And yet you all dance to your music and drown out the rest of the world."

Guilt set in, as it always did, but I had to squash it down. He had his role, just like I had mine. "After all this time, do you have even one good thing to say about them? Us?"

His severe frown eased reluctantly. "Some of the movies aren't bad."

"Any favorites?"

He nodded his head toward Gabby. "Her last was passable."

"You watched it?" That made me nervous. Of course he'd be interested in her. I loved her. He'd be interested in anything that interested *me*.

Death rolled his eyes. "A man had a heart attack in the theater and hit his head on the way down. I stayed a bit longer when I noticed her on the screen."

"Well?" I couldn't help but be curious. "What did you think?"

"She is talented. I can see why you . . . love her."

"If you're not here for Gabby, why *are* you here?"

"As I said, I'm stopping in to see an old friend."

"Is that what you think we are? Friends?"

"Given our long history, I thought the term might fit." We sat there for a while. He was a constant. The only one after decades and decades on earth. He knew the truth of me and I of him.

"Are you happy, Nella?"

Was it a mistake to admit I was? Would he cut Gabby's life short? I glanced at her, chatting with her circle, still strong, lithe, incandescent. "Yes. I am."

Death settled forlorn eyes on me. "Can you describe it?"

I sat for a minute, flummoxed. He'd never asked that before. "I can only describe happiness as a light that comes from within. You feel lighter, almost buoyant, maybe giddy. Are you?"

"No," he said. "And I thought seeing you would fix it."

I forgot how to breathe for a moment. "And did it?"

"I suppose. I find your happiness means something to me. I thought I'd take a look at it up close."

He drained the last of the second drink. "Enjoy it, Nella. You deserve it. I'd stay longer, but, alas, duty calls." He bowed and winked out of existence.

When he was gone, the music sharpened around me again, the sights and sounds of the nightclub refocused and more vibrant after his exit.

I had many years with Gabby. Death had assured me, but how many more? I tried not to think about it, but how could I not, especially as the years passed? As Death had promised, nothing unexpected happened, but I still had to watch the passage of time on her person.

In 1991, Gabby turned sixty-six, and though she was still beautiful, the effects of time were evident in small ways: the creases at the corners of her eyes, the slight thickening of her waist, the touch of gray kissing her temples. I remember one night she sat at her makeup table at our house, squinting at her reflection, pressing back the soft skin from her eyes.

"You are stunning," I said from the door, watching her.

She smiled at me. "Easy for you to say. You haven't aged a day. It's been more than thirty years since we met, and it's like you just walked through the church doors. You have to tell me your secret."

"Just good stock," I lied, then told fiction stories about my family and their slow-aging fountain of youth genes. I hated lying to her. She was more than a lover, a wife, a partner, but a trusted friend, someone I wished I could let in on the truth. But I couldn't break Death's rules.

"Still, it's a marvelous thing. Almost every actress I know would give their eyeteeth for it." Gabby glanced up at me. "To be forever young looking. A blessing—"

"And a curse." My thoughts wandered to the true price of living forever. All around me, the world had sped up: turbo jets, bullet trains, cell phones, Walkmans, VCRs, personal computers, and twenty-four-hour news cycles. The only thing remaining unchanged was me.

I'd resorted to dusting my hair with powder, overdoing my makeup, wearing longer skirts and dated blouses, and putting on thick, clear-lensed glasses that took up half my face. Despite my efforts, the comments about how good I looked for my age never stopped.

"Do you mind?" I asked her.

"Why would I?" She stood, her dressing gown sweeping behind her, and wrapped her hands around me. "Intelligent, talented, *and* beautiful? Who would complain about that? Not me, that's for certain."

I hugged her, her skin soft, her jasmine perfume wafting. Being in her arms felt like home.

"Speaking of certain," she said as we broke apart, "I did want to talk with you about something I've been thinking about for a bit."

I paused at the seriousness of her tone.

She swallowed, rubbing her hands together. "Perhaps it's time for part two of my dream—that maybe we just do that full-time."

"Does that mean what I think it means? Time for suitcases?"

She chuckled at my delight, the sound low in her throat. "I think so." She glanced around the room at the posters and trophies, evidence of her success littering the walls: pictures with other stars and blown-up movie stills. "As much as I love it, I can admit that perhaps it doesn't feel like it used to. Three a.m. calls to set, weeks on location, always being camera ready . . . I think I've done everything I wanted to do. I'm getting older," she said, putting up a hand to stop my protests, "and we still have twenty cards to go. I'd like to see them all before—you know."

"Well, we're not going to think about that."

"But we should. I'm not getting any younger. I just wanted to make plans—"

"I *have* a plan—taking care of you and Winston as long as there is breath in my body."

Gabby's eyes met mine in the mirror. "I think it's time for our next act."

"You don't hear me complaining," I said, kissing her curls. I hadn't thought she'd ever give up her career. Her stepping back meant more one-on-one time, slowing down, and exploring. I went through the cards mentally. We hadn't traveled much to South America. Maybe we'd start there. Perhaps we could find more that Death would be interested in. We could explore her retirement. As for what would happen later, we'd get there in time.

She stopped me, gently capturing my hand and searching my face. "Are you sure? We're always doing things for me—so much so I feel guilty. You moved all the way here for me—took care of Winston. I want you to accomplish your dreams as well."

"I have you, Winston, and our life together. What more could I want?"

"Well, it's decided then," she said decisively. "The final shot's tonight, and I can tell my agent at the wrap party right after. If we plan it right, we can be off in a month."

I stood beside her as she applied the blush. I loved her even more today than I had years ago. I knew every inch of her body, how she smelled after getting caught in the rain, and the micro frown lines that popped between her eyebrows when she read a new script. Our love had a depth that only time could bring.

I wondered what she'd be like, retired. It was easy to imagine long walks up the boulevards, using my gift to translate for us, or taking tours as we explored other places.

I glanced at my watch. "I need to get moving if I'm going to make it on time. I might be a smidge late to the wrap party, but I'll see you there."

"Oh?" she said, catching my eyes in the mirror. "What'll be keeping you?"

"It's a surprise."

"For me?"

I leaned down and kissed her. "Who else would it be for?"

"Well, I know it's not Winston. He was just here for Easter. So what else could it be?"

"You'll just have to see," I said, padding from the room. I hurried to finish dressing and gather my papers, sure the cab would arrive at any minute. I hadn't wanted to tell her, especially since nothing had been finalized, but Sunset Publishing had reached out about writing her memoir. If she was going to retire, this might be the perfect time to tell her story—our story.

I read through the proposal in the back of the cab, nervous.

I'd written all those stories for *The Defender*, but this was different and personal. I'd be recording her nomination for a Primetime Emmy, her work on the variety shows, and all her work in civil rights. Reading through the manuscript reminded me of how proud I was of her—how lucky I was to have her.

The traffic was surprisingly light, and we made fantastic time.

*Maybe I can even get to the party early.*

We pulled off the highway and were idling at a red light, almost there, when I felt a tingle of awareness so strong that I looked up from the papers.

It was only half a second, if even that.

One glimpse, and I was certain my life as I knew it was over.

Death stood on the corner, dressed in all black.

It was only a glance, but I knew what it meant. He hung his head as if it hurt him to hurt me, and vanished.

It was as if my lungs collapsed, the weight of an elephant there, making it impossible to draw breath.

When I could make a sound, it was a scream.

"Shit, lady! What's the matter with you," the driver said, swerving.

"Stop!" I pounded on the partition. "Turn the car around! Take me home now!"

"Hit the glass again, and you'll be walking."

"You have to take me back now. I don't care what it costs."

I held myself in the back seat, papers scattered at my feet as I prayed. *Please, no, God. It's just a coincidence. Everything is fine.*

I couldn't allow myself to think of anything else.

Gabby was fine.

Gabby was fine.

Gabby was fine.

If I thought it enough, then it would have to be true.

I checked the time. Maybe she hadn't left yet. Perhaps it was just a coincidence.

I flew out of the cab as soon as it pulled up, not even waiting for it to stop. I threw money at the driver and grabbed the papers to my chest.

"Gabby!" I screeched, running up the stairs, papers fluttering like leaves behind me as I searched the house, going room by room, scared I'd find her fallen behind a door or having suffered a heart attack.

I searched and searched, but she wasn't there.

My mind jumped to all the different scenarios. Where could she be, and what had happened?

I was running to our room to call her agent when the phone rang.

At that moment, I knew.

It *could* have been Winston checking on his mom.

It *could* have been the maid calling in sick, the wrong number, or any number of things, but at that moment, I knew.

I sat on the bed, watching it ring. But it could've been her, and she could've been fine. That was the only reason I picked up.

"Hello?"

It was her agent, Joan. "Jimi, they're taking her to Cedars-Sinai—you have to get there quick."

# A VISIT FROM DEATH

The bed dipped as Death sat beside Nella, her figure frail in the sheets.

The alarm clock read 11:45 a.m., but the thick pulled curtains shrouded the room in shadow, the space stinking of neglect and stale smoke, stubbed cigarettes spilling from the ashtray—gray dust smeared on the surface. Three fat gnats circled above the empty wine bottles littering the bedside table, and the trash can overflowed, the garbage piling onto the carpet. Gabrielle's clothes were still hanging in the closet, her brush still on the dressing table.

In the center of it all, Nella lay huddled, the spilled wine appearing like blood in the dark light.

It was bad.

Visiting now wasn't the best idea. He wanted to win their bet—prove that he had been right all those years ago—but not like this.

"Why are you here?" she said, not turning to face him, voice tired.

He had struggled with that very question himself.

He'd seen what she'd become in the two years since he'd taken Gabby.

Nihilistic and hedonistic. As bad as him. It'd been hard to watch, to see such a beautiful soul turn inward and empty. He'd thought victory would taste sweet, but it felt wrong, sitting heavily in his chest—harsh and bitter, more like guilt.

"The last time we met in that bar, I said we were friends, and I've come to learn that friends check on each other. I've never seen you like this, not with any others. I wanted . . . I wanted to know how you're doing."

She finally turned, the mascara caked to her lashes, two trails running down, and her mouth smeared red. She gestured helplessly at the stained sheets and creased nightgown—her skin wan, her hair tangled in knots. "How does it look like I'm doing?"

"Like you've given up."

She shrugged, the tattered edge of her silk nightgown slipping over her thin shoulder. "What's the point of anything else?"

She plucked an old cigarette from the ashtray and lit it, the bright end flaring in the darkness as she took a drag, emphasizing the hollows in her cheeks.

"I hate seeing you this way."

"So stop taking everyone I love," she said, blowing out a stream of smoke. "It's an easy enough solution."

"Nella, look at yourself. We've been through this." He shook his head sadly. "I've told you. We all have our roles to play. Especially you."

She turned on him then, eyes unfocused. "What is my role, then? Hmm? Exist only to keep you entertained? Live the rest of my life alone? You're always popping up, taunting me, saying you want me to lose . . . but I don't think you do."

Death scoffed. "Of course I do. I was right all those years ago, and I'm right now."

She shook her head, eyes red. "I don't think so." She laughed, the sound husky and half strangled. "I think . . . I think you love me."

His breath hitched. A thousand refusals gathered in his throat, then vanished as he tried to speak. "I—"

She pointed a finger accusingly. "You do, don't you? That's why you keep taking everyone. You want me for yourself. Take me, then. Like you take everything else."

She grabbed him, dragging him close, and smashed her lips on his.

He couldn't describe how it felt. Right and wrong simultaneously. A tension in his chest uncoiled at her touch, craving the intensity. All of it was there: the hate, the anger, the pain, the mixed feelings, all of it bubbling up in that kiss. For a moment, the emptiness ebbed away.

The phone rang, splitting the silence. She pulled away first, avoiding his eyes, rubbing her lips, and dragged the phone off the receiver.

"That's fine," she said into the phone. "See you in a bit."

She hung up, and they sat there, tense.

"Nella, I—"

She laughed again, the sound strangled and a little bit mad. "Now I know I've lost it."

"That wasn't my intent when I started this."

"Well, that's where we are. And there's no way out of it."

"There is a way. But just one." If she only said the word, she could take his hand and they could remake the whole world. A place where pain didn't exist. Not for her. Not ever.

The possibility of it rolled through his mind, the idea making him heady.

She sighed. "Then I suppose we continue this horrible dance."

He nodded, the silence settling between them as he processed her response. "Do you really mean to go on this way forever?"

"No," she said decisively. "Not forever."

It was the way she said it that made him understand. He withdrew, his face becoming masklike. "Ah. The boy."

"He's a bit more than a boy," Nella said defensively.

"Time will take its course," Death said gently. "There'll be a moment when I have no choice."

A tear slipped down her cheek. "There's no way I can end a world with a piece of her still in it."

Death stood, discombobulated, skin tingling—he no longer had a reason to stay, but he didn't want to leave her.

The front door opened and slammed. "Jimi, are you here? I've got bagels."

"I'll stay away. For a long while," Death said quietly, fading into the shadows. He meant it as a kindness even as it devastated him.

"We'll have to see, won't we."

He winked out of sight just as the door opened and Winston entered, bag in hand. "Everything okay, Jimi? I thought I heard someone talking."

Nella shook her head, unsettled. "I was on the phone. Just an old friend."

# PRESENT DAY

## Savannah, June

# Thirty

I drag a hand across my face. Midmorning arrived, and Sebastian is still here, listening to it all, recording and asking questions. He was barely able to contain himself when I talked about MLK, the boycotts, and all the movements, but he listened the entire time.

"I'm so sorry, Nella," he says, his words comforting. Talking about it makes the pain fresh.

Tears splash down, trailing down my arm. "It was just so unfair. I don't know why I thought we were above it somehow. When Death said 'years,' I thought it would be decades."

"Did he try to talk to you, at least? Make it right?"

"Not then. If he had . . ." I don't finish the thought, catching myself in time. I feel like Death plucked the light out of my life and left me shrouded in darkness, all to force me to give in, his desire to win our bet pushing him to force my hand. "That's why this is a curse, Sebastian. I am destined to lose everyone I love, but I'm forced to keep finding evidence that life is worth living."

"But does it always have to end that way?"

I pull the wooden sun from the chest, the stain mottled red, deep cracks visible. Does it always have to end that way? That had certainly been the case, though Death had gone to extra trouble with Diego. The carved sun's old wood glue chips under my fingertips as I turn back to Sebastian.

"Yes, Sebastian. I've lived too long for there to be any other conclusion."

"What happened the next time you saw him?"

I close my eyes at this, remembering the pain.

# PART VII: BUENOS AIRES

## THE GOLDEN SUN—2005

# Thirty-One

I prayed for death after burying Gabby. The light inside me extinguished as the graveyard men piled dirt on her coffin. I gripped Winston's hand as we watched our beloved, the heart of our little family, disappear into the ground, never to be seen again. I stood there until the last ray of sunlight left the sky before allowing Winston to lead me back to our car.

"You need to get some sleep, Ma." He'd taken to calling me "Ma" and Gabby "Mother" over the years. I let him take me home and put me to bed, the sweet young man now tending to my grief alongside his own. I took a long, deep look at his face, wondering how it would change as he aged and I disappeared from his life. He had his mother's eyes, and I longed to stare into them and wish I could trade some of the years I'd lived to extend hers.

I left him a letter and a forwarding address, packing one single suitcase and discarding my typewriter, notebooks, and pens. I wouldn't need much. I'd set out to end this deal with Death. He'd won. He'd taken the last thing worth writing about.

I joined bands of hikers, working my way through Mexico to Guatemala to Peru to Brazil, seeking the highest highs. I drowned my thoughts with ayahuasca and the herbal psychedelics of Vilcabamba, Ecuador, hoping it'd end consciousness altogether. I leaped off every cliff into the warm Caribbean Sea or the Bay of Campeche looking for any god who would answer. I interviewed every local, searching for superstitions about caves and grottos and rivers where darkness lingered, diving headfirst, waiting for Death to step out of the shadows as I inched closer to the end and throwing in the towel. I knew Gabby would never want me doing any of this: flirting with my own end and that of the world on her behalf. But I wanted him to tell me why he'd taken her. He'd promised me years with her, but he'd never said how many.

Death never appeared.

I'd settled in Buenos Aires, a place Gabby had wanted to go. Most midnights, I'd taken to walking through the Cementerio de la Recoleta like a wandering spirit, thinking Death would return to such a familiar space. The aboveground crypts spread out before me each night like a small city of the dead, the crosses stretching into shapes in the moonlight. I'd felt dead and could only find a sliver of peace while in the quiet of the cemetery after the world had gone to bed. Thoughts of Gabby and Winston would dull in the dark quiet.

"Mamita, please," came a voice one night.

I'd just begun my nightly routine, the graveyard long deserted and closed for the evening. I followed the noise of the voices, keeping to the shadows. I stumbled upon an elderly woman in a thin nightgown being trailed by a handsome young man who could either be her son or grandson. Only two candles and the moonlight lit the path before them.

I listened as he tried to convince her to return home. The softness of his Spanish was a beautiful melody, as if he were singing her back to where she belonged.

My foot scraped the gravel, and he whipped around, calling out, "Who's there?"

I stepped out of the shadows to not startle either of them. "Sorry, I didn't mean to frighten you. I'm just here visiting too."

His eyes found mine, and I watched his ease settle into his shoulders and his expression turn from fear to warmth. "It's no problem."

The older woman sat before a crypt, running a shaky hand gnarled by time over the plaque. She whispered nonsensical words.

"My grandmother sneaks out of the house at night," he said. "Coming here to be closer to my grandfather, her beloved."

She was probably stuck in a sundowning loop, her memories and the present fractured by the disease of dementia.

"My family wants to send her away, but I won't let them. Everyone is concerned about these episodes, but I don't mind this nightly stroll with her." His eyes combed over me, and I was taken aback by the gentle kindness he showed his grandmother. A selfless act. "And why are you out this late in the graveyard by yourself? It's not always safe."

I couldn't answer his sensible question. I should've been afraid, but I knew I couldn't die, only Death allowing me release. My entire world for the past few years felt like these midnight strolls, an aimless loop through memory, loss, and death. I could fill each crypt with something I'd lost: a friend, a lover, a home, a job.

"It's peaceful, isn't it?" I stared up at the moon as it hid behind a patch of thick clouds, shrouding us in subtle darkness. It would be fitting that I couldn't see this stranger fully.

"The quiet of the dead often is," he replied. "Reminds us how loud living is. That it's all worth it."

"Is it?" The question slipped out, crackling between us. Too intimate for strangers. I smiled sadly as his eyes flitted between me and his mourning grandmother.

"She has forgotten so much. But the memory of her love remains. It's beautiful, isn't it? Would it be better if she forgot that too?" he asked. We both watched as his grandmother kissed the tips of her fingers and touched the letters of her husband's name.

His question was one that had haunted me after every loss of every love and every city and every friend.

"Maybe if it would prevent the scars . . ."

"Isn't love nothing more than both a mark of joy and sorrow in equal measure?" he posited.

"You speak as if you've never had a broken heart." I pressed a hand to my chest, knowing I carried all my scars inside; my heart was a bruised and battered thing, barely functioning.

"This woman"—he led his grandmother to her feet—"raised me after the death of her only daughter, my mother. Seeing her fade from me . . ." His voice broke. "I'm glad to have lived and loved her, even when it comes time for me to lose her."

The perpetual knot in my chest, hardened over the last few years from the loss of Gabby, loosened just a bit.

He grasped his grandmother's hand and led her deeper into the darkness, whispering his good night. For the next few weeks, I returned to the cemetery, not just for myself, but to wait and watch in the shadows as he completed his loving midnight routine. If I had been up to it, his would've been a story worth recording, his selflessness a brief reminder that good continued to endure.

But I wasn't up to it. I wasn't up to it for a very long while.

∼

A black fan blew hot, listless air around the travel agency, ruffling the stacks of pamphlets with each pass, moving in the same rote sequence—a good metaphor for my life at the time. A boxy gray TV hulked up in the corner, suspended on a white wire shelf, a muted press conference of President George W. Bush talking, the Spanish captions covering half the screen.

I tracked the drips from the air conditioner as they raced each other down the side of the wall. A brief buzz ran through me when the drip I'd picked won and ended as the two drops plopped together, becoming one and speeding down to the floor.

I sat in my tiny cubicle, *Carmella White* printed on my name placard, a dying fern languishing in the corner, watching water drip for entertainment.

Every day was a repetition of the last.

I got up, wore a variation of a black top, black pants, and boots, stared at a screen, ate lunch, clocked out, and made my way home for glasses of rich red Argentinian wine, sinking into a dreamless sleep until the next day arrived.

Time pressed forward in this way. I observed it all like a ghost drifting through their lives, peering in and disappearing, invisible. After everything that had happened to me, it seemed like a fine place. A small existence but a safe one—proximal to life. My midnight trips to the cemetery had been the most interesting part of my day, but recently they'd stopped. The beautiful, fragile abuela and her dutiful grandson no longer came. I found myself utterly alone.

I glanced at the cubicle next to mine, the pile of Isabella's copper hair poking over the gray divider that separated me from Cat Central. She had forty-three cat-related items crammed on her shelves—calendars, plant jars, glass figurines, and a creepy cat clock, whose eyes followed you when you moved—one cat for each year of her life. She kept me updated on the happenings of Tango, Gaucho, and Maté, her three actual live cats at home, who she swore were superior to children and who, she assured me, were dying for a visit. Or Juan, creeping away from the supply closet, scalp shiny with sweat through his thinning hair, likely with a year's supply of paper clips bulging from his wrinkled slacks, off to write another memo about everyone's copier count and conserving company resources, steadfastly oblivious to Isabella's adoration of him.

"There's a new travel agent starting today," Isabella reported.

I tried to feign interest. "Oh, really?"

"He's supposed to come in—" She froze, pointing at the door, then whispered, "Now."

The man soared high above, his presence drawing the attention of everyone in the room. He had thick, wavy brown hair threaded with sun-kissed highlights, big cognac-brown eyes, and a strong jaw sporting a permanent five-o'clock shadow. He was decidedly handsome and probably poised to become the golden boy of the office.

Isabella whispered about his looks as he toured the floor. I packed my things, ready to head out to spend my lunchtime in the shade on the roof with my latest read, this time *One Hundred Years of Solitude*, by Gabriel García Márquez, to pass the time and have my own years of solitude in peace.

I heard a voice before I could go. "A beautiful book. Are you enjoying it?"

The new travel agent hovered at my cubicle. His voice sent a chill over my skin. I hadn't recognized him in the light. It was the man from the cemetery.

"So far, yes." I glanced away.

"Do we know each other?" He scratched at his temple, like he was conjuring the mystery of me. "I'm Diego."

I shook my head, my coldness ending the small talk. He began unpacking his things in the cubicle across from me.

Linda burst out of her office, drawing attention to my section. "Carmella! Glad I could catch you. Great work on your last set of brochures. The hotel loved them and wants more for another chain. Where are you at with the Hyatt project?"

I lifted my notebook, which did *not* have anything related to what she'd just asked about, and lied. "It'll be finished soon."

"Keep at it, and you might be in the running for the all-expense-paid trip next summer." She winked, a satisfied smile spreading over her pale oblong face.

I nodded in what could've been interpreted as enthusiasm. Laughter burbled up inside me.

It was ludicrous. I didn't need her trip.

At this point, I could buy her firm, this building, and all the real estate for five blocks in cash, with plenty to spare.

I snorted. I didn't have concrete plans, but I was sure I wouldn't be here next year. This job was only marginally better than sitting at home, watching telenovelas.

I retreated to my sanctuary for lunch, then dragged myself back to my cubicle and computer, ensuring not to look at Diego just across from me. I forced myself to the task, drafting the required assignment—250 perfect words to describe the Maldives. I hadn't been there in ten years, but how hard could it be to describe white sandy beaches, wooden freestanding bungalows, and clear turquoise water designed to entice travelers and help them part with their money?

I had been alone, just me, my books, and my thoughts for seven days of paradise—a specific version of hell. But I'd checked another postcard off the list.

I emailed Linda my draft and sat up, shaking off the funk. No one was forcing me to be here. I'd come to Argentina after spiraling my way through Central and South America—in search of inspiration, in search of the place Gabby had wanted to be when she retired, something new—but once I got here, I found that it was more of the same.

So I had settled for an approximation of life.

No more features.

No more books to write.

Just 1,250 words of copy a day and my glass of wine.

Okay, a bottle of wine.

Fine, bottle*s*. No judgment.

I stood up and stretched. I needed a new challenge—a project to distract me from the passing of time.

I snagged my canvas tote and headed for the fire escape that led up to the roof and down two stories to Calle Peña. We technically weren't supposed to use it, but it was quicker than the stairs, and there was something about seeing the world at your feet.

The higher I got, the better I felt, the city dropping away as I ascended. The rungs were slightly damp from a brief summer rain, washing away the day's heat. The air breezed fresh and new, smelling like opportunity.

Maybe there was a charity I could join. Get my hands dirty. Help someone else. Every time I felt a spark of motivation, I reminded myself of the lessons Death had taught me. That work was taxing, and there was always a chance that he was nearby, but it had to be better than watching water drip, my endless day ticking away.

I was halfway up the ladder, turning the idea over, when the heavy metal door banged open, spilling out a grinning Diego. His smile was so genuine, I almost felt bad for not returning it.

"We meet again. I see this is where you hide," he said. "Carmella, right?"

I grasped the rung in front of me, boots thumping on the slick metal, slinging the bag to my side as he gazed up at me.

"Did you want company?"

"I came up to read so—"

"I figured it out," he said. His energy was lively and uncontained, and not what I wanted at this very moment, or for him to have recognized me from the cemetery.

I fished out my book and flipped to the bookmarked page, ready to read about characters as tragic as me. But as I scanned the page, I could feel Diego's eyes on me. "What?"

His smile slipped for an instant, but he pasted it back quickly like the edge of curling wallpaper. "I have a question for you, but it might sound strange. It'll only take a moment if that's okay?"

I closed my book. Tapped my watch so he knew I was counting this alleged moment.

He grabbed the railing and hoisted himself up the rungs, scaling them with the ease of a rock climber. He sat beside me on the tiled roof. I'd been polite enough. Maybe it was time for more direct action.

"Such a nice day. Isabella said you come up here. I see why." He turned, taking in the Buenos Aires skyline. "It's beautiful, no?" He inhaled, his shirt molding to his sculpted figure.

"Yes, it is. Now, what is it that you need? Shouldn't you be getting settled in?"

He smiled widely. "I should and I will soon enough. But first, I must know. You're the woman from la Recoleta."

"That's not a question." I gazed out in the distance, careful not to make eye contact. My stomach fluttered with embarrassment.

"Are you?"

"Am I?" I was being obtuse because I was trying not to be rude. There was an office full of women who'd want his attention. Surely I could redirect him.

"I would never forget your voice." He fished for eye contact I wouldn't give him.

I didn't admit to anything, and I wouldn't encourage him to dig deeper. I also pushed down the desire to ask about his grandmother. Had she passed? Had his heart been broken like mine? We sat there as the noise of the city filled the silence between us.

"There will be a company hike this weekend. We're going to Costanera Sur on Saturday morning," he said. "Linda says it's for team building, since I'm new. Will you be there?"

If I went, he would ask again. And again. I would come to care for him. Something terrible would happen, and I would need to leave the life I'd made.

"Sorry. I have plans. Nothing personal." They were the same plans I had every Saturday—book and bed—but that was none of his business.

He finally got the hint. "Well, let us know if your plans change."

I held my book aloft. "Enjoy the rest of the lunch break."

"Of course," he said, shoving his hands in his pockets. I flipped to bury my nose in the middle of the book, ignoring the sting of guilt in my chest. He was just being nice. And the thing was, I wished he'd met me in another time. Sometimes you meet someone and it's simply the wrong circumstance. Perhaps things would have been different.

What happened next, I couldn't even blame on Death. He wasn't there.

The rungs were wet.

He slid down too fast.

He overcorrected, flailing backward on the ladder.

But none of that helped my guilt as I watched them cart him away, hands immobilized, neck braced, bundled into an ambulance, the sound of Isabella's wails mixing with sirens as it pulled out into the street.

# Thirty-Two

"You don't have to help me with this. I can manage. The cast is coming off tomorrow." Diego was at my side, hovering in Isabella's chair, rolled up next to his at his desk.

"Yes, but you still have it on today. I have time." I typed the information into the database and squinted at the screen. "You have to get these people to Puerto Vallarta, Mumbai, and Johannesburg in just three weeks?"

He shrugged. "International weddings for a multicultural couple. They've got the money."

With him having one arm in a sling and the other in a cast, it was hard to watch him do his work one key at a time. Even though it wasn't technically my fault, I needed to do something. I helped him complete details for several clients until near closing time.

"I'm more surprised about you. Over forty countries? Are you for real?"

He'd been pestering me about where I'd been, and I'd given him a number.

"It's no big deal. I save my money. I travel the world. I'm still working here."

"Nope. Either you're a military brat, or your parents were hippies. Which one? Ooh! Maybe you're a secret billionaire or a spy, fleeing a life of crime." He had the wildest imagination. And he wasn't far off.

"Wrong on both counts," I said, keying in the entry. "I'm an . . . orphan, of sorts. No wealthy parents here."

"But then, how *did* you travel so much?"

There was no way I could even begin to tell him the truth, nor did I need to.

I shrugged. "I started early."

*Like in the 1700s,* I thought.

"Anyway," I said, focusing on the screen again, "I still think planning three different ceremonies for one marriage is crazy."

Diego chuckled. "People do crazy things for love." The silence lingered after his statement. He must have realized, because he coughed. "But seriously, Carmella, you don't have to help me. I got this."

"I know, but we're almost done. Didn't Juan and Isabella tell you to accept the help?"

The shock of Diego's accident had forced Isabella to see that life was too short for unrequited love, and she'd ambushed Juan at Diego's bedside with her confession. It was good to see them happy, but they were perhaps a little *too* enthusiastic about their love in our *very* open office.

Juan had shown up every day since, covered in cat hair and with a lovesick grin, caring not one whit how many office supplies everyone stole. They had left together over an hour ago in a tangle of limbs.

Diego leveled me with a look. "You're only doing this because you feel guilty."

"Can't two things be true at once? Now, where's this next account need to go?"

After another thirty minutes, his email inbox was clean, and a neat stack of envelopes with printed tickets to mail sat on his desk.

I flopped back into my chair and stretched. Everyone else was gone, the muted TV still casting shadows on the wall. After twelve hours of work and an aching back, I'd had a productive day. Diego kept up a steady stream of conversation as we powered through the list. He had a story for every one of his clients: Dorcas from Córdoba, who packed her mother's urn everywhere she went, including car washes and hair appointments; Rafael, who only wore his father's suit jackets every day, even though they were three sizes too big; Alejandro, who was slowly going bald from eating his hair. My sides ached by the time I entered the information for the final travel package.

"I'll admit I wouldn't have been able to get this done without you. I really appreciate it."

"Well, I'm sure you'd appreciate having your hands back more." He had been a sight at the hospital with a broken left wrist and a fractured right from where he'd tried to break his fall, a face full of bruises, and one lost canine tooth.

"While that's true, I have enjoyed this time getting to know you. You're usually so—"

"What?"

He squinted, searching for the word. "Businesslike."

I laughed. "We are at work, a place of business."

"Yes, but you've been much more open of late. It's nice."

I didn't say anything, blushing, soaking in his words, remembering when I used to be nice to my team at the newspapers. It hadn't gotten me anything. But that didn't mean I didn't miss it.

"So, any plans for tonight?" he said, interrupting my thoughts.

"Nope, just me and a good book. And a trip to Recoleta?" I bit my bottom lip.

"So, it *was* you." He grinned.

"Yes." I swallowed down the worries about admitting to my secret midnight trips. "How's your grandmother?"

His eyes turned wistful. "She's confined to her bed now. But she's still hanging in there. Thanks for asking."

I clicked open another document on his computer to hopefully signal that this part of the conversation was over.

Diego tapped the book in my bag. "Must be some book. You're always with one." He eased his cross-body bag from his desk drawer.

I shrugged. "It's something to do." I walked back to my cubicle, then powered down my computer and grabbed my bag. The last six weeks of helping Diego had been good for me. After the big rush of guilt had subsided, I finally had to admit I liked having someone to help, even outside work—picking up dry cleaning, dropping off meals, and assisting with more dexterous tasks. I wouldn't admit it, but I'd be sad when the whole cast came off and I returned to my old routine.

"Well, it's my last night in the cast. Why don't you come out and help me with my drink to celebrate? I'll need someone to maneuver the straw."

I shot him a look. "You can't manage a straw?"

"Ah, but I'm sure you would do it so much better, cariño." I warmed at the endearment. He had started using it in the last two weeks, but I never reciprocated it.

"One drink, and then you're going home. You're not even supposed to drink on your pain meds."

He stood up straight and tried his best to give me a salute, his sling flapping. "Yes, ma'am." I just shook my head and followed him, locking the door behind us.

I turned toward a bar just a few doors from the office, but Diego shook his head, his wavy brown hair falling into his eyes. "If you've finally said yes, I have a different place in mind."

"Different, huh? Am I going to like it?"

"Who is to say?" he said, shrugging. "You'll have to let me know when we get there."

I smiled as we continued to walk, Diego telling me to turn here and cross there. This was a different Diego, unlike the one I thought I knew. Yes, he liked to party and was obsessed with the gym, still doing leg exercises and waiting for the day he could lift his weights again. But he was more reflective than I'd given him credit for—more open—and I found his brand of optimism refreshing rather than grating.

"I'm curious," he said, sidestepping a group of tourists, "why did you say yes tonight? More guilt?"

"You needed help with a straw, remember?"

He grinned, though his eyes remained somber. "I think the question stands."

"It's a Friday, and my book wasn't that good. Besides, you won't need my help after tomorrow. I don't know—I thought I'd live a little."

He nodded, thoughtful. "It's good living, no?"

I chuckled, thinking about all I'd been through. "Depends on how long you've been around."

"True. But you've done a lot of living. Traveling to over forty countries? It's amazing. When these casts come off, I'm going to travel."

"Really?" He had mentioned it before, but there was a gleam in his eye. He was serious.

"Yes, I—wait! Close your eyes. We're almost there."

"Are you sure this is going to work? With your cast and all?"

"Ah! Stop planning and be surprised for once."

I smiled and closed my eyes, listening to the sounds of cars as they rumbled past, the clink of glasses from a restaurant, and the sizzle of meat floating toward me.

"This must be one heck of a bar."

"I think it'll be something you'll like."

It wasn't long before he slowed me to a stop. "Open your eyes."

I blinked, stunned by the sudden burst of light. We'd reached an eight-story building, a bright sign reading GRAND SPLENDID arched over the entrance. The facade reminded me of where I'd lived in Paris more than 130 years ago: all white stone, black terraced balconies, and architectural detail. The string lights of the restaurant next door bobbed in the breeze like fairy magic, adding to the ambience.

"What is this? A theater?" I stopped in my tracks. As charming as he was, it was not the time for a show. My hands had cramped up from typing, and I couldn't wait to kick these boots off and sink into my bed with a glass of red wine.

"Even better," he said, winking at me, loosely tugging me inside. At the sight of his cast, I swallowed my questions and followed him to where the lobby revealed itself and the surprise beyond.

Books.

Books everywhere I looked.

They lined the lobby, forming aisles like altars.

I gasped at the size of it. My version of heaven could look just like this. Jacques's study had been the most beautiful room to me for more than a century, but this was the most beautiful book-filled space I had ever been in, and I think Diego knew it.

The deeper we went in, the more in awe I was. The place was fashioned like a Parisian opera house, ruby-red theater curtains framing the stage, flanked by two balconies; rows of books lined the main floor where the seats ought to have been. On the circular ceiling, nude lily-colored angels, partially covered by clouds, observed all. Conversation echoed through the grand room as people milled about, browsing the titles. Clusters of tables stood on the former stage, all occupied with people chatting over their coffees and books.

"Welcome to El Ateneo Grand Splendid. It just opened," he said in a hushed tone, tugging my now-unresisting body behind him as I marveled at the details—the gilded moldings, plaster reliefs decorating the cream walls, and thick red carpet underfoot. "All your breaks, I see you with a book and thought you might like it." He looked back, a small smile on his lips, his reconstructed front teeth glistening.

I didn't know if it was the recessed features or the sparkle of the chandeliers, but I was starting to see Diego in a new light.

Thoughtful.

Observant.

Considerate.

Once, this might have been a cause for joy. A chance to start anew. But even if I wanted to dig deeper, I couldn't risk it. I moved to the next display, giving myself room and time to think.

Diego wandered a short distance away to browse a display of CDs and records, still glancing at me. I watched him flip through the selection, glancing away whenever our eyes met as I considered what it would be like to explore this a bit. Not for forever, but just for now. I didn't have a great love for him, but the like was there, growing—maybe growing into enough.

He sidled up beside me. "Come, let's grab seats. We can have the best view in the house."

I followed him, and we sat in the middle of the stage, gazing out at the selection of books and the grand span of the shelves, which looked like a church for all things literary. "It's amazing what they were able to do. It's like it was built for this."

Diego nodded. "My grandmother came here once as a small girl, when it was still a theater. She would talk about the dancers on the stage and how the music would swell, making you feel bigger and lighter than you ever had in your life." He glanced around again. "I'm glad they kept it. Just because something is old doesn't mean it can't be made beautiful again."

I glanced over at him. "Who are you, and what have you done with muscly Diego from the office?"

He leaned back in the chair. "I'm more than just a pretty face." His eyes lingered on me, and I believed it. The flutter grew bigger, so I changed the subject.

"So, what books did you get?"

He spread his out, a familiar black cover near the top.

I stopped him, pulling out the copy. "I read this one a while ago."

Diego blushed. "I know. You hardly put it down. I saw it today and thought I'd discover what was so fascinating."

"You might like it. It's a story about a woman and man caught by external circumstances, and whether they have what it takes to fight for their love."

"And what of you, Carmella? Are you a lover or a fighter?"

The question caught me off guard as I reflected on a long life of love and loss. "I've been a lover sometimes, sometimes a fighter, but I suppose it hasn't mattered until now. What about you?" I said brightly, shaking off the maudlin memories always lurking in the corners of my brain.

Diego grinned. "A lover, for sure. If you must fight for your love, was it ever yours?"

Interesting take. "So, you've never fought for love before?" I placed the book back on his stack.

"I've never needed to." He shrugged, sitting forward awkwardly, gripping the book in his slinged hand. "I believe that love has . . . to come willingly. You can't force it or be scared it won't show up again." He gestured into the space around us. "It's like the oxygen in this room. We can't see it, yet it sustains us. If we're doing it right, we don't have to fight for air, nor should we fight for love."

"That's very profound."

"My abuelo, my grandfather, was a farmer who thought himself a poet. Taught me all he knew to get the girls." Diego waggled his eyebrows. "Is it working? I'd hate to let him down."

I rolled my eyes but couldn't hide my grin. "If I say yes, I'll only be encouraging you."

"That's okay. A little hope won't hurt." His eyes were playful, a dimple dotting his left cheek.

I sighed. Why did there have to be a dimple? If I had a type, Diego fit it. He wanted to see more from the world. He wanted it to rise up to meet him, instead of running away like I was doing.

Maybe . . . it would be okay, as long as I didn't get too deep. Something light, something fun. Perhaps just sticking a toe in would be all right.

"Vamos," he said, standing suddenly. "Two books don't seem like enough for you."

And that, right there, was the statement that won me over.

We browsed a bit longer while I grappled with the situation, catching glimpses of him between the stacks. The light glinted off his dark hair as he perused the aisles, carefully selecting slim volumes and scanning their covers. I glanced away as our eyes met, unused to this new Diego. He was cute and more observant than I had given him credit for. I knew I'd never fall in love again, but there was something kindling between us, a kind of heat.

We made our selections and stepped outside. The sky had faded to purply black, and the flashing streetlights surrounding us hid the stars.

We headed to that little restaurant with the charming strings of lights, finally getting his promised drink. As I suspected, he needed no help with the straw but did stick to just one drink. We split an empanada de vacio y provoleta, sharing more about ourselves as the music pumped through the black speakers.

"Tell me about your past," I said, breaking off a piece of flaky crust.

He seemed surprised that I'd even ask, but launched into his family saga. "Growing up, my family didn't have much money. My mom met my dad, and, well, you know, here come me and my brothers and baby sister Liza. We rented this tiny brown house at the bottom of this big hill in Salta. We all shared a room, even my sister, a double set of bunk beds. The house was so small you had to head outside if you thought you might sneeze. That yard was everything—you could play a little fútbol, race your friends, and pretend the yelling inside wasn't happening."

He quieted, gazing over my shoulder. "My father was not a good man." His voice was small, but the words were not. I placed my hand on his and squeezed.

He squeezed back and continued, "The best thing about that house was the hill. My brothers and I would race each other to the top to be el rey de la colina—king of the hill." He grinned, holding his hands over his head like he had won. "When we would get there, we would lie in the grass and watch the planes overhead, making up stories about where they would go and what the people in them would do when they got off. We had big dreams, too, of taking our trips and seeing the world." A smile lit up his face. I could see the small boy he had been, with dimples and thick curly hair flopping into his face.

"I made it to the big city, to Buenos Aires. I got a job. And then . . . I met you."

His eyes held mine. The silence was back, not uncomfortable, but exciting. I'd tried not to feel it at the cemetery, and I tried not to feel it then. Perhaps it was the Malbec? It was difficult to tell.

"Well, what about you?" he said, breaking the tension. "What's your dream? You don't get to interrogate me."

"Oh, well . . . um, writing, of course." I'd given a similar answer to Gabby, and it was still true. Other dreams felt too lofty.

"Writing?" His forehead wrinkled.

I sat up straighter. "Yes, writing. Why not? I write for work. I'm *pretty* good at it."

"You are. You write the most magnificent copy in the entire office. Of this, I have no doubt. But there is no passion there. A dream must have passion."

He wasn't wrong, and yet it burrowed under my skin that he could see me so plainly. "I have passion for my writing."

He gave me a look that asked me not to lie to him, or myself.

"Okay, maybe my passion's been a little lacking."

"A little?"

"Okay, a lot. What do you want from me?"

"That is too complicated to answer now. Tell me and tell me *the truth*, Carmella. When was the last time you felt passion?"

"I've had passion."

"Real passion?"

I fixed him with a look of certainty. "I've had the *best* kind. The kind where the world shrinks to the two of you, the searing connection of two souls becoming one. I *had* passion. I had it—held it, was blinded by its light, and then I lost it."

"That type of passion doesn't die."

"In my case, it does." I traced his smooth skin, tanned, a whisper of five-o'clock shadow, rough under my knuckles. He didn't know what it was to watch as that skin stretched and sagged until it had withered away.

"So that's why you're so protective of your heart. It makes sense." He looked at me thoughtfully. "Who was he? Or she?"

An image of Gabby flashed in my mind, her wide smile on set as she gazed into the camera as if lit from within. I thought all the laughter in my life had gone when she died.

He held up his cast. "It's a new millennium. I'm no judge. I happen to like the ladies myself."

"Yes, she."

"What happened?"

"Death," I said. "Death happened to her. She died, and parts of me with her." The music blared over us as the truth sat raw and unvarnished.

It was nice when his hand reached for mine, his thumb rubbing my fingers. "I am sorry," he said, his words sincere. He released my hand and held his glass up. "To . . ." He waited expectantly for me to finish.

"Gabrielle," I said, the word catching. I missed saying her name out loud.

He nodded and continued, voice resonant, "To Gabrielle, a life of love, filled with meaning. In honor of her life and for what she meant to you."

I didn't expect my own tears. As I held my glass up to his, it was as if a ghost of her was there, laughing and teasing. She'd want me to dance, have fun, find the secret spots, tell bad jokes, and live freely. She'd ask me to say yes.

We stumbled into the street, and he lifted a hand for a cab. The car pulled up, and I tumbled inside, the books banging on my knees. It had been a good night. I wondered if we were going to my place or his, when the door slammed shut behind me. I looked back, surprised, and rolled down the window.

Diego stood outside, bag balanced on his arm, short curls tousling in the breeze. He waved to the driver, his voice stern. "You make sure she gets home safe." He leaned down through the open window, reading the question on my face.

His words caressed my ears, voice soft, meant only for me. "When you're with me, I want you to be a hundred percent present, clear, and sure. No hiding. No excuses." He patted the side of the car and waved as my ride trundled into the night.

I slid back into my seat, reveling in the firefly of hope alight in my heart.

# Thirty-Three

Strawberry-scented steam blossomed from the oven; the pink cake was lightly golden.

It was the best cake I'd ever made, the center high and full. I was always good at many things, but baking was not one of them. With my right foot, I shut the door and set the cake on the wire rack to cool until it was ready for the fresh strawberry-cream frosting, Diego's favorite. All was going according to plan.

The cake was good.

Dinner would go well.

No need to worry.

I eyed the clock, ticking seven on the dot.

The time for my appointment with Death had come and gone.

According to ritual, Death had left a golden maté gourd the day before, flowers and swirls etched in the top, perfect for drinking the earthy concoction, and a note, providing the location for our meeting today at six p.m.—a restaurant near the opening of the catacombs.

Of course it would fall on my first anniversary with Diego.

It was like Death was spying on me, waiting just beyond the veil. Instinct told me it was on purpose. It had to be.

It wasn't like I could call Death.

All our meetings were one-way affairs. I got the item and a time. That was how it worked.

I had no way of rescheduling. And I had never considered asking to before, but . . .

I thought about it as I stirred the cream. Diego had said he had something special planned—even life-changing.

I loved Diego: not in the all-consuming way I had loved others in the past, but in a gentle, easy way. He was a tender place to land, which was ironic because he'd fallen off a roof when we first met. Diego's love was simple—uncomplicated. It wasn't uncontrollable passion that would burn too fast, but it would be enough for as long as it lasted.

Death would be happy, right? I knew he wanted to prove me wrong, but he cared for my welfare. Otherwise, he wouldn't have shown up at that club in LA all those years ago. I was better—less brittle. I had gathered more stories and was ready to meet his challenge. I could have one day, couldn't I? After all, I had never missed a meeting before.

At ten minutes after six, when I hadn't heard anything, it occurred to me that maybe everything would be fine. I'd left a message for the maître d'. Surely that would be enough. Diego and I would have dinner at home that night, and I'd have everything ready for Death the next day.

At half past six, I started to breathe.

And at seven, I finally started to relax.

It was one time. I hadn't heard anything. I could see it as a good sign.

I had been on time for all our meetings. One wouldn't be a problem, would it?

Death would understand.

Wouldn't he?

The thought had barely left my head when a hand reached out, snaking around my waist and yanking me backward.

"Diego!"

He pulled me closer, nuzzling my neck in that sensitive spot below my ear. "That smells delicious, mi vida. Is it almost as sweet as you?"

"You startled me!" My heart was hammering. "I didn't hear you come in."

He frowned quizzically. "But who else would it be?"

*Who, indeed?* I pushed the thought away as I pushed him physically from the kitchen, swatting him with a pot holder as he reached for the saucepan lid. "Well, it shouldn't be you. Get out of the kitchen. No sweet talk here. You're going to ruin the surprise."

"You know you must watch the time on the steak—it's a delicate thing."

"You and your meat. I've got it," I said, pushing him through the door. "I won't burn it again. Give me a little credit."

His laughter faded as he made himself at home in the living room, watching commentators debate over a fútbol match.

We hadn't moved in together, but he was here as much as he was at his place. Undoubtedly, the question would come soon. I wondered about it as I stirred the side dish of stewed tomatoes, turning down the heat so it wouldn't burn. What would a life fully together look like?

Over the past year, I'd learned all the ways we fit and all the ways we didn't. If we moved into my place, Diego would want to have a workout room and an area for making music, and I found myself reluctant to give up my writing space, complete with shelves for my books and trunk. I could afford another place where we could have it all, but that would get harder to explain, since he still didn't know my secret.

Diego and I had quit the travel agency after another three months of dating. I told him a mysterious uncle had left me some money, with explicit instructions to blow it all on love and travel. Something about him reminded me of the way I used to be. Openhearted.

Diego had been thrilled to come, and it was as if the world were brand new, seeing through his eyes the glaciers in Santa Cruz, dancing in the streets of Cali, Colombia, and hiking Machu Picchu in Peru. The time was ours to enjoy. It reminded me of taking steamers down to Monrovia on a whim. It also reminded me of my trips with Gabby and all the postcards. I didn't revisit the places we'd been—that felt like it would be crossing a line—so I planned other places that Diego and I would travel to.

I had collected so many stories, recording them as evidence for Death of all the goodness that still existed. Diego was beside me as we explored the region, learning and collecting. After learning how to make wood carvings in Antigua, Guatemala, he'd gifted me a wooden sun he'd made and painted gold, which now hung in the kitchen.

It hadn't all been easy, though.

The longer I spent with him, the more questions he had. How did I know so many languages and dialects? That couldn't be explained away with a Rosetta Stone CD. More than once, the question arose about my funds and how I could afford all this.

Anyone else would've been ecstatic to have a rich girlfriend with unlimited funds. Still, the more I knew Diego, the more I understood that having a sudden font of wealth would be a problem since I hadn't shared the truth of my situation early on.

Diego was big on truth—his one nonnegotiable—because it turned out that Diego's dad had lied.

A lot.

To Diego.

To Diego's brothers and his sister.

To the people he owed money to.

But most of all, to Diego's mom.

Despite the years of fighting and barely making ends meet, Diego's mom, Luciana, had stuck by his father's side, supporting the kids through her sewing business, making sure their family stayed whole. So when Raul died suddenly of a heart attack, Luciana planned a stellar funeral and ensured he would be remembered for the few good times.

Imagine her surprise when four other children and their mothers showed up at the funeral, the children's ages ranging from nineteen to two.

She had a nervous breakdown in the middle of the church, never making it to the graveside service.

Diego had shared all this with me in a small rental in Tikal, Guatemala, as the rain poured down, having spoiled our plans to explore the ancient Mayan pyramids. So we were staying in bed watching satellite TV with terrible reception when the topic of lying came up.

"I'm not sure, Diego. Circumstances aren't cut and dried, and sometimes lies can be necessary." I was only speaking my truth. Lies made complicated lives easier, especially mine. They made my life work.

He had sat up, thrown his legs over the side of the bed, and faced the open window, watching the rain pour down. I moved to his side and watched the struggle over his face. I could never forget how haunted it was.

"I love you, Carmella. I do, but I'm sorry, I disagree. There's no reason to lie—*not ever.*" And so, he told me all of Raul's numerous lies.

About his gambling.

About losing that small house.

Pretending to work when he had already been fired.

Stealing the money Diego had saved for a school trip.

Drinking the grocery money away.

About hitting Luciana.

"If you can lie to your loved ones," he said, "what else could you do?"

So I hadn't told him.

Any of it.

I ignored that little red flag of truth.

I needed Diego and his light, his happiness, and his optimism. Traveling with him made everything special again and reinforced my work with Death. I promised myself I would break it to him gently when the time came.

I quickly chopped the parsley for the chimichurri sauce and thought about how I would do it. He loved me. It would be okay. Diego was forgiving and kind. I had nothing to worry about.

As I turned to grab the sun-dried oregano and salt, I saw something that put my entire future in doubt. The time for truth had come sooner than I thought. Death loomed next to me, in the original form, the one I had first seen him in all those years ago on the plantation. His energy flooded the room, pressing every corner, the enormity of it stealing my breath away.

"Thought you'd be rid of me that easily?"

Anger threaded through his voice, dark and crackling, like the energy of a night storm, with destruction guaranteed to follow.

The glass saltshaker fell, shattering to pieces, a plume of white salt dust rising around my feet.

"Carmella! Everything okay?" The couch squeaked as Diego stood up. I ran to the door, blocking his view to the kitchen.

"I—dropped the saltshaker. Would you run to the store and get another one?"

Diego frowned. "I think there's a container on the shelf."

"Nope. Fresh out." I swallowed thickly. He needed to leave. Immediately.

"Let me help you clean up first." He moved toward me, and I put a hand out to stop him.

"No!" I moved away from the kitchen. "Also, it'd be great if you could get me two cans of tomatoes. I need them for the sauce."

"But we have tom—"

"I used them already. Please?" I walked over and pressed my hands against his shirt despite the sick feeling in my gut. "Please."

He kissed my temple. "I'll grab my keys."

"Don't, there's glass everywhere!" I backed up, snatched the keys from the spot by the stove, and tossed them to him.

He gave me a weird look, but with one last glance at the score, he headed to the door.

"Salt and two cans of tomatoes? Nothing else?"

"Wine?"

He grinned, his trust shining out of every pore. "Now, *that* I can do. I'll be back in a bit."

I could only exhale once the door had shut, the cheers from the fans still blaring on the screen.

I swallowed and turned around. Death glowered at me, the energy in the room ratcheting higher.

From the look on his face, the world would end that night.

# A VISIT FROM DEATH

Nella held her hands up at Death slowly, as if disarming a bomb. Smoke wafted up from the pans, shifting from gray to black. "Before you get upset, I left a message." She eased toward him, gesturing in a calming motion. She reached gingerly, touching his shoulder as if to soothe him.

It was a mistake.

A wave of excess energy rolled off him so fast and thick it was a wonder the kitchen didn't burst into flame.

"You dare?" he said, snatching himself from her touch, the rage deepening his voice.

Nella stepped back in shock, eyes wide, hands braced before her. "You need to calm down." She walked across the kitchen and plucked a black folio from the table. "I was already done. Everything is right here," she said, offering it to him. "We can talk now," she said, swallowing. "I think you'll like these—"

Death slammed a hand against the refrigerator, sending it thudding into the wall. Pictures and a golden sun leaped to the floor from the force, all shattering upon impact. "You don't set the terms of our arrangement. You're only here at my mercy. By missing this meeting, I don't think you understand what game you're playing at."

Her eyes grew wide, staring between him and the jumble of wood on the floor, clutching the folio to her chest. "I didn't think you'd be this way." She swallowed again. "It's our anniversary. It was important," she whispered.

"More important than the fate of the world." With one motion from his hand, the saucepan flew across the room, slamming into the wall, the red sauce spraying like blood over the pale-yellow paint. "More important than me!"

"No, it wasn't like that! I left word at the restaurant for us to meet tomorrow."

"Tomorrow?" he sneered, pacing to the other side of the room, the glass crunching under his feet. "You'd have me wait? For him?" he said, meaning Diego. "You still don't understand, do you? *I'm* the only priority. If our bargain is not met, then none of this matters. I'll take you and everyone else with me when I go."

She stared up at Death. His anger was terrifying, even to him. It was mixed with hurt and some kind of betrayal.

"Why are you acting like this?"

Death paced through the kitchen, glass crunching under his bare feet. "I thought you understood after all this time. I was sitting there, waiting, waiting for you, and—you're here with him? *He's not even worthy.*"

Nella gaped at him. "But I'm doing what you asked me to do. I've kept our promise for years. Why—"

"Because you picked one of *them* over your commitment to me. Do you think this one—this *boy*—is deserving? He knows the truth about that! Did he tell you what he writes in his journal? That one day you'll wake up and know he's not enough? That he knows he has nothing to offer you? Did he tell you that?"

Her eyes glittered with tears, the truth pricking at her soul. "Why are you going through his things?"

He growled with frustration. Slammed his fist, sending a crack rippling through the table. The legs sagged as the split worked itself clean through. Nella jumped back as the side nearest to her crashed.

Death gathered her in his arms, forcing her to look up at him. "It's time to choose! The choice is inevitable. Why can't you see that?"

The words had barely left his lips when the boy walked in, the cans of tomato sauce rattling together in his bags. He froze, eyes wide at the mounds of glass and wood chips, as sauce streaks oozed down the walls, Death's arms around Nella.

Nella pushed Death away, straightening her hair as if ashamed, chest heaving. How could she even hope to explain?

Diego gawked at her but stepped forward, placing himself between them. "Who the hell are you? Get out of here!"

A bitter blackening sensation rose inside Death, hardening his chest. The boy wasn't meant to be reaped for some time, but perhaps, like Nella, today was the day Death would make an exception.

Spite trickled through him, warm, oozing, and prickly. "Dear boy, that is simply not the question. The better question is, Who is she?" Death straightened and smiled, the picture of magnanimity. He would simply have to show Nella. He would prove how poor a choice the boy was.

Diego glanced at Nella, baffled, but all she could do was look away—any explanation dying on her lips.

Death's smile deepened. "Go on. Ask her name."

"Carmella?" Diego said, as if he were testing it for the first time.

She squished her eyes closed as if to not see when the truth crossed his face. "It's not Carmella."

"What? What is it then?"

She opened her eyes, the confusion on his face painful to see. "It's Nella," she whispered. "Nella Carter."

Diego's face crumpled as he staggered back, away from her lies.

Death snarled at the movement, clenching his fists, mere moments from sapping the life from Diego's body. "He proves my point. Already he shrinks from you. He'll never be there for you, not the way you need." He spun around to face Diego, his voice unctuous, the change in his mood dizzying and dangerous. "So glad we got to meet in person. Nella usually finds the redeemable ones, but I can see you're nothing of the sort. You're not creative. You don't read. You lack ambition. No, sir. You're far from redeemable. Take your relationship with your father—I'm sure she'd love to hear about that."

Diego blanched, clutching the edge of the door for support.

"What is he talking about?" Nella asked him, never taking her eyes from Death, her expression murderous.

He frowned at Diego, then leaned forward, whispering conspiratorially to Nella, "I can't imagine why he didn't tell you."

Diego stepped back, distancing himself, almost out the door and into the living room. "I don't know who you are, but you need to leave, along with your lies."

Death tsked, his smile bright against his darkness. "Diego, I'm surprised at you. Why didn't you tell 'Carmella' that you were the one who pushed your father to the ground? Right before his heart attack? You love the truth so much, I want to make sure you tell yours."

Diego flushed as his mouth opened and closed like a gasping fish, the words dying in his throat.

"You see, Nella, the fact is that Diego here had time. Plenty of time to call for help. Plenty of time to get an ambulance. But he didn't. He stood there and watched. For over thirty minutes, he watched his father writhe on the floor, clutching his chest, begging for help. He had plenty of time. If he had, his dad would be here today instead of rotting in that little cemetery."

Nella paled, spinning toward Diego, brow furrowed in horror. "Is this true?"

"Given his childhood, it makes sense, doesn't it?" Death patted Diego roughly on the back and threw an arm around his shoulder as if they were old friends. "But back to your original question. Who am I? Like Nella, I have *so* many names. Hades, Kali, Anubis—Gamab is my favorite. You little humans have created so many words to describe who I am. As if you could even begin to understand. But you, my dear Diego, you may call me Death."

With that, he unfurled himself. He expanded, the enormity of him spread across the room as his skin stretched, writhing and rippling, twisting in on itself. The faces of the damned pressed up through his skin, eyes sunken, their mouths contorted into open screams, their torment reverberating off the walls, catching them all in a tornado of sound. She fell to her knees, dropping the folio, the white pages fluttering like birds, as she covered her ears, eyes wide in horror.

Diego skittered back, clutching his head. He dropped the bag, and the contents spewed out, rolling across the floor, the broken wine bottle crashing open as its contents splattered out like blood.

Death allowed a few seconds more to pass before he came to himself. The noise faded, ebbing away until the only sounds were Nella's and Diego's labored breathing and the sizzle of burning steaks. Death shrank into himself and lounged against the counter, surveying the damage and their reactions, the fear plain on both their faces. He reveled in it. Nella had forgotten who he was and what he was capable of.

Diego slowly grasped for the counter to steady himself. He made no move to help Nella. He backed away until he bumped into the doorframe, bracing himself against it.

"It's been nice, Diego, but you should leave now while you can." Death's tone was final.

Diego glanced at Nella one last time, then turned and left, crunching through the glass and wood.

Nella's tears poured freely as the front door slammed shut behind him.

Death helped her stand, but she shook at his touch, leaning away. She needed time, Death knew. She'd see the favor he'd done for her—the time he'd saved her. His true nature would have emerged eventually. He had been wholly unworthy, and he had shown her that.

Nella snapped. With a roar, she launched herself at him, hands clawing. "Why would you do that!" She scratched at him, doing whatever she could to hurt him. She went for his eyes and ripped at his clothes. Death didn't move against her.

This was anger. This was pain.

When her hands did not affect him, she broke away and started smashing things, whipping the plates and knives at him, trying her best to do him harm. She raged, the wave of her anger rolling over him, and he let her until she broke, the last plate crashing harmlessly to his left as she collapsed, the anger ebbing away like ripples in a stream, her sobs steady.

He wrapped his arms around her limp body, but she rejected him. "Get away from me! You had no right to do that!" She struggled against him, writhing, doing all she could to get away.

He simply held her.

He held her until she'd quieted, hiccuping.

"Are you finished?"

She pushed against him but sagged at the effort, her anger finally spent. She lay in his arms as he rocked her like a small child being comforted after a tantrum.

"I can't . . ." She struggled to take a clear breath. "I can't keep doing this." Her words were quiet and clear.

He paused, shocked by the admission. He hadn't gone that far, had he? "Are you sure you mean that?"

The silence drew out. "I'm just so tired."

And she looked it—her face pale and drawn, short curls in disarray, her body limp. She sat crumpled, like a marionette cut loose from its strings.

Something moved in him then, slow and heavy. Guilt, maybe. Or something close enough to recognize.

*Perhaps it had been too far.*

"Even with Winston?" he asked, quiet but firm. Their game had gone on too long for anything less than certainty.

She turned sharply, her mouth tightening—but said nothing. Then she looked away, with the smallest shake of the head.

Relief, thin and unfamiliar, stirred in him.

He stooped and picked up the folio, plucking the white pages from among the debris, anticipating her words and what she'd prepared for him.

"Perhaps today got out of hand." She said nothing as he bent, cupping her cheek in his hand, forcing her to look up. "When you calm down, you'll see the clarity of it all. And then you'll give me your decision. But for now, all of this"—he motioned to the destruction around him—"is over." She stared at him, expression flat and listless.

He shook it off, the small golden sun crunching beneath his feet as he winked out of existence.

# PRESENT DAY

## Savannah, June

# Thirty-Four

I'm finally at the end of it all. Someone else knows my story.

Sebastian hands me a tissue, and I dry my eyes.

"Before I say anything else . . ." He lowers his head to make certain I'm looking into his eyes. "I think you are incredible. The most incredible person I've ever met. The most incredible person to ever exist. I don't know how you went through what you did, and you're still standing."

"Barely," I whisper. "I'm here, but at what cost?"

He shakes his head. "You're still here. I'm grateful. All of humanity should be."

I nod and rest my head on his chest, listening to his heartbeat, steady and soothing.

"And to think, you're able to keep going like this. It's remarkable."

It's the only part Sebastian doesn't know. That I've already made my mind up. There's no need to tell him. It's only for another day. I should be kind and let him enjoy it.

"Let's not talk anymore," I say, sitting up, facing him. If I only have one more day, I want to spend it next to him.

I can remember his touch as his gaze drops to my lips. "Are you sure?" The tension peaks between us again, and he waits for my lead even now.

"I've never been surer about anything."

He stands, bringing me with him in one motion. I wrap my arms around his neck, pressing closer as he carries me out of the room and up the steps. He's in no hurry, but I am. After all that talk, I want to feel.

He sits me on the edge of the bed. I slip out of my dress and sit naked before him, the air-conditioning cool on my fevered skin. His eyes trace the lines of my body, taking in every detail. I relish the attention, being fully seen one last time.

"No more talking," I say, leaning forward.

He nods and stands between my legs, and I reach up, untying the string on his sweatpants. I tug the waistband down, tug on his shirt until he's as naked as I am.

There's no shyness. No hesitation. This man knows everything there is to know about me. And I'm not about to wait a second longer. He kisses me on my lips before grinning as he settles comfortably between my thighs, pinning me to the mattress. This is different from our first time together, mainly because we're in a bed. Everything feels slower, like the drizzle of thick honey. He feels like sweet release as he makes sure I reach my pleasure first.

When I'm finished, I sit up and kiss him long and slow. "More."

He braces himself above me, hands tangled in my hair as he kisses the heart-shaped birthmark on my collarbone. I run my hands up and down his back, pressing him closer. No matter how I move, we fit together.

I draw my legs up on either side of his hips. He shudders from the deliciously slow way he inches inside me. It's a perfect fit, almost like he was made for me. He meets me move for move as his hand finds my face, caressing.

"Oh, Sebastian."

"Shh," he says, grinning. "You said no talking."

And there is no more talking, just our bodies coming together as I pull him to me, grinding to meet him upon every thrust.

I go over the edge again, this time taking him with me.

We lie together afterward, and everything is right and wrong all at the same time. As good as it was, I already know how bad it will be when I lose this. I will be less than dust.

That strengthens my resolve.

I wait until I hear his breath even out, a pleasant ache running through my body.

Sebastian stirs, reaching, still asleep, and pulls me toward him. I allow myself a moment, savoring his warmth and the strength of his touch. I'm happy and sick at the same time, Death's words echoing in my mind. He'll never let me have this. Or, instead, he will take it from me.

I marvel at Sebastian, still nestled in the sheets, and for an instant, an image of the not-so-distant future where we've made a life comes to mind. I can picture it all—trips to museums, flights traveling the world, lovely dinners, and long walks along the beach. Even thinking of it brings a flicker of joy that makes me incandescent. It could all be so beautiful. That is, until I'm left to live it without him—alone again.

The familiar feeling creeps in, the bleak one that tastes of despair. I can also imagine what it will be like to experience it all again: to watch Sebastian wither, struck down by an accident or old age itself; to plan another funeral under an assumed name. The thought strengthens my resolve. This will all end tonight.

I tug on a robe and creep downstairs for a glass of water. His jacket is on the banister, and it looks good there, as if it belongs. All through the living room, Sebastian's things lie about, taking up space as if they're supposed to be here.

That's when I see it. The one thing that doesn't belong. It's the object I've been waiting for.

A large golden hourglass sits on top of the piano, the sand steadily pouring through, mounding in the bottom compartment. I approach it like a bomb and read the time remaining—a little less than two hours. The white card stands out, with a familiar address not far from here.

I get my water and head upstairs.

It's time to meet Death and face his wrath.

I've told someone the truth.

I sit on the edge of the bed.

"Hey." He smiles sleepily at me.

"Hey," I say back, smiling. He is so handsome. I love how he looks up at me like I am the sun and he's caught in my orbit. I enjoy his look for a few seconds more because once he hears the truth, he won't ever see me that way again.

He shifts back, eyes more alert, searching my face. "Something's wrong." He slips his hand into mine. "Is it because we had sex?"

"No," I say, squeezing his hand. "That was perfect."

He grins and brushes his mouth against my knuckles. "What's the matter?"

Hasn't he been paying attention about what happens when people get too close to me? I want to savor these final seconds together.

"I'm just glad I could share my story with you. I'm glad you're the one who knows the whole thing."

"And I'm glad to be a part of it," he says, smiling. "There's so much left to tell . . . so much more of your story to be written."

"But that's just it, Sebastian . . ."

Lightning flashes outside as rain lashes the window, filling the room with its steady beat. Silence stretches out between us as comprehension dawns.

"You broke the rules," he says. "You weren't supposed to . . . tell the story . . ."

There's no judgment there, only a simple statement of the facts.

He pauses as if replaying the last few days in his mind. "Last night at the museum, you'd made your mind up then." He swallows. "I was so caught up in what you told me about your past that I wasn't paying attention to your future."

Another man might storm out or rage at my selfishness, perhaps argue with me and try to change my mind. But Sebastian is Sebastian and comforts me. He draws me into his arms, which only makes it worse. I can imagine a life of Sebastian helping me fulfill the terms of the deal, seeking other stories. As good as it would be, nothing would be worth what would come in the end. At some future time, I'd lose him too.

My heart twists in my chest. The pain is so great that I feel my soul might shatter.

"Nella—" He moves to my side.

"No." I hold out a hand, stopping him, and take a breath. "I've had my mind made up since Winston died three years ago. I'd fulfilled my promise to Gabby to look after him. With him gone, I tried not to make any more attachments and keep things simple. The thing was, Death never showed. Not even when I tried to force him to meet me. So I decided to wait. He had to meet me at some point. And then I met you. Perfect you. I suddenly remembered everything I'd forgotten, how good the world could feel—what it was like to be interested in life again. What it felt like to want again . . ." I take a deep breath. "I was ready to choose more time, right up until I saw those figurines in the museum. I had to tell you. I had to break the deal."

Sebastian frowns, forehead wrinkling. "Why? Because of William?"

"No," I say. "It's because of you." I cup his cheek, his beard slightly rough in my hand. I breathe in the scent of him—cinnamon, leather, and the bit of essence that is just him—savoring it for the last time.

"Because of me?" Sebastian sits back, bewildered. "What about me would make you want to end this bet?"

"To avoid the pain of losing you when the time comes." I pull away, and his grip loosens, but he doesn't let me go entirely; his fingers trail over mine. Knowing how short our time is, I crave his touch, but I can't think straight when he's touching me.

"But that's the deal," he says softly. "That's humanity. We will all lose the ones we love—either them or us. From birth, we make our way in this world. The gift is the choice of who we spend it with."

"The curse, you mean." I shake my head sadly. "That's the part people miss. I've read books about immortality, vampires that live forever, people who never age . . . They think the worst thing is death. Death is the easy part. What they miss is the loneliness, all-consuming, that occurs as everything and everyone slips away, lost to the sands of time."

All I can think about is the cost. I was so sure that the beauty and the goodness were worth it. I had no concept of how empty life could feel, how meaningless it could be.

"I have a sense of what you mean. Not to the same extent, of course. You already know about Patricia. I know how hard life can be without love."

"So, you understand. As much as I feel for you, I can't go through this again. I've done it before, too many times. I don't want to stay the same, powdering my hair, pretending I'm your niece or something the older we get. And what about you? You'll never have children. We'll never be able to grow old together." I shake my head. "This is my chance to get out, and I intend to take it."

The silence extends between us as he considers my words. "I can see how that makes sense. After knowing everything you've endured, I might have come to that conclusion myself. Hell, I wanted to. I couldn't picture a world with just me and no Patricia." He reaches over and nudges my chin. "But it happened eventually. The sun kept rising. The earth kept spinning, and I kept living, I suppose, thanks to you," he says with a small smile. "Now, I'm not saying you're wrong at all. It's been your burden, and it's your decision to make . . . I just think we can try to think of another way. Surely there must be something?"

I shake my head. "You don't think I've tried? Did you know that I can't die? That I've *tried*. But no . . . I can't pick up the gun. I can't walk out into traffic. I can't leap from the bridge or take that final bottle of pills. He won't let me. My hands go numb, my feet lock in place, or I can't get the top off the bottle, no matter how much I try. *He* won't let me leave!"

I'm vibrating, everything crashing through me. I lurch to my feet and stumble to the far corner of the room, wrapping my arms around myself like a shield. If I don't hold it all in, I'll fall apart right in front of him. This is my only choice.

"If I were him, I wouldn't let you leave either."

Sebastian's words startle me.

"Without you, who does he have to talk to? Who will write him stories? Have portraits made of him?" He pauses, thinking and exploring the theory. "Maybe that's why he hasn't shown up before now. You said you tried to end your life, and he still didn't come, even prevented you from leaving. Maybe he doesn't want the game to be over . . . because, without you, his existence would be empty too."

Sebastian's words ring with truth, but I can't help but think of what that means for me . . . for disobeying and taunting him.

"He'll never let me go. Haven't I given enough?"

He crosses the room to me. "Nella, you've given more than us all. Hearing your story proved that. I can't help but think you also did what you set out to do. You *saw* beauty. You *wrote* the stories. You *found* the evidence. You *experienced* love. So much love. Yours is not a story about loss. You showed Death the goodness of man. Because he saw *you*."

I don't want to see it. I've spent so much time in the loss that it hurts to focus on the love. I've carried their stories with me. They've made me who I am.

I swallow, my throat dry. "With Eulalie . . . I learned the beauty of self-confidence, of having a dream and making your way in the world." As I hear the words, a flood of gratitude surges forth, surprising me with its force.

"Jacques showed me the value of beauty and how to collect it. Even though he wasn't my true love, he cared for me and tried to help others." I smile, thinking of William. "William showed me what it was like to be loved for who I was inside. And he believed in me and my words. Without his encouragement, I don't know if I would have had the courage to get published in France." With every remembrance, the gratitude grows as if stretching me from the inside, making room for it all. The good and the bad. I understand his point. "For all his faults,

René showed me the power of creation. With Rohan, I expanded my world, my understanding of this life and whatever is next. Adam gave me the joy of spontaneity and being my most authentic self. Gabrielle showed me the beauty of taking risks, while Diego helped me be present. They each showed me a lesson in beauty."

He nods. "But you knew that already." He cradles my chin. "You just forgot along the way."

His simple words stop me, breaking through all my excuses. I have lost sight of it—the beauty, the magic, the wonder in the world that I used to love so much. But as his words resonate, I begin to remember. The pain's there, but so are some of the other things I've forgotten. Adam's satisfied smile after crafting a new design. Gabby's proud face after helping to successfully pull off the boycott. Diego's peace as we stood on that mountaintop in Peru. When I blocked out all those moments because of the pain, I missed all their beauty.

He traces a finger down my cheek. "You are the summation of everything you have ever seen, said, written, or done. I've found the strongest woman I've ever known in listening to you. I see you, and that's why I know you've been battling this decision. What if you didn't stop doing this from a place of fear?" He gazes down at me. "What if you did it from the beauty of love? Not because he's making you, but because you want to."

A startling clarity runs through me as I gaze at Sebastian.

I have done my job.

I have shown Death everything good and found beauty in the world, so much so that I've lost myself. Death planned to take the world long before he met me. If he hasn't accepted all that I've given him, then there's nothing left that I can do. No matter the cost.

The realization that comes is calm and peaceful. I stand on my tiptoes and kiss Sebastian with everything I have.

I know what I have to do.

# Thirty-Five

The cabin sits where it did all those years ago, near the break in the woods. Fireflies flit through the coming dark, dotting the land with flashes of their hopeful, glowing light.

It's not my original cabin, of course.

That's long gone.

This imitation is for tourists—sanitizing the truth of it all. It's missing the smell of crowded bodies, the stink of sweat from laboring under an unforgiving sun, and the acrid scent of bitter desperation that marked each day.

Light flickers from within.

He's here and it's time.

"I don't feel right leaving you alone." Sebastian takes his hands from the steering wheel and wraps them around mine.

I turn to him, thankful for this man. "But I'm not alone." I touch my heart with my free hand. "I have you here. I have all of them here. It's time for me to finish this."

I swallow and glance out the car window, pulse racing. Just because I know what to do doesn't make it easy.

A new thought creeps into my mind: Death can be cruel. "But what if he takes away my life right then and there? What if he returns me to how I was?"

Even after all these years, I remember the pain that lies on the edge of death. I think about the spots, not being able to breathe, coughing up blood . . . What if he returns me with mere minutes to live? It's one thing to have thought my deal would come with death; it's another thing to confront my agonizing mortality.

Sebastian grips my hand, his fingers dwarfing mine. "Then I will be with you until your final breath and carry you in my heart to the final one of mine."

His words, his quiet confidence, his everything, is what I've been searching for through space and time. He reminds me of all the beauty I've seen that I've promised Death exists.

I kiss him.

I kiss him with all that I have in me. The kiss is sweet, full of every emotion we feel for each other and more.

I don't want to break away, but I must.

It won't do to keep Death waiting.

"It's time," I say, Sebastian's forehead against mine.

He nods and lets me go. This is something I must do on my own.

I take a deep breath and slide out of the car.

It is time to face Death.

# A VISIT FROM DEATH

Death knew today was the end of everything.

He'd avoided it for as long as he could.

He sat at the rickety wooden table and stared into the glowing fire as it danced. He'd been there all day, preparing himself for what lay ahead. Pages and pages of her words—her previous lessons from throughout time—sat before him. He'd stored her work in a little house on an island where he'd collected a hermit nearly a century before. He would light a fire and read her work in the in-between moments. He'd brought it all here for what he knew would be their last meeting.

The portrait she'd had painted of him sat on the mantel, staring down imperiously. *Is that how she sees me?*

He remembered the times they'd met—how he had shown up to her, so sure in those early times that she would lose.

Now he sat there, certain he had finally won—that this would be their final meeting.

She had broken his rules. She had exposed the inner workings of their deal. Victory didn't feel anything like he thought it would.

The door creaked open, and she was there. She took her time, studying him, the room, taking it all in.

He sat up straighter, revealing no emotion, though the space in his chest galloped. "You came."

"Did I have a choice?" She sidled into the room, shutting the door behind her.

"I suppose you didn't." He gestured to the seat opposite him, studying her.

She settled in the chair, the light dancing over her features like it did all those years ago. Thanks to him, she hadn't aged a day; her skin was as lovely and fresh as the day he had healed her. Though she hadn't aged physically, she had hardened, all the naivete from that day in the cabin gone. She sat straight in her chair. She had nothing in her hands.

"Before we start, I want to thank you."

His eyebrows lifted with surprise. "Thank . . . me?" That was the last thing he'd thought she'd say. After all the pain she'd had . . . the way she'd cursed him . . .

"I do. I thank you for this life and all that I've had the chance to experience. I've been reminded of the beauty I said existed all that time ago. I can see it again, and I thank you for the gift of life to do so."

A feeling close to hope rose inside him.

"But . . . I come to you tonight empty handed." She held out her palms for emphasis, and whatever Death had for a heart plummeted, regret twisting around within him. "I don't have anything else for you but me."

"What?" He leaned away suspiciously. "Those weren't the terms of our deal."

"Actually, I believe they are." She paused, taking a deep breath. "I've shown you all the good of humans I could find and wrote it for you. I've collected hundreds of stories and shown you people who strive to make the world better, if not in their lifetimes, then their children's. After all of this, there's nothing more to say. So I offer myself. I want you to look at me and say that *all* humanity is weak, feckless, violent, and selfish. I want you to tell me that *none* are worth saving."

She met his gaze head-on. "That was, after all, the proposition. Those were, I believe, your words."

Humans *were* weak, feckless, violent, and supremely selfish.

But she was right. There were exceptions.

She had shown him that.

*She* was the exception.

He wondered if she must see the truth in his silence. She continued, "So tonight will be the end of this. I offer myself as proof of man's goodness and of all the beauty I promised there was." She pointed to the scattered pages in front of him. "If you don't see it by now, there's nothing else I can do."

Her words rumbled within him. She was right.

His eyes flicked up to the portrait one last time. "But you broke one of the rules of our deal . . . What if I argue that it makes all you've done null and void? What if I don't accept this response?"

She shrugged. "Then that's on you. You only asked that I prove that humans are redeemable, and I've done that."

"How can you be so sure?"

"I think you already believe it—that you know the truth. That's why you didn't let me lose. That's why you saved me from myself at the lowest points of my life, when the loneliness was so thick it was all I could see. You knew *I* was worth saving." Her voice rang out in the small cabin.

He stopped, thinking of the world without her in it. It was true that he often went years without seeing her, the time passing in a blur for him, but it was comforting to know she was there, working on their agreement. She was the bright spot in years that had none. He didn't want to contemplate his existence without her, then or now. Even if he did start the world over, he would know of her absence.

"But if you're gone, what will I have to look forward to? I have no dominion on the other side. I can't linger there to talk with you."

Nella shook her head. "You're not supposed to. Your work is here. It may feel like a punishment, but you're needed. Without you, life doesn't go on."

Death glanced away. She was right, but he wasn't ready to admit it.

"What if I don't want *them*? What if . . . it's only you?"

"But there's not only me. My mama could see you—you just never caught her. If I had been able to birth a child, maybe they would've been able to see you too. Maybe by agreeing to this, you'll have *more* and not less. I'll eventually die, yes, but I'll also finally get to live."

She reached for Death's hand, capturing it in hers. He flinched but kept it there. "I've shown you everything there is to know about humans: their strengths, their ingenuity, their kindness, and their love. I've shown you the beauty they can create and how families can take shape and make every person in them stronger. You made me immortal, but after all of this, I think I've also made you a little human. Surely after all this time, I've finally earned my freedom."

Death gazed into the fire. She was right.

He was more.

He felt more.

Because of her.

The silence sat between them, broken only by the crackle of the fire, which gave no heat. A mix of emotions ran through him, emotions he only understood because of her. She'd taught him to see and feel through her words.

He thought their deal would change her. Instead, he was the one transformed.

She was right. She had done her job.

"Do you regret saying yes to me all those years ago?" Death asked.

She turned to face him. "I did. A few days ago, I wished I had accepted my death and gone on to the next life, never having done any of it. But someone helped me see—helped remind me of what I believed back then—helped me to remember how I feel today. I can't regret the past. If I hadn't said yes, I wouldn't have had this life, and I wouldn't have had my friendship with you."

He nodded, primarily to himself. He mattered to her nearly as much as she mattered to him, and that truth allowed him to expand.

She was right, and she'd done what he'd thought impossible.

She'd made him care. She'd made him see. She'd made him love. She was the most redeemable of them all. She'd won.

"I suppose it's done." The fire crackled in the silence, the logs settling, marking the end of their time together.

"I don't mean to be rude," she said after a beat, "but what does that *mean*?"

Death chuckled. Her spirit was as bright as ever. "I suppose it means I agree to your revised terms."

She leaned forward. "Care to elaborate?"

"Our deal is complete. You can live your life. Your final lifetime. You've earned it and done me a great service."

"All of it? Without interference?" she said to be sure. He liked the sound of hope in her voice.

He supposed he deserved that. "Yes, without interference. Live, love, do whatever you wish with your life, for it is yours."

"Children?"

He shrugged. "If you still want them. I find them loud."

At the sight of her, joy shining, a new sensation crept in. From Nella's words, he knew the sensation must be happiness. It was odd, so hard and bright in his chest, as if he'd swallowed sunshine.

She stood, wrapping her arms around him, the sensation leaving him warm and feeling complete. "Thank you."

He hugged her back and shared the truth he'd been carrying with him.

"I suppose a part of me knew it would come to this. I left each of our meetings a bit more than before, but also a bit less. Less sure that *all* humans were beyond redemption. More aware of what they were capable of. All those stories you brought me showed the best of what humans could be *in spite* of their nature and propensity for greed. Your love, losses, and pain gave it all meaning. I finally understand what you meant in that small cabin all those years ago. In truth, I should have released you from our deal long ago, but that would have meant losing you."

She nodded. "You didn't want to be alone."

"You know how bad it is." Death stood, glad for the resolution, though sad for her loss. She'd have no more reason to meet with him. "I suppose you'll get all those things you wanted."

He gathered the papers and moved to the door. It was time for another collection, as always.

"Where're you going?" she called out.

Death frowned, confused.

She smiled. "Our meetings are not quite done. I still have a long life of dinners with my old friend."

He could feel his own smile as it spread across his face, and he settled back in his seat. "How about a story?"

"Let me tell you about my final love." She beamed, her smile bright enough to light the cabin as she happily complied.

# Thirty-Six

A lightness settles over me as I shut the rusting door. Even though the lights still blaze inside, I know Death is gone already, yet he's left behind the whisper of his presence. Gooseflesh covers my skin.

For the first time in years, I don't resent the fact. With our new arrangement, I hope to look forward to our talks, when we'll meet as friends on equal footing.

I enjoy the sensation of freedom, breathing easier than when I was here last, all that time gone by. My burden has shifted, and I am free.

Best of all, I am not alone.

He's sitting on the hood of the car, waiting for me. "Sebastian!"

He takes three steps, gathering me up.

I laugh, happy tears rolling down my face.

"So, no more writing? No more meetings?"

I shake my head. "Not like before. I'll write because I want to. Death won't be gone, but he's not the enemy."

"That's good." He kisses me again. "I look forward to your writing. You'll have lots to record on our new adventures together."

From that instant, I know there is nowhere I would go on this earth without him by my side. We stay that way for a while, perfectly content to stand in each other's love as the cicadas serenade us in the pale moonlight.

"What's this?" he says, pulling back a bit. His fingers brush against my scalp, teasing a strand of curls.

"What's what?"

His eyes crinkle, sending a spark of happiness from my stomach to my toes. "This," he says, gently pulling on one strand. "It looks like gray hair."

My mouth falls open in shock. "Let me see!" I tear away from his embrace and race to the sideview mirror. Like he says, a single silvery strand has sprouted at my temple.

He takes my hand. "Are you worried about getting old?"

I shake my head. "I'm just glad to have this last lifetime with you."

"You're lucky I have a thing for older women."

I laugh as he plucks the car fob from my hand and jangles the keys.

"What now?" he asks, opening my door.

I smile, gazing into the face of my love. "What, indeed?"

# PART VIII: SAVANNAH

## A Final Visit from Death—2084

# Thirty-Seven

Death watches, just beyond the veil, waiting to take his friend home. Of all the souls he's taken, hers will be his favorite, her shining light gleaming until the end. It's only because of that light that he can see the shine in others, to see beyond what humans are and who they can be.

The machine ticks by her side, pushing oxygen into her nose as another monitors her heart's steady beats.

It won't be long now.

Any world he would make would end up like this, for there are no perfect creatures, and these are the ones he knows best.

She had no idea what she agreed to all those years ago in that tiny cabin on the edge of civilization. He can see her as she was then, sweating, teetering toward nonexistence, but still defiant, her spirit rising up. It made him curious to see what she thought was worth fighting for.

It was more than that. As she talked about in their meetings, it was the importance of being seen. She did that for him. She respected his purpose and helped him to not feel alone, because he had her words and life to comfort him.

Seeing her and being seen by her made him consider all of humankind's beauty worth saving. He can admit that he only wanted to watch her, this incandescent creature who made him see the world anew, but in the end, she won their bargain fair and square.

She often found beauty where he was sure none existed. When everything was bleak and at its end, she found the light.

She did well until her light started to flicker and dim, doused by the pain of life. Then he understood the toll he had placed upon her. He had the very thing he wanted—someone to share in the loneliness—and he was snuffing her out.

It was then that he fully knew how important his role was.

He missed that light.

He missed her.

That's why he put him in her path.

Death saw him first at the bedside of his fiancée—how he had cared for her, how pure their love was—and all of Nella's work helped him see that he was one of the redeemable ones worth saving. It was then that he thought their paths should collide—that he'd be worthy of her, and Death also knew she needed him. With Winston's death, she'd been alone and ready to give up.

He takes his time and studies them together in these final moments.

He takes good care of her, Death thinks—softly toweling her forehead, making sure she's comfortable, keeping up a steady stream of conversation to entertain her, often reading to her long into the evenings.

He does a fair job of keeping the grandkids busy, often too boisterous on their visits, begging to hear of her journeys around the world.

Death knows he picked well.

He complements her and makes their life the thing of beauty she looked for all those years ago. Their book, printed in dozens of editions in a dozen languages, stands on the shelf, the bestselling "fictional" story of what she sacrificed to save the world.

As he gazes upon her family . . . Death knows she was right when they first met.

The love in the room—this is worth saving. She won long ago, when he couldn't bear being alone. He now knows he didn't have to be. Several of her grandchildren have the sight. She will live on through them, reminding him of the beauty to be found in humanity.

The machine's beeps begin to slow, and her family draws near, saying a prayer for her soul.

They need not worry.

It will be fine, for she will be with him.

He feels for Sebastian. He's losing his best friend, but he is also nearing the end of his long life. He'll get to join her soon.

All at once, it is time.

He steps forward, brushing his hand at her brow, releasing her soul. She comes forward instantly, luminous.

She is free.

She smiles at him before turning to her family, her question clear.

"They'll be all right," he promises, taking her hand. "I'll make sure of it."

"You better. I won fair and square," she reminds him, as she's done for decades. "Now, I was hoping you could take me to this afterlife I've heard so much about. It had better be worth it."

"It'll be worth it," he promises. "You wouldn't settle for anything less."

They slip together into the in-between—as equals and as true friends.

# ACKNOWLEDGMENTS

Like Nella's, my journey into writing has been shaped and changed by the wonderful people I've met along the way.

This book wouldn't exist without the brilliant minds of Dhonielle Clayton and the incomparable Carlyn Greenwald. I've learned so much from you both and wouldn't be here without you taking a chance on my writing. Thank you to the team at Electric Postcard Entertainment—Clay Morrell, Eve Peña, and Haneen Oriqat—and the wonderful editors I've been lucky enough to work with. A huge thank-you to Lizzie Skurnick for your keen eye on those early pages and research recommendations that made the first drafts possible and to Kristen Pettit for your incisive editing, lightning-quick responses, and constant support.

I'm beyond grateful for Suzie Townsend and the amazing team at New Leaf Literary—Joanna Volpe, Sophia Ramos, Sarah Gerton, and Olivia Coleman—who helped bring Nella into the world. You've made my first foray into publishing a dream.

Thank you to the incredible team at Amazon. Alicia Clancy, your kindness and vision for this project shaped it from the start. Thank you, Danielle Marshall, for championing Nella through transition, and Carmen Johnson, for taking the baton and helping her cross the finish line. Thank you to Tegan Tigani for your sharp developmental edits and insightful pushes, and a deep thanks to the wonderful copyeditors, proofreaders, fact-checkers, and sensitivity readers who helped Nella's story shine!

A special thank-you to Calah Singleton and the amazing team at Hodderscape for helping Nella find her way back to the UK and for creating a dream of a book cover.

I wouldn't be writing these acknowledgments without a host of writing friends and mentors. I'm deeply grateful to We Need Diverse Books for all their work, their mentorship program, and the chance to work with the remarkable Rajani LaRocca, who mentored me in 2021. That experience sharpened my skills and gave me the gift of typing *The End* for the first time.

My most deeply felt thanks go to the OhMGs, my weekly writing group for the past three years. Thanks to Camellia Phillips, Mariana Andrade, and Maria Marianayagam, and the deepest appreciation to Lynn Wong and the incomparable Eric Boyd for your continued and ongoing Saturday-morning support. I love how we show up consistently to support each other and our dreams, and I can't wait to see your work out in the world.

No acknowledgments would be complete without Judy Fernandez Diaz, whose friendship, accountability, and support keep me going. #Diamonds

I'm also grateful for the wisdom shared by my mentors over the years—Elana K. Arnold, Camille Pagan, and Ginny Myers Sain—which transformed my approach to writing, revision, and the business side of this career. Thank you to Betsy Bunte and Susan Smith, my wonderful ELA IB teachers.

Special thanks to the Women's Fiction Writers Association for the daily writing dates that helped Nella come to life. Thank you to all the hosts, with extra love for Michele Montgomery, Hadley Leggett, Virginia McCullough, Jen Sinclair, Carla Damron, Krista White, Catherine Matthews, and Pamela Stockwell, as well as all the other writing inmates who show up daily for their dreams. I also have to shout out my Sistah's Writing Group, especially Kelly Bates and Daphene Brown, for always showing up and putting in the work.

So many friends to thank: Kristi Burns, Danielle Ouedraogo, Amanda Tice, Kendra Mallet-Brunson, Eno Richardson, Megan Rabinowitz, and Katy Pratt—thank you for listening and encouraging me. Deep thanks to the wonderful Deborah Connelie for your kind friendship and many lunches at Taj, the incomparable Tonya Abari for those early-morning writing and hustle-planning sessions, and the inspiring Katia Raina for your friendship and all those Sunday-morning sprints! A big thank-you to all my accountability buddies—Kianti Brown, Autumn Green, Arlene Vargas-Kahn, and Maria Faqier-Hardy—for cheering me on and for crushing your own goals! I'm also ever thankful for the friendship and support of Octavia Coleman, Melisande Smith, and all my Phi Chapter Sorors.

To Sophia Hunt: Thank you for reading my early drafts and being the best second mom.

To all my colleagues from Relay Graduate School of Education, Teach For America, and my wonderful sorors of Delta Sigma Theta, Inc.: Thank you for your support throughout this journey.

Mom, Dad, Chelsey, and John—thank you for always listening as I talk about my books, plans, and ambitions and for always supporting my dreams. Get 'em, Griff!

I'm so blessed to have been born into the Mapp/McGriff family. To my grandparents, aunts, uncles, nephews, cousins, and in-laws: I love you all and thank you for your continued support.

To Kanaya, Kalia, and Carter—you are my greatest creations. When I started this book, I hadn't yet learned how to balance creating imaginary worlds while raising you in the real one. Thank you for your love and patience and for helping me grow as a person and a mom.

And Sam—thank you for your love, support, and partnership. Marrying you was the best decision I ever made. Thank you for always giving me room to dream and grow.

Finally, to all the readers—like Nella, may you always find beauty in life, even when the light seems too dim to see.

## RAISING READERS
### Books Build Bright Futures

Dear Reader,

We'd love your attention for one more page to tell you about the crisis in children's reading, and what we can all do.

Studies have shown that reading for fun is the **single biggest predictor of a child's future life chances** – more than family circumstance, parents' educational background or income. It improves academic results, mental health, wealth, communication skills, ambition and happiness.[1]

The number of children reading for fun is in rapid decline. Young people have a lot of competition for their time. In 2024, 1 in 10 children and young people in the UK aged 5 to 18 did not own a single book at home.[2]

Hachette works extensively with schools, libraries and literacy charities, but here are some ways we can all raise more readers:

- Reading to children for just 10 minutes a day makes a difference
- Don't give up if children aren't regular readers – there will be books for them!
- Visit bookshops and libraries to get recommendations
- Encourage them to listen to audiobooks
- Support school libraries
- Give books as gifts

There's a lot more information about how to encourage children to read on our website: **www.RaisingReaders.co.uk**

Thank you for reading.

---

[1] OECD, '21st-Century Readers: Developing Literacy Skills in a Digital World', 2021, https://www.oecd.org/en/publications/21st-century-readers_a83d84cb-en.html

[2] National Literacy Trust, 'Book Ownership in 2024', November 2024, https://literacytrust.org.uk/research-services/research-reports/book-ownership-in-2024

HODDERSCAPE

# WANT MORE HODDERSCAPE? JOIN US!

Sign up to our mailing list to get exclusive early sneak peeks and offers:

Follow us on our social channels:
@hodderscape

Buy our books, find out more, and discover exclusive content:
www.hodderscape.co.uk